PARTY HARD

Pixel Dust Book One

D. PETRIE

MOUNTAINDALE
PRESS

ACKNOWLEDGMENTS

Party Hard is a ridiculous story full of action and heart, but it wouldn't have happened without help and inspiration.

I'd like to thank my awesome beta-readers, Kevin Eaton, Cindy Koepp, Caite Liddell, Paul Campbell Jr., and Brad Penney. Also, a big thanks to my friend and comrade Chris Bowden, for fighting by my side throughout every zombie apocalypse, alien invasion, and war-torn city, that fostered my love of video games over the years. Most of all, a special thank you to my wife, Samantha, for supporting and encouraging me. I have accomplished more in the time since she entered my life than I ever did in the years before. So to all of you, I say thanks and party on.

PROLOGUE

Crimson light pierced through the overcast sky as Milo collapsed. His knees hit the stone with a solid thud as pebbles dug into his palms.

He couldn't believe it.

It had only been minutes since he'd fallen asleep on one of the cots in Neal's parents' basement. Hadn't it? He checked his watch. It didn't work. Just a row of zeros blinking in rhythm with his heartbeat. It made sense. It wasn't real.

Cool, dry air filled his lungs. It tasted clean and real. He breathed it in, letting an earthy scent fill his nostrils.

Tears welled up in his eyes until they stained the gray stone beneath him. He couldn't help it. Emotions swelled in his chest, overflowing.

He was just so happy.

"Do you need a moment?" Neal crouched down beside him. He held a rectangle of black glass the size of a tablet computer. Dark circles hung under his eyes, like he hadn't slept in days.

Milo didn't even dry his tears before throwing his arms around his business partner. He might have only met the man a few months ago after a class at MIT, but he didn't care. The occasion called for a hug. "Oh my god, you did it. I could kiss you."

"I'd prefer that you didn't." Neal wedged the pane of black glass between them like a spatula separating a pair of pancakes.

Milo let him go. "How does it work?"

Neal took a step back, regaining some personal space. "We're dreaming… sort of."

"What do you mean sort of?"

Neal hesitated, as if thinking of a way to dumb things down. Milo would have taken offense, but he'd gotten used to the man's condescending attitude. Besides, no matter how smart he was, Neal would always be smarter. That much was a fact.

The genius cleared his throat. "The Somno system is actually quite simple."

"Somno?" Milos asked.

"Yes, it's Latin for sleep." Neal continued without waiting for approval. "The system connects us together in a shared dream space. Beyond that, the user's brain does most of the heavy lifting. When you logged in, the Somno showed your mind a series of images that it then referenced to texture this virtual environment."

"But what about taste and smell?" Milo kicked at a few loose pebbles. "Why does it feel so real?"

"That's where the system backs off, letting your mind fill in the rest. It can override the senses when need be, but it's best to leave that up to the user's brain whenever possible."

Milo stared out across the blank expanse, the horizon curving ever so slightly in the distance. "What happens if I walk to the edge of the environment?"

"There is no edge."

Milo felt his jaw go slack. "How is that possible?"

Neal raised his head to the sky. "I call this testing environment, the Sphere. It has no end other than the clouds above. It is a blank world. "

Milo exhaled slowly. "You're wrong."

Neal arched an eyebrow. "Pardon?"

"It's more than a blank world. It's a blank canvas. It can be anything we want. And everyone will come to play in it."

Neal scoffed. "Play in it?"

Milo's heart raced at the possibilities. A lifetime of Dungeons and Dragons, video games, and comics flooded back to him. It was a lifetime of stories.

"You've created a system that can give back the time that we lose sleeping. I don't know about you, but most would kill for an escape like that. There are people working two jobs just to get by. A game using this system would change their lives.

"People could create their own stories here. Stories where they can be more. Where they can live out their fantasies." He spoke so fast that he almost stumbled his words. "This place is literally the stuff dreams are made of. We have a responsibility to make something of it. To give a new world, to the world."

Neal stepped backward. "And you could build a business on that? One that could support my work on the system? That is your job."

Milo sighed. Dreams and noble intentions aside, he did need to be realistic. The debt had already started piling up, and it had only been a few months.

"So can you sell this?" Neal probed again.

Milo unleashed a wild grin. "I already said so. Everyone will want to play our game. We won't even need to charge much."

Neal didn't even smile. He just gave a slight nod. "And what will you call this game?"

Milo thrust a finger toward the crimson sky. "Dreamland!" He held the pose for a moment, then let his hand fall back to his side. "Too juvenile?"

"A bit," Neal answered with a straight face.

"You're probably right." Milo sighed. "You said Somno was Latin for sleep, right?"

"I did."

Milo smiled as the name came to him. "Then it has to be Carpe Noctem."

Neal shook his head. "I see what you did there." He tapped

at the black pane glass he held. "If that is all for now. I still have work to do in here."

"Oh, okay." Milo deflated as lines of text began running across the tablet.

Neal looked up for a moment. "I haven't fully worked out the logout commands yet. So I'm just going to shock you a little."

"Wait, what—"

Milo shot upright in his cot as an exposed wire lit up his scalp. It took everything he had not to hurl the experimental headpiece across the basement. A part of him actually thought Neal had been joking.

He took several deep breaths.

The genius still lay in the cot beside him. Neal hadn't even said goodbye before kicking him out. No matter. There were more important things to worry about.

Milo reached straight for his backpack and pulled out his D&D binder. The image of a twenty-sided die was drawn on the cover. He flipped it open to last session's character sheet. The name Alastair Coldblood was scrawled across the top corner. It was a dumb name, but he'd been playing the character since high school. Sentimentality demanded he keep it.

A smile spread across his face. There was so much work to do.

The next few years past by in a blur as Milo's life was consumed by interviews, tech demos, and investor meetings. He and Neal pushed forward fueled by ambition and the desire to create. Well, that and hot pockets.

Eventually, Checkpoint Systems, proprietor of the Somno Unit, was born.

Milo took the stage as the public face of the company, while Neal stayed in the lab creating a system to run a game like no

other. Together, they worked around the clock, risking everything in the process.

It had all been worth it.

Pre-orders came in by the hundreds of thousands, and on
day one, they were already on top of the gaming industry. That
was when Milo put aside his character sheet and logged in as
Alastair Coldblood.

Now, three years after launch day, and nearly a decade after
Milo's first trip into the Sphere, Noctem still thrived. With their
system giving back eight to ten hours a night to its users, how
could it not? It was a dream come true.

Unfortunately, the same couldn't be said for one of its
inhabitants.

Alastair buried his face in his hands, going over the events
of his day as Milo Parker, CEO. He had logged in to escape the
relentless phone calls from the press. If he was honest, he did
owe the world an explanation. It just wasn't the one that he
wanted to give. After all, it wasn't every day that he fired his
partner, the man who made all of Noctem possible.

"Why did you make me do it?" Alastair mumbled through
his hands as the image of Neal being escorted out of his lab by
security still hung in his mind. The genius's middle finger aimed
in his direction the entire way out. The gesture had been so
uncharacteristic of Neal that it was hard to believe it had even
happened.

Alastair slumped over the railing of the balcony attached to
his virtual office. It was his only refuge, or so he thought. Even
perched high atop the Citadel's gothic towers in the bustling city
of Valain, it seemed he couldn't escape judgment. The crowd
gathering below made sure to remind him of that as the flickering light of their torches added little to the view.

Alastair glanced down at the GM band on his arm. With

the abilities it granted him, it wouldn't take much more than a few swipes of his hand to destroy the whole lot of them. He shook off the impulse. That would probably be going too far. He did seriously debate on summoning a light rainstorm to make the night uncomfortable for them, though.

A sigh escaped him. He wasn't really mad at them. In fact, it was quite the opposite. Alastair wanted to skip his next few meetings and go down there to tell them the truth.

Unfortunately, that would just get him in more trouble with his legal team. Instead, he let out another sigh and resigned himself to being the villain of the day as he squinted at the flickering lights below.

He reached into his coat pocket and pulled out a small leather-bound book. A rectangular piece of glass rested in an indented space built into its rear cover. He popped it out and held it in front of his right eye, activating an enchantment that allowed him to focus closer on the scene below.

His fingers fumbled in surprise, almost dropping the tiny window over the edge. Recovering his grasp, he clenched his hand around the item as his expression changed to one of utter indignation.

"Oh, come on, people. Really? Pitchforks? Isn't that a bit much!"

It had happened.

The gathering below had become a full-fledged angry mob complete with torches and farming equipment. There was even a man holding up a paper sign with the words 'Coldblood is Cold Blooded' written in heavy red calligraphy.

He knew the people outside couldn't hear him vent his frustrations from the distance above, but that didn't stop him from yelling at them anyway.

"Where the hell did you even get pitchforks? Those aren't even available to players! You probably looted them from some poor farmer. Now his family will starve, you monsters!" he spat the words with as much disdain as he could muster.

Then finally, he chuckled.

He had to respect the effort.

The fact that someone had made a paper sign in the first place was impressive. Sure, there were several types of books and scrolls that anyone could buy throughout the world of Noctem, but getting a sheet of what looked like card stock at poster size was a long process.

First, they had to chop down a tree for some wood, then break it down into pulp, and finally refine it several times before it would even function as something akin to paper. Not to mention that they would also have to make the ink for writing on top of all that. The range of crafting skills needed for the endeavor was immense.

Actually, now that he thought about it, Alastair wasn't even sure how to craft ink.

Crushed berries maybe?

He would have to look into that later.

Anyway, the point was, a lot of work had gone into creating a stupid sign making fun of his already ridiculous name.

Alastair lowered his head to the railing in defeat.

He hated the situation. Even more, he hated that he could do nothing about it other than attend meetings and work with his publicist to try to turn things around.

That was when a system chime sounded in his ear.

Alastair glanced at the spine of the book in his hand where an icon of a feathered quill overlapping a scroll faded into existence.

Back during testing, they had originally used a system similar to augmented reality to display the game menu. In practice, though, they found it too distracting to have people wandering around with a bunch of glowing text boxes hovering about their heads. They had tried making the windows invisible to other players, but that just left them waving their hands around in the air like a bunch of mimes. And really, nobody liked mimes.

In the end, they decided to center Noctem's system messages and menus around a physical journal item. For quick access, a player's own skin was used to display information woven into complex tattoos of digital ink.

He opened his journal and placed the rectangular piece of glass, which they had called an inspector, back into the indent in the rear cover. Then he flipped to the page that showed his inbox. Columns of text ran down the paper, displayed in a delicate cursive script that he'd chosen in his preferences as his default font. At the top of the list was a message in bold, seemingly written with a heavy pen to indicate that it was unread.

The sender read, Neal Carver.

The subject was HARD FEELINGS, all in caps.

Alastair groaned as soon as he saw the name, expecting nothing good. He touched the line with his finger and the text faded away as if staining the paper in reverse. It reformed a second later to show the selected message.

There was no text, just a decorative icon of a frame with a triangle inside representing a video attachment. Alastair tapped it and flipped back to his inspector, which among other things, was the only screen that players had access to in-game.

He popped the piece of glass out again, this time tossing it into his office where it floated into the air, ignoring gravity altogether. Thanks to an upgrade that came with his GM band, the glass grew to the size of a large monitor. His eyes narrowed into slits as Carver's face took over the portal.

A minute later, his jaw dropped as the horror of the video's contents slammed into him. His forehead burned, and his legs shook as he raised one hand to his mouth in disbelief.

He took a step backward as if trying to get away from it. The window followed, tracking his movement and reinforcing the video's message.

Escape was impossible.

The video ended and he held out his hand, prompting the pane of glass to return to normal and float back to him. He slapped it back into his journal, shoving down the fear and nausea bubbling up inside him. Alastair took three deep breaths and gradually calmed down, calling back some of the determination that he had gained over several years of building a company.

Closing his journal, he raised his caster. The elegant bracelet hugged his right wrist, a small chamber attached underneath. He snapped it open, revealing a glowing crystal. Its deep crimson light reminded him of the sky from his first trip with Neal into the system's virtual environment.

Alastair swiped the caster up to open his spell-craft menu, which appeared before him as a curved field of glowing glyphs. He spun the rows of symbols from left to right, aligning a teleportation spell into the vertical selection column. From the top down, each glyph identified a different aspect of the incantation. As soon as each row settled into place he swiped down with a decisive flourish, activating the spell and striking a rather cool pose that had become habit for him.

Threads of energy climbed and swirled around him before expanding into a solid sphere. The shell dispersed in seconds, flaking apart into shimmering particles that glowed brighter just before vanishing.

The light faded, and he was gone.

CHAPTER ONE

MaxDamage24's eye twitched in sync with the discordant sound of a harp having its strings plucked in random order.

"You're doing that on purpose, aren't you?"

Kirabell didn't answer. Instead, she continued to walk ahead of him in a comical manner, raising her legs higher than necessary and plucking away at the small instrument with each step. It reminded Max of an old cartoon. She wasn't so much playing a song as she was adding background notes to her movement.

Max kicked at the dusty ground, knocking a small rock off the edge of the wide ledge they traveled. An echo sounded as it bounced down the wall of Hunter's Canyon. "Could you knock that off? It's annoying."

She glanced back with a mischievous grin. "It wouldn't be fun for me if it wasn't."

He retaliated by dragging out a loud groan for as long as he could, his voice droning on for almost a full minute.

Kira plucked her next few notes louder.

Unsatisfied with her reaction, he gave up trying to beat her at her own game and turned his attention to his journal, holding the book at an angle to catch the light of Noctem's eternally full moon. "I have a message from someone that needs help with the *Fire Tomb*. We're way over-leveled, so we could pop on by and do a quick run through to give them a hand." He raised his eyebrows and held his journal to face her as he pointed to the message like it was a prize on a game show.

"Nope," Kira chirped without even looking back.

Max flipped the book back around and tried again. "We haven't done that last quest for the *Devil Born* expansion yet. We could check that out."

"Nope." Kira plucked another string louder than the rest.

"Or maybe we could—"

"Nope!" she cut him off. "Tonight is farming night, and we have Northern Scalefangs to murder."

Max let out another groan and dragged his feet in protest, allowing his arms to dangle limply at his sides. "But they suck and take so many bullets!" he complained, putting in as much effort as he could to sound like a guy who had been forced to go shopping. Kira was his sidekick after all, so he wasn't used to following.

She stopped short and turned to face him, forcing him to stop as well. She held her harp at her hip with one hand and poked him in the chest with the other. "You'll wish we spent the night farming scalefangs when I get killed by something stupid because I don't have the materials to craft bone charms. But at least I'll have the comfort in knowing that I won't be alone in my grave - because your ass will be joining me soon after if I'm not there to keep you alive, so to avoid that, we will need the *Bones of Predatory Beasts* and lots of them."

"Yeah, I know." He craned his neck to look down at her finger stabbing at him and held in a laugh. The fact that she was almost a foot and a half shorter than him hindered her attempt to seem intimidating.

She spun back around, her silver hair flipping around her head so that a few locks landed across her face. She blew them away with a huff and shoved the rest behind a slightly pointed ear bearing a pearl earring. "Might I remind you that this arrangement was your idea."

"Yes, dear," he said in a tone appropriate for responding to a nagging girlfriend just as a scalefang shot out of a small opening in the rock wall to the side of the sloping path that they traveled. Its scaled form, the size of a large dog, lunged at Kira; its eyes trained on her throat. The creature's mane of feathers fluttered as it moved.

On reflex, Max drew his pistols and pumped three rounds into the beast before it could make contact. Smoke and flame roared from their muzzles as the scalefang landed with a thud at Kira's feet. He swept one gun around the scene, following its iron sights with one eye to secure their perimeter while making a point of keeping his other gun trained on the dead beast just in case. Satisfied that they were safe for the moment, he slid his weapons back into the drop leg holsters he wore strapped to his thighs.

Kira released the breath she'd been holding almost as tightly as she clutched her harp against her chest. "I knew I kept you around for a reason."

Max watched her for a moment as she glanced around at the other openings in the canyon wall further down their path. "Maybe you should put that harp away and pay attention to your surroundings," he jabbed as if to say 'I told you so'.

She groaned as she tapped a small tattoo of a keyhole that sat just below her caster on the underside of her left wrist. From it blossomed an elegant design of filigree that spread, wrapping around her forearm to form what most players referred to as their *stat-sleeve*. The design varied from player to player depending on what they had chosen. In Kira's case, she had picked something delicate. Max, on the other hand, had chosen a skull surrounded by flames that he thought looked badass. Either way, it framed their party's status readout with style. Kira ran her eyes over the numbers.

MaxDamage24

Hit points: 2,960 out of 2,960
Skill points: 275 out of 275

Kirabell
Hit points: 50 out of 50
Mana: 1,420, out of 1,420

She frowned at the readout and flipped her arm to the other side where her menu options ran down her forearm woven into the pattern of curled line work. Her class emblem, a small feather, capped off the design where it ended on back of her hand. She tapped an option that read 'inventory,' and the design shifted to display a short list which showed everything she carried on her person in the small item bag she wore attached to her belt. Below that was a longer list that contained everything stored in her virtual inventory. At the bottom, near her elbow, she touched a word that read 'transfer.' The harp she held in her other hand dematerialized as if it had been made of nothing but air. The words *Harp of Ending* appeared on the list. Afterward, she continued walking, only glancing back to Max for a moment. "You coming?"

He shrugged and got moving.

The path they traveled ran down the side of Hunter's Canyon - the bottom of which was lined with a number of caves to explore. Most were filled with northern scalefangs, obviously. Max used to like the place back when his level was down in the mid-forties. It had been a great area to grind, but ever since Checkpoint Systems had decided to add an event called *The Culling* to the area, it had become more of a pain in the ass. Sure, it had been fun the first few times, but considering that the event called every scalefang out every two hours to attack anyone on the canyon floor, it had gotten old fast. Not to mention that it spawned an annoying boss named One-Eye who was missing one of his eyes, again, obviously.

Kira stopped short and spun around. "You hear that?"

Max held his breath and listened. The sound of shouting

mixed with growling drifted up the stone walls toward him. "The hell?"

Together they stepped to the edge of the path and peered over the side to find a party chipping away at a pair of scale-fangs that they had lured out into the open.

Kira blew out a low whistle. "That's kinda risky. Didn't the message boards say that The Culling was overdue? The place should be empty."

Max whipped out his journal. "Crap! We better not have missed it. I'm so not waiting another two hours." He flipped to his inspector in the back, bringing up a simple text screen without bothering to remove the glass window from the cover. He exhaled a second later. "Nope, still says overdue."

Kira looked back down at the party below. "Maybe they're here to farm like us."

"No way. Look at their gear." Max pointed down at a man wearing a set of plate armor covered in golden spikes. "No self-respecting high-level would be caught dead in something that flashy."

Kira tilted her head for a second, then shrugged. "Maybe they just don't understand fashion?"

Max looked at her sideways, pointing with his eyes at her outfit. It consisted of a gray dress with high slits on the sides that would have displayed her hips if she hadn't added a pair of short pants that covered her legs down to her knees. The mismatched garments left her looking like she wasn't sure if she was trying to be elegant or punk rock.

She glowered back at him, clearly receiving his nonverbal jab. Then she looked down at her outfit and nodded, accepting his point. She shrugged it off and spun back to the scene below, her item bag bouncing on the heavy leather belt that hung from her waist.

Max rested his hands on the butts of his guns. "Well, fashion sense or not, they're going to die down there."

Almost as soon as the words left his mouth, a low growl echoed through the canyon followed by a dozen shorter growls emanating from the caves that lined the rock walls. Then, in unison, dozens of drooling mouths emerged from the shadowed openings and closed in on the unsuspecting party. The Culling had begun.

Max watched as the players below were forced into a tight group, its members taking hits left and right. Their healer began panic-casting their strongest spells to keep them alive which never ended well since it painted a target on the mage's back from the overuse of their magic.

"Yeah, they're doomed." Max nodded, folding his arms across his chest.

Kira spun back to him. "We can't just watch."

Max attempted to hold his ground, her huge blue eyes glistening at him in the moonlight. He let out a sigh. "Fine," was the only word he could get out since she was gone before he even had time to close his mouth. A swirl of lingering sparkles circled around the spot where she'd stood as a faint trail of magic followed behind her. "Don't get yourself killed!" he called up to her as she darted twenty feet into the air above him.

She redirected and shot back down past him without saying anything.

"Show off," he mumbled to himself.

It would have been easy to mistake her for a run of the mill *Flight* magic user, but Max knew better. Her agility and the sparkling trail that followed her every move as she plummeted toward the ground made it clear what she was - a fairy. The difference between the average *Flight* spell and hers was that it wasn't a spell at all. The soft hum of wings was barely audible, and they were only visible during brief moments where the moonlight caught them at just the right angle. Max remembered Kira telling him once that learning to use the four individually controlled dragonfly wings had been like learning how to use a set of new appendages with no instinct for them. Now, he had to admit she'd been getting good, especially considering that she'd spent her first few weeks after unlocking the ability crashing into everything from the ground to other players. Hell, thanks to the learning curve, few in Noctem had even seen a fairy in flight.

Max shook his head and stepped away from the edge. There wasn't time to hang around and watch. Kira's fifty hit points weren't going to go far down there in the fray. He had to get moving. That was when a low chittering came from behind him. His breathing froze as quiet footsteps approached his back, the ruffling of feathers meeting his ears. It wasn't Kira he should have been worried about. He was just as good a target as any.

"I don't have time for this." He spun, drawing his pistols on reflex as a pair of reptilian jaws streaked toward him in the dark.

Below, Kirabell couldn't help but grin as she tucked her wings back, using them to guide her descent. Wind rushed through her hair as she let gravity take her. She could never get sick of that feeling. She flexed the virtual spellwork that ran through her body, and it twitched like a muscle tethered to her mana, sending her wings into motion. She leveled off and darted toward the party who were still clinging to life in the chaos.

A mixture of surprise and confusion met her from the ground as she passed by overhead. She snapped open a caster and tossed out a couple of *Pulse* spells that she always kept ready in her quick-cast queue. The spell delivered almost no real damage, but it carried enough force to shove the beasts away from her landing zone. She didn't want them pouncing on her the moment she touched down. That would be embarrassing.

Kira darted back up in a spiral that sent the canyon spinning around her. She tensed the imaginary muscle in her shoulders and released a wave of magic into her skin that erupted from her wings in a burst of shining energy like a sprinkler watering a dying lawn. The sparkling dust fell like rain across the lucky party. The act cost twenty percent of her mana, but because she couldn't open her spell-craft menu while airborne, it was the only way to get their health out of the red fast enough. She cut off the flow of mana, and her wings winked out of existence with a sound like wind chimes in the breeze. She dropped. "Make a hole!"

Eyes widened as the players all dove to the side to give her some space.

Kira twitched her spellwork one last time, flicking a single point of mana into the magical constructs that grew from her back. Her wings only blinked for a fraction of a second, but it was more than enough to break her fall. She came to a graceful stop as if she'd weighed nothing at all, which was close to accurate since, as a fairy, Kira was not only small but also weighed about half as much as a normal person her size.

The instant her bare feet made contact with the ground, she swiped open her spell-craft menu and set up her strongest area effect heal. She combined it with a heavy protection bonus, sending a cloud of energy through the group that brought each of them back up to full health and boosted their defense stats. It was a powerful mix of spells that she almost never used together, not because it was hard to set up on the fly, but more because it was as bad as panic-casting in terms of how much attention it drew. But that wasn't the problem right now. One thing at a time.

A few scalefangs chittered and squawked as they prowled closer. Kira responded by emptying the three remaining *Pulse* spells from her quick-cast queue to buy a few more seconds. Of course, it would have been nice if the party surrounding her had helped out a bit, but they were too busy staring at her with their dumb mouths hanging open. They acted as if she was their savior, like she was some kind of high-level badass that had already rescued them simply by showing up. Kira glanced at the fifty hit points inked across the underside of her wrist and swallowed. They didn't know how wrong they were.

She took in a breath and tried to live up to their expectations. Of course, she started by stumbling her first step. It was always hard to adjust back to using her feet after flying. She shifted what little weight she had and clutched at the small bone charm that hung from her item bag. A sigh escaped her, putting an end to the illusion that she knew what she was doing. Sure, if she had Max to lean on, things would have been different. But alone, well, there was a reason why not many players chose to play as the fairy race, though that didn't matter right now. The first wave of scalefangs was already closing back in, outnumbering the group three to one.

Kira gave up on trying to impress, settling for limping along until Max could get his ass down to her. "I didn't fly down here just to get killed. You're gonna have to do some fighting here, people!" She held out her hands to draw attention to the fact that she wasn't even carrying a weapon, not that she could anyway with her body being too weak to even lift one, let alone cause any damage. Just another drawback to being a fairy, but that didn't mean she was out of options.

She raised both arms, revealing not one but two casters. They snapped open in unison, a tranquil white glow coming from both that almost seemed soothing. At least it would have if the group wasn't about to be torn apart by ferocious slobbering mouths. Numerous sets of teeth lunged at her all at once. She avoided three with some quick footwork. Considering she could be one-shotted by everything in the world, she'd gotten good at dodging. She set up another five *Pulse* spells at the first opening and dropped them all into her queue. They were gone in under a minute since she was still receiving the focus of every scalefang in the canyon.

She glanced around the party, checking the emblems on their hands to see what classes might be helpful to her. Their leader seemed to be a *Blade*, though he wasn't doing much damage, probably due to his low level. *Let's change that.* She swiped a caster up and set up an *Infusion* spell with a spark element that carried a buff to his strength stat. The annoying thing about northern scalefangs was that they had the ability to change their elemental affinity. She didn't have time to check, but she assumed at least some of them would be weak to spark. Infusing the *Blade* class with it was better than nothing. The spell activated with a swirl of yellow energy that trailed around his body. It got her a thumbs-up in return.

Eventually, a *Shield* class player, the one whose gaudy gear made him look like a golden blowfish, got his act together. He slammed his armored fist against his chest to activate his *Taunt* skill and yelled a string of obscenities at the scalefangs that would have made a sailor blush. The words he used didn't matter, but the skill added more weight to them regardless, drawing the attention of a couple enemies.

Kira cringed at the man's use of vocabulary. It wasn't that she was bothered by swearing. Sometimes she loved it. A well-placed F-bomb or an interesting combination could be pretty funny, if timed right. More often than not, though, it showed a lack of creativity and throwing away such a great opportunity like a *Taunt* seemed like a waste. Even worse, most of the scale-fangs ignored the player altogether, still focusing on her.

Jaws snapped shut, missing Kira's toes by less than an inch as she hopped out of the way. She might have stood a better chance if she had at least picked a combat mage class such as a *Venom* or a *Cauldron*. But had she picked either of those? Nope. She had gone with *Breath* mage, which could heal, and that was pretty much it.

"Any time now, Max," she grumbled through her teeth as she swiped open her spell-craft menu and set up a *Mirage* with one hand while casting another *Pulse* at a hungry scalefang with the other. Two transparent versions of herself appeared, bracketing her on both sides and mimicking her every move. They were taken out after a couple more attacks, buying her precious little time. That was when a drooling mouth clamped down on her left arm.

A dull, simulated pain spread through her wrist, followed by a numbness that radiated from her elbow to her hand to keep it bearable. She pivoted, using the beast's momentum to swing her attacker off. She looked to her forearm where teeth marks glowed red across the digital ink of her stat-sleeve before fading away. The bone charm at her side did the same, taking the hit for her and leaving her feeling vulnerable without it. It was an item that only worked once, meaning that the next hit would be her last.

"Crap!" She regretted her decision to jump into the situation alone. Without some reliable back up, it was only a matter of time.

MaxDamage24 shoved with one hand at a scalefang as it pinned him to the ground. The beast's jaws scraped against the underside of the pistol he gripped in his other hand. He would have shot the thing, but the angle was off, leaving the muzzle of the gun sticking out the side of the creature's mouth like a cigar. Oh well. At least it wasn't biting him. There had been a second scalefang, but he'd pushed that jerk off the ledge. Granted, he'd also dropped his other gun in the process. Now it was laying on the ground just out of reach.

He shoved again at the beast above him, its over-muscled neck holding steady as it pushed back in an attempt to eat his face. A droplet of drool fell from its tongue. It would have landed in his mouth if Max's scarf hadn't slipped up over his chin a moment before. He blew a puff of air at the fabric with a frustrated grunt to clear it away from his face. Then another drop of drool fell.

"Blah! Right in my mouth." Max spat right back at the creature.

The scalefang didn't seem to care.

"Get off me, you damn lizard thing!" he growled through his teeth. He was glad Kira wasn't around. She'd never let him live down such a bland insult, or for that matter, the fact that he had been caught off guard a minute after he'd jabbed her for not paying attention to her surroundings. Thinking of her, he glanced at his party readout roasting in the tattooed flames on his wrist. She didn't have time to wait for him.

Max wasn't any stronger than he was in the real world. Sure, his stats were high enough but that only affected his weapon damage. He reached for his other gun, fingertips falling just short. He groaned. He almost would rather it be further away, as if it was teasing him by being so close, yet so far. In the end, he ignored it and opted to punch the scalefang in the neck. It let out a growl, but his bare fists couldn't do much more than chip damage. He cursed Noctem's developers for prioritizing the game's realism over giving players enhanced physical capabilities to match their character build. Although, it could be worse. He could be Kira. She'd hit him more than enough times to know how limited a fairy's physical strength was.

He punched the beast again hoping to make it flinch. Then he got a brilliant idea. He shoved his wrist into the creature's mouth and held it in place while he yanked his pistol free. Teeth clamped down, illuminating his arm in a glow of crimson puncture marks.

"Bite me." He shoved the gun into the thing's side and fired.

The scalefang reeled backward, letting Max roll out from under its weight. He snatched his other pistol from the ground and fired twice to put down the threat.

Max stood as the red glow faded from his wrist, and he spat out his scarf which had somehow gotten back in his mouth during the struggle. The light scrap of fabric hung halfway off his shoulder, leaving him looking disheveled. He pulled the accessory off and stuffed it down the front of his leather armor to keep the bump to his dexterity that it provided. He could equip it properly later. Right now, he had to get moving.

Max raced down the canyon's zigzagging path, catching a glimpse of the party below. Kira was at its center, dodging scalefangs and casting every spell she could to stay alive. He still had some way to go when she took a hit. He checked his stat-sleeve for her health, hoping she still had a bone charm equipped to take the damage for her. He exhaled when he saw her meager fifty points, right where they belonged, but even with that, he couldn't slow down. No, worse. He had to move faster. The next attack would kill her.

He examined the path, finding a place where it doubled back further down. He was still over thirty feet above the canyon floor, but the ledge below was halfway in the middle. It sparked an idea. He glanced at his own health and ran the numbers, estimating the fall damage against his defense and remaining health. He nodded to himself, then took a running leap.

His boots hit the ledge with a crunch of crumbling rock, and he lost track of which direction was up for a moment. Then it was obvious. The ground met his feet with a sudden jolt of simulated pain that faded as he tucked his body into a ball. From there, damage registered all over. He rolled, working with the momentum until he found his footing and slid to a stop on one knee between Kira and a few hungry mouths. He drew his pistols in the same motion and opened fire.

A cacophony of sound and smoke erupted from his hands, his eyes darting between enemies to make each bullet count. It was his turn to catch the scalefangs by surprise. Swirls of smoke trailed around him until his magazines ran dry, the slides of his pistols locking back empty. The first wave of The Culling was finished; lifeless reptilian bodies littered the ground around him. He stood motionless for a moment, still aiming his guns in opposite directions. A satisfied smirk grew on his face while his dumbfounded audience took in the scene. He gave Kira his most annoying wink. "Sorry, I had to do my class justice. Wouldn't be much of a *Fury* if I didn't know how to make an entrance."

She narrowed her eyes back at him.

He responded with a bow, twirling the tip of one empty gun as if it were a top hat. Having made the right impression, he stood back up and tossed one pistol into his other hand to hold it next to its twin and ejected their magazines. He shoved in a fresh pair just as the next group of scalefangs got into position.

"Nice of you to show up. Did you log out and use the bathroom on your way down?" Kira spouted in an obvious attempt to hide how relieved she must have been as she took up her position at his side.

"Yeah, that's exactly what I did, you jackass," he replied through a thick layer of sarcasm.

"That's good. I'd hate to repeat that night you ate all those tacos before logging on," she added with a musical laugh at the end that was entirely out of place in such a tense situation.

"God, you're never gonna let me live that down, are you?"

She laughed again. "Nope, it was hilarious. I'm just glad I don't have to do your laundry."

Noticing the party's unease at their banter, Max got serious again. "You ready for this?"

"It's what we came for." She turned back to the party. "We're gonna need some space for this. Before I landed, I released enough pixie dust to give you all a few minutes of *Flight*. You should have a little left. Use it to get clear."

The group did a double take at their stat-sleeves to find a tiny feather icon next to each of their names. Before Max could say good luck, they were already gone. He let out a low whistle. "Damn, they cleared out fast."

"Yeah, I'm kinda glad I didn't mention the effects of my pixie dust earlier."

Max brushed a lock of dirty blond hair off his cheek with a thumb. "Did you ever think you would use the words 'pixie dust' in a serious conversation?"

Kira snorted. "No. No, I did not."

Then, almost on cue, the next wave of scalefangs began to close in, now outnumbering them ten to two. Kira and Max turned to face each other and stepped in close, their backs to the creatures.

He gave her a smirk. "May I have this dance?"

She rolled her eyes as hard as possible and swiped her hands up to open her spell-craft menu for both casters at once, surrounding herself with glowing glyphs on either side.

Both Max and Kira were level one hundred and fourteen, but that didn't mean they were strong enough to survive with only the two of them. They could win if they had a party of five or six, but alone, it would take some strategy.

Max held his guns up in front of his forehead and breathed the words, '*Custom Rounds*' followed by, '*Low Velocity*.' He didn't need much range for what was coming, but the fifteen bullets in each magazine weren't enough to kill a wave of scalefangs before being overtaken. There was no margin for error and reducing the recoil on his guns would help him land his hits. Of course, he could have used the same skill to add an element to his bullets, but he couldn't change them a second time, and besides, that wasn't his job.

Kira spun the rows of glyphs without needing to look, skipping past the one that started *Infusion*. That spell would have worked to buff Max's hits, but it was too slow, and the scalefangs' ability to change their affinity made them versatile. She needed to be, too. Her fingers aligned three low-level spells instead, *Flame Touch, Spark Touch,* and *Wind Touch.* Most players forgot about this little group of spells as soon as they got new ones because they required the caster to actually touch a player's weapon. She dropped two of each into her queue and finished off with a *Guidance* spell which let her see the elemental weakness of each target as a colored aura around them.

Max swept the scene with his eyes as the feathered lizards closed off any possible route of escape. He took a breath and raised his pistols to a pre-planned height to allow the fairy to reach them with her short stature.

Kira turned to face the creatures and reached back over her shoulders, tapping each gun with her fingertips. Then it started.

A scalefang lunged as the pair darted in opposite directions, causing it to stumble between them. Then turning in unison, Kira pointed at it with her right hand, telling Max to use his right gun. He fired a single round, ending the creature. He looked back to his partner. She had already selected two more targets for elimination before the ejected bullet casing hit the ground.

The scalefangs swarmed, leaping two and three at a time as Max dodged and ducked attacks. Kira matched him, weaving past without ever getting in the way. She pointed. He fired. Together they took out the closest threats to make some room. They left alive the ones that didn't match their current set up. Kira ducked past him, close to his side. He responded by lowering one pistol for her to touch on her way by and she spun across his back like a dancer to update his other weapon. With both guns set to spark, he cleaned up the last of the wave, electricity arcing off each kill.

Max ejected his near-empty magazines as a new wave of enemies moved into position. Normally, he would keep firing until they were spent, but he had to make efficient use of the moment available. He didn't bother reloading; there wasn't time to get a new mag from his pouch. Instead, he held both pistols sideways so that the openings at the base of their grips faced the same direction. He didn't even have to wait. Kira was already sliding in two fresh magazines from the stock she carried as a backup.

From there, Max continued to fight while Kira pranced around him, speeding up as his confidence grew which led to an almost cocky attitude. "Hey, scaly dumbass," he called as he took out another.

"Oh, if you're doing wisecracks you can do better than that." Kira pointed out a new target.

He fired. "I think that one had a reptile dysfunction."

"Really? A dick joke?" Kira slapped one hand to her face and pointed to another scalefang with her other.

"Toothy handbag?" Max fired.

That one got a snort out of her.

"Feathers McBiteface?" he offered, pulling a trigger.

The fairy laughed and twirled past him, becoming more excessive with her movements for added style. She leapt backward and materialized her wings to float over his head. At the same time, he raised his guns for her to update. Shimmering particles fell from her wings, mixing with the swirls of smoke that drifted around him. It was impressive, but her landing put her in the path of a lunging scalefang, which forced Max to dash between them to take the hit.

He grunted with the impact and lost his balance, going down on one knee hard enough to take damage to his leg. He took a few more hits before regaining his stance. His health plummeted. Kira cast a frantic mid-level heal in an attempt to fill him back up without drawing too much attention. He recovered, but the near loss reminded him of what they were up against. From there, he quit screwing around and pushed on with renewed focus, leaving few openings for the rest of the beasts.

The whole fight, which seemed to last forever, only took about a minute. After which, he was left standing with her at his back in the middle of a circle of corpses. There was no blood, as that would have been more graphic than what the game intended for its audience, but the sheer number of bodies still gave the scene a macabre feeling.

Max took a moment to catch his breath as the same deep growl that signaled the start of the event echoed from the largest cave in the canyon. They both looked in its direction, making contact with a single massive green eye that glowed in the dark of the shadowed entrance. A glance at the shifting ink on his wrist showed him the boss's health bar as it appeared, running down the edge of his forearms to the side of his party status.

One-Eye stalked into the bright light of the moon, his size being several times that of the scalefangs that they had finished off. His feathered mane fanned out like razor blades. Despite being nothing more than a construct of the system, his low growl seemed full of contempt and rage for the ones that had put his brothers to death. He charged. Max and Kira did the same.

The fairy darted into the air, casting a *Pulse* with both casters. White puffs of energy hit the beast in the face and neck, bursting on impact. His massive scaled body faltered for a moment. He recovered and spun his head to face the fairy for a killing blow as she landed on the ground in front of him within reach. It would only take seconds for him to end her. Then the sound of a bullet being chambered came from beside the huge scalefang.

The boss hadn't seen Max approach since Kira's distraction had kept the beast's blind spot turned toward him. There was no time for it to turn or run. Instead, it just froze. For a moment, Max almost pitied the artificial beast, but only for a moment. He unloaded one pistol into the scarred indent where the creature's missing eye should've been, landing several critical hits before switching hands and emptying his other gun for good measure. Max ejected the magazines while saying one line as the beast fell. He kept his voice low as he quoted a bad action movie, "Rest in pieces."

Kira hopped over to him, grinning like a goon. There was a sharp contrast to the intensity she had carried just seconds before.

Max chuckled at the sudden cheerfulness. It suited her better. Although, he would never actually tell her that.

"That was quick. Didn't have to wait around at all," she stated, drawing a small doodle on the dusty ground with her foot.

Max's heart lifted, excitement rushing into him. "That's true. We still have a few hours before logout. We could do something else ... something that's actually fun."

Kira navigated through her stat-sleeve's options again, this time selecting the word 'loot'. It redrew itself into a list of the items gained by the fight.

Five scalefang scales
Twelve scalefang teeth
One large claw

Fifteen bones of predatory beasts

"Nice! This should cover me for a couple of weeks at least." Kira bounced on the balls of her feet as she tapped 'collect all'. The bodies faded to bones which would disappear as well over the next hour, erasing the evidence of the last few minutes of scalefang murder from the landscape.

Max checked his progress bar in his journal, finding his level hovering at ninety-five percent, even after the 51,634 experience points gained from the fight. Most of the time, he didn't bother looking because the bar took so long to fill, but he had been close to advancing for the last few days. He also needed the upgrade points to rank up his *Custom Rounds* skill. His attention was drawn away when he noticed a *Blade* class player standing behind them. It was the leader of the party that they'd rescued.

"Umm, thanks." The *Blade* seemed to be making an effort to stand tall.

Kira returned to drawing on the ground, so Max did the talking as usual. "No problem, we were here anyway."

The *Blade's* eyes shifted from Max to Kira, then down to her drawing. "Oh."

"Why were you here with The Culling overdue like that?" Max asked as he pulled his scarf out from where he had stuffed it earlier and held it out straight so he could fold it back into a triangle.

The *Blade's* eyes snapped back to him, and he scratched at the back of his head. "A friend told me that it had already happened, so we were trying to get a level." He gestured toward the rest of his party hiding up on one of the ledges.

"I'd probably have a chat with that friend. I think they just tried to get you killed." Max wrapped his scarf around his neck and tied it back on.

The *Blade's* eye widened. "Oh, damn! You might be right. Anyways, my name is DarkAssassin. Thanks for the rescue."

Max shot Kira a look, hoping she'd refrain from snorting or making a joke about the kid's name. As it was, he was pretty sure her mind was already shortening it down to DarkAss. "No problem, I'm Max, and this thing here is Kira."

She waved and went back to drawing.

Assassin gave her an awkward wave back. "I have to ask. How the hell did you do that?" He looked past them at the bones on the ground.

"It's a farming spot for us. We come here a lot."

"Sure, but I mean, the *Fury* class isn't really known for being that strong, and there's no aim assist or anything, so how did you learn all the …" Assassin finished the question by making finger guns and shooting them in all directions.

Max laughed at the gesture. It had been a while since he'd had a chance to brag, so he decided to give the guy a lesson. "It's true that *Fury* isn't a popular class, but it is versatile and can deal respectable damage, provided you can hit your targets. That's the part that's easier said than done. I mean, stats like strength and dexterity matter for damage output, but if you want to run, jump, aim, or dodge, the system can't help you there. That would mean the game would have to control your movement somehow, and honestly, I don't think the technology has come that far. So, you have to do all that on your own, like in the real world."

"Yeah?" Assassin raised his eyebrows, clearly expecting some kind of sage advice to come next.

"Now, the higher your level gets, the harder the enemies get. Which means that the only way to play at higher levels is to learn to fight. In short, git-gud."

Assassin's eyebrows fell back down. "Oh."

Max rested his hands on his guns. "Sorry. Wish I had something better to tell you. Just keep playing. Eventually, things will just click into place."

Kira stepped in, now finished with her drawing - which looked like a cartoon purse with a mouth. She'd written the words 'toothy handbag' beside it. "Tell your *Shield* thanks for protecting me while we waited for this ass to take his sweet time getting down here."

"Hey! I ran as fast as I could," Max said before realizing something important. "Actually, why the hell didn't you just dust me up before jumping down here? I could have just flown down with you."

"Ahhhh …" she started to say, but then she closed her mouth and shrugged while making a sound that suggested the words 'I don't know.'

DarkAssassin gave her a look that seemed to ask the same question, but he said nothing.

After that, they said their goodbyes and sent him on his way, getting a friend request from the player almost as soon as he was out of view.

Kira groaned as soon as she opened it. The kid had replaced each S in his name with the number 5, making him DarkA55a55in. "I hate it when people use numbers in the place of letters."

"Oh, god. Not this again," Max sighed.

"I mean, it's so hard to read." She held her journal close to re-read the friend request. "The only thing worse is when they alternate between upper and lower case 'cause that's completely illegible."

Max rubbed the bridge of his nose with his fingers as if he had a headache. "I know. I've heard this rant so many times."

"Well, it merits repeating. Is it too much to ask to just come up with something original enough not to require alternate spellings and numbers?" She walked backward in front of him.

Max sighed again. "Anyways, what you want to do next?"

She shrugged, falling back into sidekick mode. "I don't care. You pick."

He opened his journal and held it so they both could see as she slid up to his side. "Let's see if that guy still needs help with the Fire Temple."

"Tomb," she corrected.

"What?"

"I thought it was the Fire Tomb that he needed help with."

"Temple, Tomb, what's the difference?" Max argued.

Kira leaned her head to one side. "Well, one is a place of worship, and the other is a place to lay the dead to rest."

He groaned. "Thank you, Miss Dictionary."

"Hey, you got a new message." She leaned in close so their shoulders touched and pointed to a line of text at the top of the page.

"That's odd; I must have missed the system chime during the fight," he said, looking at the page.

The subject column read one word: Important. If that wasn't enough to encourage him to open the message, it was also written in red ink to signify that the sender had marked the contents as urgent.

"That's odd. The sender's unknown," Max commented.

Kira scrunched up her nose as if smelling something. "That's fishy."

"Better not be spam." Max selected the red text and read aloud. "Meet me in the back room of the Hanging Frederick tavern in the city of Valain. Bring the fairy. Cannot wait until tomorrow. Must be before logout. I have a mission for you. I repeat, come ASAP!"

"I hate when people say ASAP. It makes me feel like I'm at work reading emails. Also, I do have a name." Kira squinted her eyes as if somehow glaring at the unknown sender of the message.

Max tapped a finger on the back of his journal. "Might be interesting, though. I mean, it's piqued my curiosity."

She chuckled. "What's that they say about cats?" She drew in a breath then frowned. "Oh, yeah. Curiosity kills them."

Max snapped his journal shut. "True, but I don't think I've heard anything about it killing fairies."

"I guess so." She opened her spell-craft menu and set up a *Teleport*. "I didn't wanna do the Fire Tomb again anyways. It's too easy."

CHAPTER TWO

Water poured from the mouths of the decorative stone dragons that frolicked in the fountain at the center of the large circular park in the heart of the city of Valain. An orange sphere appeared, sparkling flakes dissipating from its surface to reveal Max and Kira standing casually as if they were used to it, which they were.

Max began making his way in the direction of the tavern, holding his journal open to a map of the city. A line highlighted the path to the new waypoint that came in the anonymous message. That was when he realized that his partner was no longer by his side. With a quick glance, he spotted her buying some form of meat on a stick at a strip of food stands lining the side of the park.

How the hell did she get over there so fast? he wondered. "Hey!" he called to her.

She turned in his direction, chewing on a skewer of chicken.

Max tried to look annoyed, but in truth, it was a kind of adorable in an unintentional sort of way. He chuckled to himself before calling to her again, "ASAP doesn't mean, 'After you buy all the food in the park.'"

She pulled the skewer from her mouth, taking a bite in the process. "That's what they get for saying ASAP. I have to rebel a bit."

Max joined her, understanding from experience that there was little point in arguing. She forced one of four sticks of food into his hand. He grumbled but took a bite without further protest. Then they sat in silence, just enjoying the atmosphere and watching players pass by.

Amongst the six major cities in Noctem, Valain was easily the largest. And since it was the only city under the direct control of Checkpoint Systems, it - and the territories that it ruled over - remained peaceful no matter what was going on in the game. Even when wars broke out between one house of players and another - which was more common than one might think.

Like most of the cities in the game, Valain had an overall fantasy look to it but with larger buildings covered in Gothic architecture that towered overhead like skyscrapers. Though Noctem might have been a world of magic, the city also had elements of technology and present-day life mixed in. A stroll through its medieval streets would find taverns full of players taking time off from questing as well as cleverly disguised night-clubs and malls catering to the less adventurous inhabitants of the world. After all, some people just used the system to take back the night while they slept which had always caused a crowd in the heart of the city.

Airships drifted through the sky, transporting people across a world that begged to be explored. Joining them was a number of private transport shuttles, mostly carrying the city's worka-holics who spent their nighttime hours making deals and racking up more money than Max would ever see in his lifetime.

In fact, business was booming in the city of Valain, so much so, that it had become something like Noctem's unofficial capital of commerce with corporations renting entire buildings of virtual space for their online operations. With a system like

Somno out there, things like international travel had become a thing of the past. Hell, Max had even heard of large corporations holding entire trade shows and conferences right there in the city. Not that he would ever be invited to one. Thanks to Checkpoint, it was all kept hidden within the well-designed towers that reached high into Noctem's sky. Business was good and all, but that didn't mean it was allowed to interfere with the game. That would have gone against everything that Carpe Noctem seemed to stand for.

Amidst all the activity, Kira finished off her three skewers and stood before Max could finish his one. She left him on the bench while she stretched out her limbs. It might have seemed needless since her body wasn't actually real, but the way the system interacted with the user's mind included subtle things such as stiff shoulders and sore legs.

She raised her arms above her head and leaned to each side, inadvertently allowing the slits on both sides of her dress to shift upwards to show a perfectly formed hip just above the low waistline of her pants. Her delicate pale skin peeked out to say, hey!

Kira's age was a little hard to judge, standing at only four and a half feet tall, but depending on who you asked, most would put her around twenty. She was cute, that much was obvious. Granted, that wasn't really saying much, since most of the users, especially the ones in the city, had designed their avatars to be easy on the eyes. This, of course, created an overall population that was pretty damn hot, but it also made the more unique characters like her stand out.

The features of the fairy race made Kira seem a little more magical than the rest, with her large eyes and slightly pointed ears adding something special into the mix. On top of that, the fact that she weighed so little compared to others infused her movements with a subtle grace that just didn't exist in the real world. Combine all that with her somewhat goofball personality, and she gained a sort of perfect storm of appeal, making it seem like a night with her in your bed might be more fun than most could imagine. A fact that had proved dangerous for Max, as it was occasionally hard for him to stop staring.

He watched absentmindedly as her back arched exquisitely. She stretched her arms behind herself and let out a quiet sound, a little moan to express her transition into relaxation. That was when Max caught himself eyeing her bare skin visible through the opening in the back of her dress meant for her wings, in what most would call an inappropriate manner. At least he wasn't drooling. Unfortunately, he realized he was leering a second too late, averting his eyes only to meet hers as she looked down at him over her shoulder. Her hair hung down, hiding half of her face and giving her a look that inadvertently radiated sex appeal.

"Don't make it weird, bro. Don't make it weird." She shook her head at him.

Max sunk into the bench, bringing one hand up to rake through his stylish yet messy hair as if trying to hide. His skin prickled hot.

She laughed at his discomfort.

Then he sat up and slapped one hand down on the bench. "You know what? No. You're the one making it weird, always wiggling that thing around in front of me." He gestured to her rear as the thing in question.

She tilted her head and placed a finger to her chin. "True, but as you remember, you chose this body for me as part the deal. So, the root cause of said weirdness is still definitely you."

The weirdness was due to the fact that in their twenty-seven years of life, they had been friends for almost all of it. Also, both of them were men. Not that there would be anything wrong with them finding love in each other's arms, but Max didn't think of her like that, and he was pretty sure she didn't either. It wasn't on the table for them. They were bros, and that was just how it was.

Back when MaxDamage24, whose real name was Wyatt Mathews, told Kirabell, also known as Seth Hase, that he wanted to get Carpe Noctem when it came out, they both decided that if they were going to play it, they were going to be the best. In the past, they had gravitated toward teamwork-based shooters. Over time, they'd learned each other's tactics inside and out. So much so that they appeared to be able to read each other's minds as they worked together in perfect sync. Hell, their friends even complained when the two of them were placed on the same team against them, claiming that it wasn't fair. So, when they read that Noctem would offer a range of experiences, from fun and simple quests to near impossible boss fights referred to appropriately as Nightmares, they were sold.

In the year before the game came out, Wyatt got a head start by looking over all the pre-release information to learn everything he could about their new world. The first thing they'd needed to decide had been the best combination of races and classes to give them the maximum potential possible - even if it meant that it might be difficult in the beginning. After all, they were far from casual gamers.

In the end, it took some convincing and a number of spreadsheets, but they settled on a human *Fury* and a fairy *Breath* mage. The convincing needed was due to the fact that fairies only came in female, meaning Seth would have to explore his feminine side since he had always preferred support classes. He'd tried to back out the deal a couple of times, but Wyatt had simply told him that 'he was being a baby' and 'not to worry about it.' Eventually, launch day came, and Kirabell was born. After that, it was too late to go back.

When they had spawned in together in their new forms three years ago, the first thing Kira had said was an awkward, "This is new." Her words had been followed by a burst of uncontrolled giggles at the sound of her own voice, which neither of them ever expected to be so pretty. Max still remembered the judgmental stares they received as she rolled around on the ground amongst the other new players at the spawn laughing her dumb little ass off.

She wasn't the only one to choose to play as the opposite sex. That had always been common in most MMOs, but since players actually had to inhabit the body they designed rather than just look at it on a screen, it did change things.

For some, Noctem meant giving people an outlet where they could live as the gender that they felt matched their identity. For others, it was just part of living in a fantasy world and making it as different as possible. Of course, there were also those that chose it for, well, less pure reasons. Granted, most of them got bored with it once the novelty wore off. Kira though never seemed to care about the difference, aside from getting used to being so short. Max had always assumed she had decided not to overthink it. That seemed to allow her to continue her dual existence as both a well-adjusted adult male and an adorable fairy mage.

As for relationships, Kira didn't seem interested in dating while online and therefore avoided most of the issue altogether. Besides, back on Earth, Seth had always done okay at attracting women.

Unfortunately, the same couldn't be said for Max, who had been single longer than most. As impressive as he was on the battlefield, he seemed equally inept when talking to women in both worlds. A fact that made it even more painful to pal around Noctem with his bro in the form of a magical enchantress.

"Arrgggg!" Max exclaimed, jumping up from the bench. "You know what? I've been single for like three years now, so at this point, I don't care. This whole thing you have going on here is hot." He waved his hand in a circular motion to indicate her general area, highlighting what he referred to as 'this whole thing.'

Kira smirked, cracking a slight smile.

He continued, "Now obviously, I don't consider you an option because that would be weird. But yeah, I'd totally hit that. And by hit that, I mean, I would wreck that."

Kira raised an eyebrow. "You done? Got that out of your system?"

"Yes, thank you very much," Max responded, almost politely.

"Okay then." A grin crept across her face. "Wanna touch my butt?" she joked in a sing-song tone as she pushed her rear in his direction.

Max feigned annoyance to humor her. Then, without warning, he slapped her square on her left butt cheek. The fairy let out a surprised squeak, making his victory clear, and he started walking. "Come on; we're late for a meeting," he added as she lagged behind, straightening her dress and stalling while she waited for the bright shade of pink to fade from her face. Max stopped to glance back. "You coming or what?"

Finally, she jogged to catch up, taking her place by his side. "You will pay for that." She stared straight ahead. "Oh yes, you will pay."

"Oh, I know." He smirked.

CHAPTER THREE

Max took a look at his map, examining the line that showed the shortest path to the tavern. He tilted his head to the side, making a dissatisfied groan before pulling out his pen and drawing in a few edits to alter the line. As leader of his two-person party, his map changes appeared in Kira's journal as well. It was a detail that didn't matter much since, besides farming, which Max hated, she tended to follow his lead and trust his judgment.

The custom path set by Max was almost twice as long as what the system's navigation had suggested moments before. He hoped that by taking a detour they could avoid some of the crowds that gathered in certain parts of the city, the worst being the entertainment district. The area was essentially a long street lined with clubs, bars, and other distractions. For those users who didn't care about questing and just wanted to take advantage of a few extra nighttime hours, it was the place to be. Well, to be more accurate, it was party central. With no risk of a hangover in the morning, the area could get pretty crazy, which was why Max and Kira avoided it at all costs.

It wasn't that they didn't like fun. There was just something about the crowd there that made them feel a little uncomfortable. It certainly didn't help that last time Kira had set foot in the area she had been forced to activate her cage, which was a failsafe option that forbade other users from touching her by creating an invisible barrier just above her skin. Players under eighteen had this option locked in active status at all times to prevent certain activities that might be considered inappropriate. Hence why it had been referred to as a cage.

Most of the party-people in question never ventured beyond the city's walls. Hell, most of them were below level ten and didn't even own a set of armor, so their impact on the game was minor, to say the least. They were background characters, not adventurers. Similar to the world's businesses, Checkpoint had gone through the trouble of designing Noctem's cities in a way that kept that part of the world hidden as well, which made the crowds easier to avoid. Hidden or not, they did still serve a valuable purpose, which was consuming virtual content like it was going out of style.

The economic setup of the game world was pretty impressive. It offered two distinct types of products and operated on a dual currency system that kept everything balanced. On one side, all equipment and items that influenced the game could only be bought with virtual credits that could be earned by simply playing. The other side of things allowed any transaction having no bearing on it could be purchased at a reasonable price with regular money. Checkpoint taking a percentage, of course.

If a user wanted to see a movie, buy a beer, or purchase a new outfit for the club, they would pay for it just like they would anything in the real world. With no way to exchange one currency for another, having a dual currency system also ensured that players would never be left struggling to afford important things like crafting items.

That didn't mean that it was impossible to purchase game items outside the system, the demand eventually giving rise to a number of websites where users could post requests for help in exchange for real money. Sometimes it was something simple like needing to purchase a transport shuttle to get around. Other times, it was something more complex like escorting users through high-level territories. It was a system that had funded a road trip up the East Coast for Max and Kira just the year before. It had been fun. They saw a deer.

Now, the pair traveled away from the bustling streets of commerce and toward the dim corners of Valain on the outskirts of town. Being a virtual world, users were never in danger anywhere in Noctem, but since the game allowed for player versus player combat as well as friendly fire, fights were not uncommon. Player-killing happened from time to time, but for the most part, it tended to gravitate toward the places in the world where that kind of behavior was encouraged. So as long as you didn't make a habit of provoking people, you could walk around most places without much worry. Nevertheless, the outskirts were rather spread out and getting around could be inconvenient. In the end, it was a place that didn't draw much of a crowd, allowing the real players to enjoy their adventures without distraction. For Max, it felt like home. He belonged there, and he knew it.

The outer districts branched out into a maze of side streets and alleyways. Lamplight flickered, casting a soft silhouette of the pair across the cobblestone path as they progressed toward the waypoint. Gone was the decorative stonework of the city's high-rises, and in its place loomed simple wooden buildings with rickety shutters covering their uneven windows. Threads of light spilled from cracks here and there, lending an air of added mystery to their already intriguing night. Random barrels and crates cluttered the edges of the winding street, making the place seem like a functioning town with its own purpose.

A lagopin, which was a sort of cross between a rabbit and a bird but larger, plodded past them, pulling a cart full of freshly cut hay. The sweet grassy odor filled Max's senses. Its driver, a hardened looking man, leered at him from under the brim of a floppy hat as he took up most of the narrow street, forcing them both to stand aside to let him pass. The animal in front shook its head as if to scratch an itch, its long ears flapping back and forth while it rustled its stubby wings. For a moment, Max feared he might have to stop Kira from petting the fictional animal, but she refrained.

The night air was crisp, feeling several degrees colder than it did in the city's center. Kira wrapped her hands around her arms and shivered but held in any complaint. Instead, she padded along, her feet bare on the stone covered ground while Max strode comfortably, dressed in his armor and scarf. Obviously, it would be ridiculous for a fairy to wear shoes, or at least, that seemed to be what the developers thought since they had made the race unable to equip any.

Soon after, the pair arrived under a dangling wooden sign bearing an image depicting a stick figure game of hangman, the blank spaces below filled in with the words *The Hanging Frederick*.

"Well, that's ominous," Max said matter-of-factly as he glanced around.

Not a soul was in sight. Apparently, it wasn't a popular spot. The door creaked as he pushed it open, causing them both to cringe at the sound. Inside, they were greeted with what they expected, a dim room with few patrons. Exposed beams ran along an uneven ceiling which was held up by a series of rough wooden pillars bearing a number of mismatched carvings. The walls were decorated with pictures of all kinds, ranging from wanted posters and maps to landscape paintings, each one in a different style of frame. Most weren't anything fancy, but the collection did give the place an eclectic feel.

A couple of parties occupied the tavern, taking a moment to unwind after a night of exploration and progress. Occasional laughter peppered the air while a lone guitar player sat on a stool in a corner singing a slow, acoustic version of 'Space Oddity.' Max wished they had come across the establishment sooner. The atmosphere was perfect.

The obvious focal point of the room was a long dusty bar that ran along the full length of the space. A burly man stood behind, wiping a mug made of dark wood with a filthy rag. As Max and Kira approached, they triggered the NPC to cease his cleaning, if that was what you wanted to call it. He leaned on the bar and said in a gruff but friendly manner, crafted to match the atmosphere, "'Ello, my young travelers. What can I get you on this fine evening?" His accent could only be described as old-timey, and his words regarded them as welcomed guests.

"Yes, We're-" Max started to say but was cut off by his partner.

"Could I get some food?" Kira asked, stepping on Max's words and somehow sounding polite and rude at the same time as she glanced at the haphazardly carved menu hanging on the wall, a dagger sticking out of it as if placed there to add items later.

The bartender stuttered for a moment like his programming was trying to figure out who to address. He started again, algorithm clicking into place, "What can I get for such a lovely young lady?" He lowered his head closer to Kira's height, ignoring Max altogether.

"Turkey leg, please." She placed her right hand on the bar to allow a transaction of ten credits to process as she bounced on her toes. She elbowed Max in the ribs to inform him that the tavern worked off in-game credits rather than dollars, which was almost unheard of. Most food items fell into the category of luxury items, so discovering a place that worked off credits was a rare find. It was the sort of secret that you only shared with your most trusted friends, which was probably why it was so quiet. Max would have to thank whoever had sent the urgent message that brought them there.

"You just ate like ten minutes ago." Max rubbed his side where she had elbowed him.

Kira shrugged as if it couldn't be helped, and the bartender walked away through one of two doors behind him, returning a moment later with a smoked leg of meat wrapped in wax paper. She took it from him with enthusiasm and raised it to

her face, leaving Max to continue his conversation unin-
terrupted.

He turned back to the bartender and started again, "Hi,
we're supposed to meet someone in the back room." He hoped
there would be some kind of prompt in place to let them past
the bar.

"What can I get for you?" the bartender repeated since Max
hadn't waited for him to speak first in the interaction. The
man's tone was gruffer than the one he used when addressing
Kira. Pretty young women must get better treatment from his
algorithm.

Max grumbled to himself and repeated his inquiry, growing
impatient with each passing moment. "We're supposed to meet
someone in the back."

There was either no prompt to proceed, or Max hadn't used
the right words because the bartender skipped back to the
beginning of his dialog loop, repeating his question in the same
unfriendly voice. "What can I get for you?"

Max placed his hands on the bar and lowered his head as he
let out the heaviest sigh ever produced by a human being.

A snicker came from Kira.

He looked at her sideways then up at the man again with
narrowed eyes. "Okay, pal. My friend and I got a message to
come here. You gonna let us back there or not?" He pointed to
the door behind the bar.

The bartender paused for a moment as his algorithm tried
to understand Max's words, giving the appearance that he was
considering it. Then he spoke, "What can I get for you?"

"Arrrggghh," Max growled, giving new input to the NPC
without meaning to.

"What can I get for you?" the man repeated.

Max stepped away from the bar and walked in a small circle
before returning.

"What can I get for you?"

He tapped his fingers on the counter, then tried a different
approach. "Hello, my good sir. I hope this evening finds you

well. My compatriot and I were asked here to this fine establishment for a clandestine meeting with persons unknown. Would you be so kind as to allow us access to your back room?" He finished with a slight bow which he held while awaiting a response.

"What can I get for you?"

"Okay, that's it!" Max ground his teeth hard enough the break a filling if he'd had any. For a moment, he let his hand travel to his pistols, the ridiculous urge to shoot something running through his head as he fingered the grips. He refrained. Instead, he hoisted himself onto the bar and stood upright on it before jumping down on the other side.

The bartender didn't seem to notice the intrusion, though several heads looked up at him from across the tables of the tavern as the lone musician ceased an acoustic rendition of 'Safety Dance' so that he could gawk properly.

"What are you looking at?" Max barked. "Go about your business." He gestured a shooing motion with both hands, then turned away from the onlookers and banged on the unused door behind the bar. "Okay, we're here. Let's get this show on the road," he called out.

Silence answered back, and Kira stopped chewing for a second to listen. Then a quiet click-clack came from the lock.

Max twisted the knob. It turned. "You coming?" he asked, looking to Kira.

She swallowed a mouth full of turkey before climbing onto a bar stool and hoisting herself onto the counter with an awkward motion, one hand still holding the large leg of salty meat. She slid her rear across the bar, dusting its surface with her dress, then dropped to the other side to join her partner.

Max shook his head.

"What?" she asked indignantly.

"Nothing. Let's go," he said with a smirk as they passed through the door and into a large shadowed room.

Something was off. The space was somehow larger than it should've been. In fact, it was larger than the tavern itself.

Decorative stonework lined the walls making it feel disjointed from the wooden beams of the previous space. It was as if the room wasn't even part of the same building, like he had walked through a door and into a different part of the city, which might have been possible. He wasn't sure.

A long stone table stretched into the empty space with several high-backed chairs lining its sides. A few small lanterns ran down the table's imposing surface, causing the shadows cast by the chairs to reach across the floor and up onto the walls, the gaps of light and dark making the room feel like the rib cage of a giant skeleton.

A lone hooded man rose from the furthest chair at the head of the table. He seemed to glide toward them without a sound in the darkness as he approached. The shadow of his hood twisted the features of his face in the dim but hard light of the lanterns.

The door slammed behind them, making Max aware of the presence of two additional figures lying in wait. They were surrounded.

Stupid, Max thought, *walking into a room without thinking. So very stupid*.

The air grew thick with tension the second he realized the trap they had just stepped into. Max's mind fired up to process the situation, his artificial muscles twitching in anticipation. That's when the man in front of them pushed back his hood. Max recognized his face from many of the presentations he'd watched online from gaming conventions.

"Thank you for accepting my invitation," greeted Alastair Coldblood.

CHAPTER FOUR

Flesh tore on impact, leaving bits of skin remaining on the stunned face of the smaller of the two figures blocking the door.

Max stood, guns drawn, his eyes darting in assessment of the trap.

In front stood Coldblood, human, a *Cauldron* class. Slow compared to other mages but capable of handing out far more destruction than any other. Max knew the man's capabilities. Hell, he was famous. Everyone did.

Behind them on the left was a tall male, his face hidden by the hooded robes of a *Venom*, the fastest of the offensive mage classes. Dangerous with debuffs and damage-over-time spells. From his height, he was probably an elf. Decent mana with moderate health. An armband on one arm marked him as one of Checkpoint's Game Masters.

To the right, a woman was still recovering from being struck in the face with a turkey leg. She had a medium build. Human. And no armband? Interesting. One of her hands was covered by a gauntlet, *Shield* class gear. Max had seen it before on other *Shield* players. It required around level one hundred and ten to wield.

Max tightened his grip on his pistols. They were out-numbered and outgunned.

"Who the hell throws a turkey leg?" the *Shield* spouted with disgust after being hit without warning by an airborne meat projectile.

It hadn't helped that Kira had yelled, "Distraction!" when she threw it.

"I mean who does that?" The *Shield* continued to wipe her face, the grease leaving a dull sheen on the brown skin of her cheek.

A few locks of black hair clung to her face, their strands peppered with bits of smoked turkey. She pushed them to one side where she ran her fingers through, removing the foreign matter before letting them fall back into place. The rest of her hair was tied back and fell down her neck in a mass of loose curls that trailed off into wisps at their ends. The sides were cut short with a single braid hanging on either side just before her ears in a way that made her look like a viking raider. Her brown eyes burned with shock and indignation, but she repressed any further complaints.

A moment passed where nobody moved as if everyone was unsure of how to proceed. Max did the talking, trying to sound calm despite the situation, "Am I to take from the fact that none of you have drawn on us yet, that we are not in any kind of trouble?" He would have batted his eyelashes, but he didn't think that would help.

"Have you done anything that would get you in trouble?" Alastair sounded like a teacher in high school fishing for information.

It rubbed Max the wrong way. "How 'bout we skip the pleasantries, and you just tell us why you called us here."

"Fair enough; have a seat. I'll explain." Alastair motioned to the chairs on one side of the table.

"We'll stand if you don't mind. Not looking to get too comfortable," Max stated, keeping one gun on Alastair and the other on the hooded *Venom* mage behind them.

Kira stood at his back, casters glowing, ready to throw a couple *Pulse* spells at the *Shield*, who now seemed to be having trouble maintaining eye contact with anyone.

"Sure, it's a free world." Alastair shrugged, holding both palms up to the ceiling. "Although, I would recommend sitting before you hear what I have to say. And by all means, keep the gun on me if it makes you feel better." He pulled out a chair and sat down opposite them, ignoring the weapon pointed in his direction as if Max was no threat to him at all. His dark, shoulder-length hair fell forward as he took his seat, red streaks running through it like blood trickling from a wound. He pushed it back with a ring-covered hand, his snow-white fingers slipping through his locks with a practiced elegance. He looked back to them, his eyes encircled by crimson streaks of eyeliner that traced angular points outward and down his nose, making him look like a cross between Ziggy Stardust and an evil Kabuki actor. His demeanor was calm, which annoyed Max as the mage continued, "To answer your question, I called you both here to request your services in completing a quest."

"Why the hell would we want to work for you?" Max spouted, knowing all about the controversy that surrounded the man. After all, he hadn't been living under a rock.

"Good question." Alastair leaned his head to the side and smirked. "For starters, this quest pays two hundred thousand U.S. dollars each."

With that, guns were slid into holsters just as fast as they had been drawn and casters snapped shut. Max stepped forward, pulling out a chair and sitting like he was at home.

Kira bowed to the *Shield*. "I sincerely apologize for assaulting you with food," she said, sounding polite, almost out of character for her.

The shield hesitated as if unsure of how to react to the fairy standing before her with her head lowered, enchanting blue eyes looking up at her through a few silver locks of hair. Max thought he saw a hint of a smile on the woman's face.

After another pause, she nodded, adding an awkward, "It's okay. We're cool."

Kira smiled back before hopping into a chair next to Max and pulling up close to the table. She leaned her face on one palm. "So what kind of quest are we talkin' about?"

Alastair held up a hand. "Let me start by saying that to move forward, you both must accept a standard non-disclosure agreement, which has just been sent to your inboxes. You can do so by placing your hands on the table and stating your approval."

"We'll bite." Kira placed her palms flat on the stone without bothering to open the message.

Max at least pretended to skim the contract before doing the same. "We thoroughly agree to keep our big mouths shut."

"Yup," added Kira.

Alastair relaxed in his chair. "Okay, now that's out of the way, here comes the part that you needed to be sitting down for." He exhaled and leaned forward on the table, letting his character's persona slip a little, giving Max a glimpse at the man underneath. "One hour ago, I received a video message from Neal Carver, who you are probably aware was just let go from Checkpoint Systems."

"I bet he didn't have anything nice to say, what with the backstabbing and all." Max leaned one elbow on the table, resting his chin on his hand to mirror Kira.

Alastair rolled his eyes. "One common misconception about him and me is that we were the best of friends back when we started this company." He spoke quickly as if he had already explained it several times.

"That is what people say," Max commented.

"Well, people are wrong. The truth is that we had a business relationship and that was all. I was just a nerdy kid that he used to get money so he could work on whatever project he wanted. I was a means to an end to him."

"Scandalous." Kira placed both hands over her mouth and

spoke in a voice that to Max sounded like fancy lady gossip. He suppressed a chuckle.

Alastair spoke louder as if defending himself, "I did everything I could to support him when I saw what this system could do. And I'd do it again in a heartbeat. Noctem … was … worth it." He jabbed his finger at the table with each word for emphasis.

Max lifted his chin from his hand and sat up straight. "Did that have something to do with the recent split?"

"Yes and no." Alastair tilted his head from side to side. "I know the media has been portraying me as a ruthless CEO that cuts people loose when they're no longer useful. But officially, the legal department and I were forced to make the decision to let him go over what the paperwork calls 'creative differences.'" He held his fingers up to form air quotes. "The 'creative differences' being that I didn't want to kill anyone."

"Wait. What?" Max sputtered, dropping his hand from his chin.

"Yeah, that was my reaction too when I found out what he did." Alastair leaned against the armrest of his chair. "Neal tried to run an unauthorized test trial last week on some volunteers. Ultimately, he put their lives at risk."

Kira leaned forward. "How?"

"From the beginning, his goal has always been to push the limits of the system, and we indulged him as long we could. But he kept pushing for more and going beyond what was reasonable. Eventually, we had to shut down his department." Alastair paused as if remembering something. "Neal didn't handle that well. But his feelings aside, the system has come far enough. From a business standpoint, we don't really need any further development right now. That was why he tried to bypass us by doing things off the record. He put a group of people in the system and disabled the safeties that bring users out after ten hours."

"How many hours were they in?" Max asked.

"Over twenty-six."

They both leaned forward in their chairs as Alastair continued.

"We found out and put a stop to it in time, but they could have died from the combination of being in too long and the mixture of sedatives he gave them to keep them under. Which was precisely why I wouldn't sign off on trials like that. Neal is not a doctor and does not know what the hell he is doing when it comes to medicine."

Kira looked worried. "How long does someone have to be logged in before it becomes dangerous?"

"Currently, we know it's safe to stay in the system for sixteen hours. That's how long we tested in the official trials using only light sedatives. We didn't go beyond that. There wasn't a need to," Alastair tilted his head as if thinking of what to say next. "But in theory, prolonged use could cause the brain to think it doesn't need a body. And that would be bad. Heart failure and what not." He raised a judgmental eyebrow at them. "This shouldn't really be news since it's in the health and safety warnings that come with the system."

Both Max and Kira claimed that they had read the booklet, which was clearly a lie 'cause really, no one ever read those things.

Alastair rolled his eyes. "In the end, Neal forced our hand, and we fired him. We've been keeping the situation quiet and paid out plenty in settlements to the subjects of his unauthorized trial. But obviously, it all kind of backfired on me public image-wise, since no one knows the real reason for his termination."

"That's one way of putting it. You have an angry mob with pitchforks out there." Max left out the fact that the two of them had stolen the farming equipment from a nearby village earlier that night and handed them out to the protesters before heading off to farm scalefangs. Kira had insisted it would be funny. It was kind of funny when Max thought about it. They didn't care enough about the issue to actually protest with the others, but at least they had contributed in their own way.

"I can live with a mob outside my door, but that will be for nothing if Carver gets his way. That's why I need you." Alastair held out both hands as if pleading.

"Okay, you have us here," Max started.

"How can we help?" Kira finished.

"We expected some kind of response when we fired him. We just didn't expect this." Alastair opened his journal and took out his inspector, flicking it out into the air between them. The small glass rectangle expanded to several times its size and the mage leaned back in his chair as if his part was done. Then he swallowed hard.

The image of what looked like a basement filled the portal. Above, there were exposed wooden beams with some of that pink foam insulation packed into the spaces between. Below, a cement wall lined with shelving full of bins contained discarded computer components. The angle of the scene was turned up a hair, like a view from a laptop webcam. In the center of the screen sat a man. Max didn't recognize him, which surprised him. *Did he really not know what the creator of the world that he spent a third of his life in looked like?*

He was thin with glasses and short, dusty blond hair. His eyes were set deep in their sockets, exacerbated by dark circles as if he hadn't slept in days. He wasn't ugly, just unkempt. Kira shuddered as if some detail about the man bothered her. Max noticed it too, though he couldn't put his finger on what it was. He just seemed empty somehow.

"Hi, Milo," Carver said in a tone that was hard to read. It wasn't angry, but it wasn't friendly either. "Looks like I'm back in the old lab, huh? Sorry, the media seems to be giving you a hard time. Well, I guess I'm not that sorry." He paused a moment before starting up again. "I'll get right to the point. I'm grateful for the opportunities that you created for me. You gave me what I needed to create a system that I hoped would help people, and so far, it has. Through it, we've found new ways to treat coma patients and gave others with conditions such as locked-in syndrome a way to interact with the world. But I know it can do more. Fortunately, with the money you helped me make, I now have the resources to branch off on my own. And, as I said, I am grateful," his expression hardened, "but you know I never meant for this system to be used for something as childish as Noctem. It's always bothered me that I had to humor your fantasies to get things done. Now that I don't have to, I can't let my system continue to be misused any longer." He let his face soften. "However, I know you love this world and its players. So, while I may not like it, I can't take it away from you without giving you a chance to save it. With that in mind, I figure the best thing to do is to give you what you want. One last adventure." He gave a halfhearted smile. "I figured that you would cut me loose eventually, so I've prepared a little something. Years ago, I added a quest to the game that would become active if I was ever locked out of the system and unable to deactivate it. If this quest is not started by a standard party of six within twenty-four hours, the world of Noctem will end." He paused to let his words sink in. And sink in they did.

Max and Kira gasped. Even the *Shield* class player standing behind them took a step back.

Carver continued, "Well, to be more accurate, it will be taken apart by..." He hesitated as if searching for the right words before dumbing them down, "let's call it a virus. I mean, it's not really a virus, but that's probably the best thing to call it so that you and whoever you find don't have to think too much about it. Anyways, I built it into the core of the original system. I'm sure that given time, you could rebuild, but without me, that will take years. And by then, the damage will be done. Don't bother trying to remove the virus; there are plenty of fail-safes in place to ensure the system is destroyed completely. Your people would take weeks to clean it out, and you just don't have that kind of time.

"Now, I know what you're thinking - you have an army of Game Masters with near god-like powers at your disposal. This will be easy." Carver smiled. "Let me put that thought to rest now. The quest will not, I repeat, will not, accept any character that has equipped a GM armband at any point since its creation." He paused again. "Your champions will have to come from the players, the very people you made me create this world for. And don't bother trying to find me, either; I'll be long gone before you see this." He held up a note card with a set of numbers on it, some kind of location code. Max didn't recognize it. "Here's where you can start the quest. You have twenty-four hours to get ready. Good luck." He reached forward with his other hand and stopped the recording, leaving a blurry image of the last frame on the screen. The note card still held up, telling them where to go.

"Holy crap!" Max and Kira blurted out in unison.

"This is bad," she added.

"Yeah," agreed Max.

"Like real bad," she added again as if once wasn't enough.

Max slapped the table. "How could he just throw all of this away?"

"He doesn't understand." Alastair sighed, sinking into his chair like someone had let the air out of him. "He never has. Games do help people. Especially now, when everyone spends too much time working. We need fantasies." He seemed heartbroken.

Max found himself feeling bad for the vampiric-looking mage. It must have been hard to face the fact that someone he had worked with for so long had never cared about him.

"Wow." Kira's face fell, the color fading from her cheeks. "All this. Gone."

"Yes. Again, that's why I need you."

"Why us?" Max shifted his tone from one disbelief to suspicion.

Alastair answered with two words, "The Nightmares." He didn't need to say more.

Considered the hardest bosses in Noctem, the Nightmares were infamous. They were battles where one wrong move could get your whole party wiped, Checkpoint's way of catering to the more hardcore players. Granted, everyone else hated them. Not only were they brutal, but they also seemed to have been designed to represent mankind's deepest fears, which added a psychological element that most found disturbing.

They were optional, of course. Although, that didn't really matter when they were the only way to get your hands on some of the most powerful items in the game. Items that could bend the rules of the world in strange and unexpected ways. Sure, some of them only worked once or came with a heavy cost to balance them out, but that was what made them interesting. Still, most players didn't have the patience or skill to suffer through the most torturous experiences that modern gaming had to offer, a fact that got a lot of people frustrated.

Max snorted at the ridiculousness of what he was hearing. "Nice try, but we aren't even on the leaderboards for any of the Nightmares."

Alastair chuckled. "That's true. I've seen a recording of your first attempt at one. You both ran around screaming with your arms flailing in the air before getting killed in one hit. It's a favorite clip amongst some of the developers. They made a blooper reel."

"Oh great." Kira folded her arms. "'Cause that really makes us want to help."

"Sorry, it was pretty funny. But the reason I mentioned it was that you kept trying. And, over time, you got better - which was the point. The Nightmares were the only feature of the game that Neal cared about. He'd even designed them person-ally. At the time, I was just glad that he was taking an interest, even if his reasons had less to do with the game."

"And those reasons were?" Kira asked.

"I already said, to make you better. It was an exercise to see how fast the brain could learn and adapt. That's why they're so hard; he wanted to push players beyond their limits within the safety of a virtual environment. The results were pretty impres-sive. And the players retained most of the skills they learned in game when they logged out, even showing improved reaction times and decision-making skills. We call it *The Nightmare Effect*.

There was even some serious interest in what kind of military applications it had." Alastair held up his hand as both Max and Kira began to argue. "Don't worry, that was the one thing that both Neal and I had always agreed on. Neither of us wanted to see what we built used to train people to kill. When that idea came up, we shot it down right quick. But all that aside, when you two went from the screaming idiots that you were to well-oiled Nightmare killing machines, it got our attention."

"So what? We weren't the first." Max waved his hand to brush away the absurd turn the conversation had taken.

"Do you know why neither of you made the leaderboards?" Alastair asked as they both stared at him blankly in response. "You didn't because we removed the original item limitations on the fights to satisfy some of the complaints we got about the Nightmares being unbalanced. Once we did that, most groups just went in with an item bag full of elixirs since they heal everything and boost their stats at the same time. Then they just chugged their way through each fight, making it more about brute force than skill."

"But that would take months of farming," Max argued.

Kira looked up to the side, remembering. "Yeah, we've only had one elixir between us, and we hoarded it for over a year before using it since it was so hard to get."

Alastair nodded. "You're right. The crafting recipe and level needed to make elixirs is huge. And we did that on purpose, so they would be hard to use like that. The thing is, most of the players above you on the leaderboards come from the top houses in Noctem, all of which have about thirty players farming supplies for them nearly non-stop. With that in place, they have a stockpile ready to go for each expansion. It may take them a couple tries before they get lucky, but they can get through a Nightmare pretty quick compared to players that don't cheat the system. So while it's true that you two may not be high in the rankings, you at least fight the way Neal intended for you to. And that is kind of impressive."

Max scoffed at his words. "There have to be other parties out there that do the same."

Alastair considered it a moment. "True, but after studying fight recordings, the two of you are the most consistent. Even when your party changes, you still create a level of teamwork that most leaders can't manage. Not to mention the fact that you've completed many without losing a player and that you've even made it through the more recent ones on your first try."

"Yay us!" Kira circled one finger in the air.

Alastair ignored her. "Anyway, that's the reason I picked you. I need people that can lead a party into any situation. I need this because I don't know what to expect." He leaned forward. "I underestimated Neal on this, and now I don't want to take any chances."

Max turned to Kira, raising his eyebrow to ask how she felt about the quest.

She tilted her head to the side and frowned, which Max understood. She'd never liked responsibility and placing the fate of an entire world onto their shoulders was too much pressure.

He nodded in agreement. He didn't love it either. Still, there was an offer of payment, and that was something they both could use. He raised his other eyebrow to join the first and pointed to Alastair with his eyes.

Kira leaned her head to the other side. The frown faded somewhat. She was still unsure.

He shifted his eyes around the room to indicate the world they would be fighting for and added a smile to remind her that they both loved it.

Finally, she nodded with a smile of her own.

Max turned back to Alastair. "Okay, we're on board.

Alastair's brow furrowed like he wasn't sure how they had come to that decision without words. "Thank you."

Max slouched back in his chair. "Can't make any promises, but we like this game, so we'll certainly try our best."

Alastair's face fell as if he'd said something wrong. "I hope so. After all, the fate of the real world will be in your hands as well."

Max gave him a puzzled expression as Kira cocked her head to the side like a confused pet hearing a recording of its human's voice.

"Okay, maybe that's a little overdramatic," Alastair bobbed his head, "but businesses have already begun to grow dependent on our system to run globally twenty-four hours a day. Not to mention the fact we are dumping enormous sums of money back into the economy through the sale of the non-game content purchased here. And since most of what we sell is user-created, all of that money goes to regular people who will actually spend it, not corporations who will horde it. My family wasn't wealthy growing up, and my parents sacrificed a lot to get me into MIT, so this is actually a part of the company that I'm particularly proud of."

Max pointed at the man. "Didn't you drop out of MIT?"

Alastair cringed. "Yeah, that didn't go over well at the time. But that's beside the point. I'm not going to say that Checkpoint is going to save the economy or anything, but it's helping. There are plenty of studies to back that up. At the very least, if we lose this system, around a million people will lose their jobs since we employ a staggering number of the world's programmers. We have to just create enough content to keep up with the demand of our users."

"Shit," Max said, unable to come up with a better response.

Kira summed things up a little better with an obligatory, "No pressure."

"Sorry, but you have to understand how serious this is," Alastair added before giving them a weak smile. "At least your team will be paid well."

"True." Max leaned back in his chair. "Speaking of which, we're only two players, so where are we supposed to get the rest of our party for this?"

"I was hoping that you two would be able to help with that. You must have some friends in mind that you work well with."

Alastair placed his hands down on the table in front of him. "This won't be an easy quest, so trusting your team may be the difference between success and failure. I don't want to jeopardize the mission because you don't know your team well enough." He paused, running his finger along the edge of the stone surface. "That being said, I'm not above trying to put at least one of my people in the group." He stood and gestured to the *Shield* class still standing by the door. "That's where Farnsworth here comes in. She works in the creative department at our headquarters, but her character is unrelated to the company, so she's never been a GM. She's a great *Shield*, which is a class you're going to need."

The woman approached the table with confidence, probably putting in the effort to compensate for the somewhat embarrassing way that they had met only moments ago. She ruined it by hesitating with her mouth open as if she had forgotten how to speak. After an awkward pause, she got out the words, "Call me Farn. Most people do."

Max stood as she offered her hand to shake. He took it, and an icon of digital ink flashed below the skull tattoo on his wrist indicating the addition of her contact information to his journal. He kept his attention on Alastair. "Okay, so we have a *Shield*. Now we, what, just invite the rest?"

"Sounds like a good place start." Alastair walked around the table to their side. "You're in the eastern time zone, meaning you only have a few hours at best before logout, right? Can you get it together by then?"

"Yeah, I think so." Max let go of the *Shield's* hand.

"Great." Alastair held out his hand to pass along his profile info. "Contact me if you need any form of support. I'll do anything I can." He shook Kira's hand as well before opening his inventory tab and selecting an item from the list on his forearm, its edges framed by a tattoo of decorative bones. A small rune stone materialized in the palm of his hand. He handed the new spell glyph to Kira. "Take this. You won't need to spend any upgrade points to learn it, and it will give you a new teleport destination that will take you to a command center that regular players can't access. Once you have your team together, take them there, and I'll brief them after they agree to the non-disclosure. Try not to say too much about the mission before then." He turned and walked toward the door as the tall *Venom* mage next to it, who had yet to say a word, took his place at his employer's side, making him look like a henchman.

"Time is of the essence, obviously, so I'll take my leave for now. Good luck. Now get going." Alastair slid back into his character's personality just before an orange shell of energy encompassed the two, leaving the three remaining adventurers in an awkward silence.

Kira clasped her hand around the rune, and a warm glow showed through her skin as the stone was consumed by the system, adding it to her character data.

Max turned to Farn. "Okay, we don't know you—" he stopped abruptly upon realizing how nervous she looked. A spattering of dark freckles ran across her nose and cheeks, blending with her skin as they spread down her face. They drew his eyes to hers, even if she was still avoiding making contact. He started again in a more pleasant tone. "Can we count on you to have our backs when things …" he searched for the right words, "hit the fan?"

She stuttered before answering, "Of course. As long as no one throws any more turkey legs in my face."

A wry smiled cracked across the fairy's face as she opened her spell-craft menu. "I make no guarantees."

CHAPTER FIVE

Kirabell stood in the middle of the new party of three as they looked up at the Everleigh Club, which was located on Cresswell Street, just a short walk from the teleport point in the City of Lucem. People drifted around her on all sides, creating an exciting yet somehow relaxed atmosphere that, upon contact, was down-right infectious. Unlike Valain, with its suffocating entertainment district, Lucem was an entire city devoted solely to fun. The colorful streets were filled with theaters, casinos, arenas, and clubs. The sheer spectacle of the place gave everyone a reason to visit. Kira appreciated the effort.

Above hung the Grand Archway, its impressive length stretching across the sky as far as she could see, all stone and silver. According to the rumors, on top of being Lucem's palace, the arch could also project a shield around the entire the city in the event of an attack. Although, there was no way to know if it was true - since the city had never been threatened thanks to a player, named Leftwitch, who had conquered it back when Noctem first launched. As Lady of the House of the Silver Tongues, she turned out to be a brilliant negotiator, keeping her territory neutral. Not all of Noctem was as lucky. The city of

Torn seemed to have a new ruling house every month, but that was beside the point. Lucem was a place for everyone to play, and no one wanted to disrupt that. It didn't hurt that it was also pretty to look at.

Kira didn't go out for a night on the town much for obvious reasons, but if she did, this would be the place. Strings of lanterns ran this way and that, while every window shined down on the people below. Even the buildings, while nowhere near as tall as the ones in Valain, were magnificent. Each one looked like its own individual piece of art, woven into the tapestry that was the city as a whole as if there had been some kind of architectural renaissance. Although, as wonderful as the place was, Kira still might have avoided Cresswell Street where pots of red flames painted the buildings in a pink glow that made her skin feel hot.

"I thought we were getting a *Coin*?" Farnsworth asked.

Max stood with his hands resting on the butts of his guns. "Oh, we are."

"So why are we outside a brothel?" She grimaced as she looked up at the Everleigh Club.

Max spun to face her, his hands moving up to his hips. "Because the best *Coin* class player we know happens to work at a brothel." He held out his hand to her. "Shall we? I hope you like nudity."

Farn backed away with an awkward step. "Thanks, but no. I'll wait outside if that's okay."

"Suit yourself. Let's go. The women await," he said, excitement in his voice as he turned in Kira's direction.

It was clear to Kira that he was trying his best to imitate what movies had taught him about how cool guys should act. She cringed a bit but held in any jokes she might have had to make at his expense. He was already embarrassing himself all on his own. She followed his lead anyways but walked backward to keep her focus on Farn. It was obvious the new addition to their party felt uncomfortable. "Sorry. We won't be long." Kira gave her reassuring smile, getting a weak nod from the *Shield*, who had only stopped stuttering her sentences a few minutes ago on the walk there.

The Everleigh Club was a large five-story building containing a bar and stage area in its lobby. Kira's ears were greeted by music and the sounds of festivities from within as soon as she stepped through the entryway, which had a strong art nouveau look to its design. She was also scanned by an invisible barrier that confirmed and logged her identity to ensure that she was of legal age to enter such an establishment. At the same time, the scan began processing a cover charge of twenty-five dollars that was subtracted from her bank account upon entry and deposited it in the club's before she was even through the threshold. Unfortunately, that was when she realized that she should have just waited outside and saved her money. Max didn't need her help anyway. Then again, the crumbling facade that he wore to look confident while walking into the place told her otherwise.

When Noctem was originally released, it revolutionized how the world did business in many ways. The adult entertainment industry was no different. With no threat of danger or disease, few cared about streaming videos online anymore when an evening beyond their wildest fantasy had become so easily within reach. Driven by temptation, legislation was passed, and a new golden age of adult entertainment was born. It also created a new, high-paying job market with massive demand. Student loans got paid, and people got their heads above water instead of drowning in debt. That was, as long as they were willing to seek a somewhat different kind of employment.

Kira hid a grin as a bead of sweat betrayed Max, forming at the edge of his forehead from the sight of barely clothed women. They were everywhere! To the left a burlesque show, to the right waitresses serving drinks in an almost nonexistent skirt. His eyes kept moving as if both trying to avoid staring as well as take in the view at the same time. It was obvious he didn't know where to look. Needless to say, it was not the kind of place that he frequented. He may not have been mister popular in either world, but she knew he would never feel comfortable paying for that sort of company. Not to mention the fact that she also knew that he didn't have that kind of money to begin with. They had to share the rent on their apartment in the real world after all.

Kira was a little less terrified of their surroundings, but only a little. The female form wasn't a mystery to her. She had never taken the time to find out what her own body looked like under her clothes, though now, her surroundings did make her a bit too aware of what she was, which left her feeling a bit vulnerable. She tugged on her dress, making sure the slits on the sides didn't ride up.

Alone with each other for the first time since leaving the Hanging Frederick, Max tore his attention away from their surroundings long enough to lean down to Kira as if to tell a secret. "Hey, what do you think of Farnsworth? I mean she's cute, right?"

Kira glared at him. "Don't go gettin' all creepy on her. You just met, and she seems nice."

"I know. I know. That's what I mean. She seems nice," he repeated her words, holding his hands up and palms out.

Kira tilted her head in consideration. "She does have an interesting face, I guess."

"What's that supposed to mean?" He stepped to the side staring down at her sideways.

"I mean, most people try too hard to make their avatar look like a model. But she looks like she put a lot of effort into crafting a character that feels unique, and that makes her seem real." Kira paused, remembering how she had spent hours designing her own character back when she had started for the same reason. "She's interesting is what I'm saying."

"True. Maybe that's what's making her stand out." Max shrugged. "Anyways, I messaged Ginger on the way over. She said she couldn't join us tonight because she was about to put her profile back in to pick up a client before logout."

"That kinda sounds like she turned you down."

Max grinned. "Not if I buy the rest of her night. She can't say no if I'm paying for her," he explained as he approached a row of kiosks by the wall, each bearing a glass screen similar to the inspector in the back of their player journals except bigger.

"Oh, god, that's your plan? I can't imagine any way that could backfire on you."

"Well, I don't really have time for adequate planning, and we need a *Coin*, so I'm going for it." He ran a search of the club's system for her name. "Nice! Found her, and she's still available."

A profile picture appeared on the glass surface, showing a gorgeous brunette with green eyes wearing a matching dress and an inviting smile on her face. She looked like she'd smell like cinnamon. Text ran underneath: Name: GingerSnaps. Age: 23. Not true. Likes: reading and watching movies. Dislikes— "Blah, blah, blah," Max said out loud as his finger searched for a checkout button. "Oh!" He stopped, his finger hovering above a tab that read additional photos.

Kira cleared her throat. "Didn't we just talk about not being creepy?"

"Hey, it's been three years," he reminded her as she continued to bore a hole in his head with her eyes, trying her best to push away his thoughts of misconduct. Eventually, he pulled his finger away from the photos tab. It looked like it took some effort. He hit the button reading 'Request' that brought him to an options screen. "Woah!" he exclaimed, looking at the price which started at just over three hundred dollars per hour. "We better get the payout on this mission." He accepted the amount without adding any of the additional services that made Kira blush just by skimming the list. He pressed the submit button.

The request was processed by the club and cross-referenced against a list of banned users to make sure that he wasn't someone unsavory. Then it was sent to a room upstairs where the requested employee had the option to decline.

"How much you wanna bet she bounces you?" Kira joked,

causing an expression to wash over Max's face that made it clear that he had not known how the transaction worked.

"I thought she would just be surprised when I got up there." His eyes widened. "Oh, god! She knows it's me down here requesting her?"

Kira nodded with a smug grin. "Yup. You basically just asked her to sleep with you."

They both watched the screen. Nothing happened. A torturous moment went by, too slow for Max, judging from his face, which had lost all color. Then a message appeared on screen: 'Approved.' Money was transferred from one account to another, and an elevator nearby covered in delicate gold leaf designs opened to grant him access to the upper floors.

Max looked back at her.

"Have fun up there." Kira shooed him inside before giving him her most obnoxious grin. "Looks like someone likes you."

Max swallowed hard. "Yeah, this was definitely a bad idea." He took a breath and tapped a button inside the lift. He looked terrified as the doors slid closed.

Kira made sure her taunting smile was the last thing he saw.

With Max gone, she became conscious of the fact that she was standing in front of a selection kiosk in a brothel. She backed away as if she couldn't get away from the thing fast enough. Then, turning in haste, she bumped into a man in mid-level *Breath* mage gear. She apologized, avoiding eye contact. He accepted in a polite manner and attempted to place a hand on her shoulder as if to steady her. She must have looked shaken. She shrunk away before he could make contact, forcing a smile so that she didn't seem awkward, or worse, scared. She apologized again and made her escape down the hall.

She debated leaving the club altogether but felt like that would've been cowardly, as if she would be admitting some kind of defeat. So, instead, she made her way to the bar area, her bare feet padding across the red carpet until she found a place against a wall next to a large potted plant that had a view of the stage where a beautiful elven woman danced.

The woman waved a pair of large fans on the raised platform while tables of patrons filled the floor below. Music played as the newer employees served drinks and flirted with the grateful public in hopes of picking up a client.

Kira did her best to blend into the background as she watched the dancer's slow, seductive moves, fans waving in sync with the music. The tempo sped up, and the fans burst into flames. Flames that traveled to the dancer's clothing, burning them away, leaving only the smoldering fans to provide cover. The routine was well practiced, keeping most of the performer hidden, but flashes of skin sent a chain of reactions through Kira's body that made her skin feel warm. She fidgeted with her item bag and lowered her head to hide her face, letting her hair fall to the sides. She felt eyes fall to her as a couple of the patrons' views shifted away from the stage, which only made her burn hotter.

A man stood from a table that he shared with a group and began to approach, sending her heart into her throat as a familiar panic began to set in. Fortunately, he was headed off by a waitress, who seemed to have been sent by an older woman that now approached Kira in his stead. "Hi there," the woman said, her voice sounding kind and reassuring.

"Hi," replied Kira in a tone that was a cross between grateful and suspicious. She looked up at the tall woman and tucked her hair behind a pointed ear on one side with a nervous hand, revealing her eyes.

"Wow," said the woman. "Not the place for such a magical creature as yourself, huh?"

Kira gave an awkward nod. "Not so much." She paused. "Sorry, I was just waiting for a friend. He's upstairs. He shouldn't take long."

The woman let out a laugh at Kira's apology, making her aware of how the words 'he shouldn't take long' were interpreted, bringing a smile back to her face.

"No need to apologize. Can I get you something from the bar? On the house, of course." The woman gave her a kind smile, but the offer of free drinks informed Kira that she wasn't being rescued at all. She was being recruited. The woman must have been a floor madam. It made sense. She was older and attractive but not so much to draw attention. Definitely not a student working herself through college, that was for sure. She must have acted as a conduit between the company that ran the brothel and the women that worked the lobby, and she had just marked Kira as a potential employee. "No thanks. As I mentioned, I shouldn't be long," she answered, sounding almost formal, trying to decrease her appeal a bit.

The woman laughed, showing a small number of teeth. "Now what would your friend want upstairs when he has something like you waiting down here?" she fished for information. Her words sounded like a compliment but also referred to Kira as a thing. It was clear what was going on.

Kira remained polite, not wanting to make a scene. "He's just a friend, so——"

"Just out of curiosity," the madam interrupted, not wasting any time. "Have you ever considered working at a place like this?"

Kira tried to act surprised at the question, despite knowing it was coming. "Oh, well, no," she answered with an unintentional innocence that must have made her more marketable.

"Yeah, I know. It's definitely not for everyone," the madam said in a way that was somehow both praising and condescending at the same time. "Although the money is amazing, and someone with your unique qualities would be in high demand."

"Yeah, but I'm not really experienced in the field, if you know what I mean," Kira responded, which was sort of true in a way.

"That's no problem. We have training programs for new employees that need a little instruction," the madam offered like she had given the pitch countless times.

Taken aback by the idea of training, Kira hid behind her most comical blank face to express that she was not taking the conversation seriously. "Oh, wow. I am very uncomfortable with the line that this conversation has taken," she said in a flat monotone.

The madam laughed at her response as if it was refreshing to hear. Then Kira noticed the woman's eye repeatedly glancing at the second caster on her wrist. The gear Kira wore was all high-level, and like most high-level equipment, it tended to be simple and unimpressive, more function than form. The result was that it was sometimes hard to tell a high-level player from a low-level one. A second caster, however, was unmistakable. After all, *dual casting* wasn't available until level ninety, and even then, it required the completion of several difficult quests.

The madam had probably pegged Kira for a low-level player, just assuming it from her race, since most fairies never made it past their first few levels. Though now, it was obvious that she'd realized that Kira was something different. The question was, did that make her more valuable or less? Kira could practically see the math going on in the madam's head, scales weighing the options.

The woman seemed to make up her mind, and her attitude shifted. It was still polite but less nurturing. "Okay, I'm just gonna lay it all out on the table here. Due to your … uniqueness … I can skip you past the entry level position and move you right upstairs. No waiting tables and parading around in your underwear to get clients." She paused as if trying to read Kira's face before continuing. "I can also start you in the middle tier. So, depending on what you're willing to do, you can make around three hundred to six hundred per hour. What do you think? Not a bad offer."

Kira was shocked, and well, if she was honest, a little tempted by the amount of money. Taking one or two clients would cover her half of the rent and then some. She shook her head before she finished doing the math and blurted out the first words that came to her mind, "I'm gay." She followed the statement with a confused expression that said, what did I just say?

The madam ignored her puzzled look and added, "That's not as much of a problem as one might think. In the end, it's all about acting."

At that point, Kira realized that there was no way to exit the conversation with her pride intact. *Okay, screw cowardice*, she thought. She was getting out of there any way she could. So, she took a deep breath, turned, and began running toward the door, leaving a stunned madam behind her. It didn't help that she yelled, "I have made a mistake!" the whole way out.

MaxDamage24 fell onto the bed in Ginger's room. "I have made a mistake!" he blurted like an idiot, after being pushed by the always stunning brunette, who did, in fact, smell like cinnamon. She climbed atop, straddling his legs and moving up his body with the grace of a cat stalking a helpless mouse. Her face reached his, and her hair fell from her shoulder to rest against his throat. The warmth of her body required every bit of willpower he had to suppress certain physiological reactions that would normally happen in such a situation.

"Sometimes it's fun to make mistakes," she whispered in his ear, letting her breath caress the side of his neck.

Max panicked as he attempted to explain. "I'm serious. I'm here for a mission, not, umm, this."

She ran one hand down his body, clasping his belt buckle with her fingers. "Oh, I have your mission right here."

He squirmed backward into a pillow, knocking her supporting arm out from under her and causing her to fall onto his lap. "Seriously, it's a real mission!" he shouted, his voice almost cracking, reminding him of how far from cool he was.

She lay still for a moment, face down in his lap, then she began convulsing like she was having a mild seizure as laughter became audible. She lifted her head and placed both hands on his belt buckle, interlocking her fingers and resting her chin on her hands. Her wide smile and green eyes shined up at him. "I figured as much, but I had to mess with you," she said as if there had been no way to avoid it. She sighed, almost sounding disappointed. "So tell me about this all-important mission that was worth three hundred bucks to recruit me for."

He held his hands up, framing her head as if to ask if she minded getting off of him?

She begrudgingly rolled over and slid up to the pillow beside him. A green baby doll top covered her chest but split open just below, revealing the rest of her body. A tiny pair of underwear covered the more important parts, giving Max a minuscule amount of comfort in the fact that she wasn't lying next to him naked. "Well, that's the problem. I can't tell you about the mission until we're ready to start."

"That's not weird at all." She sunk into a pillow. "Is the fate of the world in peril or something?" she asked without looking at him, her words dripping with sarcasm.

For a moment he said nothing. The silence was telling. She shot him a concerned look which he returned, conveying the fact that the time for jokes had ended.

She shrugged. "Okay, fine. I have to change into my gear, so I'll meet you out front in five."

Max thanked her as he slid off the bed and motioned toward the door, then stopped, looking back for a moment. "Should I leave a twenty on the dresser?"

She laughed. "I actually feel kinda bad. You paid, but I didn't earn it." She winked an emerald eye in his direction. "I'll just have to owe you one."

He opened the door as casually as he could. "Sorry, got no time for love." He stepped out of the room, leaving Ginger alone to get ready.

Leaning against the closed door for a full thirty seconds, Max attempted to calm his nerves. He couldn't help but feel a little down after seeing how easy it had been for her to throw him off balance. "I guess that's why you're still single." He shoved his hands into his pockets and made his way back to the elevators. On the ride down, he wondered for a second what would have happened if he had shown up in her room without an ulterior motive. The doors slid open before he could finish the thought and he stepped out just in time to see Kira run out the front door. She flailed her arms in the air like a cartoon as she yelled and made a scene. He quickened his pace to return to the helpless creature.

Max found Farnsworth outside with an out-of-breath Kira. "You okay there? Did the scary men harass you?" He placed a hand on her head and tousled her hair, giving the fairy a rather fluffy appearance.

She swatted at his hand, telling him to knock it off.

He ignored her attacks. "Ginger will be down in a minute."

Farn let out a short laugh at the sight. Max was glad to see her feeling a little more comfortable. "Great, we've got a *Coin*. What do we need next?"

Kira smoothed down her hair, trying to get it to lay flat again. "We need damage."

"Sure. Know any good *Cauldrons*?" Farn inquired.

Max shook his head. "We don't know what we're up against in this. A *Cauldron* could be too slow."

"We need a *Leaf*," Kira said.

Farn raised an eyebrow. "That's an odd choice,"

Kira smirked. "You haven't met our *Leaf*."

"Trust us; he can get the job done," Max assured her.

"You work fast," a voice joined in.

Max turned to find Ginger slipping through the crowd. She'd changed into a pair of canvas pants and a leather corset with a white blouse peeking out the top to cover her chest. She pulled on a short-hooded cloak that gave her an air of mystery. It was more appropriate for the mission than lingerie.

"A *Coin*, a *Breath*, and a *Shield*. You've got quite the little harem going here, Max. And I thought I was special," she joked badly, then changed the subject before he could respond. "Hey, Kira, you want a job at the club? They give me a bonus if I recruit friends."

She crossed her arms. "Already had that offer tonight, thank you very much."

"You sure? We could do doubles," Ginger suggested.

Kira started to blush but covered it with a laugh. "Haha, no. I'd make you do all the work."

Ginger didn't let up. "You might have fun. I could help you break in that little body of yours."

Kira and Farn both looked uneasy as the joke grew less vague.

"Anyways. We're off to gather a *Leaf*. There will be time to make me uncomfortable later." Kira turned away and tugged at her dress.

Farn shook Ginger's hand to exchange their contact information, looking a little uncomfortable meeting someone new. It made sense to Max considering how much more confident Ginger seemed to be compared to the *Shield*. That was when he realized that he hadn't introduced them. "Oh, sorry. Farnsworth meet Ginger; Ginger meet Farnsworth," he added after the fact.

"Nice to meet you, Farn," Ginger said, shortening her name without being told to.

"Likewise," replied Farn, her voice shaking a little.

"So, you know any more about this mystery quest than I do?" Ginger prodded the *Shield*.

Caught off guard, Farn responded with a simple, "Umm …" which seemed to tell Ginger more than enough.

"Great, I'm becoming less excited about this by the minute." She crossed her arms and glared at Max.

Rushing things along, he continued, "We don't have a ton of time here, so we should probably head out." He turned to Kira. "Can you take us to Port Han? We're going to need to rent a boat." She nodded and opened her spell-craft menu without questioning the destination.

"A boat? Where are we going?" Farn asked with a puzzled look since there were no cities near the port.

Max gave her a villainous smile. "We're going to Tartarus."

CHAPTER SIX

Max sat at the wheel as the boat shot along the coast of the dark continent of Gmork, its twin engines pushing it along at full speed. Actually, boat wasn't really the right word for it since it didn't touch the water. Instead, it hovered just above, skimming the surface and giving it a smoother ride than any regular watercraft would have. Nevertheless, it was called a boat. The whole thing was white and would have looked like something straight out of Miami Vice if not for the figurehead of a goat that sat on the bow and the two detailed wings that fanned off the back at an upward angle.

In the back, Kira and Ginger argued about whether it would be funny or stupid to climb onto the front of the boat and yell 'I'm king of the world!' Ginger insisted that it was a classic that bore repeating, while Kira felt it was overdone and an insult to comedy. Eventually, they agreed to disagree and settled for quoting a few random lines from a song about being on a boat.

Max shook his head as the pair behind him belted out a few ridiculous lyrics. Next to him sat Farn, chewing on her lip like it had wronged her.

He tried to think of a way to take her mind off what was bothering her, which, if he had to guess, was the mission. "So, are you a big Futurama fan?"

"What?" She looked at him with a blank expression.

"Your name. Is it a reference to Professor Farnsworth from Futurama?"

"Oh, no, it's from the show Fringe. Agent Farnsworth …" she trailed off awkwardly before starting back up. "I liked the character."

Max grinned. "You just got a lot nerdier."

She leaned away from him and crossed her arms. "How is Fringe worse than Futurama?"

He shrugged with one hand on the wheel. "I don't know, but it is. I only saw some of the first season, though."

"Oh, I get it, you're too cool to like Fringe," Farn said, almost looking sad for him and coming out of her shell a bit.

Max dismissed her comment with a wave of his free hand. "Nah. I'm more into movies than TV; I'd rather a self-contained story over episodic things. That's more Kira's style since she has trouble committing to a two-hour runtime."

"Well, you have to watch the rest. Fringe is worth seeing once." Farn leaned on one hand and smiled.

"Maybe I will when this is done, you know, if the world doesn't end and all."

She nodded. "Yeah, you should put it on your bucket list now then."

He leaned back over his seat. "Hey, Kira! Guess where Farn's name comes from?"

The fairy tilted her head a moment before guessing, "Fringe?"

"Ha! Yes!" Farn hopped around in her seat to face the back of the boat. "And you called me a nerd," she argued over her shoulder at Max.

"Yeah, and I stand by it. You're both nerds," he said as Kira slid up to sit behind Farn, Ginger joining them out of curiosity and putting her feet up on the back of his seat.

The two began chatting about their favorite parts of the show, causing a pleasant atmosphere to take over the craft as they sped toward the dark destination ahead.

"What about you?" Farn asked. "Where does MaxDamage24 come from?"

"Nowhere." Max shrugged. "I picked it at random."

She looked at him sideways with judgment in her eyes.

"What? I'm not good at coming up with names."

"What about the twenty-four?" she asked.

Kira butted in to field the question. "It was his age. At least it was three years ago. Apparently, he didn't realize that he would get older because, you know, time is a thing that exists and all."

Farn laughed, bringing a reluctant smile to Max's face. "Like I said, I'm not great at names." He pulled back on the throttle, signaling that their ride was coming to an end despite there being no marker on the world map.

Tartarus was different from the other cities in Noctem in the sense that it wasn't a city. At least, not technically. It sat on the coast of Gmork, the dark continent, which was a dangerous place, crawling with high-level monsters. The perfect place for a city like Tartarus. From the sea, where most visitors approached, it looked like nothing but a crack in the side of a massive coastal cliff with a river flowing out into the ocean from within.

Max steered the craft over the turbulent waters as they passed in through the narrow entrance. After a few hundred feet of nothingness, the crack grew wider into a full-sized canyon. Its walls were lined with structures, stacked and supported by all manner of ropes and chains. It was a patchwork of architecture with no overall plan or design.

Numerous bridges stretched across the gap, connecting both sides of the canyon. A few were made of sturdy wood held up by complex support systems of cables and pulleys. In contrast, most of the others were just a bunch of ropes strung together with barely enough stability to support the weight of a few people at a time. On more than a few occasions in the past, bridges had actually snapped, dropping parties into the river below. Hell, even Max had come close to dying once when an entire tavern fell off the side of the canyon. Fortunately for him, Kira had been there to catch him and slow his descent just enough so he didn't take damage from the fall. There was no lamplight like the other cities; just torches placed randomly throughout its various walkways and platforms. It was strictly a place built to fulfill a purpose, not to look nice.

The reason for its lack of presence on the world map and its overall terrible workmanship was that it wasn't created by Checkpoint as part of the game. It didn't have a teleport point or stores selling official items. It was just a crack in a cliff. The city had even been built on the walls to avoid the monsters that spawned on the banks of the river underneath. The place had been built using nothing but farmed or crafted materials, and the dangerously sub-par construction was thanks to the fact that most of its builders had no experience whatsoever. The hodge-podge city had become sort of a hobby for some players. Some people like to build model cars, and some people like to build a bunch of crappy tree houses on the side of a cliff in unsafe conditions. To each their own.

As for how it got started, no one really knew. It just became a thing, and no one questioned it, not even Checkpoint. Over time, it had become a sort of a black market for the world of Noctem. Nothing technically illegal went on there, but much of it was questionable, to say the least. If you needed to broker a shady deal, such as an assassination of a house lord, it was the place go. It was also the place to go if you needed to recruit a shady *Leaf* class named Kegan.

The boat drifted under the bridges as noises filtered down. Farn jumped at the sound of a gunshot as they pulled up to a rickety dock and disembarked. Max tied off the boat as haphazardly as the city above was built, and they proceeded down the river bank toward a ladder. They passed a few players on their way who wasted no time in boarding and stealing their vessel.

"Hey, they're taking our boat!" Farn pointed an urgent finger in their direction.

"That's how it works here. Leave something unattended, and it's not yours anymore." Max stuffed his hands in his pockets without looking back. It wasn't like the boat had been rented by the hour, so it didn't matter where it ended up. He assumed it would just dematerialize if someone left it somewhere for too long.

Farn looked confused anyway.

Ginger slinked up behind her. "First time here, huh?"

Farn nodded. "Yeah, it's not exactly a place that I've heard good things about."

"It's not that bad," Max insisted.

"Just different," added Kira as they approached the ladder leading up to the bottom-most platform of the city.

Just as Max was about to set foot on the first rung, a loud reptilian hiss came from behind them. "Damn, basilisk. Everybody climb fast and don't look at its eyes!" He leapt up the ladder several rungs at a time to make room for the others.

"I looked at its eyes, Max," Farn said from behind.

Max looked down to find her unable to move and locked in a gaze with a ten-foot-tall, black serpent. It bobbed its head from left to right, its paralyzing stare boring a hole through the helpless *Shield*. It dashed forward for a critical strike, a blur of dark scales. He motioned to jump back down, but Kira bolted toward Farn, beating him to her by materializing her wings for added speed. She plowed into the *Shield* with what little weight she had, shoving her out of the way enough get her to safety and to break the snake's hold on her in time for it get a mouthful of sand. They toppled to one side, landing in a heap, Kira on top, straddling one of Farn's legs.

"Sorry," she chirped.

The creature wasn't that dangerous, Max thought as he considered their options. Granted, their party wasn't complete, and they lacked some damage, which could make the encounter risky if they weren't careful. He decided to stay put for the moment to see how things played out.

Ginger dodged an attack by weaving around the serpent as it struck past her. She countered, striking with a curved dagger drawn from a sheath at her lower back. Scraping a number of thick black scales from the monster, she tossed them in her bag. Basilisk scales were valuable after all. She avoided its eyes by hiding under the large hood of her short cloak. She bobbed to the left and fired a grappling line from her wrist into the canyon wall, using it to pull herself to the side to dodge another attack. The wrist launcher, equipment exclusive to her class, sat on the opposite arm from her stat-sleeve. Her cloak trailed behind her as she touched her forehead with two fingers and quietly said the word *Blur* to activate a skill to lower the creature's targeting capability. The thing lost track of her soon after.

Farn, who was recovering from her earlier blunder, pushed herself out of the sand and drew her weapon, baring her teeth as she joined the fight. Max didn't recognize her sword as he had her gauntlet. It wasn't particularly long, but what it lacked in reach, it seemed to make up for in power. Its sturdy blade sat in a reinforced hilt with a grip resembling a set of brass knuckles. The sword had an extended handle that gave her the option of wielding it with both hands, although the blade was too short to call it a bastard sword. It wasn't flashy, but still, it carried an aura of strength and ferocity. Similarly, Farnsworth herself seemed to radiate power now that she had gotten serious. Her eyes burned with an intensity that Max hadn't noticed before. Even Kira had paused to watch as she got into position.

The *Shield* wore a long, sleeveless tunic of light gray cloth that split on the sides of her waist and tapered off in the front and back. Below that, the black fabric of a pair of loose fitting pants billowed out before being gathered up tight into the tops of her knee-high boots, a lining of white fur peeking out where they met. A thick sash of faded blue cloth wrapped her middle, circling her hips multiple times before tying off in the front where the excess hung over the ends of her tunic. Her leather armor fit snugly around her back and abdomen, a metal plate covering her chest. She wore the collar of her tunic flipped up so that it stuck out from the top of her armor, the light material sitting in contrast against the dark skin of her throat. She let out a growl as she darted forward. Apparently, she intended to pull her weight or die trying.

Farn pounded a fist against her breastplate and yelled, "I'm right here you overgrown nope rope!"

Ginger stumbled with a snort at the ridiculous taunt while Kira exploded with giddy laughter.

The words hit the beast like a blow to the head, and it focused its attention on Farn in response. She lifted her left arm in front to block the hit that was coming. Unlike her right, which she had kept bare, her left shoulder and upper arm were protected by a few overlapping pieces of metal and leather. They looked tough but were still light enough to allow for easy movement.

She braced with one leg and activated her gauntlet. The heavy looking steel glove covered her hand and upper wrist, its hinged fingers making her fist look much larger than it was. It hummed to life as the shield generator located on her forearm flipped open, forming a shining X at the back of her wrist as it rotated into place. Blue energy poured out from its center, creating a transparent barrier of protection. The snake lunged, only to be deflected and shoved to the side by a well-timed parry. She taunted the beast again and strafed to the side to remain in its view while making a point to focus her sight on its fangs and not its eyes.

Max watched from his place on the ladder, an impressed smile creeping across his face. It was what he had been waiting for. Alastair was right. She was good. In fact, she looked like she could block the thing all day. Although, just defending wasn't going to kill the creature, unless it could die of old age, which he didn't consider an option. He paused and looked for an opening. Seconds later, he saw his moment. He brought his legs up and sprang off with all his strength. In the same motion, he drew his pistols. They didn't have all day.

Farnsworth stood, stunned as Max soared overhead.

He flipped in mid-air, taking aim at the basilisk. His pistols barked one after another until the sounds blurred together. He landed in a perfect action movie crouch, guns crossed against his chest as if he'd practiced it. The snake reeled from the attack, losing most of its health after being hit by every shot. Afterward, Max just stood there as if he wasn't even paying attention. Farn didn't know much about guns, but she could tell at least one was empty from the position of its slide.

The snake recovered, flicking its head back at him as he placed a spent magazine in the pouch at his waist.

Farn struck its tail with her sword to get its focus back on her where it belonged. That should have been enough, but he had dealt too much damage too fast. She would need to get between them to protect him, but it was too late. She wasn't close enough.

For an instant, it looked like Alastair had made a mistake in trusting Max. The *Fury* was breaking one of the most basic rules of combat. He had ignored his team. Even worse, he was showing off.

The snake was already coiling to attack.

Thoughts raced through her head as her eyes darted around the scene for a way to help. Her gaze stopped hard at Ginger and Kira, who were just standing there doing nothing by the river. The *Coin* actually had her journal out, and the fairy was dipping a foot in the water. Farn furrowed her brow, and she looked back to Max. That was when she noticed his expression. It was calm, more so than any player she'd ever seen.

Fangs streaked toward him, and the basilisk came to an abrupt stop, its body flopping off balance, its hiss choked off.

Fangs scraped against the pistol that Max had shoved down the beast's throat as it lunged. Its eyes went wide in some kind of artificial panic, pupils struggling to find him. Max just stood there, his eyes closed as he said two words, "Eat this." With a twitch of his finger and a muffled bang, the creature went limp, smoke wafting from its mouth.

Kira hopped past Farn and leaned over to look at the fallen serpent. "Nice. I didn't even have to heal anyone." She collected the item drops, her bare feet in the sand next to the giant serpent like it wasn't even there while its body faded to bones.

Farnsworth couldn't help but think back to the conversation she had overheard in the tavern's back room earlier about why Alastair had chosen the pair. There was even term for it, *The Nightmare Effect*. She had heard of it before, although many users still claimed it was a myth despite the evidence to the contrary.

Of the first Nightmares present at launch, which had been named after historical figures, Rasputin, who represented destruction, had been the hardest. He had seemed almost unkillable. His damage was insane, and he was invulnerable except for brief moments between his attacks. Over time, the absurd challenge of the fight gained players enormous amounts of skill. Provided they did more than just stockpile powerful items to get through it as Alastair had mentioned. Farn, herself, had even found that it improved her reaction speeds. But in her time playing Noctem, she had never witnessed the Nightmare Effect on the level that Max had just displayed. She let out a quiet, "Woah," as he wiped venom from his gun.

Seeing his pistols drawn for the first time, she noticed that even his weapons weren't like anything she had seen before either. They almost looked modern. Most firearms in the game were fantasy based, all covered with filigree, pearl handles, and random gears. His were matte black with simple wood grips bearing the icon of a skull. Small text engraved on the sides, naming the weapons. Mary on one, and Anne on the other. Each was tipped with a heavy compensator, giving them an aggressive look. They fit him well, almost like they were forged for his use only.

"Are those *contract items*?" she blurted out without thinking.

The Nightmares were powerful, and in turn, so were the rewards for defeating one. They came in the form of a contract, awarded to one party member who was chosen at random. To make matters worse, any player who completed a fight could never attempt it again, whether they were picked or not. This meant that for one player to form a contract, they must be chosen and that the five people that helped them get it got nothing, not even experience points. On top of that, the contract wasn't free. Upon defeating a Nightmare, the player would be asked to make an offering as a sacrifice. It could be anything. Depending on who was chosen and what they offered, the results were unpredictable. The reward could be overpowered, balanced, or too valuable to even use. Sometimes it could have no purpose at all.

Max looked down at his weapons. "The girls? Yeah. Got them from the Rackham fight. The critical damage is pretty good, and they scale off my dexterity really well."

Farn thought about the weapons, not seeing what made them special. Her sword was also a contract item with similar stats, but it at least had an additional ability to make it stand out, even if she didn't use it much. If anything, his guns were convenient more than anything else, since the dex scaling would let them grow in damage as he leveled, making it so he would never need to replace them. She assumed he was leaving out a detail. "I didn't know anyone had beaten Rackham yet other than the usual houses."

"Oh, we did that one a while ago. When was that?" He looked to Kira.

"Had to be last year, I think."

Farn took a moment to process the information. "That would be just after the *Dead Men* expansion came out. You beat it that fast?"

"We beat all the Nightmares from the pirate expansion.

Well, actually, we've beaten all the Nightmares released so far," Kira added over her shoulder, dipping her toes in the river again.

At that, Farn tried her best to keep her jaw from hitting the ground. "Seriously?"

Kira shrugged without offering more.

Out of curiosity, Farn tapped the tattoo of Celtic knotwork that sat on the underside of her wrist to reopen her party read-out. The fight had ended so fast that she hadn't looked at anyone's health, but now, she had to know what kind of players could speak so casually about fighting Nightmares. Her previous efforts of keeping her jaw off the ground failed as the bold lines of dark black ink filled in her party's names. "Fifty hit points!"

Kira jumped like a startled animal. "What?"

"How do you only have fifty HP?" Farn screwed up her eyes. "That's how much I had at level one."

Kira dismissed Farn's concern with a wave of her hand. "I'm a fairy, so my constitution stat started with a soft-cap. Putting points into health doesn't do enough to make it worth it."

"So, you what, just didn't upgrade it?"

Max burst out laughing. "Oh no, she started at ten hit points."

"That's right." Kira puffed out her chest with pride. "I put a whole four points in to get myself up to fifty."

"And why did you do that?" Max asked, still laughing.

Kira deflated, glaring back at him. "Because I stubbed my toe on a door frame and died … twice."

Ginger snorted a laugh, setting Max off again.

"It's not that funny." Kira stomped one foot in the sand.

Farn just stared ahead at the little *Breath* mage, trying to comprehend what she was hearing. "So what did you put your points in?"

The fairy tilted her head back and forth. "Mostly focus and wisdom for the mana and healing potency. The rest went to learning spell glyphs and agility to get my flight speed up. Oh, and I threw a little in luck for fun."

Max wiped a tear from his eye and settled down. "All kidding aside, she should be one of the most powerful *Breath* mages in the game in terms of raw healing ability. At least, that was how the math worked out when we planned it back when we started."

"As long as a slight breeze doesn't take her out," Ginger added.

Kira puffed back up. "Not really. A good party should be able to keep me safe, especially with a good *Shield* watching out for me."

Farn threw up her hands in resignation. "I guess I have my work cut out for me."

"You'll do fine." Max kicked at the basilisk's skull with his boot. "Hell, you handled this thing better than most."

"Speaking of snakes. There are more of them around here," Ginger reminded while herding Max and Kira back toward the ladder with a shooing motion, "And as fun as all this is, we should probably get moving before we have to fight another one."

CHAPTER SEVEN

Boards creaked under Farn's feet as she climbed the stairs beyond the ladder that lead up to the city, some so loud that she was sure one would break at any moment. Tartarus was like one giant tree house built by an inebriated child. Actually, speaking of drunk children, they passed an open-air bar with a few patrons arguing and slurring their speech.

Alcohol worked the same way as most things in Noctem. The sensation of being drunk was pulled from each of the players' memories. As long as they had been drunk at some point, it had the same effect in game. Supposedly, this kept it from working on those who were under age for the most part since they lacked the memory data to load, or at least, they should lack that information. For everyone else, it was time to get wasted with no consequences. Whether that was positive or negative was out for debate. To Farnsworth, it was just a fact. A fact that was demonstrated when two players knocked over a table and smashed through the railing in front of them.

The pair fell over the edge, one of them dropping a dagger as they went. It fell with a solid thunk as it stuck into the floorboards at an angle. A distant splash could be heard from below.

Farn froze from the shock of what had happened.

Max, on the other hand, didn't skip a beat as he continued on his way, only stopping for a second to nudge the fallen dagger over the edge with his foot. In a way, it was the honorable thing to do. The weapon should remain with its owner, Farn acknowledged, starting to understand how the place worked a little more.

As they made their way up the next flight of stairs, one step broke part way under her foot, causing her to fall against an uncomfortably thin railing with nothing but the river below to fill her view. She recovered from the stumble, her face blank with terror.

In response, Kira hung back, taking a place at her side. "Don't worry. If you fall, I'll catch you." She gave the *Shield* a gentle smile.

"It's true. She's good at being there when you need her," Max added over his shoulder.

Farn looked at them both, a warm feeling in her chest from the trust that they seemed to share in each other. It was actually really sweet. *They make a nice couple*, she thought as she began to feel like a third wheel.

At least she wasn't alone with Ginger strolling along behind her, just as much an extra wheel as she was. The *Coin* snapped in a fresh spool of wire into her wrist launcher, causing Farn to look back at the sound. For a moment, she accidentally made eye contact with the stunning woman. Then she made it worse by freezing like that for a second without saying anything before turning back. She cringed at her own actions. *Nice, Farn, now she probably thinks you're special.* She couldn't help but be reminded of all the times she had embarrassed herself in the real world. Like with every store clerk she had ever interacted with. She tried to shake off the thought as the group climbed a few more levels of precariously placed structures.

Cheers and curse words met her ears when they arrived at a large square cage that sat on a platform, surrounded by walkways filled well beyond capacity with spectators. Inside, a *Coin* player darted around the makeshift arena, striking at a *Shield* class, getting a lucky strike through his defenses every now and then.

"Well, that makes sense," she whispered under her breath. Tartarus was a city of considerably shady nature, so of course, it would have cage fights. That much should have been obvious.

Max made his way to a raised platform that looked down on the event and approached a *Whip* class player with a large ferret wearing a tiny chest plate and lounging across his shoulders.

"Maximum Damage, you want in?" the *Whip* asked.

"Has Kegan been up yet?"

"No. He's up next though. You should see the guy he's matched with; it's gonna be hilarious." He laughed.

The ferret seemed to laugh as well, but that might have been Farn's imagination.

"Ha, I bet. Give me twenty on Kegan," Max threw into the mix.

"Seriously?" The guy raised an eyebrow. "He's up against a *Rage*."

"Oh, I know. It's going to be hilarious," Max repeated with a smug grin.

The *Whip* shrugged, adding, "It's your money." He held out a worn, leather-bound book and opened it to a blank page in the middle. He allowed Max to place a hand flat on the paper, a line of text appearing on the page.

Farn grew suspicious. "A portable payment ledger. How does he have that?" she asked Kira, leaning close so as not to disturb the questionable transaction going down in front of her.

Kira leaned in to meet her and held a hand in front of her mouth to keep quiet. "He runs a business in one of the other cities. I forget which. But he got the book through it. He just uses it to make a little extra managing the fights here."

"There are arenas in the other cities. Why don't the duelists just go there?"

"The arenas in the cities place bets in credits, here you can place them in dollars. Hence, the payment ledger," Kira explained.

"What?" Farn raised her voice, drawing the attention of a few of the spectators around them. "Sorry." She quieted down. "Isn't that ... kind of illegal?" Her shoulders fell when she realized how naive she sounded.

"Not really. It's really more of a gray area," the fairy said, looking up as if the answer was hanging above her head. "The laws haven't really caught up with the technology in some ways. They'll probably crack down eventually, but until they do ..." She finished her sentence by gesturing at the cage.

A mixture of cheers and groans filled the air as the fight within was coming to an end.

Inside, the *Coin* had gotten behind his opponent and slipped a narrow dagger into his back, far enough so that the tip stuck out of the *Shield's* chest. The flesh around the end of the blade glowed red in place of blood, and the large man winced.

Some spectators watched through their inspectors to view a green bar hovering over the man's head as it dropped down to a third remaining. Others just eyed the class emblem on the back of his hand as it faded from black to red.

The attack had missed the *Shield's* heart, which might have killed him outright no matter what level he was. Still, it was quite damaging, since it counted as a backstab, delivering a hefty critical damage bonus. The *Coin* laughed as he twisted the knife. A grin crept over his face as victory fell into his grasp. Then, just as the *Coin* drew back his knife to repeat the strike, the *Shield*, who had stood helplessly until now, thrust back an elbow, throwing his attacker off balance. He rushed backward, not giving the *Coin* a chance to recover as he flipped his sword under his right arm and drove the blade through the shocked man behind him.

The strike hit home, delivering maximum damage and destroying the *Coin's* smaller health pool. The *Shield* dislodged his sword and shoved backward with his shoulder against the *Coin*, leaving him to fall in a crumpled mess on the floor. His limp body lay still for a moment, then it shimmered and dissi- pated into particles of white light that drifted off into the air like snow falling from the ground up.

Upon his death, the *Coin's* Somno system would be forced into an auto-restart sequence before reconnecting to his sleeping brain to let him back into the game. How long it took to reestablish the link and log back in varied from person to person. For Farn, it always took around fifteen minutes. After that, the *Coin* would appear alive and well again at the last spawn point visited. Although, he would lose any progress he'd made during the night as well as any items he hadn't stored in his virtual inventory.

The *Shield* inside the cage raised one hand in victory while an elven man, wearing only a pair of shorts and a caster, ran into the cage to administer a few recovery spells. Half the crowd cheered while the other hurled curse words at the player.

The victor exited the cage as a tall, attractive woman wearing a small breastplate and short leather skirt entered. The long, fluffy tail of a reynard swayed softly behind her, lifting the back of her skirt almost high enough to see where it connected at the base of her spine. A tall set of pointy, fox-like ears sat atop her head. The reynard race was the more popular of Noctem's two beastkin-themed avatar models that had been added to the game in the first expansion a few months after launch. They still weren't as common as human players, but they gave some much-needed diversity to the game.

There were also several less-human races, but the system couldn't get the user's brain to sync with a body that was too far removed from what they were used to, which was probably why they only existed as the game's non-player characters. As far as users went, a cute pair of ears and a tail were as exotic as it got.

"That was a decent match," announced the reynard woman. "Let's hear it for the victor, BadMatt69!" She arched an eyebrow in his direction. "Really? 69? How old are you? Thirteen?" she asked, getting a laugh from the crowd. "Okay, anyway, for this next match we're doing something a little different. We tried to say no to this, but what the hell, it will probably be pretty funny. So, without further ado, I give you, MurderStorm!"

A hulking man, who had apparently named himself MurderStorm, ducked as he entered the cage dressed in the tattered leather armor of a *Rage* class. The twisted horns of a ram on his head marked him as a faunus, the other beastkin race. He held a short but wide axe in one hand, his muscles twitching as his fingers curled around the grip. The crowd cheered as he approached the pretty reynard woman in the center, towering over her by at least a foot.

"Wow, you're a big fella, huh? What're you doing after the fight? You like foxes?" She allowed her tail to brush against his leg.

MurderStorm answered with an impolite grunt.

"Okay then," she added in an awkward tone before making her second announcement. "And now, for our challenger, the *Leaf* that wouldn't take no for an answer, Kegan!" The crowd went quiet.

A well-tanned, dark-eyed elf made his way out of the crowd at the gate and stepped into the cage. He wore a simple sleeveless top with a v-neck and a pair of wide flowing pants with several red and brown sashes wrapped around his waist, hanging to one side. His hair was styled with an asymmetrical cut, spiked up at an angle on top and long on one side. Streaks of maroon wove through his otherwise black locks which, on top of being Asian, made him look like a Korean pop star. None of that mattered now because the fact that all he carried was a bow and a handful of arrows made him look ridiculous in front of the massive *Rage* as he approached.

Laughter burst out all around the cage as some of the crowd rushed to place last minute bets.

Farnsworth turned to look at Max with one thumb hooked back at the *Leaf* in the cage.

He responded with a hard to read smile as if he knew something that she didn't.

She groaned and turned back to the cage.

"Alright, everyone, no more bets." The tall reynard woman held out her hands, palms facing the crowd. "Combatants take your places." She pointed to two opposite corners of the cage. Kegan took his place in one where a faded circle on the floor marked his starting point. MurderStorm did the same on the other side. The *Leaf* shook out his arms and did some light stretching to limber up while the crowd's laughter continued. MurderStorm just cracked his neck with an audible pop that could be heard over the noise. The reynard woman rushed to the gate as if she didn't want to get caught in the middle of what was about to happen. A bell rang as soon as she made her escape.

Kegan nocked an arrow while holding the rest in his draw hand before making eye contact with his opponent. The *Rage*, being a class made for all-out attacks, wasted no time. He rushed forward, axe in front of him ready to block an arrow or two. Kegan let one fly, and as predicted, the *Rage* swatted it out of the air causing it to ricochet, hitting a spectator with a surprised yelp, having made the mistake of standing in the front.

Kira snorted a laugh.

With the first arrow deflected, MurderStorm should have been able to close the gap before Kegan could find time to fire again. He drew back his axe for a swing guaranteed to do maximum damage. He looked like he wasn't going to be satisfied unless he could cut the elf clean in half, but as soon as he moved the axe from in front of him, an arrow pierced his shoulder. He didn't seem to wonder how the elf had followed his first shot so quickly. If he had, he might have been able to come up with a better strategy, but honestly, Farn didn't expect that level of thought from someone named MurderStorm. Instead, he kept going, since for his class, taking a couple arrows was probably an acceptable risk. But it wasn't a couple. Arrows pierced his body one after another at a speed unheard of. They hit in quick succession. Three, four, no, six. Farn almost couldn't keep track.

MurderStorm attempted to bring his axe back to block, but he had swung too far behind in preparation to attack. It took too long, leaving him helpless as Kegan flipped arrows from his draw hand onto the bowstring and fired in almost the same motion. It wasn't a skill or ability, but rather, it was sleight-of-hand, a trick that Kegan had somehow mastered.

Finally, the *Leaf* stood with his hand empty as the *Rage* stumbled toward him, losing all momentum as the eight poison-tipped arrows that had pierced his skin did their work. Kegan stepped to the side, exiting his starting circle for the first time during the fight to make room for the falling brute. The lifeless corpse of MurderStorm slammed into the floor, arrows snapping underneath while a few pushed through his body like a pin cushion. Kegan then held out his hands and gave a little bow as if to say 'ta-da.'

Sparkling particles rose from the body on the floor as the reynard woman came back in. She looked confused like she had somehow missed the fight altogether. Which was possible, since the whole thing had taken less than ten seconds.

Farn looked back at Max, who again gave the same annoying smile as before. She saw him glance at a page in his journal, probably checking the balance of his bank account that had just received his winnings. Then he led the party down to the cage entrance as Kegan was exiting to a mixture of boos, laughter, and curse words. He took one more bow just before stepping outside. More curse words were launched in his direction.

"You're not making many friends here are you, Kegel?" asked Max in greeting.

Kegan faked a laugh through a layer of sarcasm. "I get it; my name sounds like a groin exercise. That joke never gets old." He threw his bow over his shoulder and slung it across his body at an angle.

"Have you ever known him to let a joke die when its time has passed?" Kira asked.

"Repetition." Max held up a finger. "It's repetition that makes things funny."

Kegan tilted his head and nodded as if seeing Max's point, but then turned to Kira and Ginger, ignoring him completely. "Anyway, how are you two? You're looking pretty as usual." He glanced to Farn with a smile. "Who's your friend?"

"This is Farnsworth. She's working with us on this one," Max explained as the leaf shook her hand.

Farn forced out a quick, "Nice to meet you."

With introductions out of the way, they got down to business.

"So, what's this mission all about?" Kegan asked.

Ginger butted in, "Don't bother; it's apparently a big secret." She still looked irritated at the lack of information.

"Oh, okay." Kegan shrugged without a hint of curiosity. He must not have been bothered by it as much as she was.

Farn gathered with the group close to Kira so her teleport could accommodate their larger number. She selected a destination and swiped down to activate the spell. That was when a loud creak struck the air, followed by several deafening cracks. The overcrowded platform shifted below Farn's feet, dropping a few inches.

She glanced at Kira in panic as the orange shell of the teleport spell began to form around them ever so slowly. Too slowly. Several more cracks sounded out along with a cacophony of screams from all around them as the platform gave way and fell into the river below.

CHAPTER EIGHT

Screams filled Max's ears as he took a deep breath and let out one of his own. He clung to the only thing within reach that might save him from the fall. The rest of the party did the same, each holding tight until the glowing shell of a teleport spell dispersed.

"Everybody off NOW!" Kira cried in protest.

Max let his voice trail off into surprised silence, his feet once again on solid ground. The central park in the city of Valain surrounded him. A few players that happened to be hanging around the teleport point made it their business to stop and stare. Something told him it had to do with the sudden screaming that had accompanied his party's arrival. Although, it could also have been the fact that four high-level adventurers, including himself, were clinging to an uncomfortable-looking fairy as if their lives depended on it.

"I'm so not kidding!" Kira continued as Max released his small savior, the others following his lead. "Whichever of you grabbed my ass is gonna die," she added, shoving at him and Kegan even after she was free.

Max held his hands in front of him as if pleading, hoping to stop her long enough so he could explain. "Relax. I touched your butt earlier. So really, it's old news at this point."

She did not relax. Instead, she wound up and threw a punch with all her strength. It impacted weakly against his shoulder, a frustrated growl percolating in her throat as her nostrils flared.

"Okay, okay, I'm kidding. I'm pretty sure it wasn't me anyway." Max brushed off his shoulder, pretending that her attack had hurt.

Farnsworth laughed at the exchange but stopped herself short, looking somewhat guilty. Like a cat that swallowed the canary. Max wondered if she had been the real transgressor of the butt-touching in question.

Ginger stepped in to referee, "Okay, little one, if it makes you feel better you can touch his butt."

Kira crossed her arms and stamped one foot. "I don't want to. His butt is full of farts."

"Then it's settled," Ginger put an end to the dispute. "Go get some food and leave the adults to get things done," she commanded in a tone that was somehow kind and strict at the same time.

Kira perked up at the mention of food and made her way back to the stands that she had visited earlier that night, this time buying a paper bag filled with some form of pastries. One thing about eating in a virtual world was that it wasn't possible to get full, a fact that Max had seen demonstrated numerous times as Kira gave new meaning to the word binge.

Ginger watched the fairy. "That was easier than expected."

"Food always works with her. She has a one-track mind," Max commented.

"Wait, why were you touching her ass earlier?" asked Kegan, shoving up next to him.

Ginger jumped on the subject as well, as if she had completely forgotten what she had said about being adults, "Yeah, you passed up an opportunity with me earlier, and now I hear you're running around groping her all night."

Max held up his hands again in defense. "Woah, I wasn't groping her all night. I slapped her on the ass once tonight. Once! And it was strictly for comedic value."

That was when Farn spoke up, looking confused, "I have to ask, are you two not a couple? Because I thought—"

"Oh, god no!" Max cut her off. "You thought she and I were?"

"Uh huh." Farn nodded.

"Nooooooo, no, no, no, no. We're friends. Have been since elementary school. And let's just say, she's not my type." He avoided the full explanation.

Kira returned a moment later with a danish hanging out of her mouth before handing the paper bag she had purchased to Farn, implying that there was one inside for everyone.

The *Shield* took one and passed it along.

"What'd I miss?" asked Kira, talking with her mouth full.

"Nothing important," Max answered as he took the bag of pastries.

Kira snatched it back. "You don't get one." She squinted at him as hard as she could.

"Anyway, what class do we need for our last member?" Farn asked, reminding Max that they were still on a mission.

Kira ceased her squinting but continued to look at Max to hear his answer.

"I was thinking a *Venom* mage. I already messaged one before we got here."

Farn nodded. "Great! Where do we need to go to meet them?"

"Nowhere, he's right there." Max pointed to a young reynard in black robes sitting on a bench near the edge of the park engrossed in a book. "He wasn't busy, and he can teleport, so he came to meet us."

"Oh," Farn sounded a little disappointed.

"That kinda kills our recruitment montage," Kira commented while examining her danish as if trying to find the perfect bite.

"Yeah, but what are you gonna do?" Max shrugged before calling out to the mage. "Hey, Corvin!"

Corvin's tall black ears twitched upwards at the sound of his name. He lifted his head, his attention drawn away from the small, leather-bound book that he had been holding sideways, the inside of which held a screen running an emulator of a Sega Genesis. It was a third-party app that he had purchased a while back. His one good eye followed the sound of Max's voice, while his other hid behind a heavy cloth that wrapped diagonally around his head, covering almost half his face. A shaggy mop of black hair matched his tail and ears, and combined with his thick black robes, it gave him a rather dark presence. He slid the emulator into one of his inner pockets and stood up quietly. Despite his somber appearance, a smile showed on his face as he approached the party as if he was just happy to be there. "Hey, Max, thanks for the invite."

"No probs. Thanks for meeting us."

"Nice to see you too, Kira," the boy added.

"Likewise," she chirped, rewarding him with a smile and a fresh pastry from the bag.

Corvin took the danish and nibbled politely without saying anything more to the rest of the group. The mage had always been quiet, and considering he didn't know anyone other than Max and Kira, his silence wasn't a surprise.

Max slapped a hand to the mage's back, not wanting him to fade into the background like he usually did. "This guy here has taken down a number of Nightmares with us. So, don't let the gentle face and fluffy ears fool you. He's a badass through and through."

Corvin brushed pastry crumbs off his face, having been startled mid-bite by Max's introduction. "I, ah, thanks."

"Glad to have you." Kegan held out his hand to shake.

The others shook the *Venom's* hand as well, passing their contact info along.

Once it seemed like they were finished, Max cleared his

throat to get everyone's attention. It ended up being louder than he had intended, which caused him to pause when everyone looked in his direction. He reached a hand back and scratched the back of his head. "Ahh, okay. This quest is gonna be a little different in that we will be the only party in Noctem to participate in it. Also, it will probably be the hardest that any of us have ever attempted. That being said, if anyone wants to change their mind, this might be your last chance." He glanced around as the group remained silent. "Okay then. Kira, will you do the honors?" He motioned to her as he finished his mediocre pep-talk.

Kira nodded and swiped open her spell-craft menu.

Corvin, the only other magic user, watched as she snapped the rows of glowing glyphs into alignment. His eyes widened as she selected a destination that wasn't available to the public.

Tendrils of orange light wove around Max and his party, enveloping them in silence as it blocked out the city beyond. Only the sound of nervous breathing reached his ears as the team's shared body heat raised the temperature inside, increasing the tension in the air along with it until finally, cool air rushed in. Particles of light vanished in an upwards sweep revealing the bridge of an airship. Sitting in the captain's chair was Alastair.

Gray steel and hardwood lined the floor, giving the craft a classy yet militaristic appearance. Most airships didn't have a crew since they just followed a preset schedule and path, but this one was different. Control stations were placed around the sides of the room with crew members bustling about them.

A faunas stood with her hands on an old-style ship wheel in front of a gigantic window. Its panes consisted of circular sections riveted together, suggesting the nose of a World War II bomber. Two more crew, an elf and a human, sat at consoles behind her. The three were dressed in uniforms bearing patches with the Checkpoint logo. They must have been the ship's main navigators. At the back of the bridge, Alastair had gained two

Shields bracketing him as if they were his personal guards. He had also had changed into a long gray coat with a high collar and epaulets that fit him as if painstakingly tailored. The change made him look like a vampiric version of a military general.

Gasps sounded from Kegan and Ginger while Corvin choked on the danish that he had been eating when they left.

"Welcome to the Nostromo." Alastair gestured to the ship around him with both hands as he stood up. "You're just in time."

Ginger ignored him altogether. "What the hell did you get us into?" she demanded of Max, bewildered.

"Yeah, what the hell, man?" added Kegan, his hand twitching like he might go for an arrow.

Corvin remained silent, as he was still recovering from choking.

Kira patted him on the back.

"Just hear him out." Max held up his hands to stop the questioning.

"Thank you; I've asked Max and Kira to gather a party …" Alastair trailed off, looking at Farn who was half done with her danish. "Are you eating a pastry on the bridge of my airship?"

Farn paused for a moment, then committed to the act by shoving the remaining half into her mouth all at once and replying with a muffled, "No?" There was an upwards inflection at the end like she was asking a question. Crumbs fell as she spoke, causing her to raise one hand to cover her mouth.

Kira snorted and shot her a smile.

Alastair sighed and rolled his eyes at the speed of which Kira and Max had seemed to rub off on his employee. Then he continued, "As I was saying, I asked you all here to take on a mission of the utmost importance." He explained some of the situation, then triggered a non-disclosure agreement for everyone aboard the airship. Once the legal part of his presentation was covered, he cut to the video of Carver, which played in a circular portal appearing at the center of the ship's massive front window.

The group watched in silence as the truth of the situation unfolded, looks of horror becoming visible on each of their faces as they realized the severity of what was going on. Even Max, who had seen it earlier, grew fearful, the potential impact of failure setting in again as the video came to a close.

Silence fell across the bridge for a long moment until it was finally broken by Ginger. "I feel sick." The *Coin* looked down at the floor for a second before snapping her eyes back up. "I have two kids," she said, revealing a detail about herself that Max wasn't aware of. "I'm doing it alone. I can't go back to working seventy hours a week to make ends meet. I'll never see them." Her eyes welled up. "I need this game."

Corvin looked from Ginger back to Max. "I'll do my best."

Then all eyes turn to Kegan, who shrugged, "I'd be kind of a dick if I backed out after watching that."

"Thank you." Alastair released a tension in his shoulders that Max hadn't noticed before. "As an added bonus, the mission pays two hundred thousand dollars to each of you upon completion," he turned to Ginger, "so let's do our best and get those kids of yours into a good college."

"Seriously?" Kegan's eyes darted back to Max.

The rest of the group followed suit, their gaze falling on him all at once.

Max cracked half a smile and gave them a slight nod.

"Now, that's what I'm talkin' about." Kegan clapped his hands while Ginger gripped a nearby railing for support. Her face shifting between fear and excitement.

Alastair continued, "Now, we still have about twenty-one hours before we have to start the actual mission. So, we'll take the day to get prepared. Someone from Checkpoint will contact each of you as soon as you wake up to arrange travel accommodations to get you to our main office in New York."

Max stopped him. "I'm sorry, what's this about travel?"

Alastair looked at him as if it should have been obvious.

"We can't afford to take any chances on this. I think the safest thing would be to conduct the operation from our main testing lab."

"Is that really necessary?" Kira stepped in beside Max.

Alastair nodded. "Definitely. What if one of you have a power outage or your internet lags out at the wrong time? There's a lot that could go wrong here. Our facility has its own power system and a secure internet connection. Plus, the rigs we use for testing are significantly more advanced than the home versions you use. They'll allow us to monitor your vitals the whole time you're logged in. I'm also bringing in a full medical team to keep an eye on you just in case."

"That's a little scary." Ginger shrank back.

Alastair took a decisive step forward and gripped the railing in front of him. "Look, I'm not gonna lie here, Carver has always found ways to push the system's limits. And we don't know what to expect from this quest. It's important that we do this safely." He let some of the businessman inside him take over.

Max moved into the center of the group. "Alright, but we can quit at any time if we feel it's getting out of hand."

"That's fair." Alastair nodded.

Ginger blew out a sigh. "I guess I can try to get my sister to take the kids for a day."

Alastair pushed off the railing and clapped his hands together. "Great. I'll be taking my leave then. I have a lot to get ready before tonight. I suggest you all do the same."

The others looked to one another as nervous tension filled the air again.

"Okay, I guess we'll all meet up in New York," declared Max, a little unsure of what he was saying.

Everyone nodded in agreement, and one by one, they vanished from the world. The last to log out were Max and Kira. "See you in a minute," Max reassured himself as much as his partner.

Kira nodded with a smile that felt a little forced. He suspected it was more for his benefit than hers.

He selected the sign off option from his stat-sleeve, and after a brief countdown, his system powered down, allowing his body to enter the natural waking process. Then, only minutes later, he opened his eyes to greet the morning.

CHAPTER NINE

Wyatt struggled to come up with a good story to explain to his department manager at the electronics store where he worked why he wouldn't be able to come in for the next couple days. Things were so much easier as Max back in Noctem. There he could just shoot anything that got in his way. Seth wasn't making the phone call any easier as he critiqued his performance like an acting coach. At least in the real world, Wyatt didn't have to worry about his fairy friend getting hurt by something stupid. Which was why he whipped a half-empty water bottle at Seth as soon as he hung up.

"I'd like to see you do better."

Seth took on the challenge with gusto, pulling out his phone and clutching his stomach. Thirty seconds and a theatrical performance of having a stomach virus later, he had the next few days off. According to Seth, if you tell your employer that you're quote 'firing out both ends uncontrollably' they don't want you anywhere near them.

From there, the sudden trip was quite comfortable. A little before noon, a black limousine pulled up outside the apartment that

Wyatt and Seth shared in their hometown of Sarasota, Florida. Then it was off to the airport where they caught a non-stop flight to JFK International. Wyatt spent the time watching a movie on his phone, trying to reconcile the realization that he had been thrust into the position of having to save the world, just like the heroes he had always watched on screen. Seth occupied himself by working his way through a pile of comics that he'd purchased that morning after forcing their limo to stop at the shop near their apartment.

Their seats were first class, which was a new experience for Wyatt, never having seen beyond the curtain before. So, when they pulled up to the main office of Checkpoint Systems in upstate New York later that afternoon, he was feeling pretty good about the day.

The building, if you could call it that, was huge, making it clear why they picked somewhere so remote for their headquarters. It shared a resemblance to the Citadel in Valain, which must have been an intentional design choice and an expensive one at that. Looking closer, it was more like a fortress, with multiple guards patrolling its grounds at regular intervals. The tight security made sense, considering how much personal information the company had on its users.

Wyatt entered the building's massive lobby through a pair of equally massive glass doors, becoming a little more over-whelmed with each step he took. He had played Noctem almost every night with Seth for the last three years. He had just never expected they would be standing where it was all built. He couldn't help but pause just to take it all in.

Light poured into the thirty-story room from a ceiling full of skylights, the only shadows being cast by a line of balconies running all the way to the top, one on each floor. A Checkpoint logo made of three-dimensional lettering marked one wall while concept art on hung around it, printed on twenty-foot tall fabric banners.

Wyatt pointed up at an image of a delicate young fairy being embraced by a brave warrior. "Hey, look; it's you."

Seth gave him a sarcastic laugh and pointed to a different banner featuring a hideous orc. "They have one of you too."

Wyatt groaned in response as he walked in the direction of the front desk, where a receptionist was expecting them.

After a call upstairs, a security guard came down to escort them up. Wyatt stepped into a spacious elevator that had him wondering if it was larger than his room back in their apartment. It rose several floors, and they exited into a hallway leading to a large but somehow inviting waiting room which was where they met a woman in her late thirties sitting between a well-behaved teenage girl and boy.

Wyatt had one of those faces that used to look okay in an unconventionally attractive sort of way. Although, after he'd lost his hair back when he was twenty-three, he'd lost most of his confidence along with it. He didn't look good bald. Which was why adding his hair back on had been the only major change he had made to his avatar when creating it. Other than that, he looked similar to how he did online.

The woman glanced up at him as he entered the room, a look of instant recognition appearing on her face as a grin took over. She stood and hugged him without hesitation. She was short and had a dusting of gray in her hair that made her look a little older than she probably was. But even though she didn't look anything like the *Coin* that had tortured him with her powers of seduction ten hours before, he could tell it was her just the same. Plus, she still smelled a little like cinnamon.

"Hey, Ginger. Good to, ah, meet you." He held his arms limp in her embrace, not sure what to do with them.

"Great to meet you too. It's Marisa Price, by the way," she gave him her real name before spinning to face Seth. "And you must be Kira," she added without him needing to say anything. "You're even more handsome than I thought you'd be."

Wyatt's face dropped in surprise. Not because she had called Seth handsome. He figured that she was just being nice, but what was surprising was the fact that she had recognized him at all.

Seth started to turn red but covered with a graceful smile and nod that he must have picked up from his time spent as a fairy in Noctem. "You're looking nice as well."

Marisa grinned. "Cute and charming, don't you have it all."

"Good lord, Mom. You gotta not flirt in front of us," commented the teenage girl, looking up from a schoolbook.

"Yeah, that's wicked inapropes," added the boy.

Marisa jabbed a finger in their direction. "Hey, if I never flirted with anyone, the two of you wouldn't exist."

They both shuddered at the thought.

"Sorry, these are my kids. The big one's Toby. He's sixteen. And this lovely young lady here is Wren. She just turned fifteen." They both gave a polite but sarcastic wave.

Seth waved back with an awkward smile.

Wyatt didn't, trying to look cool and aloof. He didn't want to come off as lame in front of the teenagers.

Toby looked like the kind of kid that you wanted to hire to mow your lawn. The kind that had an honest, easy to read face. Wren, on the other hand, was more of a mystery. She seemed nice enough but also more guarded than her brother like she'd had a more difficult life than most teenagers. It probably had something to do with the large hearing aids that she wore in both ears.

"Your sister couldn't take the kids for the day, huh?" Wyatt recalled what she'd said back on the Nostromo's bridge.

Marisa's jaw tightened at the mere mention of her sister. "My bitchy sister felt it was more important to spend the day with some guy she just met at a farmer's market than to watch my children while I save the world, so I had to bring them along."

"Ha! You called Aunt Linda a bitch," laughed Wren.

"No, I said she WAS bitchy. There's a difference." Marisa smiled down at her daughter.

That was when a Checkpoint employee snuck into the room. An ID badge with 'Sarah Williams' printed below her picture hung from a lanyard around her neck.

Wyatt took one look at her and let out the first words that popped into his head, "Holy crap."

She froze like a deer in headlights.

"You look exactly the same," he added.

Seth agreed, staring at Farnsworth's real-world doppelgänger like she had just achieved something incredible. "Amazing." He released the word on a slow breath. The only visible difference was the absence of the two braids that she wore in the game.

"Ahh, thanks? I think." She took a step back and fidgeted with her ID badge. "And you are?" Her face dropped in shock the instant the words left her mouth.

Seth glanced away at the floor as he scratched the back of his head with one hand. "Sorry, umm, hi."

Wyatt choked out a laugh.

"Oh, wow, that is not what I expected." Sarah stared at Seth in amazement.

"Really? I always assumed Kira was a guy," Marisa said in a casual tone like it should have been obvious.

Sarah looked at her with confusion for a second, then she glanced at the two teenagers and clearly put two and two together.

"Really?" Wyatt arched an eyebrow still surprised that not one but two people recognized his fairy companion in the flesh.

"How could you tell?" Seth asked, almost wincing like he was about to tear off a band-aid.

Marisa tapped one finger on her other arm before answering. "As Kira, you seem conflicted? Not in a bad way, though," she explained, not really making much sense. "It's actually kind of endearing for some reason. Makes people want to hold you and tell you it's okay."

"Gee, that's not weird at all." Wyatt sat in one of the chairs as Seth took a seat next to him.

"Yeah that is kinda weird," added Wren, closing her book as if she'd given up trying to study with everyone talking around her.

"You're kinda weird." Seth matched the maturity level of the fifteen-year-old.

Wren looked to her mother. "Are you gonna let your weird friend call your children weird?"

Marisa shrugged. "If the shoe fits, dear."

Seth gave Wren a look that said 'Ha, I win.'

The group talked for a while more before being joined by two more guests. Wyatt held up his hand, stopping the two before they had a chance to speak. Then he pointed to each of them, guessing their identities. He got them right, mostly going by the fact one of them was Korean.

Kegan, or Kevin Park, as he was known in the real world, eyed Wyatt. "You only got that right cause I'm Asian, didn't you?"

"Ah, maybe?" Wyatt responded, unsure if that made him sound racist.

Marisa stepped forward. "Wow, you look like an older version of your avatar."

Kevin shrugged. "Well, yeah, I based it off a photo of myself when I was twenty. I'm over forty now."

Next to him stood Corvin, who turned out to be a six-foot, three-inch college student with long black hair named Bastian Castillo, who had started at the University of Massachusetts. He was rather dashing according to Marisa, who made a point of telling him.

He responded with a nervous, "Thanks."

Kevin started to speak but paused as he surveyed the group, gears clearly turning in his head. Something wasn't adding up. His eyes stopped at Seth, "Hold on, are you …?" he trailed off unable to finish the thought.

Seth shoved his hands into his pockets. "Yup."

"Holy crap!" Kevin said. "I've been picturing you naked for like, the last two years," he cringed, "and now I've said that out loud. Soooo, that's embarrassing."

Bastian also looked a little red, possibly thinking something similar but being less vocal about it. At that, the group shared a laugh worthy of the end of a Scooby Doo episode, all gathered round with the monster tied up and the day saved. That was when Milo entered the room, his face lighting up like a Christmas tree upon seeing them together in the flesh.

In sharp contrast to the dark and powerful presence that he had online as Alastair, Milo looked more disheveled than anything else. His short hair was a mess, his shirt was wrinkled, and his narrow tie hung loosely around his neck. Even his glasses seemed a little askew. It must have been a long day so far, but as stressed as he seemed, there was still a glimmer of wild excitement in his eyes. Wyatt understood why. After all, it probably wasn't every day that he got to assemble a team to save the world.

"I'm glad to see everybody has gotten to know each other." He looked around the room. "I thought about providing you all with name tags, but then I thought it would be more fun to let you guess." He glanced at the clock on the wall. "Damn, how did it get so late?" He glanced back at the door. "How about I give you a quick tour of the testing facility where you'll be spending the night? Sound good?" He didn't wait for them to answer before turning toward the door.

Wyatt noticed the rest of the group looking to him as if waiting for him to go first. Apparently, they had all joined his party and made him leader in the real world as well. The thought gave him a slight boost of confidence as he spun and headed out. Seth joined him, followed by the others. In the end, even the two teenagers fell in line.

He followed Milo through a long hallway as the frazzled man pointed out a few noteworthy offices to the group. Wyatt didn't pay much attention as he trailed behind the man who had built an entire company from the ground up. He couldn't help but feel a little star struck even if Milo's appearance wasn't all that impressive. Perhaps it was the fact he was so ordinary that drove the point home. Wyatt could easily forget who Milo was when talking to him online, where he wore the form of a ridiculous fantasy villain. Seeing him as he really was now, Wyatt finally realized that he was just a regular guy like him.

He wasn't even that much older.

The fact he had achieved so much made Wyatt feel more than just a little small. Hell, earlier that morning his main concern was about a stupid job at an electronics store. It put things into perspective as the thought chased away some of the confidence that he'd found moments before. He tried his best not to show it, following in silence until they came to a stop at a heavy set of double doors. A silver-embossed plate mounted on the wall to the right bore the words, Nemo Unit.

Bastian let out a chuckle at the name.

Catching his reaction, Milo stopped before opening the door. "I'm surprised someone got the reference, especially someone so young," he said, addressing the youngest member of the party with a smile on his face.

Bastian didn't seem like someone who spoke unless spoken to, so all he said was a quiet, "It's clever."

Milo continued to look at up at the young man as if he expected more, eventually beckoning with one hand to coax a few more words from him.

"Oh," Bastian continued, "Little Nemo was an old movie and video game about a dream world." He shifted his hand in his coat pocket as if holding onto something. "I have the game on my phone. There's an app that runs all the classic Nintendo games. I've been working my way through its library."

Milo grinned from ear to ear. "You know, you remind me of myself when I was your age. I would have loved something like that. Now, if you remember, what did you do in the game?"

Bastian's eyes rolled up and to the side. "Umm, you rode various animals through the dreamland and used their abilities to make progress."

"Ha, YES! Exactly," Milo slapped a hand against his leg. "How about we meet the animals you'll be riding tonight."

With that, he pushed open the double doors dramatically, revealing a wide room full of high-tech looking equipment. The far wall contained a massive multi-screened terminal with heavy cables running out and around the edge of the room, each disappearing into one of eight identical machines that lined the space. At their hearts sat a cushioned chair that reclined into a position almost parallel to the floor. Screens and electronics surrounded them with coils of thick wires running in and out in all directions. A large Somno system, attached to the headrest, completed each machine. They were all black, which Wyatt would have liked but, instead, found more than a little intimidating. From the expressions he saw all around him, so did everyone else. Well, everyone but Milo who was walking backward with his hands spread apart, directing the group's attention to the chairs that would be their beds for the night.

"These are our test rigs," he said, almost taking a bow. "On top of providing you with the best possible connection, they can also monitor your vitals and brain activity. So, if anything goes wrong, we'll know about it." He called to a middle-aged man with glasses wearing a white lab coat who was inspecting some of the monitoring equipment. "This is Doctor Narang. He's leading the team that'll be keeping an eye on you during the mission."

The man let out a sigh before turning to the group. "What is it?"

"I wanted to introduce you to the team you'll be monitoring." Milo gestured toward Max and the others.

The man made no motion to shake anyone's hand. "Yes. It's very nice to meet everyone."

A moment passed where no one said anything before Milo took the hint. "Ah, yes. Well, we should let you get back to work."

Narang nodded without saying anything more, which appeared to be Milo's cue to take his guests back out into the hall before he got them all yelled at. "I guess we should get out of their way." He pushed the side of his glasses up before changing the subject. "I've had a meal prepared for everyone. You know, trying to be a good host and all," he said, leading

Wyatt and the others into a conference room where a table full of food waited.

A few employees from the building's commissary were still bringing in a few dishes as they entered. Milo took a seat at the head of the table and motioned for them to do the same. "There's plenty for everyone, so dig in. We're going to have to get an early start tonight, so we should relax now while we can."

It was the first time Wyatt had seen food since the flight, and the limo ride from the airport had been longer than expected. He glanced at Seth with half a smile to apologize before piling a plate high with chicken fingers.

Seth nodded in return.

Wyatt passed the tray along to Marisa's kids who devoured the rest while the others selected more refined options.

"I hope everyone can find something they like," Milo said. "I had an intern pull some of your food purchases to find out what you preferred." His mouth hung open for a moment. "Now that I've said that, I realized that was probably an invasion of privacy. Sorry." The group stopped eating, but Milo continued regardless, not giving them the chance to get upset. "Oh well, it's done now. If there is anything else I can get, just let me know."

Everyone looked to Wyatt, who shrugged and continued to eat. The others followed his lead. Well, everyone except Seth.

"You feel okay?" Marisa asked, noticing that he hadn't touched anything.

He sipped a glass of water. "I'm fine."

Wyatt glanced around the table, hoping to find something that might be okay. "Oh, there's some mashed potatoes. You should be okay with that, right?"

"Sure, that should be fine, as long as I don't have a lot," Seth said, reaching for the bowl of fluffy white starch. "Sorry, I have a thing with my stomach," he explained in a casual tone as if it was no big deal. "I can't actually digest solid foods."

The group stopped eating mid-chew, a look of horror on

Milo's face. "I'm so sorry. I didn't know. What about soup or something like that?"

"Yeah, as long as there's no chunks in it." Seth leaned back. He was used to explaining it. Wyatt still remembered when he'd first heard about it. His friend had tried to make a joke of it. "But really," Seth continued, "don't worry about it. I know it's kind of a weird thing. I don't expect people to go out of their way."

Milo pulled out a large smartphone and typed a quick text, tapping send like it was the period at the end of a sentence. "Okay, liquid sustenance is on the way," he said as if he could have produced anything with another few taps.

"You really don't have to worry about it, but I do appreciate the effort." Seth smiled.

"How come you can't eat stuff?" Kevin asked while picking up another fork full of food.

"Nothing major, just unlucky. Caught a virus, it did some nerve damage that affected the muscles in my stomach; could've happened to anybody. It was about ten years ago."

"That sucks." Wren pushed a bite of food around her plate. Her sympathetic tone sounded more mature than a fifteen-year-old should.

Seth chuckled with a sad smile. "Yeah, it does."

Marisa slapped a hand down on the table. "That's why you're so obsessed with food online."

"Pretty much. It had been seven years since I had solid food when Noctem came out. I went on a several-day-long binge when I realized there was a way I could eat again. It wasn't real, but I didn't care."

"Yeah, we barely gained a level in our first week thanks to this one's compulsive eating," Wyatt added, remembering how many nights he'd sat in a tavern drinking while his partner consumed the menu line by line.

Seth grinned. "It was amazing; I can't tell you how much it meant to have that back. I mean, talk about delayed gratification. The years of nothing but shakes and broth before then made everything taste so much better than I remembered. First thing I had was some kind of meat pie. I didn't even know what was in it. You could have told me it was rat pie, and I still would have eaten it." He paused, almost salivating. "I still remember that pie like it was yesterday."

Milo looked dumbfounded. "I had no idea that the system had an impact like that for somebody."

"One more reason for us to get this done," Wyatt said through a mouthful of breaded chicken, reminding the others of the reason they were there without meaning to. They fell silent.

Not long after, a serious looking man entered, pushing a cart containing beef consume and some form of protein shake.

"Sorry there isn't something more," Milo apologized. "I asked my assistant, Jeff here, to find someone from our fitness center to tell him how to make a decent shake."

Jeff didn't look thrilled to be used as a gopher, wearing a stern expression on his face as he placed the bowl of liquid in front of Seth, who thanked him. Jeff said nothing in return, then he approached Milo, handing him a thin tablet computer.

Milo took it and looked over the screen, deflating as a frown gnawed at his face. "Damn, they need me down the hall." He excused himself, leaving Wyatt and the others to spend the next hour without him, getting to know more about each other's lives.

The standard questions were asked all around. Where you from and what not. As it turned out, Sarah had grown up in Georgia and had only moved to New York in the last two years. Kevin, on the other hand, had lived in Denver his entire life. And by sheer coincidence, Bastian's new dorm at U. Mass was only a half hour from where Marisa lived in Haverhill, Massachusetts. They would have been on the same flight too, but he had a couple classes in the morning that he couldn't skip.

Just as Kevin and Marisa's kids were polishing off what was left of the food, Jeff returned with several plastic packages, each containing a pair of hospital-like pajamas. He handed one out to each of them. "You may use the offices down the hall to change," he informed in a formal tone before turning to Marisa. "Mr. Parker has a small apartment in the building that will be comfortable for the children to spend the night, and there will be someone available at all times if they should need anything. If you would follow me, I'll show you there."

"Oh, okay," she agreed, trepidation in her voice as her small family followed him from the room.

Wyatt spoke as soon as they were gone, hooking a thumb at the door. "That guy's loads of fun, huh?"

Seth joined in with an impression of the assistant's no-nonsense demeanor. He continued the act as he took over leading the party down the hall to the offices, getting a few laughs on the way and showing the others more of the resemblance between him and his ridiculous online persona.

There was no shortage of offices, so the others just picked whichever one was closest and shut the door. Wyatt hesitated in the hall alone for a moment and took a slow breath. Eventually, he took a room on the far right, closing the door behind him.

The office belonged to a young woman. He assumed this from a pair of slip-on shoes sitting by the door, a backup for when fancier ones became uncomfortable. On a shelf sat both boyfriend and dog, lovingly photographed. A Hello Kitty calendar hung on the wall, one week highlighted, where excited handwriting had scribbled the words 'England trip'. Wyatt tried his best not to disturb the room.

He tore open the plastic package, removing the cotton pajamas and holding them in front of himself as he let them unfold in his hands. The day had passed by so fast that he hadn't really considered that it had been leading up to something. Now, standing there in a stranger's office with a pair of white hospital jammies, reality sunk in. A feeling of dread swelled, more worry than fear, but worry of what, he didn't know. He shook it off and disrobed, slipping into the PJs and pulling the front across his chest to where they tied on the side. They fit well. At least he'd be comfortable.

Gathering his things, he exited the room and rejoined his companions who had also finished.

Kevin eyed Bastian. "Well, this is embarrassing, we wore the same outfit." No one laughed. "You know, cause the ..." He gestured to his attire, exacerbating the failed joke by explaining it. Although, in his defense, the air had grown tense, making his words feel forced, like he was struggling to distract himself. Evidently, it wasn't just Wyatt that was sensing the weight of what they were about to do hanging over them.

With most of the group waiting, the only one missing was Seth, who was taking longer to get changed than he should've, prompting Wyatt to knock on his door. "You okay in there?"

"Yeah, umm, I'm fine," Seth responded from inside, followed by a low clunk, like the sound of someone bumping into a chair. Wyatt raised an eyebrow but leaned against the wall to wait anyways. Finally, he emerged. One look at Seth told him what the issue was, and he coughed an abrupt laugh in reflex.

Seth held his top out like a tent, the strings tied off in all the wrong places, making it look almost as if he was wearing it side-ways. "I have done something wrong."

Wyatt shook his head and moved to aid his clothing chal-lenged friend, tugging at the knots Seth had tied. "How the hell did you even do this?"

"I don't know. I panicked. Just started tying things," Seth said as if it was a reasonable explanation.

"Good plan." Wyatt struggled with a tangle of string. "Who in their right mind ties a triple knot? Have you never tied a shoe before?"

"Obviously I've tied a shoe before," Seth defended in an annoyed tone, sounding far too much like the fairy he played online.

Wyatt laughed again. "You sure about that? I could go get Marisa's kids to teach you." Seth rolled his eyes at the comment as the scene continued for longer than was comfortable for either of them. Wyatt began looking for other options. His first thought was to ask Sarah for help, hoping that she might have longer fingernails, being the only woman there at the moment. That would require him to talk to her, though, and she looked a little self-conscious standing there in just a pair of pajamas which, in turn, made him nervous. So that was out.

Fortunately, Seth got a better idea, disappearing back into one of the offices. The sound of scissors snipping strings was heard, followed by a few staples. He reemerged looking put together, for the most part, giving the room a little strut as if he was walking the runway during fashion week. He held one hand out at his side and finished with a proper turn as he looked at the group over his shoulder stating a simple, "Problem solved."

"I'm not sure—" Wyatt started to say before being interrupted.

"I believe I said, 'problem solved,'" Seth insisted, getting a smirk from Sarah.

A minute later, Marisa returned, her face reading like an open book as she hugged herself and frowned. She must not have been accustomed to being separated from her family in a strange place.

Not long after, Milo came to collect them. He had also changed into matching pajamas, giving the group a ridiculous appearance, like some kind of adult slumber party. Hail the conquering heroes and their jammies.

Wyatt pointed at the man's clothes with his eyes. "I take it you're going in with us?"

Milo looked wounded. "Of course. I may not be able to share the full burden of this, but I can support you from the airship as much as possible." He placed one hand on his chest as if making a promise, and with that, he led them back to the Nemo Unit in a parade of white cotton.

Again, the room was abuzz with activity, adding to the tension in the air. Doctor Narang gave orders to staff in green scrubs as they got things into place. Trays of small vials and plastic wrapped hypodermic needles sat beside each machine. The terminal at the end was manned by two technicians talking in complex techno-jargon that Wyatt thought sounded made up.

To his surprise, Jeff, the far-too-serious assistant, was coming with them as well. Either that or he had developed a compulsion for wearing pajamas for some other reason.

Wyatt gravitated toward one of the Somno rigs, and the others spread out around the room to pick one of their own. Seth lingered by his side a moment longer than the rest. They exchanged panicked looks as the staff descended upon them, getting them into their chairs and sticking electrodes to their skin as last-minute checks were done. The monitors came alive with readouts of their heart rates and blood pressure as they danced across the screens like an excited raver, waiting for the beat to drop. Then, one by one, the padded chairs reclined, sliding back into a table-like position. Breathing grew heavy as the large headsets began to slide into place over their faces, emitting various electronic sounds louder than normal, being so close to their ears.

Wyatt stole one last glance at the room before his vision was cut off, only catching a small detail. The image of Seth's thumb jittering about on the armrest of his rig, the sound of him tap, tap, tapping still audible over the start-up noises of Wyatt's Somno. It was a nervous tick that Seth had always done when he was feeling overwhelmed. Something about the action stirred the fear bubbling in his stomach, forcing him to swallow it back down before it ran away with him. Then, from his other side where Sarah lay, he heard something else.

"Everything will be fine. You can do this," she said, probably talking to herself but at a higher volume to compensate for the noises around her.

It was an awkward little pep talk, but Wyatt appreciated it. He let the words echo in his head. *Everything will be fine. You can do this.*

CHAPTER TEN

Max opened his eyes, finding Kira waiting for him on the bridge of the Nostromo as soon as he got logged in, her small form slouching into the captain's chair as if she owned the place. The others trickled in behind him, their expressions grateful just to be out of the testing room - despite the fact that they never really left it. Even Alastair looked a little relieved as he raised an eyebrow at the fairy taking up his seat.

She took the hint and slid from the chair, taking a couple steps to the side with her hands behind her back as if she hadn't been there in the first place.

Alastair ignored her and reclaimed his set.

A moment later a tall *Venom* mage appeared, the same one who had accompanied Alastair in the tavern the previous night, this time with his hood lowered. He wore a severe expression on his face that looked like he might release an annoyed sigh at any moment. Connections formed in Max's head, identifying the elf as Jeff, the no-nonsense assistant that had brought them their pajamas back in the real world. He would have said something to him, but his attention was torn away by Alastair who stood to address the entire bridge. His voice was clear and professional.

"Aboard this airship are the only people aware of the situation at hand. It will most likely be the biggest challenge that any of us will ever face in our lives. The consequences of failure could be devastating to this company and the world as we know it." He jabbed two fingers downward against the railing in front of him. "However, among us, we have some of the finest players to ever set foot in Noctem as well as the best support staff that I have ever had the pleasure of working with. In short, it will be hard, but I believe in this crew. We can do this. Neal simply doesn't know who he's messing with." There was a heavy dose of pride in his words, and the speech rallied the crew more than Max would have expected, like the man genuinely had their respect. Alastair turned back to take his place in the captain's chair, filling it well as he pointed forward and added, "Full speed ahead."

Max stood between Kira and Farn as the Nostromo flew toward the starting point given to them by Carver's video. It had helped that they had been near their destination when they logged out the night before. At first glance, their starting point didn't look like much, just a small hut placed at random in a vast, empty desert. It was nowhere near a city or even a village. Max walked out onto the deck of the ship for a better look, but there wasn't much more to see from there either. Although, outside the Nostromo for the first time, he was curious about what the ship looked like. It was a cross between a navy destroyer and a vintage plane with some fantasy styling thrown in for good measure. It was a distinctive design choice, like it was somehow part of Noctem's military. Max liked the aesthetics but questioned why the game world needed something like a warship.

The craft descended toward the ground, stopping to hover above the tiny shack, dust billowing out in wide circles as it was pushed away by the ship's vertical engines. Alastair walked them to an opening in the railing where he pulled a lever. A rope ladder that almost reached the ground unfurled from the deck like a tongue. "There's nowhere for us to dock, so this will have to do."

Max peered over the edge at the ladder flipping around in the wind. "It's cool. This looks safe."

"Would you rather walk the plank? And yes, before you ask, we have a plank." Alastair waggled his eyebrows.

Kira shoved at Max, pushing him so close to the edge that he had to catch himself with one hand on the railing nearby. "Get going, fearless leader; we don't have all day."

"Alright, alright, cut it out." He laughed at her playful attempt to murder him as he placed his foot onto the first rung, making sure to not to let go of the ship's handrail as he found his footing. Kira hopped up on the railing, sitting a couple of feet from his hand before letting herself fall back like a scuba diver to plummet toward the ground.

"Well that makes sense," Max muttered to himself as he began to climb down.

He dropped from the last rung of the ladder, landing so hard on the dry, brittle ground that he took a small amount of damage in the process, as did the rest of the team behind him. He opened his mouth to comment, but Kira streaked through the air above before he got a word out, dropping a wave of healing energy like a plane dumping napalm. Max looked up as her trail of dust sparkled through Noctem's eternal night sky. It was dark, but the full moon provided plenty of light to see where he was going as he made his way over to the broken-down shack, finding Kira waiting at the entrance, her arms crossed and tapping one foot.

"Don't even say it," he pleaded.

She flashed him a dopey grin. "Took you long enough."

He ignored her and knocked on the door while the others looked at him questioningly. He responded with a shrug that asked, got any better ideas? No one answered. He drew one of his guns and stood to the side of the door with his back against the wall, the way he'd seen police do in so many movies. He reached down to hover just above the wooden handle. Before opening it, he nodded to Farn, indicating for her to take the other side. The rest of the group stood back. He turned it and nudged the door open a crack as Farn kicked it in the rest of the way, her sword at the ready. He followed, drawing his other gun and they fell into formation. They made a good team.

The room was empty, empty except for Max and Farn who now occupied the space inside. Their badass formation lost its impressive status with its overall lack of purpose. One at a time, the four heads of the rest of the party peered in from the sides of the door, silhouetted by the moonlight behind them. They relaxed as Max broke the silence.

"What the hell? Nothing." Just then, the dusty stone floor beneath his feet began to sink, causing him to jump back like a startled animal, making an embarrassing sound in the process. Segments of stone fell into place to form stairs and the entrance of a dungeon. "Well, that answers that." He brushed off a bit of dust from his pants.

Max took a moment to do a last-minute equipment check of what he carried in his item bag and ammo pouches since he would be unable to retrieve anything else from his virtual inventory once they entered the dungeon. Then, satisfied with his choices in carry items, he made his way down the stairs.

Alastair's voice reached his ears, sounding as if he were standing right there with them, his name listed in Max's chat group. "Talk to me, people. What's down there?"

Max raised a silver com-ring to his mouth. "It's a dungeon entrance." The enchantment on the item carried his voice back up to the airship. "We're going in. Over."

"Okay, keep me posted," Alastair said.

"Roger."

There was a short pause, about long enough for someone to execute an exaggerated eye roll, before Alastair added, "You can leave out the 'overs' and 'rogers,' Max. It's a fantasy game, not Call of Duty."

There was a second pause in the transmission, followed by Kira's voice, "Ha, you said 'duty.' Over."

Alastair didn't respond.

The stairs let out into a massive cylindrical room, a staircase spiraling down along the walls into its depths. The empty space in the middle spanned hundreds of feet across and well over a thousand down. Thick links of metal hung from the center of the ceiling, supporting a daisy chain of wrought iron chandeliers fastened to the walls in places with heavy support ropes, each layer decorated with silver statues of angels. An eerie glow filled the cavernous space as shadows played on the stonework of the walls. Max cringed. He'd played enough survival horror games to know how places like this treated their guests.

Corvin turned to the others while pointing at the statues, "Don't blink, am I right, guys?"

The joke was received by most with puzzled looks, but a couple of chuckles told him that at least Kira and Farn got the reference.

Kegan looked down over the railing-less side. "If Kira gives everyone *Flight*, we might be able to get down there fast."

"That sounds too easy. I assume something would stop us," Kira thought out loud while tilting her head back and forth as if weighing the risks. "I can try it alone and go down a couple levels, see what happens."

Max nodded, giving approval to the idea and she stepped off the edge without hesitation, hovering in mid-air like a hummingbird sipping from a flower. She dropped a level, stopping in the same abrupt motion and scanned the area from below while Max did the same from above.

"We've got movement!" Kegan shouted, pointing with an arrow at the chandelier as the statues came to life.

They hopped from one branch of the iron structure to another until they all stood facing Kira. Bows were drawn from behind their silver wings, and arrowheads found the fairy in their path. She darted from side to side, avoiding the first few shots. Her maneuverability kept her in the air while Max and Kegan laid down some cover fire to give her some breathing room so she could make her way back up. The bullets ricocheted with metallic clangs as they impacted with a statue's extended wings. Kira landed with an uncharacteristic stumble, and Farn moved in to brace her impact, preventing her from tumbling down the seemingly endless stairs.

"Okay, bad idea," Kira sputtered while regaining her balance, leaning on Farn.

As soon as her wings dematerialized, all but one of the statutes halted their attack and returned to their starting positions, leaving the remaining angel to take flight in their direction. It landed right in their path, a short sword clasped in its hand.

The uneven nature of the stairs made it hard to move, but the party worked with it as Max called out his commands. "Ginger, get behind it. I'll meet you there. Farn, keep it focused on the front. Kegan, find its weak points, and Corvin, lay down some debuffs." He didn't bother telling Kira what to do as she took up a position furthest from the fight to support the team and keep Farn's health from falling.

Like clockwork, the team clicked into action. Ginger fired a line into the wall above and leapt to the side, swinging off the edge of the stairs over the empty space below. She arched back around to land behind the statue for a quick strike that carried the critical damage of a backstab. The angel staggered, giving Max a moment to sneak by while Farn shouted a ridiculous taunt in its direction.

The thing stared at her for an instant, looking dumb as a spiral of green and gray smoke circled its head. Corvin snapped his caster shut as the poison spell he'd cast took hold, adding a fragile defense status along with it. A second later, Kegan fired three arrows, hitting his target in the head, neck, and chest. The neck was critical, the damage almost doubled by the active debuff. Max fired a few rounds into the statue's back as Kegan loosed another arrow at its neck, their attacks delivering a one-two punch that brought the angel down.

All in all, it was a pretty standard fight. Without the other statues firing at them from a distance, the thing turned out to be a bit of a pushover. Ginger even seized the opportunity to snatch a couple feathers from its wings as it fell. In the end, the only resource lost was time.

They regrouped, and Max reported the encounter back to Alastair on the Nostromo. Then, with no reason to stand around, they continued their descent, the occasional statue swooping over for a visit only to end with Ginger getting another handful of silver feathers. After traveling around the massive spiral a few more times and removing a modest number of angels from the dungeon, Max was starting to feel pretty good about their chances.

"This isn't so bad." Kegan looked over his progress in his journal. "The experience is crap, but at least these guys are easy."

"Plus, I'm getting a ton of these feathers," Ginger added brushing a few against her cheek. "You want to buy some off me later, Kegan? I'm thinking they would craft some good arrows."

"Buy some?" the *Leaf* waved his journal at her like she had just committed a crime. "We're on an epic quest to save the world together, and you want to charge me for feathers?"

"It is a material world." She shrugged.

Kira rolled her body against the curved wall of the chamber until she stood with her back against it looking up at the flights above. "I wish there weren't so many stairs, though. I mean how long is this gonna take?"

"About another hour. Maybe a little more?" Max peered over the side.

Corvin chuckled. "Anyone ever play Ghostbusters for the original Nintendo?"

Kira slapped a hand against her forehead. "OH GOD! The damn stairway at the end. Why would they make you press a button forty thousand times to climb each individual stair when you have a perfectly good d-pad available."

"I know, right? At least there aren't any ghosts chasing us." Corvin smiled as he passed her.

She tensed her body as if the memory brought her physical pain. "Don't get me started on the ghosts——"

"We got another statue," Max interrupted before she got into full-on rant mode.

They repeated the process of fighting a silver annoyance and traveling down a level several more times, the continuous victories building up their confidence the whole way. In fact, it started to seem as though Carver had underestimated their capabilities when he had created the quest. It was to a point where not even the decorative mosaic of death and destruction that sat on the floor of the chamber could shake Max's faith in his team.

He stepped off the stairs and onto the tiles, the others doing the same one at a time behind him. The image below his feet depicted what looked like the end of the world, cities falling and the souls of people being drawn in toward the center of the circular room. It was typical for a standard role-playing game. Each square tile reminded him of the 8-bit sprite graphics of games past. He hadn't played any from back then like Corvin or Kira, but there had been a few retro-styled releases that he'd gotten his hands on. Now, a part of him expected the tiles underfoot to come to life and play out some kind of macabre, animated cut-scene.

At the center of the image sat a pedestal of coiled serpents holding a wide basin filled with a dark liquid. At six points around its edge were detailed skulls of polished black stone, their eyes turned upwards toward the angels above. Max looked up to see light glinting off their silver wings as the statues hopped down to the lowest chandelier for a better view as if they were curious - some even finding perches around the stairway a couple levels up when space became limited. Their blank eyes seemed to watch with intense anticipation.

Taking their places around the basin in line with the placement of the six skulls, the group stopped. Kira leaned down for a closer look at the grim shape in front of her. Max couldn't be sure, but for a moment, he thought that hers was somewhat smaller than the rest, like it had resized to match her own skull. He shook off the thought with a shudder before he let his nerves run away with him.

They each inspected their edge of the basin for some kind of indication of what to do next. Hands reached out in curiosity but stopped just short of touching as if that would be an action that couldn't be taken back. But after losing close to two hours on their descent down the stairs, they couldn't afford to be cautious now, and Max knew it.

He let his fingers fall to the bony face below his hand; its surface was far colder than what he imagined, almost like ice. He jerked his hand back again, expecting the tips of his fingers to adhere to the skull with frozen moisture. They didn't. Instead, the skull's expression shifted, jaw contorting into a wide scream that tore through the cavernous space before it echoed back down to where it started. The flapping of silver wings followed as the angels above shifted, as if frightened by the sound. Max cringed along with them. Then, as if set off by a chain reaction, the rest of the skulls did the same, each member of the group jumping backward. Out of each gaping mouth rose a small, empty glass about the size of a single shot, the purpose for the dark liquid becoming clear.

"I was afraid of that." Kegan placed a hand over his eyes, expressing the group's reluctance at the prospect of drinking any form of mystery fluid.

Max raised his com-ring ring to his mouth. "Hey, Alastair, we got some kind of black water here. It looks like we have to drink it to get this thing started." He didn't know why he was reporting it. It wasn't like Coldblood would respond with a casual never mind and send them home.

Instead, he got an expected, "Bottoms up," from their temporary employer over the group chat.

"Well, you heard the boss." Max sighed and reached for the glass, taking it from the skull unceremoniously.

Without warning, its jaw snapped shut with an implied murderous intent, causing him to yank his hand back again, dropping the glass. It fell with an echoing chime that reverberated through the chamber.

"Argh!" he yelled up at the angels. "I'm getting sick of all the jump scares. It's not even original anymore!" He growled in frustration as he looked for the dropped glass.

He found it under the basin where it had rolled to a stop. Despite being made of what looked like well-crafted crystal, it didn't break on the tile floor like it would have if it had been real. After all, it would have been foolish to have programmed something so important with the ability to break. He picked it up and dusted it off with his scarf. The others watched him. Kira snickered.

The surface of the black water was as still as death, like an obsidian mirror. His dim reflection vanished as he dipped his hand in, consumed by the ripples that spread out around it. The same unexpected cold chilled his fingers to the bone as he filled the tiny glass. As much as he wanted to hesitate, he didn't. Waiting would only let his imagination run wild with the idea of what the liquid was.

He tipped back the glass, and its icy contents hit his tongue, immediately changing temperature to scalding, like hot coffee that had been served without warning. An acrid taste filled his mouth, and an intense tingling swam across his taste buds as if he'd just placed a nine-volt battery to them. The sensation connected with something inside him that made him feel weak. He wasn't sure why, but fear climbed up in his throat. He choked it back down along with the liquid, coughing as it burned his insides.

The others waited in silence for a minute, eyes focused on him as if half expecting him to drop dead. Nothing happened.

"That looked like it sucked," Kira observed.

Max leaned on the basin for support. "Yeah, well I'm guessing we all have to drink it to activate the quest, so get to it."

Without a word, Corvin snatched his glass from the skull; its jaw snapped shut in response. In a single motion, he filled and downed the shot.

Max watched, expecting the same response that he'd had, but the mage just winced, placing a few fingers against his mouth as if his teeth hurt. His eyes widened, and he fell to his knees clutching his jaw. His eyes watered as he struggled not to spit it out. He forced it down, gagging, and then panted for a good thirty seconds, touching a few specific teeth as if he was trying to make sure they were still there. After a long moment, he regained his composure and pulled himself back up. "Sorry, I-I didn't expect that. It tasted like blood."

Max leaned on the basin. "Mine was like boiling acid."

"Well, shit." Kegan looked anxiously toward Ginger.

She shrugged. "It's a game. How bad could it be?"

They both picked up their glasses, filling them in unison and clinking them against each other before downing the evil cocktail at the same time. At first, they both seemed fine, then Kegan keeled over clutching his mouth as if he were about to vomit. Ginger's reaction was less visceral, staggering with one hand on her stomach. Her eyes welled up, and she blinked away tears. Kegan swallowed and proceeded to dry heave since the game wouldn't let him actually throw up.

Farnsworth was next in line, and she stared at the crystal glass of pure darkness. She started to take a step backward but stopped herself. Then she froze, her hand wavering as if hitting a barrier that she couldn't cross alone.

Kira responded by sliding her glass gently out of the small skull's mouth, its teeth snapping shut with a painful sounding crack as the others had. She scooped up the liquid and raised the shot to her mouth, stopping as a drop that balanced on the rim, passed to her bottom lip. It spread across the pink skin of her mouth, shining in the dim light. She looked to Farn, making eye contact. Then together, they sipped.

Max winced as they swallowed, expecting them to react as the others had. Farn grimaced, but that was it. She swallowed, then ran her tongue around her mouth as if trying to remove an aftertaste. She scrunched her nose as if smelling something along with it. "It's sweet." Her voice shook as if there was something more that she wasn't saying.

He turned to Kira, her eyes staring forward at nothing in particular as she let the water flow into her mouth and swirl around her tongue. She swallowed without reaction and lowered the glass, placing it on the rim of the basin. One hand raised to her lips, her fingertip ensuring the removal of any uncooperative droplets. Her face was hard to read, and Max wondered if she was doing it on purpose like she didn't want them to know what she felt. Then she blinked a few times and placed the glass back down. "Sorry, tasted like nothing."

Before Max could say anything back, the basin lit up. The still surface of the water filling with a video portal, similar to the previous one he had been shown the night before, the same basement wall with the same man in front of it, Carver.

"Hi there. Welcome to the end of the world," he said matter-of-factly but without malice, like he was reading from a script. "Good to see Milo was able to get you all signed on for this. He is good at negotiations." He paused, leaning back from the camera, swiveling back and forth in his chair for a moment. "Anyway, for this quest, I've planned something a little special. Think of it as a Nightmare expansion made just for you. And since it is a battle to stop the destruction of this world, it seemed fitting that you should face some of the biggest fears shared by humanity, the Four Horsemen of the Apocalypse to be exact. Each time you defeat one, the location of the next will become available.

"However, before I can set you loose on the world, there are some rules that we should cover. The reason that you were required to drink this stuff to start the mission was so the quest could mark you as participants and make some small changes to your character data." He leaned forward again. "Number one." He held up a finger. "You'll notice that you no longer have the glyph required to start a teleport spell. It has been disabled. You'll get it back upon completion."

Kira and Corvin swiped open their menus to confirm his claim as he continued.

"So, if you want to get anywhere, you'll have to physically travel there. No shortcuts.

"Rule number two - you can no longer accept transfers of any kind from anyone outside of your current party. So no asking Milo for infinite items. You must do this on your own with the resources that you have available or else it won't mean anything.

"Rule three is simple. Long distance communication is out. You can't use com-rings or send messages. If someone isn't in earshot, then they can't help you.

"Number four is important, so pay attention. At any given time, no more than four of your team may be logged out. If at any point more than four of you are offline, a failure will trigger, and the world will end. There is no way to stop this, so don't take any chances."

Puzzled looks met across the basin as Max considered the purpose of such a condition.

"And, last but not least, is rule number five which is more of an extension of rule four. Since your whole team can't log out together, it should go without saying that you can't all die at any point either; that would count as a disconnect since it forces a brief logout before putting you back in. So if your team wipes, the world will end."

He placed his hands on his desk, interlocking his fingers. "I apologize for not being able to be there myself to send you on your way, but I've never been that interested in role-playing. So, without further ado, here is the location of the first Horseman," a system chime sounded, indicating the addition of a waypoint to their maps. "But before you go, I want you to know that I do hope you win. In all honesty, nothing would make me happier. So be careful, and do the best you can." He reached forward to stop the recording but paused before hitting the button. "Oh, almost forgot. You will have thirty hours to complete the quest. Also, as soon as this video terminates, you will have five minutes to escape this dungeon before it collapses. Good luck." His finger tapped a button, and the basin went dark.

A timer appeared at the bottom of Max's stat-sleeve, blinking five-zero-zero before ticking down each second. A second timer faded into existence in the space the beneath that, showing the mission clock's thirty hours.

"Crap!" Max looked to Kira for ideas.

In battle, he'd always been a take-charge kind of guy with quick tactical thinking being his strength, but when he needed some outside the box thinking, she could usually come up with something. She might not have always had the most common sense, but when it came to complex thought with a dash of the absurd, she was his girl. It was part of why they complimented each other so well.

She took a moment to think as Ginger and Kegan glanced toward the stairs, numbers counting down on their wrists. Kira spoke as if responding to what they were thinking. "No, it took hours to get down here, we'll never make it up that way." She stood still for a moment looking up. "I think I might be able to fly out."

That was all Max needed to hear. "Okay, Farn, you're with Kira. Everyone else, log out."

"What?" Kegan blurted.

Kira nodded in line with his decision. "If you're not here when the place comes down, you won't be killed. I should be able to make my way up without getting hit by debris, and Farn should be able to take a few hits while flying if she uses her shield." She turned to Farn and stepped closer. "We'll need to stay close so I can keep your health up, and I might need to get under your shield if things get bad."

Farn nodded, though her eyes looked like they were screaming.

"What about the angels?" Max fluttered his hands together to mime a pair of wings.

Kira looked up again. "We'll wait until it all starts to come down. They'll have to deal with the collapse too. I'd rather dodge falling objects than dodge arrows that are specifically aimed at me."

"Okay, sounds good. We're out," agreed Max as he signaled to the rest to head out. They didn't seem confident, but they selected the sign-off option on their sleeves anyway.

Max knelt down to make sure he didn't cancel his logout request by moving around too much as the short wait-period passed. He couldn't help but notice how anxious both Farn and his sidekick looked as they stood like an awkward pair of teens thrown together at a junior high school dance. He figured he should say something encouraging. He turned toward the fairy. "Try not to screw this up."

Kira crossed her arms, unamused.

Then he turned to Farn, adding, "Try to make sure Kira doesn't screw this up."

Farn's mouth fell open, but no words came out.

"You done?" Kira glared at him on the ground.

He laughed at his own joke before raising his hands and lowering them as if he was melting. "Good luuuuuuuck …" he said, dragging out the words and letting them waver like a ghost as he attempted to time it with his log out. Then he held the pose, looking foolish.

"You timed it wrong." Kira's arms remained crossed.

Max dropped his hands and let out a single, "Damn," that echoed as the world faded out of existence around him.

CHAPTER ELEVEN

Farnsworth stared at the timer on her forearm, regret setting in as soon as Max was gone. She looked up at the dozens of enormous chandeliers hanging above her head. It was insane, the idea that she could somehow fly out of there. She glanced at Kira and wanted to shout at Max for volunteering her to protect the fairy. She had only known her for a day, and while it may have been fun, she wasn't ready to jump into a situation where they had to depend on each other to survive.

Even worse, Farn was angry at herself. She actually had a contract ability that could have shielded the entire party, but she hadn't spoken up fast enough. *Classic Farn*, she scolded herself as she touched her gauntlet against her chest plate and remembered the words to activate the contract. She yanked her hand away. It was too late. With only two party members logged in, the ability was out of the question. She just couldn't pay the cost to activate it.

Kira glanced up at her, making eye contact for the briefest of moments before looking back to the scene above. The fairy's body trembled, and she took a deep breath as if she was struggling to hold herself steady. It actually made Farn feel a little better, knowing that she wasn't alone. Kira was probably just as freaked out as she was.

At the thirty second mark, Kira set up a *Flight* spell with an added protection buff that felt warm and tingled as it activated around Farn's body in a spiral of sparkling silver dust.

The timer hit zero, and for a moment, all was silent. Then a low foreboding rumble came from above, reaching down into the back of Farn's mind, fanning the flames of doubt. She motioned to take off, but Kira reached out, her hand stopping a few inches before making contact with Farn's wrist as if telling her, not yet. The sound of stone crumbling above reached her ears as slits of moonlight found their way through the falling rubble that was once the ceiling. Iron chandeliers clanged and crashed against each other as they tore their support ropes from the walls and tumbled down the shaft, their echo reverberating as Farn stood below. She held her ground, looking up at the sight, more intimidating than any she had ever seen. Her heart raced as she fought the urge to launch. Timing was everything.

Finally, as the volume grew to a deafening level, Kira yelled, "now!" and shot up into the air.

Farn followed close behind, her shield glowing, hoping to plow through whatever might be in her way. She moved fast to meet the falling rubble, the familiar twinge of doubt reminding her of the insanity of the plan she'd agreed to. It vanished as she watched Kira weave around the first of the chandeliers that fell toward them as if it was nothing, its heavy chain whipping by as she passed.

Farn did the same but with far less grace, the chain glancing off her shield as she watched the sparkling fairy above slip through the branches of two more iron shapes like a thread through the eye of a needle. The angel statues screamed in horror as they fell victim to their crumbling home. Farn took a few large hits to her shield, her health dropping about half way from the spillover.

Kira responded by firing off a heal from her queue, making it obvious to Farn that the mage was hanging back to stay in

range. Farn gritted her teeth and sped up to force her way
through, not wanting to slow them down any more than she
had. The light from above grew brighter as they streaked
toward the surface until, suddenly, it was gone, blotted out by
the debris. They were so close.

The iron and stone simply became too dense. Through the
energy of her shield, Farnsworth saw the fairy juke from side to
side before freezing in the air, her last moments slipping away
before her death became inevitable. *It was over already*, Farn
thought, but that was when she heard something unexpected:
her own voice yelling.

Farn's body moved on its own, guided by the instinct developed over the course of three years of protecting others, telling
her mind to shut the hell up with all its stupid doubts and fears.
She wasn't shouting anything in particular, just a long roar of
ferocity. It snapped Kira out of her panic as well, and she
glanced back down at Farn speeding toward her. Then it all fell
into place.

Kira's wings blinked out of existence for a moment, and she
dropped to meet Farn halfway. Farn reached out and caught her
wrist, pulling her in. Kira let out a squeak as Farn let go for a
second only to wrap her free arm around the fairy's back to
keep her within the protection of her shield. She clenched her
fist to push the *Flight* spell's speed to full, still yelling at the falling
rubble as she rushed straight toward it. Kira shut her eyes tight
and ducked her head close to the safety of Farn's body, just as
they hit.

The sound of rock, metal, and shouting blurred together as
impact rocked the pair again and again. Their forms smashing
through layer after layer; Farn didn't have to look at her status
to know that she was close to death. Then light engulfed her as
Kira's wings reappeared with an eruption of shining dust that
brought Farn's health back up and held it steady as she forced
her way through. She just hoped the mage had enough mana to
keep it going.

The shack, through which they had entered the dungeon,

fell along with everything else, somehow still intact. At least it was until Farnsworth smashed through its doorway with the force of a cannonball, a fairy held close like a damsel in distress. Dark clouds billowed around them, forced up by the collapse of their surroundings. Farn had no way to tell if there were more obstacles in their path or even which way was up.

With her arm still clutching the mage, she felt Kira hold her breath as if clinging to the hope that it was over, that they were out. Farn did the same, finally letting her endless war cry die out. For a moment, it seemed like the world was gone, like it was just them, floating in a void of sand and dust. Then, just as Farn expected it to go on forever, the sky filled her view.

Kira let out a long, "Whoooooooo!" in celebration as Farn released the fairy from her grip, freeing her to fly in circles around her as they made their way back to the Nostromo hovering not far above.

Farn's legs gave out as soon as she landed on the deck. Kira toppled down next to her, laughing hard enough to shed tears. Farn couldn't help but laugh too at the absurdity of what she had just done.

Alastair rushed out onto the deck, his face somehow even whiter than it had been already. He held his com-ring in his hand rather than wearing it on his finger as if he had taken it off when the group chat had gone dead. He must have been panicking without a way to know what to make of the rest of the party's sudden logoffs.

Farn was pretty sure she saw his eye twitch. She ignored him for the moment. Instead, she sat up and leaned against Kira who was still far too consumed by endless guffaws to be able to stand up quite yet.

Finally, the pair settled down, the mad laughter dying into just a few chuckles as Farn voiced what they both were thinking. "How the hell did we survive that?"

CHAPTER TWELVE

After suffering through a rather long debriefing aboard the Nostromo, Farnsworth was forced to return to Valain. Since the dungeon that the others had been occupying when they had logged out no longer existed, the system defaulted to the last city they had entered as a new login point. This was a function she had already expected, as she had encountered it before while accessing a number of temporary dungeons that were available at certain times per year. Although, they didn't tend to self-destruct so spectacularly.

A look at the mission counter told her they had lost a little over a half an hour on the return to the city. There was still plenty of time. So, while the rest of the team took a short break in the real world, unsure of when they would get another chance, Kira had insisted that she and Farn run a few errands. Farn suspected that the fairy just didn't want to be cooped up in the ship with nothing to do. Considering that the inability to accept transfers from anyone outside the party would make it difficult for the team to get supplies during the night, it wasn't a bad idea.

The Nostromo took port at a private dock, belonging to a

major footwear manufacturer, atop one of the taller buildings in Valain in an attempt not to draw attention to the irregular airship. Farn followed Kira as she hopped off the retractable stairs.

An overly serious elven assistant stepped onto the dock behind her acting as their corporate chaperone. Farn could tell Kira wasn't a fan of the arrangement from the near constant eye rolls and scowling. She wasn't being subtle. There was something insulting about being assigned a babysitter after all.

Out of curiosity, the fairy removed her inspector from the back of her journal and looked at the elf through it. He hadn't introduced himself in game yet or passed on his contact information, so no one knew his character's name. Kira let out a sudden snort. "Really? Jeff with a three?" she asked as she read the name above the man's head.

Farn leaned down to see as well, curious about the what she meant by the question. Apparently, he had tried to use his real name but had spelled it with the number three in place of the letter E. It must have been picked by another user before him.

The elf looked annoyed. "Yes. Is that a problem?" responded Jeff-with-a-three, which was now what Farn remembered him as.

"Not for me, I guess." Kira shrugged and moved past it.

The dock was made of polished stone slabs held up by a series of buttresses, and being on one of the tallest buildings in Valain, it gave them an almost unobstructed view of the city surrounding them.

Farn watched as Kira rushed to the edge without warning and leaned a little too far over a railing to remark on the people walking below. She reached into her item bag and retrieved a small piece of iron ore meant for crafting. Then, holding the clump of metal out in her hand, she dropped it.

Jeff-with-a-three gasped at the action.

She then turned to the archway that concealed an elevator at the end of the dock and ran toward it. "Come on; we gotta see if it hit anyone." The cheerful notes of the fairy's laugh convinced Farn to follow, and Kira tapped the call button as soon as she reached the large stone doors.

Their chaperone expressed his reluctance by keeping his pace slow as to make them wait. This, of course, turned out to be a mistake when the fairy slipped through the elevator doors as they opened and hit the button to close as soon as Farn stepped in behind her.

Farn couldn't help but smirk as she watched Kira wave goodbye to the elf. His eyes narrowed the moment before the doors slid shut. It was probably for the best. Farn didn't think he wanted to be there any more than Kira wanted him to be. Not to mention that he made no motion to chase after them.

The elevator was round with a panel of polished silver floor buttons following the curve of the wall. Decorative stone carvings covered the chamber's floor and ceiling, and four matching pillars were distributed around its perimeter. In most cases, an elevator made of stone would be a terrible idea, what with weight limits being a thing. But since there were no cables holding it up to begin with, that didn't matter. Farn wondered for a second how it actually worked within the game's system, assuming that there was some kind of plate in the floor that removed gravity's hold on it.

Despite being modeled after the same medieval style as the rest of Valain, the elevator had some more modern elements in the form of wall graphics between the pillars that Checkpoint must have allowed to be customized. The panels featured crisp black and white images of avatars from the game with high-end footwear from the real world being the one thing in color. Kira leaned against a portrait on the back wall of an attractive reynard woman wearing a short pair of pants, her bright green sneakers laced up tight, with perspiration on her skin as if she'd been running.

The two stood in silence, Farn feeling a little self-conscious, being alone together without the threat of being crushed to distract her. The lift came to a stop part way down, where a group of the building's employees boarded. Dressed in the closest things to business wear available, the sharp-looking group crowded in around them, forcing Farn to pull her sword in close to make room. They received more than a few odd looks, as if it was obvious to everyone but them that they were not supposed to be there.

Pressed up against the wall, Farn, who was rather tall, couldn't help but notice the fact that Kira's short stature caused the group to dwarf her completely. It made her look small and a bit weak. Both of which were true.

The fairy let out an annoyed huff as the middle of people's backs became the one view available, giving off an unintentional vibe of vulnerability that made Farn want to stay by her side and keep her safe. It also taught her a lesson in what made Kira so appealing. She was easily the most adorable player Farn had met. The thought caused a strange disconnect between the character that stood beside her and the person she knew played her. It was as if the fairy's current form had overwritten her real one in Farn's brain, making it hard for her to see the small woman as anything else.

After a few floors, the group of formal men and women exited, leaving them alone. Kira blew out a sigh of relief and stretched into the space again. A few floors later, they reached the lobby. Outside, Farn walked past a mid-level *Shield* player in full, shining armor complaining while waving around a familiar piece of ore. "I'm telling you, it fell straight out of the sky!" The man rubbed at his head.

Kira marked the victory with a quiet, "Yes."

Farn assumed she had to take what she could get. Part of her was tempted to check the man's health to see how much damage had been done.

They passed through a business district, meaning that there wasn't much in the way of item stores, just large buildings full of boring offices. The towers were well designed, but they were still boring all the same. At least it gave them something to look at as they made their way through the street. Kira didn't seem to notice, as she was staring at her map.

It was obvious to Farn that she was trying to figure out where they were going without letting on that she was lost. Instead of speaking up to help, though, Farn just followed in awkward silence. Silence that went on for far too long. She searched her brain for a subject to start a conversation with. Most couldn't tell by looking at her, but making friends was not something that she was adept at. No, Farnsworth was more the type to spend her nights and weekends making a complicated meal for one and binge-watching media content before going to bed, spooning a Japanese body pillow.

It wasn't that she was antisocial. Far from it. She did want people in her life, quite badly if she was honest, but after losing all of her friends back in high school, she had been left with a fear of others that she had trouble overcoming. So she hid in the corner at office parties and went to the movies alone. In fact, Noctem was the only place that she ever socialized, but that was because her capability as a *Shield* made it easy to find party invites. Although, even under the protection of anonymity that the game provided, she still hadn't forged any close relationships. Her friends' list was long, but really, it was more of an acquaintance list, her only real interactions being based entirely on gameplay. In the end, she had given up on having any form of social life.

Then, last night, Alastair, the head of Checkpoint Systems, messaged her, threw her into a party of people that had played together for years, and tasked her with saving the world. It was intimidating, to say the least. She would have declined the invitation as soon as she got it, but she felt uncomfortable turning him down since he was her boss. Not to mention she did still kind of owe him.

She had hidden her concerns as best she could as she waited in the tavern for her new companions to arrive the night before. She had been sure that her presence being forced into the team would've been met with hostility, and being struck in the face by a turkey leg was not the best foot to start off on. Then something odd happened. After a couple of teleports, she seemed to have been welcomed into their group. No one even batted an eye. Max and Kira even seemed nice. Before she realized it, she was having fun. They were trusting her with their lives and encouraging her to do things that she would never have attempted a night earlier. In fact, if it hadn't been for Kira, she never would have escaped the dungeon collapse a half hour before. She wouldn't have even considered the strategy. She would have just frozen up and gotten crushed.

Without meaning to, Farn quickened her stride, bringing her next to the cheerful fairy that had finally seemed to have figured out where they were. *It's now or never*, she thought and let a single word slip out, "Thanks."

"No problem," Kira responded without looking up from her map. Then she slowed to a stop and looked up. "For what?"

"The dungeon earlier. I know I wouldn't have made it without you. So, thanks."

"Oh, sure. We're a team. Besides, I wouldn't have made it without you either, so that makes us even." Kira flashed a smile of genuine appreciation.

"I guess that's true," Farn smiled too but kept her face down, "but really, that was crazy. I mean, is that sort of thing normal for you guys?"

"Kinda." Kira turned to walk backward with her hands behind her. "I guess it depends on the situation."

Farn laughed at the nonchalance of her answer. "So you're all just ridiculous badasses then?"

Kira let out another one of her unintentional pretty laughs. "Yup!" She spun around to walk forward again. "Don't worry. You're well on your way to epic badassery. Just stick with us."

Farn nodded, attempting not to get her hopes up for the potential friendship.

"So how did you end up working at Checkpoint?" Kira slowed her pace to stay next to her.

Farn let out a long, "Ummmm," while she considered her answer. "I don't really do much there. Mostly I just format internal reports so they look nice."

"Still, it must be a hard company to land a job at," Kira said.

"I sort of, just got lucky," Farn rested her hand on the hilt of her sword. "I moved out on my own kinda young and waited tables for a few years, but that got old quick as you would expect. So I took out a ton of loans and got an art degree. Then I waited tables for a couple more years."

"Ha, yeah. They didn't tell us in school that there aren't many opportunities for people in creative fields these days."

"Us, you say?" Farn stared down at the fairy. "Are you also the proud owner of an art degree?"

"Caught me." Kira held up her hands as if admitting guilt. "I went for illustration."

Farn raised an eyebrow. "How did that work out?"

"It did not. I work at a service center of a car dealership. I write up paperwork all day. It is the worst," she said in a flat monotone.

"Sorry to hear. What kind of stuff did you draw?"

"Oh, pretty much anything: comics, portraits, animals. I've been drawing since I was a kid. Although I don't really have time now with work. Plus, I got lazy, so I'm kinda rusty."

"I know what you mean." Farn nodded. "I used to paint, but I'm way out of practice at this point. I wish I could get back into it."

Kira frowned. "You should. I always tell myself I will. Granted, I never do." Her shoulders sunk a little before picking back up. "How's working for Alastair?"

"Good, I guess. But I'm just a low-level employee, so I don't really have any contact with him. Although, if it wasn't for him, I'd still be putting up with people complaining about their undercooked or overcooked steak."

Kira looked puzzled. "You knew Coldblood before working for him?"

"Sort of, not really." Farn tucked her thumbs into the sash at her waist. "He plays Noctem a lot in his spare time, and I happened to party with him as a rando. He tried to make conversation while we waited for a *Breath* mage to join. Found out what I went to school for and that I wasn't thrilled with what I was doing. Next day, I got a message from him with a link to a job posting suggesting that I apply."

"Hmm," Kira pondered. "So he really does cares about the players? I kinda thought that might be an act."

"He must. He's trusting us with this quest." Farn raised both hands, palms up like she was lifting the weight of the responsibility that had been thrust upon her. "Anyways, I wasn't going to apply to the job, but after closing that night, a drunk driver drove their car through the steakhouse I worked at, and we were forced to shut down. So I figured why not send in a resume."

"I guess that worked out."

"Not for the drunk driver. She died," Farn said letting her hands fall back to her sides as she remembered the aftermath of the tragedy. "It was actually really sad. It was some girl on the way home from a college party."

"That sucks," Kira concluded, her tone sounding somber.

They walked in silence for a minute before Farn came up with a new, less depressing subject. "Oh, okay, so people talk at work, and sometimes, I overhear things."

"Yeah?" Kira's head tilted to the side as she looked up at Farn with an inquisitive eyebrow pump.

"Did you know that Max's class used to be called something else?"

"It wasn't always *Fury*?"

"Nope. It was originally called an *Ash*, but they changed it right before they released the class info to the public before launch. Some of the creative team noticed that it sounded too much like the word 'ass' when said in conversation."

"Ha! Nice," Kira snorted.

"I know, you'd be surprised how much that stuff happens. Anyway, they needed a name and didn't have time to go through a long process. So according to a guy in the sound department, the creatives pretty much phoned it in by stealing a word off a movie poster hanging on the wall of their break room. It was for one of those over the top car films."

Kira slapped a hand against her thigh. "Oh god, that is such an appropriate source for Max's class title. He dragged me to every single one of those movies."

"It gets better though." Farn held up a finger. "As a joke, one of the developers added a mural related to it somewhere in Valain. Supposedly, there's a Dodge Challenger behind it."

"Really? Anybody find it?" asked Kira, looking tempted to abandon their shopping trip and run off in search of the thing.

"Nope. But it's just a rumor, so it might not be real," Farn answered, letting her excitement fade.

"I guess we have no choice then," Kira said cryptically.

"About what?"

"About the fact that, when this is over, you and I are going to have to scour this entire city to find that car. Just imagine the look on Max's face when we pull up in a fantasy world driving the car from Vanishing Point. He would literally die right there," Kira said, bouncing on her toes.

Farn cracked a stupid grin at the idea, accepting the obligation. "I understand. We must do what we must."

Farn continued bonding with the fairy all the way to the merchant square where they entered a series of shops, leaving with a new stock of health and mana vials to keep the team alive through the ordeal to come. They finished their shopping excursion in a tiny store down a dark alley that was easy to miss, a small sign hanging by its door read 'Arcane Imports'. It was the sort of place that didn't see many customers. This was largely because the items it sold were expensive, powerful, but expensive all the same. But now was not the time to be pinching credits, and besides, Farn figured that they could get reimbursed by Alastair when things were over and done with anyway. It was time to splurge.

The two spent their remaining credits on a variety of things. Special bullets for Max, a new dagger for Ginger, and a *Shrapnel* rune for Corvin cleaned out Kira's wallet faster than Farn would have expected. She let out a sigh as she looked at what remained written in her journal's account page.

Farn found a number of rare items, but not much stood out as she wandered around the shop, stopping at a display case of rings which were always useful. She peered through her inspector to read the stats and descriptions hovering above each item. There was one with a regeneration effect that she considered and another with a hefty dexterity increase that she thought might work well for Max. Then her mouth dropped open, her eyes locked on the lines of text hanging over a small dusty box. She couldn't believe what she read.

"Excuse me?" she leaned onto the counter, looking for an NPC to handle the transaction. She flinched when a step-stool shoved itself against the case from the other side. At first, she thought that it had moved on its own, but a second later, a small jerobin in a black waistcoat and tie hopped up the steps until he was almost eye level with her. She stifled a laugh at the sight, since she'd never seen a member of the jerobin race dressed so formally. The NPC looked like a small kangaroo with gray fur and a mousy face. A pair of long ears topped his head with a puff of white hair between them. Despite its strangeness, Farn had to admit that the little guy's clothes fit him well, like they had been tailored just for him. The cuffs of his sleeves were gently frayed as if he'd been wearing the shirt for years.

The jerobin leveled his black eyes on her. "Yes, how might I help you?" His voice came out sounding older than she expected for a creature so small.

For a moment, Farn almost forgot what item she'd wanted to ask about, too distracted by the unique NPC. After an awkward pause, she pointed to the box in the case. "May I see this set here?"

The small creature hopped down from the step-stool and opened the case, fishing around a little before removing the small, black enamel box that Farn had chosen. It had no markings on it whatsoever.

Kira eyed Farn suspiciously. Then her eyes fell to the box as the small clerk set it down on the counter, a thick layer of dust coating its surface as if no one had touched it in decades. Of course, that was impossible since the game had only been out for three years and the box was not real to begin with, but despite that, the NPC treated the container with the utmost respect, wiping away the dust with a cloth to bring back its reflective surface.

"Now, this is an interesting item," the jerobin exclaimed, keeping his words vague so that they could be applied to any of the shop's wonders. Despite all appearances, he was just a point-of-sale system, no matter how interesting his design was. There were some NPCs in the world that had more complex programming to allow for more complex interactions, but most were just there to serve a purpose. He allowed Farn to do the honors of opening the lid, which she did with respect, mirroring the shopkeeper without meaning to. Inside was a set of two rings, resting in a black felt pad. Both were silver. One was large with a thick band bearing two shields protecting a round onyx stone between them. The other was small, a design of delicate filigree flowing across its surface and swirling around a smaller onyx that matched its mate.

Farn paused, letting Kira wonder a little longer. Only when she looked like she might burst with curiosity did Farn speak up, "Someone sold a contract item."

"Seriously?" Kira scrunched her nose.

"I know. I thought contract items were bound to the player that received it."

Kira shook her head. "No, I got one once that was transferable. But I would never sell it. Not after everything I did to get it." She frowned and stared at the black box. "That just seems wrong. Like selling a part of yourself."

"True." Farn gripped the handle of her sword, wondering what someone would have to offer for her to sell it, provided it hadn't already been bound to her. She shook off the thought and looked back to the description text on her glass. "Maybe we should give these a new home. They're a little weird, but given

your low health, they may be a good thing to have as a backup."
Farn pushed the box over for her to see.

"Oooooh, pretty." Kira lifted up on her toes to look closer at
the set on the high counter. "What they do?" she asked, not
bothering to check for herself.

Farn hesitated a moment before reading the long string of
information.

Contract name: *Rings of the Willing*
Type: accessory
Equip slot: left ring finger
Ownership: unbound
Usage: one-time only
Basic enchantment: plus six luck, not stackable
Item given to form contract: intelligence ring, quantity, 1
Advanced enchantment: ability, *The Willing*
Ability description: once equipped, if shared between two play-
ers, the wearer of the small ring will survive one fatal blow. In
exchange, the wearer of the large ring will die after five minutes
time, during which they will be given increased strength,
defense, and dexterity.

"Damn," Kira commented in a flat tone, making it hard for
Farn to gauge her reaction. "That's risky."

"But possibly helpful," Farn added. "Granted, it could backfire spectacularly if handled wrong, but we're pretty much dead
without you. So it could save the team in a pinch. Plus, the additional stats for five minutes is pretty strong on its own, not to
mention the plus six luck. I mean, everyone could use more
luck." Farn explained her thinking.

"So, who's the lucky one that gets to be my hero?" Kira
asked.

"Well, it's my idea, so …" Farn trailed off, holding up a
hand like she was volunteering.

"That's a tough choice." Kira tapped a finger on her chin

before dropping her hand back to the counter. "It's up to you I guess." She sounded a little hesitant.

Farn ignored the voice in her head that warned her that she was coming on too strong and, instead, listened to the one that told her to buy the fairy a friendship ring. She asked the shopkeeper to complete the transaction without thinking on it further and claimed the shield ring as her own. "Anything to give us an edge, right?" she said, not expecting an answer as she offered the small ring to Kira.

The fairy stood looking at the item but not taking it, a wry smile sneaking across her face. Kira cleared her throat and tilted her head to the floor. "I'm not that easy; you're gonna have to do this right."

Farn froze for a few seconds as she realized what Kira was hinting at but recovered by feigning annoyance. She glanced around to make sure that no one was in the shop with them before reluctantly dropping to one knee. She sighed her heaviest sigh, holding up the ring for Kira to take.

Kira continued to ignore the offer. "Well?" She waved her hand in a circular motion as if time was a factor, which it technically was.

"Would you wear the stupid ring, please," Farn spouted, resisting Kira's influence but also getting a strange feeling of acceptance as she realized that the fairy was antagonizing her the way she did the others.

"You're gonna have to do better than—" Kira started to say before being cut off.

Farn raised her other hand up in front of Kira's face to signify that it was time for her to stop talking. Emboldened by the fact that she had been included in the fairy's games, Farn lowered her hand. Then she raised her head to look straight into Kira's eyes, resisting her instinct to look away from the shining pools of blue. She spoke, "My dearest Kirabell, may you accept this token of our meeting in hopes that our new friendship be filled with joy and laughter and not the collapse of the world that we met in?" Farn held a look of smoldering intensity in her eyes that may have been more charming than she realized.

It delivered a decisive blow that showed on Kira's face, forcing her to look away. She reached out to take the ring to put an end to the scene that she had started, but Farn caught her hand. Kira's face snapped back, a look of panic in her eyes as the joke backfired.

Farn swallowed but followed with an honest smile that she hoped would hide the fact that her cheeks were beginning to turn a rosier shade of brown. She slipped the ring onto the mage's finger, and the silver band resized itself in an instant to fit. She continued to hold Kira's hand to make her squirm in place until finally, she released her. Farn then rose back to her full height, a foot taller than the fairy, a proud grin on her face.

"Okay then." Kira cleared her throat, lowering her hand and holding it with the other, running her finger over the ring "Now that the shopping is handled. We should get going. Max will be back online soon." She turned to the door and walked out of the store without looking back.

Farn made sure to snicker as loudly as she could before Kira disappeared through the door. Her smile reached from ear to ear as she laughed to herself alone in the shop. At least the mission ahead might be fun. She turned to the store clerk, who she had forgotten was even in the room. He looked like he wanted to say something, although she knew that it was just her imagination. She eyed him for a moment. "Don't judge me."

Farn and Kira arrived at the large cathedral that housed the city's spawn crystal just as Max and the others were getting logged back in.

"We took care of the shopping while you guys were sitting on your asses," Kira said with her arms folded.

"You all rested up and ready to do this?" Farn added as she threw a box of *homing rounds* that she'd purchased to Max.

"We're good to go," he replied with his usual attitude, catching the item, "and there was no sitting on our asses."

"Yeah, mostly Max just ate some Doritos," Kegan chimed in, pointing a thumb in his direction.

Kira laughed. "That sounds about right. Back when we used mics to talk, he used to crunch nacho cheese flavor in my ear nonstop whenever we played anything."

"Shut up. I don't do that anymore," Max responded.

Kira didn't relent. "At least you're not yelling to your mom to bring you snacks anymore."

"Oh, come on, that was one time." Max held up a finger.

"HEY, MA! Maaaaaa! Get me some bagel bites!"

Max's face grew serious, and he pointed straight at the small mage. "Hey! When pizza's on a bagel, you can have pizza anytime!" he shouted back, drawing confused looks from a few nearby adventurers.

Kira laughed and changed the subject, "Look what Farn bought me." She shoved her hand in his face like a character in a romantic comedy showing off an engagement ring to people who didn't care. Apparently, she had gotten over the embarrassment of how she had received the item.

"That's very nice." He glanced at Farn, who held up her hand to show the ring's mate, making a point of being less obnoxious about it than Kira. "So I'm gone for all of an hour and you two become BFFs?" Max added.

"Yup, you've been replaced." Kira danced around him before settling into her place at Farn's side.

Joining in, Farnsworth gave him a smug look. "Sorry, if you liked it, you shoulda put a ring on it."

Max looked at the two with one eyebrow raised. "I'm sure you two will be very happy together. Now, let's go. We still have a world to save."

Farn smiled, feeling lighter than she had in a long time. Then she fell in line behind him as he headed back toward the airship dock. She looked back for Kira, finding her place empty. Kira was lagging behind to buy some last-minute snacks for the trip. Farn snickered to herself. "I guess that makes sense."

CHAPTER THIRTEEN

Kirabell tapped her foot on the floor of the Nostromo's bridge. The flight to their next destination had consumed a full thirty-five minutes of the mission clock. She just wanted to get on with things already, realizing how spoiled she'd become since getting access to her fast-travel teleports. Part of her wanted to take over for the helms-woman and fly the ship herself, not that she knew how to fly it anyway. But still.

The ship approached the waypoint. It didn't tell them an exact location, but they found it easily enough, nestled into the lifeless dark stone of the Teln mountain range. This time, Carver had at least placed an airship dock by the dungeon's gates which were set into the side of a massive wall of jagged rock. A smoky river of molten lava flowed below.

Max leaned against the window as the helms-woman pulled the ship up to the dock. "At least we don't have to climb down that ladder again."

Kira swallowed and let out a quiet, "Yikes," at the view, regretting her thoughts about wanting to land sooner.

Alastair stood from his chair and walked the team down to the platform, a worried expression on his face after the close call of the previous dungeon's collapse. "We'll be right here waiting for you, so make sure to come back."

Max nodded, then turned to the open archway embedded into the rock face beyond. Thin clouds of smoke carried embers up from below as they walked. "Let's go see what Horseman we have first. Anyone want to place bets?"

Kegan's face lit up. "I'll take you up on that," he said as they all passed through the entrance, a chill running down Kira's spine despite the warmth of the air.

Corvin pulled out a small piece of yellow candy from a pocket in his robes and tossed it to Kira. "I made plenty, so let me know if you need more."

"Thanks, man." It was nice having him around. He was always well prepared. She cast a number of support spells on the group in preparation for whatever lay ahead, not wanting to be caught off guard by more creepy angel statues. Or worse. Corvin added on a couple spells of his own while Kira pulled the twisted ends of the foil candy wrapper she had been given, the familiar crinkling sound taking her back to childhood. A memory of grandma candy danced through her mind.

The bright yellow lemon drop inside would have the effect of regenerating three points of mana every two seconds as long as it remained in her mouth. It also had a light citrus flavor that she liked, or at least it should have. Instead, she didn't know how to describe it. It was like someone had somehow combined the worst possible flavors known to man, like rancid garbage and dirt swimming in warm Moxie cola. No sooner had she popped it in her mouth than she spat it back out to the floor with a surprised, "Ack!" She sputtered, wiping her tongue on the shoulder of her dress. "You might wanna check your crafting recipe next time; that was awful," she said to Corvin, her tongue still hanging out.

His brow furrowed as he looked at the candy. Then he tossed one into his own mouth. His face contorted immediately, though he held it without spitting it out.

Kira cringed as his knuckles turned white with effort. Then

she felt a little dumb when she realized why he hadn't gotten rid of it like she had. He was forcing himself to hold the evil thing in his mouth long enough to confirm what she now feared. She glanced at her wrist to check his mana. It didn't increase. Not one point.

He took the lemon drop out of his mouth with his fingers and held it under his nose, sniffing. He licked it and winced.

"Dude, stop tasting it." Kira looked away, unable to watch him. "You're gonna make me sympathy hurl."

He tossed the candy to the floor and spat as discreetly as possible to remove the lingering taste in his mouth. "So food items have no effect. I'm guessing the rest of our items are duds, too."

Kira pulled a silver vial containing a mana tonic from her item bag and poured the sparkling blue liquid into her mouth. Panic flooded through her as she realized her mistake.

Max burst out laughing.

She responded by performing an exaggerated spit take in his direction, a fine mist covering his hand and arms as he shielded his face.

"It tastes like garbage water!" She spat the remaining residue from her mouth. She still had a slight mana regeneration effect attached to an anklet that she wore, but the inability to get a quick boost from her consumable items was going to be a problem. She would have to be conservative.

Farn rubbed at her chin. "So it's looking like we're up against Famine."

Ginger erupted with a loud, "Yes! That was my guess. Everybody pay up."

"Damn it!" Max spouted as he begrudgingly settled the bet.

Kira laughed at his misfortune, feeling he deserved it for laughing at her a moment before. Plus, she had lost nothing, since she had been too poor to participate in the bet after spending all her credits shopping.

Max glared at her in response. Afterward, they continued on their way.

The hallway seemed to go on forever. The walls were smooth, bare stone as far as the eye could see. It was bleak, empty and void of any kind of detail. In short, it was boring. The only thing of interest was the fact that it seemed to bend to one side as if she was walking in one massive circle. Around what, Kira didn't know. Either way, it didn't take long to hit a dead end, a door blocking the hall, a circle carved into its surface like an open mouth.

Max shrugged and knocked like he had earlier at the entrance to the last dungeon.

There was no answer.

"Pretty sure no one lives here." Ginger leaned against the wall.

Max gave her a stupid grin. "But how will we know that if we don't knock?"

Corvin cleared his throat, looking at the barrier through his inspector. "Umm, it has a health bar."

At that, Kira leapt away from the door and sprinted to the back of the group to hide behind him. The others all stared at her as she peeked out from his side. "What? It might be an enemy."

"I don't think so." He held the inspector lower so she could see through it as well.

The door did indeed have a health bar hovering over its carved circle, but it wasn't full. Instead, it was empty, blinking as if the gateway was in danger of dying. Kira stepped out from behind her teammate and swiped open her spell-craft menu to cast a mid-level heal on the door. She hadn't really thought about what she was doing, just that the bar was low, and that every instinct she had told her to fill it back up. She looked back over her shoulder at Corvin who was still watching through the window of glass in his hand.

"It went up but not much. Maybe a percent or two."

Kira turned back to the door with a frown and cast another heal, this time, opting for her strongest.

Corvin's furry ears drooped like a dog being left home alone. "That only got it to five percent."

Kira dropped her arms limply by her sides. "Okay, this is gonna take a while."

A few minutes of casting later, the door's bar reached its limit, and it slid open to reveal another hallway complete with another door further down.

As soon as they reached the next gate, Max stepped to the side and gestured for Kira to get to work.

She grimaced as she opened her menu. "I hate this place already." She set up another heal but stopped before activating it. Kira let a grin creep across her face and cleared her selection column. She turned and looked around the empty hall, then spun a glyph into place that she almost never used. It would at least be fun to see Max's reaction.

Max's eyes widened as soon as he saw what she'd picked. "Wait, don't—"

She swiped down before he could get another word out. The spell flooded the hallway with power and the door opened instantly. At the same time, Max drew his pistols and aimed them in both directions down the empty hall. His eyes narrowed with an intensity that looked ready for anything. He stood in silence like that for several long seconds.

Finally, Kegan spoke up, "Hey, ah, Max?"

"Yeah." He didn't take his eyes off the hall.

"What are we looking at?"

He didn't answer for a long beat. Then finally, Max relaxed and shoved his pistols back into his holsters. "What the hell, Kira? I thought we agreed that you wouldn't use that contract."

She waved a hand at him dismissively. "It's fine. There are no enemies here. And if there were, we have a solid bottleneck to work with."

Max rolled his eyes. "I know but still."

Farn's eyes shifted between him and Kira. "I'm sorry, what's the problem here?"

He raised his arm to show her his stat-sleeve. "See for yourself."

She looked closer, then snapped her eyes to her own party read out where a dozen tiny icons now appeared surrounding her own name. "Holy crap, I've never seen so many active buffs."

Kira's chest swelled with pride. "I know. It's every buff in the game plus a full heal and regeneration effect that lasts for five minutes."

Max scoffed. "Yeah, and why don't we use it?"

She let her shoulders fall a little. "Because it aggros every monster in range."

Max held out his hand as if he didn't need to say more.

"Got the door open fast though," Kira grumbled under her breath, making sure it was loud enough for him to hear.

Max dropped his hand to rest on one of his guns and shook his head before cracking a smile. "True."

"Knew you'd see it my way." Kira nudged him in the ribs with her elbow and marched forward, looking back to give him her most annoying smile. She didn't get far before running into another door. She could almost sense an aura of smugness as he approached behind her.

"Too bad you're out of mana. Now we have to wait for it to refill." He folded his arms and grinned.

Kira let out a groan and plopped herself down in front of the door to let her mana regenerate faster by holding still. She sunk her cheek into one hand. "I still hate this place."

CHAPTER FOURTEEN

After walking and opening doors for longer than Max would have liked, he came across a large opening on the inner wall of the hallway. "Finally, I was starting to feel like this dungeon was designed just to waste time."

The others followed him through the gateway and into a massive chamber. Actually, massive was an understatement. It was more like someone had hollowed out the entire mountain.

Max looked around the space. "At least, now we know what we've been circling."

The hallway outside must have wrapped around the chamber's edge. Other than its size, though, it was quite plain. The only thing worthy of note was a giant bell hanging from the center of the ceiling. From a distance, he couldn't really make out any details, just that it was a large cylinder the size of a five-story building with a dome at the top connected to a ring and anchored to the ceiling with several thick chains.

I hope that isn't a dinner bell.

He turned back for a moment to make sure everyone was inside the chamber just as Corvin, the last of their group, passed through the entryway. The moment he did, a slab of solid rock slid down from a pocket above the door to seal them inside. It hit the floor with a loud bang that sent the *Venom* mage leaping. Max drew his guns just in case, then stood in the stillness of the room for what felt like an eternity.

Kira interrupted the silence with an uncomfortable whine that drew Max's attention behind him, where he found her fidgeting, repeatedly lifting up one foot after the other like she was standing on a hot beach. He raised an eyebrow at her in question, then he knelt down and touched the floor. It was hot. "That's not a good sign."

"Kind of smells like sulfur, too," Kegan added.

Ginger took a step away from him. "Really? I thought that was you."

Kira and Farn laughed as Kegan glowered at them both.

Max shook his head before moving things along, "Hey, Famine, we're here to wreck you!" he shouted into the chamber. His voice echoed off into the distance and faded away. Silence answered back. "Maybe we have to ring that bell."

As if in answer to his suggestion, a long foreboding creak groaned through the air, like the sound of metal tearing under a tremendous strain. Suddenly, the chains that held the bell tore from the ceiling, sending the huge object crashing to the floor. The deafening volume of its fall ripped through the cavern as the object landed, vibrations pulsing through the floor so strong that Max could feel them in his teeth. Rocks clanged against the bell's surface as they fell all around it, pulled free from the ceiling above. Shafts of moonlight shined down through cracks above as it rocked back and forth, almost falling over before settling into a stable position. The din subsided, and Max looked around the party, each still hunched and cringing from the noise. He turned back to the bell, something inside him telling him that more was coming. Silence set in again.

Then it started.

Max spun around just in time to see the floor beneath Corvin and Farn crumble away, surprise and terror filling their faces as they dropped through. He shot Kira an urgent glance, unable to form the words fast enough. It was enough. She nodded and dove after them with the precision of a competitive diver. He hoped she might be able to save at least one. Then the holes grew wider. It wasn't over. The ground continued to collapse everywhere, starting at the edges of the room and moving inward, forcing Max and the remaining party members to run toward the bell like their lives depended on it.

He sprinted away from the crumbling edge as it gained on them with unyielding momentum. He looked back at Ginger as she trailed behind due to a late start. The floor beneath her feet fell away as she jumped with everything she had. She landed, solid ground meeting her feet only to fall away once more. She jumped again and again as the ground beneath her lost its form with each leap. Max slowed hoping that he could do something to help, but his options were slim as the rumbling sound of pure terror bit at their heels. Then Ginger's luck ran out.

She pushed against the loose debris, but her foot passed through it, making it impossible to get enough momentum to bridge the ever-increasing gap.

As if part of some cruel joke, the collapsing floor stopped, leaving Max safe as he watched her disappear through the ground a few feet behind him. He threw out his hand, but she was already gone. He leaped toward the edge anyways hoping that maybe the fall wasn't that far, that maybe she might survive it. His heart sank as soon as he looked down, molten rock and fire filling his view. Then he heard a small pop.

"Oh, crap." Max blurted out as a grappling line flew straight at his head causing him to dodge on instinct and roll to one side. He let out a short, "Nice," and pumped his fist as he watched the line soar into the air, knowing full well that Ginger was on the other end. The hook flew straight up, and then it stopped. "Oh, crap," he said again, realizing that she must have fired it blind while falling as a last-ditch effort not to die. She hadn't actually aimed at anything. "Oh, crap," he said yet again as the line began to fall back down without hooking on anything. Then he reached out and grabbed it.

Max knew it was a dumb thing to do. He knew the weight of the falling *Coin* at the other end was far more than he could hold. But the stupid part of his brain, the one that had seen too many movies, had told the other parts of his brain, the ones in charge of reason and math, to kindly sit down and mind their own business.

The line cut into his hand as pain surged up his arm, challenging the game's system to dull it back down to a manageable level. It whipped him forward, almost yanking him over the edge and forcing him to let the line slip through his hand to slow it rather than stop it all at once. Thinking he might as well go all in, he grabbed it with his other hand, noting his health dropping on the status readout displayed on his wrist. After a few uncomfortable seconds, it stopped, the line holding steady in his hands as they glowed bright red with damage. He took one breath and shouted over the edge. "You might want to climb back up now!"

Max glanced back to Kegan, finding him standing at the ready with his bow drawn. He didn't blame the *Leaf* for leaving him and Ginger behind. It made more sense to have someone to watch their backs. After all, there was probably a Nightmare lurking around the chamber waiting to ambush them. If he was honest, he felt a little better knowing that Kegan was ready to fight. Well, at least, he did before the floor in the center of the room collapsed all at once, leaving nothing left of the ground but a stone ring a few dozen feet wide floating in the massive space, Kegan standing on the edge.

He fired an arrow by accident, sending it off at an odd angle. If he had been a few inches back, he would have plummeted to a fiery death. Even as it was, the collapse left him flailing his arms like a cartoon as he struggled to regain his balance, looking like he might fall anyway. A string of expletives erupted from the elf, and Max assumed the guy would be fine.

Finally, Ginger appeared, her arm reaching up over the edge. Max grabbed it, helping her to her feet as they both regained their bearings.

"That sucked," the *Coin* said, half shouting.

"Tell me about it!" Kegan shouted back from where he stood on the other side of the stone ring.

Max raised his arm to check his party status, hoping to find Kira and the others alive and well, but before he could look, a realization hit him like a truck. If the center of the room had collapsed, then why was the bell still there, floating in mid-air. He could practically feel the color drain from his face as the massive object began to rotate, a glowing circle on its surface like an eye.

"IT'S THE BELL!" he yelled to Kegan who was standing with his back to it.

The *Leaf* reached for an arrow as a beam of golden light erupted from the Nightmare that had been hidden in plain sight. It swept across the ground where he stood, a trail of explosions in its wake. Then, he was gone. Just gone. It happened so fast.

Max froze, still holding up his arm to check on the others. His eye dropped to his stat-sleeve. Kegan was dead, and worse, he wasn't the only one.

The glowing circle on Famine's surface turned as if searching to find more targets.

Ginger looked to Max for what to do next.

He swallowed, then gave the only order he could, "Run!"

CHAPTER FIFTEEN

The floor crumbled as Kirabell hurled herself downward, parting ways with Max as he ran with the others toward the bell. She flew as fast as her wings could take her, the trail of sparkles behind her flaring as if ignited by the heat below. She was like a comet streaking toward her two friends who were helpless in free fall. She just hoped that Max and the others could keep their feet on the ground. She had to focus on the two that were already in danger. The others would have to wait.

Of course, her first thought was to somehow cast *Flight* on both Corvin and Farn, but the spell took too long to activate, and she only had seconds. She would have to grab someone with the hope of slowing them long enough for her dust to take effect. At best, she could save one. The thought of it bit into her as soon as it entered her mind. She had to let one of them die.

Kira had dived through the same hole that Corvin had fallen, which set her closer to him. Her eyes, though, shifted between him and Farn. She shoved her feelings to the back of her mind, sweeping them into a closet and shutting it tight like a lazy child cleaning their room. She had to think about them as a team, not friends. Her mind raced through the variables of the situation as she weighed her options. What would the boss be like? What would they need? The room lacked one thing, cover. And lack of items meant they needed to conserve their health and resources. The result, they needed protection. In the end, there was only one choice.

She looked down at Corvin, his one good eye locking with hers. The closet door in her mind rattled, threatening to burst open. She clutched at her chest, shoving an imaginary chair up against the door to hold it in place. She hated it. Kira wasn't one of those *Breath* mages that withheld healing out of spite. No, she loved healing, and she was good at it. Letting him die went against everything she was. Not to mention that he was her friend, and he deserved better. Even if none of it was real.

It didn't matter, she told herself. She had to make a decision. If she didn't, she might lose them both, and then where would she be? Nowhere, that's where. Flares of pixie dust flowed out of her. She wasn't even doing it on purpose. She felt like she was going to explode. Then Corvin smiled.

Kira's eyes welled up, and she fought to hold back anything more. Corvin was smart, so of course, he had worked out the choice that had been thrust upon her. He must have known what she had to do just as well as she did. He nodded, giving her another smile and making the decision for her by folding his arms around himself. It hurt, but she nodded back anyways, forcing a cheerful smile as his robes ignited.

Kira's throat felt raw as her friend's name vanished from her skin. Then, without wasting any more time, she darted toward Farn who was almost out of time, falling face first.

The *Shield* held still, as if trying to make herself easier to catch. Either that or she had made peace with her fate. Kira wasn't sure which. Although, she seemed surprised when Kira caught a strap near the back of her armor. Not that Kira could see much with her eyes shut tight as she struggled to slow them down, hoping to save at least one of her friends. She didn't have anywhere near the physical strength to carry the *Shield*; she knew that much. Instead, she just dumped half her mana's worth of pixie dust on the woman.

The scorching heat licked at the bare skin of Kira's feet and back, and she let out a small yelp. She didn't have to look to know that her bone charm had already been sacrificed to the flames. If it wasn't for the healing effect of her dust keeping her meager health pool full, she would have burned up long before. Her fingers slipped, and she spat out a frustrated growl in protest, clutching her friend tighter. Finally, the pair slowed to a stop, her dust taking hold.

Farnsworth floated up beside her as soon as she was able. Kira panted from the continued effort of keeping them both alive.

Farn smiled at her. "Max was right. You really are good at being there when someone needs you."

Kira shook her head between gasps of air. "Not good enough." She pointed to the space on her wrist where Corvin's name should have been.

Farn's smile fell as she said a quiet, "Oh." Before she had a chance to say more, she was interrupted by a flash of light from above followed by the sound of explosions.

Kira's mouth dropped open in horror as Kegan's name vanished from her party list as well. She looked to Farn, her face conveying everything she was feeling. They had to get up there.

The pair had only been separated from the Max and the others for about a minute, but in that time, everything had changed. So much so that Kira could hardly believe what she saw when they made it topside. It was chaos.

Bursts of what looked like golden lasers streaked across what was left of the chamber's floor, even hitting the walls in the distance. A massive stone ring floated in space, the bell at its center. No, Kira thought. That thing was no bell. It was a dungeon boss. Actually, it was THE Dungeon Boss.

Kira took a moment to spot Max and Ginger through the

madness. Once she had, it didn't take long to see that they were screwed. In fact, it seemed the best they could manage was a frantic run for their lives. Kira motioned to fly toward them, hoping that she could help, and help she did. Just not in the way that she intended.

Famine turned, giving Max and Ginger a moment of peace as Kira found herself in the line of fire. Golden light cut a wide swath through the air, nearly blinding her. She would have dodged, but she wasn't ready. She'd thought she was out of range. She wasn't.

The world spun, a blur of gold and fire. Then strangely, she heard herself let out an embarrassing, "Oof," as she impacted with something soft. It was Farn. The *Shield* had yanked her backward by her foot and shoved her to one side before taking a direct hit to her gauntlet's barrier.

Kira righted herself in time to see her friend slam into the wall at the far end of the chamber. A glance at her health showed it drop nearly a quarter even with the damage absorption of her active shield gauntlet. Her first instinct was to get close and start healing, but then she remembered that Famine was still aiming at her. She turned, another beam streaking toward her. This time she was ready. She dodged, her maneuverability proving to be just enough to keep her breathing. That's when she realized that she might be more useful as bait. She couldn't stay airborne forever - not with her mana below half - but she could buy time for the others to figure something out. Even if it was only a little.

Below her, Max ran, firing an occasional shot in Famine's direction, causing a minuscule amount of damage to the enormous health bar that now ran along the side of Kira's forearm. *At least that's something*, she thought as she dodged another beam that tracked her movement, coming uncomfortably close. The air crackled in its wake.

It was only a matter of time until the boss switched targets to one of her friends, and there was no cover to hide in. Max looked like he could stay ahead of things for the moment, but Ginger was starting to slow down.

The *Coin* seemed to come to the same conclusion, firing her grappling line straight down into the stone ring and leaping off the edge in a dramatic swan dive to find safety dangling against the side.

Kira breathed a little easier. It might not have the bravest thing to do, but for a *Coin*, it was the best option to get out of the fight. At least, that was what Kira thought. Famine had other plans.

The enormous bell turned, seemingly fed up with firing at a fairy that it couldn't hit and fired at the ground. The beam cut across the ring near where Ginger hung, as if it knew right where she was. It couldn't hit her through the solid rock of the floating platform, but it didn't have to. The line supporting the *Coin* snapped as the golden light sliced clean through.

Kira's heart sank when she realized what had happened. She reached out, catching a glance of her mana in the digital ink of her stat-sleeve. Only thirty percent left. There wasn't enough.

Ginger fell, her body bursting into flames moments before she hit the lake of molten rock below. Her friend's name faded from her arm. Half the party was dead.

There wasn't time to process what it all meant, but Kira knew they didn't stand a chance with only three remaining. They had to retreat. Below, Max ran toward the edge of the ring. Ginger had had the right idea. Over the side, there was cover. She just didn't know the Nightmare would hit her grappling line. If Max could reach the edge and climb down, he might be able to find somewhere to wait for the others to get back online. If he could make it, that was.

Famine turned as Kira tried to get its attention. It ignored her, letting off one beam after another in Max's direction. Her heart slammed against the wall of her chest as she watched, flying above him. He moved in an irregular pattern, keeping his path from becoming too predictable to help avoid the constant blasts as explosions trailed behind him. Splash damage ate away at his health.

Kira threw out a couple of *Pulse* spells in a desperate attempt to pull the boss's attention away. They may as well have been gentle kisses for all the good they did. Max's progress slowed, Famine cutting off his path to the edge as if it knew what he was trying to do. Then it happened. A beam clipped his boot.

The resulting explosion hit Max from behind, throwing smoke and debris all around him as it tossed him into the air like a rag doll. Kira lost sight of him for a moment until he fell to the ground hard, rolling to a stop where he remained motionless. She glanced at his health. There was still a hair left, though he lay on his side as if dazed by the impact as the bell fired another beam. It was a direct hit. At least, it would have been if Farn hadn't dropped in. She slammed her gauntlet against her chest plate and shouted the words, *"BLOOD SHELL!"*

The beam struck her like a freight train, but unlike Famine's previous attack that had sent Farn flying across the map into the wall, she took this one without flinching. Kira checked her health. There wasn't even any spillover damage. Instead, the shaft of energy simply bounced off her, reflecting up and at an angle. It hit the ceiling with a crash, sending bits of rock and pieces of the mountain falling as the entire chamber rumbled. Kira ducked her head on instinct, feeling like the place might come down around her. As it was, a column of moonlight pierced through from the outside. She turned back to Farn, her mouth hanging open in shock. She wasn't sure what kind of ability the shell was, but it couldn't have been anything ordinary. She shook her head; it didn't matter now, and she wasn't going to question it.

Kira dropped to the ground, landing next to Max inside the strange protective barrier and gave him a small heal to get him back in the game. She would have done more, but she was running on fumes.

Max rolled back over and pushed himself up with his hands, stumbling a bit as he did. "I lost Ginger and Kegan." His voice sounded crestfallen.

Kira lowered her eyes. "I know. I lost Corvin."

"Yeah, but you're both still breathing." Farn looked back over her shoulder at where Kira knelt on the ground. A crimson glow emanated from her fingertips creating a shell around them.

Kira felt her mouth open to silently form the word, "Wow." She couldn't ignore how impressive the ability was, not to mention how cool Farnsworth looked holding back one blast after another, her figure silhouetted by golden light.

"This is a contract ability. It can shield us like this for one minute," Farn explained before glancing at a timer nestled into a pattern of heavy Celtic line work that stood out on the dark skin of her wrist. "Umm, actually, make that forty-five seconds," she added, sounding a little less cool.

"Okay, let's make the most of it." Max turned to Kira. "That hole in the ceiling that Farn just made, do you think you can get out through there?"

She looked up at the shaft of light shining down. It seemed pretty wide. "Should be able to."

"Nice. As soon as Farn's shell drops, get to safety. We don't really have time to come up with a strategy to fight this thing now, so I want you to regroup with everyone and figure out a plan. I don't care how crazy it is, just come up with something."

Kira saluted formally. "Gotcha. One crazy plan. I'll do my best."

Max then turned to Farn. "Can you move while you protect us?"

She nodded. "Yeah."

"Okay, let's make our way toward the edge. We can climb down and hide until Kira gets the others back in here."

Farn looked away, Kira catching a forlorn expression on her face as she began to move. It worried her, but she didn't have time to say anything. Instead, the three of them backed their way to the edge, blasts hammering the shell the whole way.

Once they reached the side of the stone ring, Max began looking for a space to climb down. "Stay close, Farn. You're going to have to get down here quick once the barrier drops. I'll try to get as stable as I can, so I can help."

Farn shook her head. "No need. I'm not coming."

Kira's flicked her eyes back to her. She didn't need to say anything more. Her feelings on the matter may as well have been written all over her face.

"Well, don't look at me like that." Farn gave her a sad smile. "This contract is called *Blood Shell*. It has a price."

Max lowered his head in understanding. "You were dead the moment you used it."

"Yeah." Her voice sounded apologetic. "I can block any attack, but my health is going to hit zero as soon as the timer runs out."

Kira started to argue, but before she could say anything, Max cut her off.

"Well, that sucks, but it was a good move." He looked up at Kira from the edge. "Now get going."

She stomped once in protest, her bare foot patting the rough stone with a slap. She looked back to Farn who was making a point of avoiding eye contact. Then she let out an immature huff and took off toward the hole in the ceiling.

Using what little remained of her mana, Kira weaved around a beam that had targeted her as soon as she left the protection of Farn's Blood Shell. It seemed that Famine was just happy to have something to shoot at again. She dodged another few blasts on her way when a streak of red on her wrist caught her attention just in time to see Farn's name fade out of the party list.

Kira looked back as the *Shield* dropped to her knees, the glowing particles of her body drifting away. Her chest tightened at the sight so much it hurt. She had let too many of her friends die. She knew it wasn't real, but she had always had trouble separating the game from reality once she was in the thick of it. Noctem had a way of taking her over. She knew she shouldn't let it get to her, but still, it did. She turned back up toward the exit. It didn't matter; she had planning to do. So again, she just shoved an imaginary chair against the closet of emotions in her mind and flew into the light, explosions following in her wake.

CHAPTER SIXTEEN

Alastair stood on the bridge of the Nostromo as terror washed over the room. He gripped the railing with white knuckles, his eyes locked on a readout showing the party's connection status. In only a couple minutes, four of them had been killed and kicked into the reconnection process, leaving just two remaining. Any second, they would lose another, and his world would be torn apart. He fought back tears. It had been his life's work. His dream. He would have done anything to save it. Risked anything!

Desperately, he wanted to rush into the dungeon or at least do something other than sit on his hands. The fact of how powerless he was stabbed him right in the chest. Anger at Carver surged. Max and his team had the best chance of succeeding. If they couldn't win, then the quest was impossible. That was when the last thing he expected happened.

Kirabell burst through the door of the bridge, a confusing expression on her face. It was a mixture of exhaustion and annoyance. She stopped short as soon as his panicked eyes met hers. "It's not as bad as it looks."

Alastair froze for a moment, unable to pick up the pieces of himself enough to get back into character. Then the questions started, "What happened in there? Where's Max? What killed everyone?" Alastair asked one after another, his voice rising with each question.

The diminutive player's face dropped, a panicked expression taking over as she stepped back and glanced around the bridge like she was looking for someone else to take charge. *It was probably an instinct for her*, Alastair thought, remembering how she had let Max do most of the talking during their meeting back in the tavern the night before.

Kira opened her mouth. The words, "I, ah," were all she got out.

Alastair backed off a little, giving her a moment to gather her thoughts. "Sorry, I know there's a lot going on, but are we okay here?"

"For now, yes, I think." She fidgeted before settling down. "Max is still in there hiding in the only cover available. As long as he can stay hidden long enough for the others to get back in, we have a chance."

"What happened?" Alastair asked again, softening his tone, not wanting to push her too far.

Kira shuddered as if remembering a recent trauma. "It was like nothing we've ever encountered. The Nightmare is a five-story bell that shoots some kind of freaking laser beam that can kill in one hit with no cooldown. We just can't move fast enough to dodge, let alone cause any damage. Oh, and all of our consumable items are useless in there."

Alastair sat down and sunk into his chair, placing a hand to his brow. "Is it possible to beat it?"

"No," she answered without hesitation.

He released an exasperated sigh. "So what can we do?"

Kira was silent for a second, then cracked a wry smile. "We change the fight. If we can't move fast enough, we just have to move faster."

Ginger was the first to get logged back in, her figure appearing under the spawn crystal within the grand cathedral in Valain. She ripped off her cloak and patted her body in an attempt to put out any lingering flames. The fact that they were imaginary gained her several odd looks from the surrounding players. She glowered back at them and plopped herself down on a bench to wait for the others as the figures in the stained-glass windows above stared down at her. She rolled her eyes at them and checked her journal to pass the time.

The experience points she'd earned that night had been meager to say the least, so she hadn't actually lost much for dying. She was just glad she'd stored the feathers she'd taken from the first dungeon in her virtual inventory. She would have lost them too if she'd been too lazy and just stuffed them in her item bag. *That would have been tragic.* She still intended to sell them.

After a few minutes, Corvin showed up, looking apologetic, followed by Kegan, who just seemed stunned after being killed so fast.

Ginger stood and stuffed her journal back in her pouch. "Finally."

Kegan checked his quiver and pulled a couple bundles of arrows out of his inventory. "Should we wait here for the ship to come back and pick us up or get our own transport shuttle?"

The inability to communicate with the rest of the party over the distance was crippling, but at least, Farn was able to fill them in on the situation when she arrived.

After listening to the *Shield's* account of the events, Ginger decided. "We take a transport. We can get there faster than having them come all the way back here to get us. I have one stored at the port. I was going to sell it, but I guess we can use it once before I do."

Kegan looked up from counting the arrows in his quiver. "What if they come back for us and we miss them?"

Ginger turned and marched to the door, pushing through a group of players loitering in the way. "Don't worry, Kira's smarter than she looks. She'll keep them there. We'll just have to trust her. Right now, we need to get to port."

Max winced at the sound of explosions. *They better get back here fast,* he thought as he clung to the side of the stone ring in the dungeon, bits of debris dropping down on him as Famine slashed at the floor above in artificial frustration. The boss seemed to know right where he was despite not having a line of sight. Not that it had eyes anyway.

A few blasts from above came too close for comfort, eroding the wall of stone between them. The damage forced him to climb sideways in the hope of finding better cover. He had once gone rock climbing in the real world. At the time, he had been good at it, but that was in a gym with an employee holding a safety line attached to a harness. This was different. There were no handholds, just jagged stone. He struggled to find a spot to grab onto as he climbed, occasionally finding a ledge large enough for him to stand upright on, giving him a place to rest and catch his breath. Nevertheless, the relentless pounding from above never stopped.

He switched out his gun's magazines with two more loaded with the homing rounds that Kira had given him earlier. It was a shame to use such a rare ammunition with no one around to see, but now wasn't the time to worry about what looked cool. He aimed upwards and fired a test shot.

Homing rounds were less of a bullet and more of a tiny monster encased in lead that sought out whatever target was closest. It found its mark and the massive health bar that ran along the tattooed flames on his forearm dropped by an almost imperceptible amount.

"At least that's something," Max said to himself as he fired off the rest of the magazine, doing a small but respectable amount of damage. He laughed and yelled up at the boss, "That's right, I don't have to see you either!" He emptied his other pistol into the air, getting the same result. It made him feel a little better. A part of him was tempted to climb up and take the thing on, a ridiculous fantasy going through his head of everyone getting back only to find that he'd soloed the thing. Then a blast from above that dislodged a boulder, which fell straight for him, caused him to rethink the idea. He leapt off the ledge on reflex, catching a handhold with his fingertips as the spot he had occupied was smashed beyond recognition. A view of glowing magma filled his vision as he fumbled for a better grip.

"Never mind; I'll wait."

Farnsworth's heart beat hard in her chest as she stood in the rear of the Karura class transport shuttle that Ginger had liberated from a clan of sky pirates a few weeks prior. It wasn't technically stolen, but that didn't stop Ginger from making air quotes around the word liberate when she explained it.

As far as ships went, it was small, fast, and durable. Its armored front bore decorative patterns that flowed down onto large engines on either side of its body with a narrow window running vertically down the front. It had a powerful look, like a battering ram with stubby wings. Although, as far as comfort was concerned, it was far from first class. The cabin was bare with nothing but a handrail running along the ceiling. There wasn't even a bench to sit on. Of course, Ginger could've upgraded the interior at a *shipsmith*, but that would have cost real money, and as she had explained, she'd leave that to whatever fat-cat decided to buy it. That being said, Farn's legs were getting tired after standing for the entire half hour ride back to the dungeon. She might have sprawled out on the floor like Kegan, but she had too much on her mind to relax.

Her thoughts ran around in circles, thinking about Famine and how it had handed them their asses in less than five minutes. She knew Kira was back on the dock, tasked with coming up with some kind of plan, but no matter how Farn looked at it, she couldn't see a way to win. She hoped she was wrong. That was when Ginger looked back over her shoulder.

"I see the dungeon. We're almost there," the *Coin* announced.

Farn tightened her grip on the handrail. "You can do this," she said under her breath, trying to gather her shaking nerves.

The ship set down hard, a little too close to one edge of the dock. Evidently, landing was not one of Ginger's strengths.

Farn jumped out as soon as she could, scanning the area to find Kira sitting at the bottom of the Nostromo's retractable stairs. She would have run to her, but she didn't want to seem too enthusiastic, having only met her the night before. Plus, the fairy hadn't seemed to appreciate her heroic sacrifice earlier. She hoped Kira wasn't still angry. Farn motioned to wave, but she looked away. Farn swallowed. "What's the plan here?" She tried to sound nonchalant.

Kira answered with an annoyed, "Humph," and crossed her arms.

"You mad?" Farn winced a little.

Kira didn't look at her. "I'm giving you the silent treatment."

"You're not very good at it."

"No, I am not. You're lucky I like you." The fairy pouted.

"And I did kinda save us in there," added Farn.

Kira groaned. "Maybe. Just don't go killing yourself all willy-nilly." She ran a finger over the ring that tied their lives together in a one-way bond.

Farn lowered her head. "I promise."

With that, Kira's body relaxed as if it had been taking significant effort to stay mad. Her smile returned. "Now, let's go get Max before he kills this thing without us."

Farn laughed at the thought.

"I'm not kidding," Kira added, pointing to Famine's health bar that still showed on her forearm. "Max has been getting impatient in there. Famine's actually taken a little damage. I'm just hoping he waits for us before he tries anything badass or stupid or both."

"Well, he better not get himself killed," Ginger jumped in. "I don't want to have to fly all the way back to Valain to get him."

Kira sent out a round of invites to get the others back into the party, and Farn fell in line behind Ginger who seemed to take charge while Max wasn't around. Then, back together again, the team began walking toward the door to begrudgingly re-enter the dungeon. Or at least, they would have if Kira hadn't spoken up, "Wrong way."

Farn turned to find the fairy boarding Ginger's shiny new transport ship, a new bone charm hanging from her item bag.

"That hole I escaped through was pretty big, so I'm thinking we can get this thing through." Kira slapped her hand against the side of the ship, emitting a hollow sounding tang.

Farn's eyes widened at the realization of what she meant.

Kira continued, "We'll never be able to dodge that thing on foot or even with *Flight* magic, since y'all are too slow. But if we can circle it in this, we should be able to move way faster than its targeting system." She wore a goofy grin on her face, clearly proud of the absurdity of the plan. "Also, I'm gonna need all the explosive items that you have in your inventories."

Farn boarded the ship with the others, leaving Alastair again to sweat it out in his captain's chair as they took off for where Kira had escaped earlier.

Ginger approached slowly, her knuckles tight on the stick. Her face dropped as the opening came into view. "What the hell? That's not big enough!"

Kira immediately gave Kegan a dirty look before he had the chance to blurt out an obligatory 'that's what she said.' "It's plenty big," she said, continuing to glare at him.

"Have you seen how long this thing is? It will never fit in there," Ginger added.

Kegan began to shake visibly as if holding something in.

Kira pointed a finger at him. "Don't you dare. That joke got old years ago." She turned back to Ginger. "You'll just have to go at it at an angle and kinda bust your way through."

Kegan nudged Corvin with an elbow, who looked annoyed at the jabbing.

"This isn't a fighter jet; it's more like a helicopter. You can't just dive in there," Ginger explained.

"Cut it out, man." Corvin shoved Kegan to the side in the cramped space of the cabin for the continued nudging.

"Just get the nose pointed down at it and cut the engines, the weight of the armor in the front should pull us down in the right direction," Kira said as if it was just that simple.

"Your funeral. Well, ours, I guess." Ginger shrugged and tipped the nose of the craft downward before reaching for the engine's toggle switch. "Hold on; this is gonna get rough!"

Farn and Kira both looked at Kegan who remained strangely silent.

Ginger flicked the switch, and the ship dropped out of the air. Gravity did the rest.

The craft's nose rammed into one side of the entrance, sliding into the space, the lack of seat belts becoming a problem.

Farn anchored herself to the handrails at the rear and pushed Kira behind her to keep the fairy from rattling around the cabin and losing a few precious hit points.

Kegan glommed onto Corvin as the two fell to one side, flipping one of his furry ears inside out as they landed against the wall.

Corvin squirmed. "Aww, come on!"

"Shut up, you love it," Kegan argued.

Ginger's whole body tensed as the cavern came into view through the windshield. "It's gonna be tight, but we're almost in!"

Kegan, still holding tight to Corvin, finally shouted back, "THAT'S WHAT SHE–!"

CHAPTER SEVENTEEN

"Oh good, this is familiar," Farnsworth said through a thick layer of sarcasm, as she plummeted toward a lake of fire for the second time in less than an hour. At least this time she was in a vehicle. Granted, the engines hadn't fired back up yet, but really, that was several problems down the list at the moment.

Farn braced her legs against the floor of the cabin to keep herself from falling into the cockpit that was now directly below her. She didn't want to end up like Kegan and Corvin who were tumbling around on the windshield with Ginger yelling at them both to get out of the way so she could see. Kira, on the other hand, just laughed in Farn's ear like a mad woman as she remained safe, sandwiched between the rear of the cabin and Farn's back. Farn gained a greater appreciation for how little the fairy weighed as she tried to hold her in place with her butt.

Ginger leaned to one side to see through the small windshield, made even smaller by Kegan's armpit being in the way. "Oh shit!" the *Coin* shouted as the top of the massive bell filled the window.

The ship lurched to the side with a crash, followed by a few seconds of continuous grinding coming from the other side of the metal plating near Farn's head. Out of the corner of her eye, she caught Famine's health bar drop. They must have hit the boss on the way down and scraped it as they fell. She tilted her head to the side in approval. It had caused a decent chunk of damage.

Ginger yanked back on the stick. "Come on, come on. I still intend to sell you. You're not about to give up on me here," she spoke directly to the vehicle. Golden light swept past them, illuminating the tiny porthole windows on one side as it almost grazed the craft. Finally, the engines kicked back in, allowing the *Coin* at the stick to pull out of the dive. Molten rock erupted into the air in one huge wave as the beam cut a wide swath through the lake of fire. Ginger spun the craft to avoid the deadly obstacle before pulling up.

Kira slid down Farn's back as the ship righted itself, ending up sitting on her rear on the floor with one arm around Farn's boot. Kegan and Corvin dropped as well, the mage ending up on the floor while the *Leaf* found himself sitting across Ginger's lap. He smiled at her for a moment before she shoved him off so that she could adjust their flight path to one that would keep them in the cover of the ring.

Farn rushed toward the front, stepping over the mage sprawled out on the floor on her way. She leaned on Ginger's seat so she could see over her shoulder to look for Max. "Do you see him?"

"Not yet," Ginger answered, before adding, "Wait a sec, I think that's him."

"Oh damn," Farn said on reflex as she saw Max dangling from a ledge by his fingertips. The ship blew past him without slowing. Farn shot Ginger a questioning look.

"What? I'm not slowing down. You want us to get shot?"

Farn thought about it. Ginger was right. Max was pretty well hidden where he was, but the ship would have to get under him to pick him up. As it was, there was only a small area of space around the stone ring that was safe for the ship. If they went any lower, they'd be in the open. Farn glanced up at a hatch in the ceiling above her head, wondering if she could climb up and try to catch him. Ginger put a stop to that line of thought.

"Open the side door!" she called over her shoulder to the guys in the back, who were just now getting to their feet. They probably would have questioned her plan, but there wasn't enough time. Instead, Kegan pulled on the handle of the wide door that ran along the side of the cabin. It slid to the side about an inch, then stopped. The close encounter with Famine on the way down must've damaged the door's track.

Farn rushed to help, grabbing the edge of the door and shoving it with all her strength while the others pulled. It opened with a metallic scrape, and she grabbed the handrail to lean out. There he was. Farn caught his eyes for a moment. Then he dropped.

The ship tilted with a sudden lurch, throwing everyone inside against the wall of the cabin as Ginger banked to the side to angle the open door upwards. She timed it perfectly.

Max, however, did not.

Something squishy hit the craft, followed by a loud, "Son of a..."

Farn looked up to the door, finding Max hanging halfway out. It must not have been easy to land on top of a moving aircraft. Farn lunged for his hand as the ship leveled out again, catching it in time to pull him back in before he slipped off the side. She stumbled backward as she did, causing them both to fall on top of each other in the cabin.

An involuntary, "Yarg," left his mouth, only to be cut off when his face impacted against her neck, his mouth feeling both soft and weird against her skin. She righted herself to the sound of Kira snickering.

Max took a moment to take in what was happening as Famine fired a beam at the ship. It missed, unable to get a solid bead on the craft with it flying faster than anything it was programmed for. Recognition fell across Max's face. Then he looked at Kira. "I guess I did ask for a crazy plan."

Kira cast a quick heal on him, then took a deep bow, a Cheshire grin reaching from ear to ear. "Ask and ye shall receive."

Farn helped him back to his feet, and he gripped the handrail to the side of the open door.

"Everybody that can, start shooting," he ordered, taking back leadership of the team without skipping a beat.

Kegan began firing before he could say another word, using a charge skill to boost his damage, while Corvin got a combination of debuff spells to stick. Unable to add to the attack, Kira cast *Flight* on everyone in case one of them fell out. She added on every buff she could before sitting down to regenerate her mana.

Farnsworth took that as her cue to open the bag that they had tied to the bottom of Ginger's seat. Inside was every explosive that the party had among them. Well, except for a few small bombs that Ginger had insisted she might need later. Farn grabbed a handful of fireworks and fired the crude missiles by lighting the fuses and holding the sticks at the ends to aim. They were low tech, but they did decent damage and lit up the map like the Fourth of July.

She looked to Max, who grinned wildly as he unloaded two magazines at the boss. It was working. Before long, Famine's health was down to half, and they still had plenty of explosives, arrows, and bullets left. That was when its attack pattern changed.

A lot of games broke boss fights up into phases that would change as their health depleted. It was usually a nice feature that stopped things from getting boring and kept the players feeling challenged. That being said, using the transport ship in the fight did feel like cheating. Which was why when it happened, a part of Farn felt like they deserved it.

The bell tipped to one side, pausing for a second at an angle.

"That can't be good," Max said, speaking the obvious before it swung hard in the opposite direction to ring itself.

A shock wave radiated outward from the bell, hitting the ship and throwing everyone against the wall again as the craft took the impact. A wave of dull pain echoed through Farn's head. She checked her sleeve. She'd been hit hard, and it wasn't just her. Everyone but Kira had lost two-thirds of their health.

"We can't take many hits like that!" Ginger called back, looking at the damage gauge on the ship's controls. "Not if we want to stay in the air."

Without the use of items, it was all up to Kira to get the team back up to fighting condition. She had enough mana to get them back to full, but it wouldn't last long. Fortunately, the basic enchantment on Kira's new Ring of the Willing seemed to be doing its job, as the slight increase in luck had caused Famine's area attack to miss her. Although, they couldn't count on something like that happening a second time.

Max hoisted himself back up to the handrails. "That was probably triggered when we got its health below half. We're gonna have to change the plan."

"You think it's time?" Kira asked as she rested on the floor.

"Time for what?" Farn shifted her eyes between the two of them.

Max held up one hand flat and shoved his fist into it. "We ram it."

"What?" Ginger shouted back from the cockpit.

"We light a fuse on the bomb bag and kamikaze the thing just before it does that attack again," he answered, sounding far too casual about it.

"That might actually work." Farn glanced out at the bell, then back at everyone in the ship. "Especially if everyone flies out and attacks from the sides. We could do a lot of damage all at once."

Corvin turned to Farn, joining in on the planning. "Could you hit it with a melee attack just after the impact? Something really strong?"

"Yeah, I have something that might work," she said, patting her hand on the handle of her sword. "Especially if I get some buffs first. Although, I'd fall into the lava afterward since I can't use *Flight* while wielding a weapon." She turned to Kira. "Think you could come get me?"

"Sure," the fairy nodded.

As if sensing their plan, the bell hit them again with its chime attack, the damage hitting them just as hard as before. This time Kira's luck ran out and her new bone charm faded out of existence, leaving her defenseless. Another hit would kill her.

"We need to be ready for the next one," Max turned toward the cockpit. "Ginger, take us back down below the ring. We'll let everyone out, so we can attack together."

She growled at the whole situation. "Okay! But I'm doing this under protest. And someone's gonna owe me a ship."

"I think Alastair will take care of it," Max replied as Kira started to heal the team. He stopped her. "Don't bother; it's all or nothing. Full health won't save us, and you're going to need mana to stay airborne."

She nodded and just refreshed everyone's *Flight* instead. Then Ginger took the ship down to dispense the team around the ring to take positions against its outer walls causing Famine to fire erratically as targets spread out around it. Beams pummeled the stone, unable to hit any of them as they hid in the cover of the ring.

The ship came back up with only Kira, Farn and Ginger on board. Kira swiped open her spell-craft menu, setting up a spell for Farn to give her the maximum strength and dexterity values. As soon as she was finished, the fairy took one step toward the open door then stopped, turning back to Ginger. "Make sure you say something cool just before you bail out."

To which Ginger grumbled, "Yeah, yeah, just get out already."

With that, Kira gave a quick good luck to Farn, saluted dramatically and dropped backward out of the door.

"Okay, just you and me, Farn," Ginger said, before letting out a sigh, adding, "I was really starting to like this ship."

Farn placed one hand on the back of her chair, a little unsure of what to say, not having been alone with the *Coin* before. "It served us well. At least there's that."

Ginger nodded, "Yeah, maybe I should give it a name. A ship should have a name. That would be respectful, right?"

Farn pushed open the hatch in the roof near the cockpit. "Frank?"

Ginger snorted. "Yeah, okay, that's good enough."

Farn hoisted herself up, kicking Ginger's seat as she wriggled through the small door. "Why the hell is there no ladder?"

"Ladders cost money!" Ginger called back up.

Farn shuffled around on top of the ship to get her head back to the hatch so she could look down into the cockpit. She activated her shield to keep the wind out of her face. "I feel like Frank is worth a ladder." She patted the ship with her gauntlet, so it made a low clanking sound.

Ginger, in turn, patted the bag of explosives. "Not for much longer," she responded as she pulled in closer to wait for Famine to stop firing and tilt back.

Farn turned her attention back to the boss. It fired, but Ginger weaved to the side, the beam passing by close enough for its heat to warm Farn's cheek. She ducked down lower just in case. Then it started.

The bell tipped away and Ginger punched the throttle. It was all about timing. They had to use the moment before its chime, when it stopped firing, to approach without being shot down. After that, they still had to hit it before it swung back and killed them all with the area attack that followed.

The craft rocketed toward it, the massive bell seeming even larger up close. Farn looked down at the *Coin* as she placed her fingers to the end of a short fuse that stuck out of the top of the explosive bag.

Ginger started to speak, then for an instant, she paused, a stupid look falling across her face. "Oh, crap, I can't think of anything to say," she blurted out before snapping her fingers against the fuse and running toward the door.

Just before impact, Farn leapt off the ship and hovered above as the craft slammed into the boss's side, detonating in a spectacular display of destruction. She watched as one burst of smoke and fire after another rocked the helpless Nightmare, the shock wave blowing her upwards as she fought to stay in place. She hid behind her shield to protect herself, her hair whipping behind her with the force of the blast. The impact pushed the bell backward, interrupting its attack and Famine's health dropped to only ten percent remaining.

The explosions subsided as the burning wreckage of the ship toppled down to the fire below. It was Farn's turn. She drew her sword, canceling the *Flight* spell and activated the contract item's enchantment for which it was named, *Feral Edge*. In an instant, the glow of her gauntlet went dark and her overall defense dropped by half. Energy surged up her arm from her shield generator, pulled through her body to reach her blade as she began to fall. The weapon split down the back and red energy flowed out, wrapping around it to form a blade, both wider and longer by double its original size. It was an all-out attack she almost never used, since it reallocated half her defense stat into her strength while in use. But defense didn't matter now.

She didn't really mean to slide down the side of the unsuspecting dungeon boss, but she wasn't able to get decent footing with her momentum. The result was a beautifully executed attack that slashed the entire bell as she skipped along its surface, leaving a trail of sparks behind her until the tip of her crimson blade got stuck near the bottom. Fortunately, the brass knuckle grip of the Feral Edge kept her grasp firm as she swung up and around the handle, shaking it loose. It may not have been on purpose, but it sure as hell looked like it was.

She continued to fall as the others let loose from all sides. Max unloaded two mags worth of custom rounds. Corvin hit it with a few *Shrapnel* spells, thanks to the rune that Kira had purchased for him earlier. Kegan unleashed a handful of arrows. Ginger even turned up firing off a few fireworks after swinging up and over the stone ring from a line to stop herself from falling.

The team came together as Farn fell away from the series of explosions. She didn't panic. Instead, she just sheathed her sword and held her arms out wide. She couldn't help but smile as she looked up at Kira who slowed their descent to a graceful stop, pixie dust dancing across her skin.

It was actually over. Famine, the first of the Nightmares that threatened their world, fell into the molten rock, sending a tidal wave of fire splashing against the walls below as it sank.

The party regrouped to a round of celebratory high fives and fist bumps. Farn even took a bow for delivering such an impressive blow. She bent low at the waist, placing one hand on her stomach while the other stretched out beside her. A stupid grin covered her face. At least it did until she heard her name echo through the cavern in an uneven voice. "Farnsworth!"

She expected it, of course. They had just beaten a Nightmare after all, so a contract had to go to someone. She just didn't think it would pick her.

The voice echoed through the chamber, rumbling like thunder so deep that Farn could feel it in the pit of her stomach as it dragged out her name. It was the voice of mankind's first Nightmare. The fear that children learn before all others. The darkness. And it had chosen her.

Of course, it wasn't really the age-old darkness calling her name. It was just a system message given a creepy voice, but that didn't stop her from cringing as it brought her back to the point in her life when the still hid under the covers, afraid of shadows in her room.

Farn lifted her head with caution. "Yes?" she said, sounding unsure.

The darkness responded. "Make your offer!"

Farn stood up straight feeling a little less scared as she fell into the routine of forming a contract, which she had done twice before. "Oh, okay," she mumbled as she shoved a hand into her item bag and began rummaging through it for something to give. Her hand came back out with a scrap of cloth meant for crafting. "Umm, here you go," she added as she tossed the item over the edge toward the sinking bell, getting a few odd looks from the others at the fact that she had chosen something so random. Following that, she waited for a long moment. It was almost as if the voice was waiting for her to relax before speaking again.

"Accepted!" it called out, sounding satisfied as Farn felt a cold chill encircle her wrist just above her party readout where a pair of black beaded bracelets materialized.

Kira hopped a little closer to see, but before she could ask what they were, a section of the stone ring collapsed. It crashed into fire below, sending another wave of molten rock into the walls, signaling that they should probably get out of there. The fairy recast *Flight* for the party and pointed up at the hole in the ceiling.

Max looked over the edge at the red-hot remains of the fallen Horseman then gestured back to Farn's new bracelets. "I hope you got something good, 'cause we have three more of these things to fight."

CHAPTER EIGHTEEN

Max strode onto the bridge of the Nostromo with his chest puffed out, feeling pretty damn pleased with himself after pulling off such an impossible win. He might have looked cool if it weren't for Ginger shoving past him.

"You!" she shouted at an unsuspecting Alastair, one finger pointing in his direction. "Pay up." She closed the gap and poked him in the chest. "I could have sold that ship."

He looked down at her finger and then back up at her, slowly pushing her hand away with his own. "How much would it have gone for?"

Ginger paused a moment before answering. "Six hundred dollars." She inflated the price by at least double. Max had sold a similar ship once before, so he knew what they went for.

Alastair rolled his eyes at the amount. "Currently, we are unable to issue a transfer due to the block on your accounts that came with taking on the quest, but I'll have Jeff send out a check."

"Jeff-with-a-three," Kira corrected, grinning at the annoyed elf and getting a confused look from Alastair.

Ginger stepped away, her hands shoved behind her back. "Oh, thanks," she said in a meek voice that seemed almost out of character for her. She probably didn't expect to get away with overcharging him.

"Hey, since you're giving things out. Can I get a free ship?" Max butted in. "Maybe like … a black one?"

Alastair sighed. "Sure, why not. Free ships all around."

The mention of free stuff prompted a loud, "Wooooo!" from Kira, doing her best impression of a bachelorette party.

Farn joined in, obviously still feeling pretty good about her new contract. Max couldn't help but wonder what it did.

Alastair's face grew serious, cutting the levity short. "Gather round." He motioned them toward the captain's chair.

They approached, Farn leaning against a railing with Max taking a position next to her. Kira hopped it altogether, floating over the rail as she found a perch next to him.

"Now that the first boss is down, we have been able to view a recording of the fight," his expression softened, "and I have to say, wow. How you were able to turn that around was incredible. But—" He paused for a moment as a serious expression returned to his face. "Despite the overall success, it was absolutely terrifying how close we came to losing."

Max felt less proud of his performance as the severity of the near loss set in.

"I know it wasn't your fault. I mean, that was something that no one could have been prepared for," Alastair leaned an elbow on the back of his chair, "but it tells us two things about the nature of this quest. First, after watching the fight, it seemed to be designed to be impossible. If you hadn't gone back in with that absurd plan, you wouldn't have survived. I was hoping that Neal was going to give us a chance at winning here, but it looks like he really does intend to take down the system."

"And the second thing?" Max inquired.

"That you can do this." A smug smile crept across Alastair's face. "It only took a couple minutes for that thing to kill four people, but you rolled with the punches and figured out a way to win. That tells me I picked the right people. If you can just out-think whatever Neal throws at you, we might be able to get through this." The group lifted, giving Max back some of his confidence from earlier.

Alastair looked to each of them once more, then he changed the subject. "We still have plenty of time on the mission clock, but that didn't start until you reached the bottom of the first dungeon. So, we have to remember to add your time getting down there as well. Currently, Kira has been logged in the longest with just over seven hours, and since you stay in for around ten most nights, I was thinking we could try to take down the next one before taking a break." She nodded.

"Sounds good." Max opened his journal to its map and handed it to Alastair, so he could see their new waypoint. "Here's the next one."

Alastair groaned as soon as his gaze fell to the page. "Damn, that's in the Verdant region."

Max put his journal away. "Yeah, we haven't actually been there before."

"That's because there's nothing there. It's just an empty forest. We haven't used it for anything yet. Noctem's a big world; there are a lot of places like that set aside for future expansions," Alastair brought the map up in the front window and zoomed in on the area. "With all the trees, we probably won't be able to find the dungeon entrance from the air like we did with the last one. Unless Neal has done something to make it stand out, which I doubt. So, you might have to search for it on the ground."

"Well that kinda sucks." Max folded his arms across his chest. "I'm starting to feel like Carver's quest was designed to waste time."

"We'll have to drop you here since we can't land in the forest." He pointed to a small clearing. "There's a lagopin stable there. You'll have to ride in the rest of the way. It will be faster than searching on foot."

Ginger's face lit up at the mention of the animals, and she let out a quiet, "Nice."

Max shot her a questioning look.

"What? I like them; they're cute."

He shrugged, giving his approval. "Can't argue with that."

Alastair closed the map image in the ship's window. "It will take about half an hour to get there. If anyone wants, there's a mess hall down below with a merchant booth. You can get food and some basic items. It's not much, but it's something."

Without a word, Kira was out the door.

"That's not surprising," Ginger smirked and turned to follow. "I guess I could go for a snack, too."

Kegan motioned toward the door. "I'll come, too. You can give me some of those feathers."

"Sure, how much you paying?" she asked as they headed out the door.

Corvin hesitated for a moment before making an awkward exit in the direction of the others.

Max pushed off the railing. "I was thinking of exploring the ship." He turned to Farn. "Wanna come?"

Before she had a chance to answer, Alastair interrupted. "Actually, do you mind hanging back? I need to ask some more questions about the last fight."

She paused for a moment, looking torn between her options. "Ahhh, sure," she answered before apologizing to Max.

"No problem. Next time." He hid his disappointment. It wasn't like he had a thing for her or anything. Then again, Farn was an attractive member of the opposite sex, and he had been single for far too long. So it wasn't that he didn't have a thing for her either. That being said, he couldn't really blame her for choosing to stay with Alastair. He was technically her boss.

"What about you, Jeff-with-a-three? Up for some exploring?" he joked, pointing at Alastair's assistant as he passed by.

The tall elf just looked at him, one eyebrow raised in annoyance at the fact that Kira's change to his name seemed to be sticking.

"Nope? Okay then." Max shoved his hands in his pockets. "I'll just wander around alone. So enjoy being here and having no fun," he added before exiting the bridge. "That was mildly embarrassing," he muttered to himself before disappearing down a narrow hallway.

CHAPTER NINETEEN

After being interrogated by her employer on every possible detail about the group's actions in the last fight for almost twenty minutes, Farnsworth headed out to the deck of the ship alone. She would have liked to go down to meet up with Kira and the others, but she felt weird about just showing up and inviting herself. Instead, she fell into her standard pattern of finding a quiet place and waiting until she was needed.

"I'm surprised you're not down with the others," a voice called from behind, startling her as she took in the view. She turned to find Max climbing up through a hatch in the deck. He looked just as surprised as she was. His exploration must have had led him back to her.

"Find anything interesting?" Farn asked, making an effort to seem as casual as she could.

"Yeah, found a treasure chest. Not sure why there was one on the ship, but I'm not complaining."

Farn laughed. "They're randomly generated. It happens whenever they add content to the game. There's no way for them to place all of the chests in the world, so they only set the important ones and let an algorithm do the rest."

"Oh," Max frowned, "and I thought I might have found something rare."

"What was in it?"

"Ear cuff," he said with a grin, brushing back his dusty blond hair to display his ear proudly. "Plus two dex."

"It's very nice," she said to be polite while withholding any further comments. If she had been honest, the cuff was a little flashy since the rest of his gear was so simple. All he wore was a gray short sleeve shirt and a pair of canvas pants with a leather chest piece that seemed to suggest a modern bulletproof vest. True there was a decorative laced seam running up the sides of his shirt that brought him back to the fantasy setting, but other than that, he reminded her more of a modern-day soldier. Especially with that scarf tied lose around his neck.

"Speaking of very nice, how about that last attack of yours back there?" Max interrupted her train of thought and joined her by the deck's rail. "You're really turning out to be one hell of a badass."

She smiled with pride but ruined it a second later by telling the truth. "It was by accident. I basically fell and made the best of it."

He laughed. "Yeah, that happens. A year back, I tripped while trying to find cover and ended up falling into a perfect dive roll. Kira saved a recording of it. It looked epic. The key is to just go with the flow and pretend it was on purpose."

She laughed, feeling more comfortable knowing that they had shared an experience. Farn hadn't spent any time alone with Max, but he did seem kind of cool in a way. And Kira got along well with him. "I'll have to get her to show me the video sometime."

"So what do your shiny new accessories do?" he motioned to the strings of dark beads around her wrist.

"Oh yeah," she said, realizing that she hadn't had the chance to look over their details until now. She opened her journal to her equipment page and read the text aloud. "Okay, let's see."

Contract name: *Shift Beads*
Type: accessory
Equip slot: wrists or ankles
Ownership: unbound
Item given to form contract: scrap of cloth, quantity one
Basic enchantment: plus five defense each, stackable

"Nice!" Max commented at the hefty boost to her class's main stat. "And you can wear them both together, so they don't take up two slots."

Farn paused and gave him a knowing smile, as if there was more. There was. Max's eyebrow raised as she continued.

Advanced enchantment: *Shift*
Usage: limited
Description: If shared between two players, they may swap positions by touching either bracelet with two fingers. Does not require line of sight. May carry anything held.

"That sounds awesome." Max's face shifted from excited to confused. "But what the hell does it mean by limited-use? I've never seen that before."

Farn shrugged. "I don't know. I've seen single-use and unlimited, but I've never seen one listed just as limited either. Why do contracts have to be so cryptic with their text?"

"I know what you mean. Kira had one once that had no description at all."

"That's weird." Farn furrowed her brow, wondering what that could mean.

"Yeah. Anyway, are you going to use the ability on yours or keep both bracelets and stack the defense?"

Farn thought about it, then pulled on one of the strings of beads. It stretched to fit over her hand and she held it out to him. "Here, it will be more useful if you have one. I could swap in to get you out of danger, which would free you up to do more damage. Plus, a little extra defense couldn't hurt you."

He took the item, giving her a warm smile as he slid it onto his wrist and admired it. "You know, it's really cool how you think."

Farn laughed. "What's that mean?"

"I mean, you always seem to be thinking like a *Shield*. You plan ahead on how you can protect the team. You know your class inside and out, and you have the discipline to stick with it. That's actually rare for players. Half the time I see *Shields* drop their guard and try to go offense."

Farn nodded. "Being a *Shield* isn't glamorous. We can fight if we have to, like I did against Famine, but that isn't what makes us strong. A party is far better off if we leave that stuff to the more damage-centered classes like you. All I care about is that I'm carrying my weight."

"Well, I'd say you're doing that just fine."

Farn fell silent for a moment. "I feel kind of bad though."

"Why?"

She sighed. "I think it bothered Kira that I sacrificed myself back there. And if that wasn't bad enough, I went ahead and bought her a ring that pretty much does the same thing. She didn't say anything at the time, but it probably made her uncomfortable."

"Don't worry about that little goon." Max waved his hand dismissively. "She lets herself get immersed in the game too much, and it makes it weird for her seeing people die. But she'll give up her own life just as easily. One time she even sacrificed herself to save an NPC."

Farn raised an eyebrow. "When was that?"

"It was during the *Shingetsu* fight."

"Oh," Farn said, remembering the strangest and most upsetting Nightmare that she had faced during her time playing Noctem.

It had been an escort mission based off Japanese folklore rather than a boss fight like most of the others. The object had been to get a large white rabbit up a long flight of stairs to a shrine at the top where a bonfire burned. She shuddered as she remembered how the rabbit had thrown itself into the fire as soon as they reached the top. There was something about losing something that she had protected that bothered her.

"What happened?" she asked.

Max snorted. "We'd heard about what was supposed to happen at the end of that one before starting it, so Kira ran ahead and jumped into the fire before the rabbit had the chance to kill itself. Fun fact, apparently the fire only needs a life, be it bunny or fairy, so it counted as a win. She even got the contract when she spawned back in miles away. It was that full heal with all the buffs that she used back in the last dungeon."

"I bet it freaked people out when she got it, hearing the darkness calling to her in the middle of the spawn point."

"Actually no. Another fun fact, only the participants of the fight can hear the darkness." Max tapped his ear. "Anyway, she claimed she just did it 'cause she hates escort missions."

"Well, that's understandable. Everyone hates escort missions."

"True, but I'm pretty sure she just didn't want to see the rabbit die."

Farn smiled. "That's actually really sweet."

"Yeah, except she left rest of the party at the shrine with a rabbit, waiting for something to happen while she got back online. After a while, we just left the rabbit there eating some grass," he shook his head, "but my point is, don't worry about upsetting that little hypocrite. Besides, she can't hold a grudge any more than she can throw a punch. She pretty much forgives people immediately. So go nuts and piss her off as much as you want. That's what I do."

"Well, that's good to know," Farn said, not quite sure if she should listen to his advice or not.

"What was up with offering a random scrap of cloth for your contract back there?" Max asked, looking curious. "I mean, you got something good, so it worked out, but still, it's kind of odd."

Farn tilted her head to one side. "I kind of learned my

lesson for getting creative with what I'm willing to trade back when I got my Blood Shell."

"Really? What did you offer?"

"I ..." she started to speak but paused, remembering the offer, "I gave one month of my life."

Max's mouth fell open. "What does that even mean?"

"It was my first contract, and I just blurted it out. The system responded by erasing every level, quest, and ability that I'd earned for one month. I had to re-do it all as if it never happened."

"Damn."

"Yeah, damn is right. That's why I decided, that from then on, I would just grab whatever in my bag had the lowest value."

"That kind of reminds me of what Corvin offered when we fought *Kafka*."

Farn tried to remember which Nightmare that was. "That's the one that starts as a person but turns into a giant insect throughout the fight, right?

"Yeah," Max answered. "I think it was supposed to represent a fear of change."

"What did Corvin offer?"

Max paused before answering to build suspense. "His left eye."

Farn slapped her hand on the railing. "Oh my god, that's why he has the eye patch? I thought it was just for looks."

"No, part of his face is messed up, too," Max added, sounding somehow proud of the *Venom* mage.

"Contracts are weird."

"Tell me about it." Max turned to lean back against the railing. "Next time you see Kira, check out the earring that she has in her right ear, the one with the pearl dangling from it."

Farn stepped closer to him. "Is it a contract item?"

Max slouched back a little. "If you're looking for weird, that one has one of the strangest activation requirements. She actually has to swallow the whole earing."

Farn flinched back. "That sounds horrible. What Nightmare gave it?"

Max shot her a smirk. "Rasputin."

Farn's mouth fell at the name of the first Nightmare to fall in Noctem. "She's had that one for years then."

"She's a hoarder. Always saving things for a rainy day." Max shrugged. "I have to respect her discipline though. I burnt through the few that I got almost as soon as I got them."

Farn smiled. It was actually quite fitting. He didn't seem to be the type to wring his hands about whether or not he should use something powerful. She wanted to ask him more, but before she could, the ship tilted to one side to begin its descent toward their destination, forcing Farn to cling to the railing to keep from losing her balance.

A massive forest filled the horizon as they dropped below the cloud cover, dark green as far as the eye could see.

"Damn. We have to search that for the next boss?" Max added, clearly forgetting what they had been talking about a moment before.

"I guess they called it the Verdant region for a reason," Farn stated the obvious.

"We should go find the others," Max concluded, almost sounding sad.

Farn took a deep breath. "Yeah, I hope this one goes a little smoother."

CHAPTER TWENTY

Max dropped from the Nostromo's dangling ladder, grateful for the soft grass of the clearing as he planted his feet with a subtle thud, free of damage. He stepped aside just in time to avoid a shrieking Kegan, who must have been equally grateful for the soft landing as he tumbled to the ground with a perfect face plant.

"You stepped on my hand!" he sputtered up at Ginger as she dropped down beside him with all the grace that one would expect from a woman with legs as long as hers.

She apologized with little enthusiasm but offered her hand to help him up anyway. Kegan responded by spitting bits of dirt from his mouth.

Max let out a loud laugh at the two, taking in a lung full of fresh air at the same time.

"I don't know why you guys are using the ladder." Kira set down beside him, Farn and Corvin floating down behind her.

To Max's surprise, they were joined at the bottom by Alastair, who must have wanted to accompany them as far as he could before leaving the rest in their hands. Max understood the sentiment. If the situation was reversed, he would have trouble letting go, too. He would at least need to feel his feet on the ground.

Ahead was small stable with an equally sized fenced-in paddock where the lagopin could graze. Max assumed they didn't really need to eat, but the behavior added to their lifelike appearance, so he decided not to question it. A few of the over-sized animals meandered about, long ears pricking up as he and his team approached.

Ginger held out an eager hand to call one of the enormous rabbit-like creatures over to the fence. Its dark eyes focused on her with caution as it moved in her direction. When in reach, she placed a hand flat on its forehead. The animal responded by pushing against her palm and rotating its head, so she could slide her hand down its cheek and under its chin to scratch it. It closed its eyes and ruffled the stubby pair of wings at its sides.

"You know, originally, we were going to have regular horses," Alastair gave a lesson in the creation of the creatures.

"Really?" Max asked as a solid black lagopin plodded its way over to him. "What made you choose something so fluffy?"

Ginger continued to pet the animal but craned her head back to listen.

"It was one of our designer's ideas actually." Alastair shoved his hands into his coat pockets casually. "I wanna say his name was Craig." He looked off into the distance as if he wasn't sure, but he went with it anyway. "Back before all this existed, we spent months coming up with the designs for all creatures to populate the world. We delegated the horses to him, but he took it in a different direction."

"And he just thought he'd create something cute?" Max assumed.

Corvin jumped in. "No, the lagopin isn't something new," he corrected. "I think they're based off a skvader, which was a hoax from the early 20th century. It was built by a taxidermist in Sweden using multiple animals. It's in a museum somewhere."

"Huh. I didn't know that," Alastair ran his hand up the

back of his neck and into his hair, "but when we logged into the Sphere to see the horse presentation." He paused. "Sorry, the Sphere was the testing platform we used back then." He glanced around at the others before continuing, "Anyway, we expected to ride a bunch of majestic steeds. Instead we got these goofy looking things." He smiled. "We were pissed at first, but with some convincing, we gave them a chance. After riding them, we were sold. The way they move is so unique. A plain old horse wasn't the same afterward."

"Plus, they're adorable." Ginger nuzzled her head into her new friend's furry cheek. She looked so happy that one might mistake her for a child who had just been given a pony for her birthday.

Max smiled at the sight.

The group paid an NPC and saddled up, Max choosing the black one that had approached him moments before, its color representing the creature's overall speed capabilities.

Farn followed his lead, selecting a similar one.

Max nodded with approval.

Kira though, despite being used to performing high-speed aerial maneuvers, had always been uncomfortable with riding another creature while traveling that fast. It didn't surprise Max when she picked a gentle looking runt, colored a dusty brown. The animal's face looked a little dumb. She climbed into the small saddle between its wings and hunched down low, holding on tightly to its harness. She probably planned to cling to the animal's back and hope for it to be over soon like usual.

Before heading out, Alastair stopped the team to feed each of their mounts a carrot that glowed a purplish green color to further increase their speed.

Max appreciated it.

Kira did not.

Then with an obligatory, "Yee-haw!" they bounded off in the direction of the area located on their map. Max looked back at Alastair who watched enviously as they vanished into the tree line. He felt a little bad for the man, but the feeling passed. It was hard to frown while riding a giant, winged black rabbit through a forest.

Max gripped the harness with both hands, steering his mount by shifting the weight of his body. He leaned forward toward the creature's ears and clicked his tongue twice in quick succession to signal his lagopin to increase speed. In the real world, rabbits only really have two settings. One being a slow and casual hop, and the other being frantic dash like a bat out of hell. It was a detail that their online counterparts shared. Which was why Max grinned like a madman as he demonstrated the reason that all lawn mowers have a hare icon next to their fastest setting.

"Oh, come on!" Kira shouted as he left her in the dust. She'd always kept her mount preferences set to auto-follow her party leader. It was a feature that allowed the fairy to cling to the animal with her eyes shut and her face buried in the fur of its neck without having to worry about steering. Unfortunately for her, this also meant that Max could make her ride as gentle or as rough as he chose, since her little runt would follow his path. His grin grew wider.

Farn, choosing not to use the auto-follow function, bounded close behind.

Max glanced back as she gave her mount the same double click of her tongue, pushing the animal to its top speed. The race was on.

Trees whipped by as Max slipped between them, his mount bobbing and weaving on its own, using its small wings to help stabilize tight maneuvers. Every now and then, he felt bark graze his feet and legs as he cut his turns close.

The tiny hairs on the back of his neck stood up as the *Shield* closed on him, Farn's midnight black mount gaining ground every second. He couldn't help but love the challenge as the darkness and lack of a developed path through the unused forest served to make things more interesting.

Ahead, the approaching ground gave way to a sharp decline. He didn't slow. Instead, he readied himself for the fall, whispering a pointless apology to Kira who he knew would be following in his path.

The animal's powerful hind legs pushed off, and for a moment, they were almost flying. Its stubby wings stretched as wide as they could, extending their leap and slowing the fall. Standing high in the stirrups while the air flowed past him, Max kept his legs loose to absorb the coming impact. He landed well, and his lagopin let out an excited squeal almost as if it, too, was enjoying itself.

Despite knowing that looking back would shave a few seconds off his lead, he couldn't resist. He had to see Farn take the jump, but when he looked, she wasn't there. Questions raced through his head. *Did she give up? Did she see the drop coming and get scared? Did she lose interest?* Then the sound of breaking twigs and the crushing of fallen leaves caused him to flip his head forward.

A black shape landed, kicking up dirt and stumbling before recovering, Farn on its back. She looked back at him with a wide smile.

Max's jaw dropped. She had leapt clear over him. The race was over, and in a way, he was glad he lost.

CHAPTER TWENTY-ONE

Max slowed his mount as they approached the search area on the map, eventually coming to a stop to allow the others who had trailed behind to catch up. A blanket of dense fog lowered their visibility to almost zero, making it even more important that he wait there. He and Farn meandered about, keeping an eye out for anything that looked out of place until the others arrived on the scene.

"You both suck," Kegan commented as he appeared through the fog.

Ginger agreed, straightening her hair which had gained a somewhat wind-blown appearance like she had been riding in a convertible.

"We got places to be. Can't spend all night waiting for all you slow people." Max shoved aside his cocky attitude as soon as Kira's mount came into view, sans its small passenger. "Crap. Did we lose her?"

The lagopin stopped short as the fairy raised her body which had been glued so tightly against its back that the two had almost become one. "No, you didn't," she said with as much annoyance as her voice could muster. "Not for lack of trying, though."

Farn lowered her head. "Sorry. We got carried away."

"That's okay." All traces of anger left her voice, though her continued glare at Max told him that he was not yet forgiven.

Max ignored the dissatisfied fairy and steered his mount to face the group. "Okay, we've got a pretty big area to search here. I say we spread out in a line and ride in a circle to cover the most ground." He waved one finger in the air, indicating a circle.

They followed his orders and moved into position, making sure to stay within earshot. The last thing they needed was one of them getting lost. The moon was doing what it could to light their way, but with the tree cover and the fog, their visibility had been cut drastically.

It wasn't long before the group found a large pond sitting in the middle of the search area, its edges surrounded by swamplands. The mounts hopped along, their progress slowing as the ground became soft and wet. Ginger frowned as her lagopin's fur became caked with mud and it stumbled in the muck. She reached forward to stroke it with her hand and whispered apologies in its ear, despite it not being real to begin with. Max lost sight of her after that.

He slogged through the seemingly endless swampland, hoping that each step would bring a dungeon entrance into view. None did. His mount struggled as its legs also sank deep into the wet ground, its belly dragging in the mud. He usually had little trouble separating the game world from reality, but now, a pang of guilt bit at his chest because of the ordeal that the fictional animals were forced to endure. He was also grateful, since without them, it would have taken several times longer to reach the area and even longer to search it on foot.

He scanned his surroundings, catching a glimpse of something moving in the murky water but failing to get a decent look through the fog. It rattled his nerves despite the knowledge that he was safe on his mount, since the monsters of Noctem ignored anyone riding atop one. They had always been the simplest way to make it through high-level areas without getting killed.

He scanned his surroundings but saw nothing that stuck out. He worried they might have passed the entrance without noticing. If the search took much longer, they would have to log out in shifts and try again later after resting. He shuddered at the thought of it. The idea of leaving two of his teammates in the swamp to wait for the others didn't sit well with him. He decided that if it came to that, he would take the first shift inside. After all, he was the one that got the party into this insanity in the first place.

His train of thought was broken by the sound of a low hissing, like air escaping from a leaky tire. Searching for the source, he turned his attention to a dead looking tree near the water's edge where a black snake the size of a boa constrictor was slithering up its trunk at a leisurely pace. He gave thanks again to his furry protector beneath him for keeping him safe.

The serpent turned toward him, lifting its head away from the tree a few inches and giving Max a better look at the creature. He steered closer, curious but not too concerned. The shape was indeed that of a snake, but from what he could tell, it had no mouth or eyes, just two nostrils from which the hiss emanated. It separated more of its body from the tree, moving toward him but making no motion to attack. He had never seen a creature like it before and wondered if it had been added by Carver for the quest.

He shifted in his saddle. "Why would he make a snake with no mouth?" Then panic alarms went off in his head as the answer hit him like a bolt of lightning. It wasn't a snake. It was a tail.

The hissing form whipped away as the concealed threat struck from below. Jaws came at him through swirling fog, a wide mouth filled with needle-like teeth, the bottom row splitting apart in the middle in an unnatural manner. An ear-splitting screech came from the creature as it rushed him. No, not him. His mount.

To his horror, it clamped down on the front leg of the rabbit and yanked. They toppled over, Max landing in the mud. His arms sank in to the elbow. The lagopin screamed, a sound never before heard in the world. It was like a squeal, combined with a howl, and merged with a child's cry. It cut through him, connecting with something instinctive deep inside, something primal that remained from the days of Neanderthals. Terror gripped him like a chain around his chest, cold links digging in as they took his breath away. He froze as the helpless animal squirmed in the monster's grip. There was no blood, but its flesh glowed red and the cracking of bones popped from the limb in the monster's mouth as the screaming continued without end.

The lagopin turned to Max for an instant, its eyes meeting his. In them, he saw fear. Real, honest to god fear, and in that fear, he saw himself. He hated it, struggled against it, forcing it down inside and locking it away so he could find the courage to climb up out of the mud. Lunging onto the animal's side, he grabbed the harness with one hand while drawing a pistol with the other. He fired several shots into the eyeless head of the creature.

It let go, sinking back into the swamp only to be replaced by another. It's webbed, frog-like hands stretched around his mount's back and abdomen, yanking the harness from Max's hand. Another came at them, grabbing the back end of the helpless animal and pulling it away.

He tried to hold onto the fur of its neck, but his fingers slipped through its muddy hair. For just a moment, he held the animal's face in his arms, its screams muffled by his chest as he hunched over it. His own head pressed between its large ears. "I'm sorry," Max choked without really intending to as the two creatures yanked at once. He lost his grip, and the lagopin was torn away, swallowed by the fog with only its screams and the sound of splashing reaching back toward him. Screams that brought tears to his eyes. Then there was silence.

It didn't last.

The monsters came for Max next. He scrambled backward like a crab, drawing his other pistol, the deep muck preventing him from regaining his footing and matting his hair against his face. He fired at the toad creatures from the ground, their insatiable mouths snapping at his feet. The only thing holding them back was his dwindling ammunition. Without an opening to reload, once he was out, it would be over. Then the slides locked back empty.

In desperation, he used a class skill by placing both pistols against his forehead and breathing the words, *Life Shot*. He snapped the slides back into place and continued to fire as the skill created rounds from his hit points, keeping him alive by draining his health with every bullet.

Less than a minute had passed since he first noticed the tail, but already, he was at his limit. There were too many for one person to take on. His health fell into the red, but he fired regardless as they closed in on him. Then, from behind, came the slopping sound of a lagopin running at full speed in the swamp. Through the air flew Farn, having leaped from the back of her mount. To Max, she seemed to appear from the fog itself as she landed sword first on top of one of the creatures. The rest of the team converged on his location almost at once.

Still on the ground, he yelled to the others. "They target the mounts!"

Horror washed over Ginger's face and she jumped down without hesitation, slapping the winged rabbit on the rear to give the command to return to the stable. Her furry friend took off at full speed.

The rest of the group did the same, despite the fact that losing the mounts put them at a disadvantage. It wasn't the best strategic move, but Max was relieved knowing that the rest of the animals wouldn't suffer the same fate as his. He never wanted to hear that scream again, and from the look on Ginger's face, neither did she.

Back together, they stood a chance. Kira set up a number of spells to bring Max back to full health as well as a few to boost the rest of the party's stats, her rapid casting drawing the attention of the monsters. She slipped behind Farn who took the hits to her shield and pulled their attention back to her. Ginger threw out a couple of stun mines to slow the creatures' advance while they waited for Kira to be able to cast again. Bursts of orange electricity pushed the toads back each time they triggered the items. Jumping into the fray, Corvin targeted the creatures, casting a few spells to weaken them as Kegan helped Max to his feet.

In the first few minutes, it seemed like they could hold their own against the endless supply of enemies, but as time went by, they were forced to fall back several times to put in some distance. It was then that Max noticed they were being pushed in one direction, south. They weren't escaping; they were being herded. He was sure of it. *But toward what? The boss? Was that possible? Was there no dungeon? Just this evil swamp?* It would make sense with Alastair's theory that Carver had no intention of letting them win, but something told him that wasn't right. When they saw the video at the start of the mission, Carver was a dick, but he hadn't seemed like he wanted them to fail. It was possible that the creatures pushing them southward might be his way of making sure that they found the dungeon entrance within the gloom of the fog. Like Carver wanted them rattled but didn't want to stop their progress.

No sooner than Max had the thought, his hopes were dashed as they hit a dead end. Their path blocked by a single, massive tree, his back pressed up against its rotting trunk. The smell of damp mold filled the air as the enemies seemed to double in number around them.

No longer herding, the monsters surrounded them. Shapes moved in the fog all around, impossible to count. There could have been twenty or a thousand. A chorus of screeching cries scraped against Max's mind like rusty nails on a chalkboard. There was no way out.

The creatures didn't attack all at once. It was more like they just wanted to keep them from running away. Then Max remembered Famine, the first Nightmare of the night. It had been a bell, and it had caught them off guard because it didn't look like the monster they expected it to. *So what if the boss here didn't look like one either?* At that, his eyes went wide with terror. There he was, pushed up against a giant twisting tree, almost the size of the bell. He was afraid to turn around but didn't hesitate. He looked up at its dead branches, a skeleton of something that once lived. He placed his hand against the black bark of its trunk. It was warm and wet, and almost seemed to be breathing. It had to be his imagination. At least he hoped it was.

He waited a moment. If it was a boss, it hadn't moved yet. Then Max aimed one gun at the decaying surface of the trunk, getting a few confused looks from his teammates who were still focused on the monsters. He fired, blowing a hole in the bark the size of his fist. Nothing happened. Then a sickly draft flowed from the hole. It was hollow! Relief washed over him as he realized what it was. It wasn't a boss at all; it was a dungeon entrance.

He called to Farn who didn't ask questions. She just started chopping. Moments later, the tree splintered as her blade hacked into it, sending bits of soft wood and rotting bark everywhere. Max leaned in through the hole, aiming his guns downward just in case. The inside of the tree dropped off into the ground. It was definitely an entrance.

Corvin pulled a small bottle from his pouch, shook it, and tossed it in as it lit up like a magical glow stick.

Max watched it fall as it slid off to one side, disappearing into the dark. "Only one way to know for sure," he said, climbing through the hole. He looked back to Kira who attempted to cast *Flight* only to find that the area didn't allow it. Apparently, she was the only one that could fly, her wings being the one method that wasn't blocked.

She motioned to go first, but Max stopped her. "It's too tight a space; if something's down there, we won't be able to get to you fast enough."

Kegan put another couple arrows in the enemies surrounding them. "Well, someone better get down there," he said over his shoulder before letting off another volley.

"Agreed," Max prepared to jump. "Watch my health. If I'm still alive in thirty seconds, follow."

Farn and Kira nodded.

Max took a deep breath and added, "Geronimo? I guess," as if asking a question more than anything else. Then, without wasting any more time, he leaped into the darkness.

CHAPTER TWENTY-TWO

Max fell a dozen feet before the wall of the dank pit curved off to form a crude slide. He shot downwards against the mud-slicked surface, cutting through the warm moist air like a bullet through flesh. An updraft hit him like the exhalation of some foul creature, its breath ripe with sickness. It was as if he had just jumped down the throat of the world itself. The descent was pitch black, and he struggled to keep track of how far he slid below the surface. He moved so fast that he didn't even have time to let out a sigh of relief when light from below rushed toward him. The steep incline decreased, curving off to align with the floor and dampen the inertia of his fall before spitting him out into a long hallway like a slide in some grotesque water park. He continued along the ground for at least twenty feet before finally coming to a stop.

Still covered in the mud of the swamp, Max slipped twice before getting to his feet. He glanced around the hallway in an attempt to get his bearings. It was far rougher than the Famine dungeon earlier. Its walls were made up of large stone blocks, stacked and cemented together with what looked like more mud. Dusty cobwebs covered nearly every surface, and torches lit the dim space from four sconces placed along the hall. Black char marked the ceiling above them as if they had been burning there for years.

Max walked back toward the entrance. He was alive which meant the others should be right behind him. Just as he remembered his own words telling them to follow, a chorus of screams echoed from above, growing louder as their source sped down the slide toward him. He took a stance, ready for anything as Ginger and Kegan rocketed into the hall, Corvin close behind. Max turned, allowing the first two to pass by him on either side, then jumped the third.

A gentle glow grew at the entrance, clearly Kira drifting down on her wings, but before she came into view, Farn sped past her into the hall.

She shifted her weight and rolled into a crouch, planting one knee on the ground, her hands outstretched for stability. She came to a controlled stop.

Max looked down at her as she lifted her head, and he offered his hand to help her up.

Finally, Kira floated in while Corvin assisted the others to their feet.

For the moment, none of the creatures seemed to be following, allowing the group to spend a brief period recovering from the fight above in relative safety. It had taken a lot out of them, in both mind and body.

Ginger stood with tears in her eyes, arms folded as if hugging herself. She looked to Max.

"You okay?" he asked, not knowing what else to say.

Before he could finish the question, she collapsed into him. "That scream ..." She sobbed without embarrassment. "Oh god, why? It hurt, " she continued, not really making any sense.

Unsure of what to do, Max just wrapped his arms around her as she clung to him, her face buried in his shoulder. He could feel her body shaking against his.

Farn stepped closer to Kira. The fairy responded by leaning against her.

No one spoke for a long while, not until Ginger had composed herself. "I'm sorry. I know it's not real, but—"

"It's fine." Max moved his hands to her shoulders and held her so he could look her in the eyes. As uncomfortable as he was consoling her, he understood how she felt. "I can't forget that scream either."

She dried her eyes on his scarf. "Thank you."

Everyone stood in the torchlight, each still covered in mud from the swamp. Well, all of them but Kira, whose dress and pants remained clean for the most part thanks to her wings keeping her out of the muck.

Max paced, looking the walls up and down before speaking. "A muddy swamp, horrible toad monsters, rotting trees, and a filthy dungeon filled with cobwebs," he observed. "I'm guessing the next Horseman is Plague."

"Looks like it," Kira blew out a long sigh, "and biblically speaking, it's Pestilence, by the way. Not Plague."

Max sighed back. "Since when are you a bible expert?"

"She's right." Farn stepped in. "I grew up in the south. Religion is kind of a thing there."

"Well, they mean the same thing," Max argued, "and that's harder to say, so we're calling it Plague."

"That makes sense." Corvin tossed a lemon drop into his mouth. "Also, our items are good by the way," he added, finding a silver lining in the situation.

"No *Flight*, though," Kira said, bringing back the glass half empty feeling by accident. "The spell's locked in my menu, and my dust doesn't seem to have any effect other than healing."

"Well, at least there's that," Farn said.

Kegan slapped dried mud from his pants. "Man, this place is a downer."

The party chuckled at his comment, as if drawing attention to the situation had helped them to face it and move on.

Max pulled a torch from one of the sconces since the path ahead was shrouded in darkness. "Can't go back. I guess we go forward."

The others followed his lead, taking torches one by one, all except Kegan and Kira, who needed both hands free to make use of their capabilities. Then they pushed onward, firelight cutting through the blanket of shadow ahead. It didn't take long before they hit a dead end.

The archway ahead was blocked by a solid slab of stone with two large cobweb-covered levers sticking out of the floor on either side. Max handed his torch to Ginger as he and Corvin brushed off the handles. Farn kept a watchful eye on the back, just in case.

Satisfied that enough of the dusty webs had been removed to give them an adequate grip, Max and Corvin pulled back on the handles. They didn't budge. Max struggled, only being able to move his lever a couple inches by placing one foot on the wall and pushing off with all his strength. In unison, they let go, Corvin hunching over to catch his breath.

"They move, but they're really heavy," Max said with a huff.

"Maybe they just take more than one person," Farn suggested, handing off her torch to Kegan and stepping to Max's side. They pulled the lever together, and with significant effort, it moved. Max heard the sound of mechanisms turning within the walls. Other than that, nothing happened, apparently needing both levers to be pulled at once.

A couple of empty sconces gave the rest of the group somewhere to put their torches as they approached the other lever. It took everyone to move the two devices. Well, minus Kira, of course. She was too small to be of much help, though she did offer some helpful tips like, "Put your back into it," and asked questions like, "Have you tried pulling harder?"

Max didn't find her to be as helpful as she seemed to think she was.

Finally, the second lever reached its furthest point with both Kegan and Corvin pulling while Ginger pushed with her legs, her back against the wall for leverage. A loud click-clack sound came from an unseen source, and the stone slab blocking their path began to rise. Then it stopped, opening a small gap underneath, barely big enough for one of them to slip through.

They released the levers and it dropped back down.

"What the hell!? We have to keep holding them?" Max kicked at one of the levers in disgust.

The others gave a united sigh at yet another aggravating design on Carver's part.

Max waved his hand in a circle to indicate for them to start over, and moments later, the gap reopened, the team holding the levers in place with a firm grip. "Can you see underneath?" Max grunted to Kira, who dropped to the ground and peered into the space.

"Crap," she said, sounding surprised. "It just keeps going." The light of the torches reached out but couldn't find the end. With nothing to see, she stood back up.

"Okay, let it down," Max instructed and everyone released the levers once again.

"I was hoping it was just a door that I could crawl under," Kira ran a toe along the bottom of the slab, "but it's more like a giant block covering the entire length of the hall. The space underneath just keeps going on like that."

"Damn." Max sat down on the floor to think. Then he noticed Kira fidgeting, her thumb tapping against her item bag. She was making a face that he recognized. It was the one she always made when she had an idea but didn't want to share it.

She spoke anyway, "I know I'm going to regret this, but I think I could still fit under it."

Max looked up at her with an expression that he felt was appropriate for such a terrible idea. "I don't think that's the best plan you've come up with. We don't know what's in there."

"True. But we have to assume there will be a lever on the other side to open it the rest of the way or, at least, some kind of clue to give us more information. We've seen puzzle-based dungeons before."

"Or the other side might be filled with more of those toad monsters," he responded, the group flinching at the mere mention of the creatures. "Also, you'll pop like a grape if we drop it."

"I know. But I trust you." She gave him a look of sincerity that drove the point home.

Max paused, then let out a long, defeated sigh before standing back up. "Alright, but if you run into trouble on the other side, you get in the air if you can and stay safe."

He signaled to the others to return to the levers, and the enormous block rose once again.

Kira dropped to the floor and snapped open her casters to activate a low-level spell, giving their crystals a brighter glow to light her way. Then without looking back at the others, she took one last deep breath. "See you on the other side."

CHAPTER TWENTY-THREE

Kirabell regretted suggesting the plan the moment she slipped her head into the gap, the danger of being crushed suddenly feeling real with the weight of the stone slab above her. Unable to fit her head in upright, she was forced to tilt it to one side, making things even more uncomfortable. Fear bubbled in the pit of her stomach as she slid her slender body into the space. She swallowed it back down, keeping it in check with her will. She was stronger than she looked, and she knew it. The fear subsided, slithering into the back of her mind where it waited, coiled and ready. The feeling of the unmoving stone against her back as she slipped forward reaffirmed the knowledge of what would happen if her friends let go.

Kira wasn't claustrophobic, or at least, she wasn't aware of it if she was. She'd never really been put in a situation that had tested her before. Sure, she'd hid in small places to jump out at Max, but she still had the ability to get out if she wanted. This was different. She couldn't turn over or even take a full breath, since there wasn't enough room to accommodate the expansion of her chest. The space was too small. She only made about ten feet before the realization hit her.

Oh shit! I am claustrophobic! The fear came for her again, and the strength she thought she possessed tore like wet tissue paper. It was as if it had never been more than a thin wrapper around her heart, hiding a soft, fuzzy center from herself as much as others. The shock of how fast panic hit her, took what little breath she had from her chest.

Kira wanted to turn back, even debated it. She tried to look behind but couldn't get the angle right. She froze, lying in the space, her head flat against the floor, each breath pushing dust into the air around her face.

Then she heard Max call out from the entrance, his voice distant, but echoing toward her. "You okay in there?"

Of course, she knew he could see her health on his wrist, so he must have known she was fine. It wasn't the question that really mattered. He was just reminding her that he was there. That she wasn't alone. It was as if he knew she was freaking out, like his bro sense was tingling. His words were meant to calm her. It worked.

Other voices called out, Farn and Corvin showing their concern.

She slowed her breathing, making sure her words came out clear as she called back. The last thing she wanted was quiver in her voice exposing how scared she really was. "I'm okay. Just … just taking a short break," she said as calmly as she could, regaining her composure, if only by a little.

Then with the voices of her friends encouraging her, she pushed forward into the dark. The soft glow from her wrists lit her way as she fought for every inch of progress, barely able to lift herself in the space.

The tightness of the gap gave her reason to be thankful that she hadn't created her avatar to be over-endowed in the chest area like many players. Her focus had been more concerned with function over form. After all, she hadn't been trying to make her character sexy, just unique and comfortable. Granted, on the petite frame of a fairy, her proportions fit a little too well. Thinking about it now, though, it didn't help her to stay calm in the darkness, so she kept moving, calling back to the others in the distance to keep her sanity.

Kira went on like that for at least another thirty feet, and still, there was no end in sight. Then a noise sprang out from inside the wall. She couldn't tell from where or even if she had imagined it or not. It was just a loud, ka-chunk, like a gear slipping. Her eyes widened as the panic rushed back at full force. *Did the others drop a lever?* The question shot through her mind like an arrow.

It was possible, her mind answered. They must have been struggling against the weight the whole time.

It didn't matter.

She had to move.

So move she did, too afraid of what might happen if she didn't. From there, her mind went blank. Her movements became frantic, and she twisted her waist, getting stuck for an instant as her hands slipped helplessly.

It didn't actually matter if she got crushed beneath the slab. Her real body, Seth's body, was safe back in the Nemo Unit. Kira was never real to begin with, just a character Seth played in a game, but in that moment, to her mind, her existence was undeniable. She was small, frail, and most of all, frightened. She didn't want to die. Not like that.

Again the sound from inside the wall reached for her, its echo slithering around her body like rotting vines, thorns of cold fear piercing her flesh. She struggled to move faster which only caused her breathing to grow more erratic. She inhaled too deeply, and the gap closed in on her as her chest expanded to fill the space. Again, she got stuck. She slipped, scraping her face on the ground as she squirmed. It didn't cause any real damage, though it rattled her further. She tried to expel the air from her body but wound up coughing as she exhaled too fast. The cough came out like a sob, making her aware of the tears filling her eyes.

The strange sound hit again, ripping through what was left of her as her mind failed to control her movements. She reached out for something to grab onto, despite knowing she would find nothing on the smooth floor. Her feet flailed, getting some momentum but getting them stuck just as often. Her heart raced, trying to tear itself out of her chest in an attempt to leave her dumb ass behind to die. The voices of her friends were no longer audible over the distance and the panicked sounds of her hands and feet scraping. She was alone.

Again came the sound. It might have been her imagination, but she thought she felt the stone slab above drop a bit against her rear as she slid forward. She cried out in a muffled yelp, followed by more coughing. Her out of control gasps stirred the dust around her face, getting it in her eyes and nose. More tears flowed.

Any second the slab would drop, she knew it. The dark space would never end. There was no way out. No hope. She would die there. The glow from her caster reflected against the bottom of the slab, and then it didn't. Her hand was out. She could feel it. There was open air ahead. She scrambled forward, foregoing the graceful movements that came naturally to her as a fairy.

Once out, she collapsed in front of the gap from where she came from. She had made it.

It was dark.

Too dark.

Without thinking, she cast a high-level light spell, throwing a ball of glowing energy into the air to illuminate the unknown room. It struck a low ceiling and bounced down to the floor, coming to rest a few inches above the stone. Alone in the room, she knew she should be looking for a lever to open the door, but she didn't. Instead, she just sobbed against the entrance, her arms wrapped around herself.

Kira thought about the last time she cried. It was years ago, in the real world, as Seth. It had been after he'd been forced to put his cat to sleep. He'd had the adorable thing for most of his life, but pets don't live forever, no matter how much you love them. He wasn't a child, though, and had known he shouldn't act like one, so he'd kept himself together throughout the procedure only to fall apart when he was alone.

Now, as a small creature huddled against a wall, she did the same, crying so hard that it choked her when she struggled to stay quiet.

When Ginger broke down and clung to Max a short while ago, Kira had thought that it seemed reasonable at the time, but now, with herself in the same situation, she just felt weak. Shame washed over her as she pulled her legs close and buried her face in her knees. She was just glad that no one was around to see.

Finally, after a minute or so of full weeping, she recovered enough to realize that the gap was still open, meaning that the others were still fighting to hold the levers back on the other side. Guilt stabbed at her breast as she dried her eyes and looked for a switch. She found it near the entrance, just where she expected to, a small handle protruding from a slot in the wall. It was the perfect size for her.

CHAPTER TWENTY-FOUR

Farnsworth stared at her hands as she gripped the handle of the lever, her arms feeling sore and exhausted. There was no way she was going to let go.

"Oh, god, how long is this going to take?" Kegan grunted as he clung to one of the devices.

Max said nothing, clearly focused on the task at hand.

Farn had passed her limit a while ago and was now holding the device back by sheer will alone.

She hadn't heard anything from the gap in almost a minute. Farn checked Kira's health. She was fine. Then, without warning, the levers released, moving past their stopping points as if all the resistance that she had been fighting against had vanished. The surprise drop caused the others to fall backward, their hands slipping from the handles.

Farn was the only one still standing, horror washing over her as the resistance returned and the lever pulled away, back to its starting position. She tried to stop it but couldn't. She looked to the gap, expecting it to slam shut at any moment. It didn't.

The party looked at each other in question. Then several loud noises sounded from the wall, followed by the motion of the slab rising up to ceiling height. They were already running before it even came to a stop, Farn and Max in the lead.

She expected to find Kira standing there on the other side, waiting and laughing about making them hold the levers for so long. Instead, they found her leaning against the wall next to a small switch. Her arms folded tight, holding her sides like she was cold. She looked away, in the direction of the far side of the next hallway, clearly trying to avoid eye contact with anyone. For a moment, silence engulfed the space.

"At least there aren't any monsters on this side," Max commented as if ignoring the mage altogether.

Farn assumed he was trying to distract the group from his partner's condition and give her time to recover, so with that, she moved onward without saying more.

The group followed Max down the hall, the fairy trailing behind. Farn hung back to walk next to her.

Kira looked down at the ground and shuffled along beside her, then stepped closer without saying anything.

Farn felt Kira's shoulder brush against her own. She was shocked to feel her shaking. She looked down, and Kira glanced up before turning away just as fast. It had only been for a second, but Farn saw so much in her eyes. She looked desperate for comfort, like she wanted nothing more than to be held by someone. Farn raised her hand to place it on the shaken fairy's back but stopped just short, afraid to actually touch her, afraid she might make things worse. Then she let it fall back to her side.

The hall widened, and the ceiling grew higher, relieving the claustrophobic feeling of the place. Farn noticed Kira breathing deeper, her shoulders relaxing now that the walls weren't closing in on her.

Max pointed toward the ceiling. "I hope this big hallway is a design choice and not Carver making room for large monsters."

It was a bad joke, but Kira smiled anyway. It made sense. She probably just appreciated the distraction.

Kegan jogged to the front of the group and turned. "I kind

of hope we do run into some enemies. I have a couple new arrows to try out."

Max looked at him sideways, "Really? Did you break down and buy those feathers from Ginger?"

"Not all of them. Just enough to craft two." Kegan pointed to his quiver, where a couple arrows glinted in the firelight with silver fletching. "I wasn't going to pay that much for all of them - no matter how cool they are."

"Oh, you will." Ginger rubbed her hands together like a villain. "You can't resist me forever."

"What do the arrows do?" Corvin asked out of curiosity.

Kegan shrugged. "No idea. They don't even have a name in their description."

"Must be a new item." Corvin sounded impressed.

"I know." Kegan clapped his hands together. "Apparently, no one's ever crafted them before. According to my journal, I get to name them."

"Any ideas?" Corvin sped up to catch up to him.

"Nah, I'm going to wait 'til I know what they do first."

"Hold up," Max butted in, cutting the chatter as they came to a split junction with two paths heading in opposite directions.

There was a brief debate on which path to take, but strangely, Corvin was the one to decide. His authority on the subject came from a piece of chalk that he pulled from his pouch. He drew a simple arrow facing right to mark the direction that they chose. Not long after, they hit another junction.

Max let out a sigh as it became apparent what kind of dungeon they were in. "It's a labyrinth." His arms dangled in front of him.

"So much for getting this one done quickly." Kegan held out his hands empty as if giving up.

Corvin abandoned the idea of drawing arrows at each of the forks in the path and just placed the chalk against the wall as they walked. That way, as long as they followed one side, they would be able to find their way through without having to think about it. It was cheating a little, but it was also the fastest solution.

Max held his torch in one hand and holstered his gun with the other. The previous dungeon had lacked any form of monsters other than the boss, so it stood to reason that this one might be the same. He relaxed and placed one hand to his chin. "So I have a question."

"Yeah?" Kira responded, her voice coming out weak.

He continued, "Now, this is really just me thinking out loud. But the gap under that door was just big enough for you to fit through."

Kira sighed and rolled her eyes.

Farn took over in an attempt to spare her from being involved in the conversation and thinking about her ordeal. "What's your point?"

"How did he know?" Max answered her question with a question.

Farn wasn't sure what he meant by it.

"What I mean is, this whole quest was something Carver set up way in advance and hid within the system years ago, so it had already been here for a while before tonight."

"Okay," Farn answered, still not quite seeing what he was getting at.

Corvin jumped in. "You're wondering how he could have known to set the gap at that height when most players wouldn't fit through it?"

"Exactly!" Max turned and walked backward to face the others as he spoke. "How could he have known that we would have a fairy in our party that could squeeze through when all other races would have just gotten their fat asses stuck?"

"Hey! My ass isn't fat." Kegan spun around to look at his own butt.

Everyone else ignored him.

Corvin stopped walking for a moment. "It could be that the door was designed so that it would only open just enough for our smallest party member. Carver probably set it with a variable to keep the space as small as possible to maximize the psychological effect."

"Well, it worked. That was easily the worst experience of my life." Kira shuddered and stepped closer to Farn.

This time, Farn raised one hand to Kira's back, making contact and giving a gentle pat in an attempt to console her. With that, the tension in the fairy's body melted.

Kira returned the gesture with an appreciative smile, the slight physical contact clearly doing wonders for her mood.

Then, almost on cue, they came to another door.

CHAPTER TWENTY-FIVE

Max winced as Kira's face fell at the sight of another stone slab blocking their path. He was pretty sure he knew what she was thinking. She was debating on if it would be okay to turn tail and run, though he also knew she wouldn't, not after going through so much already.

To the side of the door was a single lever. Max gripped with both hands, not wanting to drag things out. He pulled back with all his strength, expecting the same struggle as before but was caught by surprise when the lever slid back without resistance. He stumbled backward, letting out a sudden, "Fuc'," as he lost his balance.

The lever snapped back to its starting position as he fell into Kegan, who did nothing to catch him as he slid down to the floor. Max grabbed at the *Leaf's* sash for stability, almost pulling his pants down.

"Yar! What the hell?" the elf squealed as he struggled to hold them up.

"Sorry." Max released the *Leaf's* clothing.

Kegan straightened himself out. "You should be. I'm not ready for that kind of relationship. I mean, sure, maybe I've thought about it, but really, there's just too much of an age gap between us. What would people say?"

Max ignored him as he got back up, hearing a couple snorts of laughter from Ginger. He ignored her as well and went back to the lever. Again, it moved easily. A loud metallic clank came from the walls, and the slab began to move.

Relief swept over Kira's face as it rose higher than before, continuing until it was even with the ceiling. It was still a massive slab of stone hanging above their path that could crush them if it fell, but at least there was enough room to walk under it upright.

Max released the lever, half expecting the path to slam shut the moment he let go. It didn't.

Not fully trusting the passageway, Max decided to go through in two groups. Corvin, Ginger, and Kegan went first, leaving Max and Farn to tend to Kira, who still seemed a little shaken.

If he was honest with himself, Max regretted letting her crawl into the gap earlier, despite it being the only way to proceed. He hadn't thought it was that big of a deal at the time, but in the years that he had spent with Kira, he had never actually seen her upset in either world - real or virtual. Annoyed sure, but never on the verge of tears. For it to affect her that much, the ordeal must have been far worse than he imagined.

He felt stupid, almost like he had taken her for granted. He wanted to ask how she was doing, but he had trouble expressing his concern. They were, after all, bros, and bros didn't ask about their feelings. Instead, he waited until an awkward silence fell over the three of them, which wasn't long. Then he let out a quiet sound from the corner of his mouth. An unmistakable sound executed with precision.

Farn looked at him sideways with one of her eyebrows raised as the slow, airy sound of a quiet fart slipped from his lips.

Kira snorted a laugh as it caught her off guard. "That was a good one."

He laughed too. "Yeah, I totally nailed it."

Kira repeated the noise, this time getting a chuckle out of Farn as well, who made an attempt of her own. It came out a squeaky with an unexpected turn at the end that got a big laugh.

Impressed by her version, Max spent the next few moments trying to imitate it. The somewhat immature noises grew louder as he demonstrated the healing power of fart sounds.

Kira smiled, looking more like her usual self. Then, from down the hall in the direction of the other half of their party, came the loudest sound of flatulence that Max had ever heard in his life. The source of which became clear when he heard Ginger, of all people, laughing.

Max turned to look down the hall, making out her figure in the firelight of the torches. He almost couldn't believe his eyes as she placed both hands against her mouth to produce another textbook example of the standard elementary school fart noise. She had raised two kids after all. She must have learned things. It echoed down the hall toward them which only increased the silliness factor of it.

Kegan called out, "I can't believe that I'm the one who has to say this, but if we get attacked by some kind of monster because you guys gave away our position with farts, it won't go over well."

"Sorry," Max apologized, followed by a few giggles from Farn, the musical quality of Kira's laugh joining in. It was good to hear again.

"Anyway, we're out the other side!" Kegan shouted back.

Max responded with a simple, "Okay," and entered the passage with Farn and Kira in tow. He moved quickly, not wanting to take his time in the situation. Kira walked in the middle, as if it was safer, despite the fact that the formation would do nothing if the slab above them were to fall. Max tried his best to forget about it, telling himself that the path had remained open for a few minutes already, so it would probably stay that way. He was wrong.

A loud ticking began from an unseen source inside the walls at regular intervals, then faster. Max had played enough puzzle games in his life to know what the sound meant. It must have been triggered when the last of them entered the passage. The slab was on a timer, and it was running out.

Max turned to Kira and told her to leave them behind in a tone that told her not to argue.

She obeyed without protest, sprouting a glowing pair of wings and taking off down the hall, leaving a trail of magic in her wake as he and Farn ran for their lives behind her.

He threw down his torch in the hope that it would help him move.

Farn did the same and as the ticking grew faster.

Together they sprinted toward the flickering light of their friends at the end of the passage. *Almost there!* Just twenty more feet. They could make it. Then the ticking merged into one long buzz as the intervals between them disappeared. They had seconds at best.

A loud bang came from behind, followed by another, causing Farn to glance back at the slab hanging over the hall. She gasped. "It's falling in segments!"

Max didn't bother to look back, fearing the loss of a few precious milliseconds. He just assumed from the terrified expression on her face that it was bad and that he didn't need to see it, too. From the sound of the impact of each section slamming into the floor, there had to be enough force to make sure no one would recognize his body if he got caught under one. He ran faster.

The air pushed past him, thick and moist, as it was displaced by the falling blocks. It felt like the dungeon itself was breathing down his neck. The faces of the others became visible as they approached the end, each a shade of ghostly white. The section behind fell just as Farn passed out from under it. Max couldn't be sure, but he thought he heard it whack the tip of her sword's sheath on its way down. Then the final segment released.

The solid block of stone fell in what, to Max, seemed like slow motion as his mind raced at speeds faster than ever before. He jumped with everything he had, shoving Farn with one hand. Not enough to knock her over but just enough to give her a slight boost of speed. They made it just as the last slab fell into place, grazing Max's boot as he leapt to safety.

He rolled and shifted his weight when he hit the ground, making use of his momentum to help him recover. He came to rest upright with one knee planted to the ground. Then there was silence.

It was dark, and the loss of two of their torches made it hard to see more than a few feet in the large room.

"Well, that sucked." Max rested to catch his breath. "Starting to feel like that's my new catchphrase," he added before looking around the room for Kira.

"I got a problem here!" she yelled to the rest of the party from somewhere above. Max looked up into the shadowed space of the room's high ceiling, the soft glow of the fairy's wings being the only source of light illuminating her figure. She seemed to be stuck in the air, one arm behind her back while her wings buzzed uselessly. With her free hand, she cast a light spell, throwing a ball of bright energy into the air. Max wished she hadn't.

A massive spider web stretched across the ceiling of the room, complete with an equally massive spider in one of its corners. Its legs were pulled in tight to its body as if sleeping, but when enticed by the vibrations of Kira's wings, it moved. Eight legs extended, far longer than what he expected. It was huge, like a cargo van with fangs.

"Holy crap! What the hell?" Kira yelled as the light of her spell reflected in the monster's eight gigantic eyes.

Max drew his guns. "Don't worry; we got you!" he shouted to let her know he was there. The webbing around her was probably bringing the poor fairy right back to the claustrophobic feeling from before. He fired a few rounds at the spider, hoping they would at least push the thing back.

Kegan did the same, but the spider only winced.

Kira threw out a couple of *Pulse* spells aimed at its face, which did no damage but bought a few more valuable seconds.

"Hey! You don't want that scrawny thing!" Farn shouted at the beast with her taunt active to give the words more weight to the spider. It looked at her for a moment but, eventually, turned back to the already captured prey.

"I'm petite, not scrawny!" Kira yelled back as a bullet passed by her head so close that it displaced her hair. "The hell, man!" she shouted at Max while the spider crept closer.

"Hold still, will you!" he shouted back as he fired at the webbing around her. She locked her body in position, putting her trust in his aim. He was just glad the webbing was thick enough to target.

Kegan focused on buying time, and the creature took a critical in the abdomen. "The underside has a weak point. It's small, right between the second set of legs," the *Leaf* called out.

"Perfect. I almost have Kira free," Max called back as the helpless fairy struggled to lean away from the enemy. He kept firing until, finally, a section of the web broke free, and Kira dropped out, dangling from one last troublesome thread.

Kira spun in the air upside down, causing a portion of the loose web to wrap around her, securing her arm to her back and her legs to each other. "I'm not sure how this is helping!" she yelled as the room spun around her.

Max aimed, taking in a slow breath as he took out the last strand, causing Kira to release an uncharacteristic scream, that probably surprised herself as much as Max, as she dropped.

Considering that the fall could very well kill her with her lack of hit points, Farn dashed in to catch her. Well, catch wasn't really the right word. It was more like a backward dive to break her fall. The lightweight fairy landed on top of her, still bound with webbing. Farn wrapped her arms around her like an action hero to make sure she was safe, Kira's head resting under her chin.

Before either of them could recover, the spider dropped

down to the floor with a loud thud, still focused on the tasty morsel flopping around on top of the *Shield*. "Oh crap," they blurted out in unison.

Max reacted on instinct, jumping between them to block the creature's path. He hoped he could take a couple hits before he had to worry. He pumped a few rounds into the thing as it struck him in the leg, its contact dealing poison on top of damage. His health dropped by almost half as the status settled into the pit of his stomach, making him feel sick while depleting his remaining hit points little by little. He ignored it and stood his ground, firing another few shots. The spider wound up again, its other leg coming at him faster than he expected, and suddenly, the world winked out of existence.

For a moment, Max thought he was dead as he floated in a void of endless gloom. Then, a fraction of a second later, his feet hit the ground. He lost his balance and fell back on his rear. His stomach lurched from the poison status. He glanced around, finding Farn standing in the space where he had been a moment before. He watched in confusion as she took a hit to her shield. Then it dawned on him. He held up the bracelet that she had given him just as one of the beads faded from black to red. She had used her newfound Shift ability to get him out of danger. *They must consume a bead each time they activate*, he thought, understanding what the item's limited-use description meant.

Max relaxed as Farn stood, stopping the creature from getting anywhere near the fairy behind her, still helpless on the ground. Then a heavy blow impacted with the light of her shield, sending sparks flying as it pushed her off balance, leaving her side open. She tried to deflect the next attack with her sword, but it grazed her in the ribs, putting her in the same position Max was in a moment before. She needed help.

He pushed himself off the ground and pulled a health vial from his bag with the intent of tossing it up to the *Shield*. Then he stopped and burst out laughing.

Kira gave him an annoyed glare as she squirmed around on her stomach and struggled to get to her feet. Once upright, she wasted no time, her free hand swiping her spell-craft menu open above her head. She must have selected the glyphs from memory because she couldn't have seen the menu at such an odd angle. She tossed out a quick heal spell to get both Farn and Max out of danger and followed it with a more complex combination to remove the poison and stop them from getting it again.

Farn smiled back to Kira as the poison's effect faded but had trouble containing her laughter at the sight of the uncoordinated fairy hopping around with one arm flailing over her head.

Kira attempted to cast another heal but fell over, a short, "Yarr," escaping her mouth as she dropped to the ground.

Kegan fired several shots, failing to get a critical, then erupted in full guffaws when he saw Kira inching toward Ginger like a worm trying to escape a bird. Instant karma kicked in as the spider took a swing at him while he was distracted.

"A little help?" Kira called to Ginger who lent a hand in freeing her, laughing the whole time.

Even Corvin let out a chuckle at her expense.

Clearly, the fairy was not pleased. "You're all massive jerks, and I hope a spider crawls in your mouth while you're sleeping!" Kira shouted as she got to her newly freed feet, one arm still stuck to her back. She threw out another light spell to replace the first, which was beginning to die out. Then Ginger continued working to release the impatient fairy's arm.

Kegan, still chuckling to himself, called out a warning, "I'm using a silver arrow."

Max ducked his head and fell back to a safe position just in case the *Leaf's* new item turned out to be some kind of explosive.

Kegan stood proud, taking aim at the spider's weak point, just beneath its head. He drew back his bow and held it to make sure his aim was true. Then he fired.

In the moment that followed, a few things happen. First, the arrow flew straight into the spider's underside. Next, the same arrow bounced off harmlessly just before coming to a stop on the floor beneath the monster. Max shifted his view back to Kegan, who looked back at him, equally confused as his body began to glow before imploding into a single point of energy that streaked straight toward the spider. The terrified *Leaf* burst back into existence under the spider holding the fired arrow in his hand, its silver feathers fading back to a dull gray color.

"Huh," Max mumbled as he realized that Kegan had both discovered his own shift ability and teleported himself directly into danger.

Kegan let out a string of sounds, none which formed any words, though Max assumed from the *Leaf's* flailing limbs that, if translated, he was saying something close to, "Eek! A spider!" He followed this up by stabbing the beast with the arrow. It was obvious he was out of ideas. Fortunately, he hit its weak point, causing the spider to rear up in an attempt to impale him with its legs on its way back down.

Max took the opportunity to fire two rounds into the soft spot on the creature's underbelly. It reeled from the damage, giving Kegan an opening to roll to the side out of danger.

From there, the *Leaf* scooted back on his rear, repeating the words, "Oh shit," as he fired arrows one after another, landing a respectable amount of hits before getting to his feet.

Max reloaded. "It wasn't pretty, but you did some solid damage there."

"Yeah, well, I try," Kegan replied, failing to convince everyone that he had done it all on purpose.

Farn could really give him lessons.

Complete once again, Max and the team fell into formation around the spider. It hit hard, but Farn was doing an excellent job of keeping it focused on her. It was tough, but with an organized party, it proved manageable, provided no one else teleported into the thing's face.

It's fights like this that make it clear why we're the right team for the mission, Max thought. Not long after, they brought down the beast, Ginger snatching an item from the thing as it fell. She inspected her prize as Kira recovered everyone back to full health.

"Oh, gross," Ginger commented as she read the description of the spider egg that she now held in her hand. She wasn't about to throw away a rare item, though, gross or not. She shrugged and placed it in her pouch for later, regardless of the ick factor.

Max holstered his pistols just as the game's system played a few happy sounding tones in his ear, inaudible to the others. "Yes!" he shouted. "I just leveled."

"Seriously?" Ginger asked, sounding surprised. "The experience has been terrible all night."

Max grinned and took out his journal. "Yeah, but I was close to begin with. Now let's see …" he trailed off, adding, "Well, crap," a moment later. "I've been saving my points to learn a new skill, and I just got enough."

"So? That sounds like a good thing," Ginger commented.

"It is. But now I'm torn. I could just dump it all into dex to boost my damage instead. I'm not really sure what I'm gonna need tonight."

"What skill is it?" Corvin asked.

Max flipped a page. "It's just level five for *Custom Rounds*. It lets me make explosive bullets. It would be good for crowd control, but it's not really ideal for single bosses like the Nightmares."

"So just save the points and decide later," Kira chimed in. "That's what I do."

"Yeah, maybe," Max accepted.

"Oh, speaking of," Kegan took out his own journal. "I have an item to name."

He spoke aloud as he wrote.

Item name: *Shift Arrow*
Type: Consumable
Description: Do not shoot at spiders. That is all.

He snapped his journal shut and shoved it in his bag before gesturing toward Kira. "You got a thing in your hair. I think it's webbing,"

"Oh," she responded, running her hand through her hair in an attempt to find it. "Did I get it?"

"No, the other side," he answered.

She tried again. "How 'bout now?"

"No, it's higher."

This time she brushed past it, removing some but not all. "Good?"

"No, there's still some."

She let out an aggravated groan and squirmed in a ridiculous but adorable manner. "Would someone just get it out," she cried, issuing an order rather than a request.

"Come here," Farn said in a warm tone that shut down the fairy's attitude as she beckoned her closer. Kira shuffled over, head lowered to give a better angle. She looked up with her huge blue eyes, drawing a smile out of the *Shield* that Max found charming.

Ginger interrupted the moment, "You know I love you, Kira, but there are times when I really hate how cute you are."

Turning around so that Farn could check the back of her head for more of the dusty webs, Kira wiggled her butt in a sort of dance. "Sorry, can't help it."

Ginger stuck out her tongue. "Ugh, now I'm gonna be sick." Then she smiled reluctantly. "But I'm glad to see you're back to normal. Now, if only I could convince you to put that ass to work at the club."

Kira froze at the implications on the statement, probably regretting the butt wiggle.

Max shook his head and shoved his journal back into his bag. "Come on; we got Nightmares to kill, people." He walked toward the room's exit, followed by the rest of the party.

Kira hurried back to his side, her face still a healthy shade of pink.

CHAPTER TWENTY-SIX

Kirabell followed Max deeper into the labyrinth, fortunately not running into any more giant spiders. They did, however, come to another dead end in a large room, complete with another slab of stone blocking their path.

"Okay. This is getting old." Kira sighed as the dungeon began to feel a bit repetitive. It seemed like it had been hours since they had left Alastair back at the lagopin stable. She looked at the mission clock. "Crap, I've been logged in for twelve hours, this one better not take much longer."

"All the more reason to get this over with." Max stepped up to the single lever to the side of the door. He pulled, probably expecting it to move like the last one. It didn't. The others piled onto the device. Again, it took all but Kira to budge the thing. Not that she would have been any help.

As the lever clicked into place, she held her breath and watched the door, hoping that it would at least open all the way. It didn't. In fact, it didn't open at all. Instead, she heard the sound of stone moving against stone, followed by the sound of water coming from behind as a small square hole opened in the floor.

Still holding onto the lever, the others craned their necks back to face the opening, puzzled expressions all around.

"You mind checking that out? We kind of have our hands full." Max grunted to Kira.

She sighed and begrudgingly stepped over to the hole, water sloshing around inside it. "It's just a hole." She dropped to her knees and dipped her fingers in to splash around a bit.

It was warm, almost inviting. She reached in with one arm to see how deep it was. The thought crossed her mind to pretend that something had grabbed her. She decided against it. It wasn't that the situation was too serious for the prank, that she was too mature, or even that she wasn't in the mood after going through so much, but simply because she felt it was too obvious.

"Anything?" inquired Max.

She felt around. "Yeah, one side is open a couple feet down, I think it might be a tunnel. Maybe the way through," she said with little enthusiasm.

"Okay, get out of there. We're gonna let go of this," he instructed. They released the lever, and the hole closed again.

Max turned back to Kira. "Man, this dungeon has been hard on you."

"Yeah," she answered, rolling her eyes. She could guess what he was going to say next.

"I am really sorry," he prefaced his next sentence.

"I know, just say it," she got straight to the point.

He sucked his teeth and made a face prepared for the worst. "Yeah, we're gonna need you to go in there."

"And there it is." She dropped her head in submission. "Sure, why not?"

Corvin folded his arms, looking pensive. "I'm guessing that this is another one of those things where Carver is forcing our weakest player into something traumatic like before."

"Well, the joke's on him. I'm a fantastic swimmer." Kira stood with her hands on her hips and puffed up a bit. "I did swim team all through high school."

"That's right. Although, you didn't win much," Max added.

"Well, win or lose, what's important is that you play the game. Also, shut up. I seem to recall someone trying out for football and getting their ass handed to them."

"That's fair." Max shrugged.

She started to say something back but stopped as a thought occurred to her. Horror fell across her face as her body flooded with nervous tension.

"What?" Max asked.

She paused before speaking, "I'm gonna need you guys to turn around."

"Why?"

The question annoyed her. "Because I don't know how far that tunnel goes, and the amount of time I can stay underwater is limited by how much gear I have equipped. Plus, it's hard to swim while fully clothed." She fidgeted with her dress. "I didn't exactly think to pack a bathing suit in my item bag before we left."

A laugh erupted from Kegan. "Oh, no way. I gotta see this."

She shot him an angry look. "I'm not kidding."

"Seriously? It's an avatar?" Max held out a hand in her direction. "Who cares?"

Kira avoided making eye contact. "Look, it weirds me out, okay. And the fact that it weirds me out weirds me out even more. So just turn around, and let it go," she demanded in a tone that made it clear that she was quite serious and did not want any further discussion.

Ginger stepped in, waving her finger in a circle. "You heard her, guys. Turn around. This ain't no burlesque show."

Corvin did so without comment while the other two groaned in protest as they complied.

Kira mouthed the words, "Thank you," to Ginger before starting to disrobe. A moment later, she handed her item bag and pants to the *Coin*, who folded them neatly. Now standing there in just a dress, Kira couldn't help but feel a bit vulnerable, the high slits on her sides revealing her hips and thighs. She continued, taking a deep breath as she pulled the remaining fabric up and over her head.

She had never gone through the trouble of customizing her avatar's underwear as she had not expected anyone to ever see them. This left her in the fairy's default garments that some game designer thought would be appropriate. As such, they were nothing fancy. On top was a simple rectangle of white fabric attached to thin straps that looped around her back and neck to conceal her chest, the size of which didn't require anything more in terms of support. On the bottom was just a plain white pair of panties, cut low to a point where they were almost scandalous. It was worth noting that the word 'panties' was one that Kira had never felt comfortable saying and therefore avoided at all costs.

Overall, as far as undergarments went, they were nothing fancy, but they were also more than a little revealing. So if she felt exposed in just a dress the moment before, she was pretty much on display now, her face showing as much of her emotions as her lack of clothing showed skin.

Farn let out a surprised, "Oh," and glanced around, eventually resigning to turn around and stand with the guys. They looked to the side at her in question, but she just gave them an awkward shrug.

"Hey, no peeking over there," Ginger commanded, noticing the guys' heads turning.

"Hey, Kira," Kegan said without looking back.

"Yeah?" She held her arms at her sides, unsure what to do with them.

"I just want you to respect the restraint that I'm showing by not turning around. Because I really want to."

Ginger smacked him on the back of the head before giving her attention back to Kira. "Alright. I'll hold your gear for you since you won't be able to get it back out if you put it in your inventory."

Kira thanked her before turning to the men. "Okay, let's

hurry up and pull that thing and get this show on the road," she said, referring to the lever.

"That's what—" Kegan started to say but was once again smacked by Ginger before he could finish.

The others converged around the lever, being careful not to look in Kira's direction. With some effort, the stone panel in the floor slid open once again, leaving her to stare at the water's surface.

The warm, moist air caressed every inch of her, sending a tingling sensation through her body that was a little too intimate. "Have I mentioned that I hate this place?" Kira added before dipping one foot in the water. At least it wasn't cold.

She threw another ball of light in first, feeling relieved when she saw it reflect off the walls of the inside of the underwater tunnel. It looked big enough to move around in without trouble, so her newfound claustrophobia shouldn't be an issue. She sat down on the edge, letting her legs dangle in the pool. The stone floor beneath was uncomfortably warm against her skin. She slid into the water up to her neck, holding onto one side with her hands.

Now that she was submerged, Max looked back to her. "Be careful."

She nodded back, biting her bottom lip, then ducked under. The darkness was chased away by her light spell and the soft glow of her casters which were now the only pieces of equipment she had on other than a few rings and an anklet on each foot.

She'd gone swimming once before in game. It had been in a dungeon that required the entire party to traverse a small underwater cave, which she had done clothed since it wasn't that far. Despite that, she almost hadn't made it back then. For the most part, swimming in Noctem was the same as swimming in the real world. Well, almost the same. The major difference was that she didn't feel the pressure to breathe since the system governed the need of oxygen differently while underwater. The main reason being that if a player was down for too long without the system's help, they could literally drown. The mind would create a realistic sensation of their death before disconnecting them. Kira assumed it had been decided that would be too traumatic for a game. Instead, they had an imposed simple time limit. Once it was reached, she would just lose twenty percent of her hit points every ten seconds until they hit zero. So, in total, she could stay under for about three minutes while unencumbered before resulting in an instant death and disconnect.

Back when she had swum through the cave before, she only had a minute of air since she had worn her full gear in. Now, wearing almost nothing, she had plenty of time which took some of the pressure off. She swam well, and there were no monsters, so for once, things were easy on her. She actually kind of enjoyed herself.

CHAPTER TWENTY-SEVEN

The lever was heavy. So heavy, in fact, that it took everyone to hold it in place - some even holding onto each other like a human chain when room on the handle became limited. It was a point that made Corvin more than a little uncomfortable as Ginger wrapped her arms around his waist and pressed her breasts against his back. He understood that she didn't really care about that sort of thing, but still, for him, it felt weird.

It wasn't so much that he thought Ginger was hot. Well, he did. Anybody would. She was gorgeous. It was more that after meeting her, he knew she was almost old enough to be his mother. Which was even stranger considering that he was adopted and had never even had a mother. Sure, he loved both of his fathers. He had put them through a lot over the last few years, and they had always stuck by him. But that was really beside the point. No, the point was that meeting her out in the real world had caught him off guard. Actually, it wasn't just meeting her, it was meeting everyone.

He wasn't sure why, but he had always assumed that at least Max and Kira were close to his age. So it was jarring to find out that not only was he wrong, but that he was the youngest of the group by far. Even worse, he was closer in age to Ginger's children than to any of the others, which left him feeling like he should be sitting at the kids' table. He couldn't help but doubt his placement in the party. There must have been someone more experienced than him. He cringed, the thought threatening to send him into a downward spiral of mental anguish. It didn't help that his tail kept brushing against the inside of Ginger's thigh, making her chortle in his ear. He tried his best not to think about it.

Without the use of party chat, they struggled to hold the small hole open just in case there was an emergency and Kira needed to come back for air. Max had told them he was afraid that if they let it close, she might return to find a dead end.

The way that Max worried about his friend was cool. That's when Corvin realized that it wasn't Kira that they should've been worrying about.

Two massive sections of the wall opened on either side of the room - most likely triggered by the progress that Kira was making in the water below. He looked at the open spaces for a moment, foolishly hoping that it was nothing to worry about. His hopes were lost when two massive spiders, just like the one before, emerged.

"Seriously?" Max cried, glancing back at the hole they held open. "We're going to have to let go and hope for the best."

"Wait," Corvin heard himself say as he spoke up without thinking.

The others looked at him all at once, catching him off guard. He didn't offer an explanation. Instead, he just shoved his hand into his item bag and pulled out a small stone, holding it out in front of Max's face like an offering of food at a petting zoo.

"Nice." The *Fury's* face lit up, recognizing the item as an echo stone. He thanked him with a quick, "Good thinking."

Corvin closed and opened his hand twice in quick succession, activating the enchantment on the item.

Being mostly used for distraction purposes, an echo stone

had the ability to record audio and play it back on a loop. One would imprint a sound of their choice and throw it in another direction to draw enemies away, but Corvin had something different in mind.

As prompted, Max proceeded to yell into Corvin's hand to convey a sense of urgency. "We got two spiders here, hurry! We won't last long!"

That's an understatement, Corvin thought, knowing that they would be done in pretty fast without someone to heal and remove the poison effects.

They released the lever just as the spindly legs of the beasts came into range. Corvin made a break for the pool of water, hoping to get close before it closed. He didn't think he had the athletic ability to make the shot if he threw it, but in the end, he didn't have a choice. He let the echo stone fly, shouting out a loud, "Yes!" when it dropped into the space with a quiet plop. He hoped that the water would carry the stone's message to Kira, like a whale singing to another in the ocean. He pumped his fist once in victory. It was an uncharacteristic gesture for him, but he had let his excitement get the better of him. Then he ran for his life like a frightened mouse.

"What's the plan here?" Farn asked as soon as Corvin made it back to the group.

Max paused as if coming up with things on the fly. "Umm, we run around in circles and stay away from them as long as we can until Kira gets the door open."

"Seriously?" Ginger questioned, her tone rising.

"What if she doesn't make it to the other side?" Kegan added.

"She will; don't worry," Max answered as if it were a fact.

It really was cool, thought Corvin again, seeing how sure Max was that the fairy would make it. Then Max fired a few rounds behind him without even glancing back to aim. *Yeah, definitely cool.*

Farn looked back. "They're gaining on us!"

"Damn, these things are fast," commented Kegan, stating

the obvious.

"What do you expect? Spiders are fast when they're small, and these ones have a longer stride," Corvin informed, not sure if he was trying to be funny or not.

"My kids always take care of them for me." Ginger gasped for a lungful of air. "I'm not a fan."

"Just keep running!" Max ordered to cut the chatter as the five of them circled the perimeter of the room, the two giant spiders close at their heels. "You got any bombs left?"

Ginger responded by lighting a fuse and tossing a small round explosive over her shoulder. It detonated under one of the spiders. There wasn't much damage, but the blast caused it to stumble. The other spider didn't even slow down, climbing over its partner as it recovered.

"Any more ideas?" she asked.

Corvin thought about it but came up with nothing. If there had been one enemy, he might have some options, but there wasn't much he could do in such a large room against two. He was only a *Venom* mage after all.

That was when the sound of stone dragging against stone reached his ears like music as the huge door began to move. What was odd was that the passage didn't open from the ground up like the others had. Instead, it split in the middle into two enormous slabs. There must have been a reason for the difference, but the out of breath cheers that erupted from the group around him told him that no one cared to think about it now.

"Okay, we make one more pass and head for the door," Max commanded as soon as the new walls of the open passage stopped moving.

The others agreed. Then, running faster, encouraged by the open door, they sprinted into the hallway.

Corvin brought up the rear, panting and wishing he was more of a runner.

The corridor was only wide enough for one of the spiders to fit through at a time, but unfortunately, they didn't seem to care.

Instead, they just skittered over each other through the passage in a tangled mass of legs and eyes. Their progress slowed but not by much.

Max's shoulders fell as he ran. "Damn. I was hoping they wouldn't follow us in."

Corvin glanced back, regretting the decision as soon as he did. Judging by the last fight, he wasn't sure they could win against two of the creatures at once. Then things got worse as the same ticking sound from before signaled that the passage was about to close. He did the math in his head, feeling relieved. The intervals between ticks were longer than before, telling him that they had enough of time to make it to the other side. Although, this brought back the first problem of the spiders, since, from what he could tell, they would have plenty of time to make it through the passage as well.

"Maybe we can get the spiders caught in the hallway as it closes?" Farn suggested.

Max shook his head before coughing an exhausted, "No." He must have been running the same numbers.

"They're too fast," Corvin added, breathing heavily.

"What if I hang back and act as bait." Farn huffed, her pace slowing. "I think I can hold them long enough."

Max gestured for her to keep up. "I'm sure you could, but you might not make it back out, and we're going to need you for whatever's next."

He was right; their *Shield* was far too valuable to risk, but a *Venom* mage, on the other hand, was almost always expendable, and Corvin knew it. He reevaluated the situation. There wasn't much he could do in the previous room, but in the narrow space of the hall, things were different.

"I might have a plan." Corvin tried to sound confident. "Whatever happens, keep running."

Max started to ask a question, but it was too late, Corvin had already stopped and turned to face the monsters. Max paused, slowing down with him a for a moment. He looked worried, but he didn't argue.

Corvin's knees trembled as the click-clack of the spider's legs hitting the floor shook him to his core. He wanted to run, but he held his ground nonetheless. Then, just as they were almost upon him, he grabbed the thick cloth that covered half of his face and yanked it off.

The spider in front skidded to a stop, locked in position as if unable to move.

Max gave Corvin an approving slap on the shoulder that almost made him stumble. "Don't stay too long. We still need you." With that, Max turned and jogged away.

The spider at the rear scraped and scratched to climb over its frozen counterpart until it could shove its way through. Corvin took a few steps back and shifted his gaze to meet with the second monster's shining black eyes. Having eight to choose from made it easy as it, too, froze. Now trapped underneath its partner, the first spider regained control of itself and began struggling to get free.

Corvin winced and placed a hand to his face, making sure not to cover the bright yellow eye that needed to stay focused on his captive. The patch of dark scales that surrounded it was rough under his fingertips as he pressed them against his face, reminding him of the contract he had made. Normally kept hidden under the fabric that wrapped around his head, he had almost forgotten the gift that he had received from the Nightmare Kafka after offering his left eye.

Corvin stepped backward, alternating between the spiders to keep them in the hallway as long as possible while he waited out the clock. He couldn't tell how much of the passage was left without looking back, but the ticking grew faster, reminding him to keep moving. He shuffled backward, making sure to keep the monsters in the effective range of his eye.

Max called from behind, telling him he had twenty feet left. He also heard Kegan call out to tell him that he was, "The Man." He smiled, then winced again, almost losing both spiders as he struggled not to blink, the pain in his head growing from the continued use. Why the developers had added such a large amount of simulated pain to go along with his one of a kind ocular ability was beyond him, but he couldn't argue with the result.

He counted his steps and figured that he only had about ten feet left as the ticking merged into a steady buzz. Then he slapped a hand over his eye and ran for the exit just as the walls started to close in. He assumed that they would move as slowly as they had opened. He was wrong, but not dead wrong. He could still make it, probably.

With only a couple feet left, he was forced to turn sideways as the walls left no room for his shoulders, their sides almost squashing him as he cleared the space. There was a brief screech from the two spiders, followed by a nauseating squelch as the doors shut inches behind him, close enough to catch the end of his robe as he ran. He let out a sudden, "urk!" as the fabric pulled tight and he fell to the floor like a cartoon character, ruining his first ever moment of epic badassery.

To his surprise, no one laughed as Max helped him up and attempted to free his robe from the door. Both of them pulled until the black fabric tore at the end, causing them to fall once again.

Corvin stood, shoving himself up from the stone with both hands and forgetting to cover his eye. It throbbed, the tendrils of dull pain reaching into his brain as he briefly caught Farn's gaze by accident.

The *Shield* froze in place, only moving her lips as the words, "Holy shit," fell out of her mouth.

Corvin broke the connection for both their sakes, uttering a quiet, "Sorry."

Farn shook out her limbs and added, "That's a basilisk eye." She sounded impressed.

"Yeah, it's a souvenir from …" Corvin started to say but stopped when he noticed Max's face, the *Fury's* eyes glued to a point behind him as if dumbstruck. Corvin turned to follow his gaze, hoping it wasn't another oversized spider. It wasn't.

CHAPTER TWENTY-EIGHT

Kira enjoyed a rather calm moment floating through the water in the passage beneath her friends. She still had a full minute before her health would start to deplete, and she could already see light at the end. She hummed a happy little tune to herself as she let the water wash away the anxiety and fear she had filled her earlier. It was like hitting a reset button on her mind, turning it off and on again for a better result.

The moment was ruined the instant Max's voice reached her, the sound traveling through the water. The result was the same as if he was right there yelling in her ear.

"We got two spiders here, hurry! We won't last long!"

At first, she wondered how he was sending the message. Then she heard it again.

"We got two spiders here, hurry! We won't last long!"

She rolled her eyes as she realized she was going to keep hearing the echo stone yelling at her on a loop until she got out of the water. Something about the amount of science used in the delivery of the message told her she had Corvin to thank.

Kira sped up toward the light ahead, exiting the passage into some kind of channel that curved off to the side like a moat. The bottom of the tunnel dropped into a deep pit, from which nothing but darkness could be seen. It made her nervous, like at any moment, some Lovecraftian horror would rise from its depths and wrap its tentacles around her body. She regretted that thought as soon as she had it, her legs kicking faster to outrun her imagination.

She was met with more darkness as soon as she broke through the surface. It wasn't that the lighting was poor but more that her wet hair had plastered itself to her face, blinding her behind a curtain of silver locks. She attempted to blow one away with a firm puff of air, but it fell back into place, the tip landing in her mouth. The water tasted foul, reminding her she needed to get out sooner rather than later. In frustration, she ducked her head again, only to burst from the water a second later with her wings aglow. Droplets of liquid flew through the air around her as she arched her back and whipped her hair out of her face.

She landed and glanced around the room, not taking in much detail other than making sure that there was nothing lurking in the space that might have an interest in eating her. With her safety confirmed, she ran toward the door, her bare feet leaving a trail of fairy-sized prints in her wake.

The lever was right where she expected it. Another basic switch a few feet from the door. She grabbed it, and a moment later, the door was opening in a vertical split. She stepped toward the new passage and peeked in from the side. She let out surprised a squeak as the silhouette of two spiders chasing her friends came into view.

Panic settled across her body with an unnerving shiver as the remaining water from her swim slid down her skin. One of those creatures had been hard enough. She wasn't sure what they could do against two of them, but she was an experienced adventurer. With that in mind, she did what any reasonable person would do. She took three large hops backward, then ran in a little circle whilst flailing her arms a bit. Once that was out of her system, she swiped open her spell-craft menu, dropping several heals into her quick-cast queue in preparation. She made sure to add in some antidote and protection effects for good measure.

Seconds later, Kegan, Farn, and Ginger shot out of the hall at full speed, turning back as soon as they were out to shout encouragement at Corvin while ignoring Kira altogether. Which was probably for the best, considering she was still wearing nothing but her unmentionables. Max jogged out after them, turning with the others to help the *Venom* mage by telling him how much farther he had left.

Drawn by curiosity, Kira snuck in behind the others to see what all the excitement was about. What she saw made her grin. She'd seen Corvin use his basilisk eye once before, but she had to admit that the way he was using it now was genius. She watched, almost enthralled, as he switched between the two spiders, always using one to trap the other in the hallway. He stepped backward until finally, the ticking sound merged into the same singular tone as before. The mage turned and ran, the others taking a step back to make room. Kira stepped back as well, and in seconds, he was out.

She cringed on instinct with her eyes closed as the doors slammed shut. The sound of insects bursting met her ears, the same as it would in the real world except louder and considerably wetter.

It took a moment for everyone to get themselves together after such a tense situation, including Corvin who kept falling over. After that, they were ready to move on.

With all the excitement of the spiders, the group seemed to have forgotten about Kira who had braved the waters below to open the passage for their escape. In fact, with everything going on, she herself had forgotten that she was still lacking in the clothing department, a problem that came rushing back to her as the group's attention returned. They fell silent one by one, all eyes on her.

It was at that point that she realized that when white fabric gets wet, it becomes transparent, and thus, the water from her swim had rendered what little clothing she had pointless as it clung to every detail of her skin.

She glanced down at the pair of small yet perky breasts showing through the sheer piece of cloth that attempted to pass for a bra. She gasped in horror.

Max froze, his mouth gaping, before blurting out an involuntary, "Oh god."

Even worse was Corvin, who turned to make eye contact with her, obviously trying not to stare at anything he shouldn't. Although, he must have forgotten that his basilisk eye was still exposed, as he ended up locking her in place, which prevented her from covering herself.

In response, Kira released a sound, like the whine of a kicked puppy as her mouth failed to form words.

The young mage realized his mistake and dropped his gaze to break the contract's hold, which of course, left him staring at an area of her body that one could only describe as intimate. At this, he yelped as if it might bite him and resigned to shoving his eye patch back on and pulling it down over both eyes to form a crude blindfold. At least he was trying to be a gentleman.

Kegan however, stood his ground and summed up the situation with the words, "My boy parts are confused." A comment that led Ginger to slap him in the head again.

Kira's face and chest heated up, but with nowhere to hide, she just stood there helpless, looking from left to right as if begging for someone to rescue her.

Farn stepped up to the role. The *Shield* didn't have any spare clothing to offer, so she just stepped in front, giving Kira someplace to hide.

She leaned close to Farn's back and peaked around her heroin's shoulder at the rest of the group, staring daggers at the offending members.

Max burst out laughing. It was probably the only way that he could deal with what he'd seen.

"It's not funny," cried Kira as Kegan joined the laughter.

"It is a little funny," the *Leaf* responded.

She looked to Farn for defense, but the *Shield* was too busy looking away at the ground.

That was when Ginger stepped in and wrapped one arm around her shoulder. "I'm sorry everyone saw you naked. But I think it's just as weird for the guys, if that makes you feel better."

"No. No, it doesn't." Kira squirmed.

Corvin spoke up, still blindfolded by his eye patch. "Is it okay to look? Are you good now?"

Kira frowned and answered from behind Farn. "Yeah, I'm fine." She turned to Ginger. "Can I get my gear back?"

Ginger responded by pulling her close into a nurturing hug. "Oh, Kira, my nauseatingly adorable little Kira," she said in a gentle tone. "Is there anything else I can do for you?"

"No. Mostly I'd just like my stuff back," Kira cut through her friend's attempt to stall as she was pressed against the *Coin* in an uncomfortable embrace.

Ginger paused, squeezing her tighter. "Well, I can't give your things back right now."

"Why is that?" Kira asked, her voice almost a growl.

"Mostly because you're just so cute like this, and I wouldn't want to hinder your progress in becoming more comfortable with your body as a woman." She paused again before adding, "Also, I totally dropped your stuff in the passage while being chased by the spiders."

"What!" Kira cried out just as Ginger pulled the fairy's face into her chest for an involuntary motorboat, holding her there until her stream of muffled obscenities ended.

Finally, after she had given up trying to get free, the *Coin* released her captive and apologized. "I am really sorry." She at least sounded sincere

Kira let out a sigh, unable hold onto the anger. "I know you are. It's okay." She lowered her head.

"Do you think we could open the door again and see if anything's salvageable?" Farn looked in Max's direction.

He shook his head. "I'm not sure anything could survive

that. It probably got deleted along with the spiders. We can look, but I wouldn't get your hopes up."

Before any of them could say anything further, a low gurgling echoed through the room.

"What was that?" Kira ducked and looked around the space, now realizing the size of it.

They stood in a wide circle, surrounded by tall stone pillars attached to a ceiling at least fifty feet high. Torches lit the space, one on each column. Around the outer perimeter ran a deep channel of water that formed the moat that Kira had emerged from when she'd entered. A wooden bridge crossed the gap near the entrance. Looking up at the domed ceiling, Kira saw a strange glass orb embedded in its center about six feet wide and colored a deep crimson.

Corvin cringed a little. "Does anyone else feel like this room looks like an arena?"

"Yeah, it kinda screams boss fight to me," Max gave words to what Kira was feeling.

The low gurgle sounded again, followed by scraping, and then a moan.

"It's coming from over there." Max pointed, just as it came again from the opposite side. Then again and again from all around them. Whatever it was, they were surrounded.

A hand rose from the moat, gray flesh gripping the side of the channel and pulling the source of the sound into view. Then another behind the group, then more beside them, then every-where. Hands of rotted flesh reached out as the creatures dragged themselves out of the water. They looked … hungry.

CHAPTER TWENTY-NINE

Max had always loved zombies. Hell, everyone did. Zombie movies, zombie games, and zombie television shows had always done well. Ever since people started to fantasize about the collapse of modern society to get out of work, debt, and other responsibilities, they'd had a surge of popularity. Despite all that, he didn't want to actually meet one. In a fully immersive fantasy game where players actually had to stand face to face with their enemy, Max had always assumed that the developers had decided that zombies were a little too intense.

That was probably why, in the world of Noctem, zombies had been replaced by a less scary version of themselves in the form of ghouls. Now, ghouls weren't exactly pretty to look at either, but they at least had the majority of their skin and didn't try to eat you.

The forms that emerged from the water all around him were not ghouls. No, these were full-on, rotting flesh, tattered clothing, gory wounds, dangling organs, try to eat your face, high on bath-salts zombies.

Max ordered the team together in the center of the room,

their backs against each other to form a protective circle around Kira as nearly twenty of the foes closed in.

A drop of water fell from the glowing red orb in the ceiling, landing on Kira's nose. She wiped it off on her wrist as Max tried his best not to look at her from the neck down.

"I guess this is definitely Plague then," he commented, stating the obvious identity of the new Horseman they faced.

Kira released a heavy sigh before surprising him by stepping out from behind everyone. "I'll get in the air," she stated before Max had a chance to suggest it himself. She took a deep breath as if savoring one last moment before abandoning whatever sense of modesty she had left. Then she took flight.

Having his *Breath* mage safely in the air, Max ordered the others to fan out to split up the growing enemy horde. "Keep moving, and don't get boxed in," he added as even more of the foul creatures emerged from the water.

"Oh god. I can't believe I was swimming in there with those things." Kira shuddered while hovering in the air above. "I knew that water tasted gross."

Despite being outnumbered, Max still felt confident, as handling large quantities of moderate enemies was his strong suit. Of course, that was when he remembered he still had a skill he could learn. He holstered his guns and took out his journal, dodging the grabby hands of the dead as he did.

"Not really the best time for that," Ginger commented as a few enemies closed on her.

"Sorry!" Max yelled in a muffled voice as he held his pen in his mouth and searched for his skills page.

Farnsworth looked like she had the situation under control, since her strength stat increased her weapon damage enough to cut through multiple limbs in a single swing. She didn't get many kills that way, but she did leave a trail of legless zombies crawling in her wake. When she got swarmed, she just activated her shield and shoved her way through like a truck.

Corvin wasn't so lucky. Sure, he carried a small club as an

equipped weapon, but he hardly ever used it. He usually just left it hanging under his robe since it wasn't his job to hit things. He was better off staying on the sidelines, but when each zombie took more than two *Shrapnel* spells before dropping, he didn't have much of an option. In an endurance fight against a horde like this, he needed to be conservative. Their mana vials wouldn't last forever.

Like Corvin, Ginger was also having trouble. Her dagger lacked the range of other weapons. Max cringed as he watched her stab her way through the crowd, getting clawed and bit as she went. She shrieked and clutched her stomach as the poison inflicted by each hit stacked, evolving into a sickness status that made her impossible to heal until it was removed.

Finally, scrawling a few numbers in his journal and adding a check mark at the end to accept the changes, Max learned level five of his *Custom Rounds* skill. "Things are about to get explosive," he said to himself as he converted his magazines. He just hoped that, like ghouls, the zombies shared the same weak point.

They did.

Crimson chunks of glowing flesh detonated from the back of their skulls as he dashed from one to another. Run, duck, dodge, slide, fire, repeat. Simple as that.

Max weaved between two of the monsters just as Corvin started to get overwhelmed, firing twice without looking to take out both. He spun and dropped three more at close range as one closed in behind him. Just before being grabbed, he fired from a low angle up through the chin of his attacker. The top of its skull exploded in a way that was viscerally satisfying. He moved on before it hit the floor, leaving Corvin speechless.

Ginger fell as one of the creatures grabbed her, a crimson glow swelling across her shoulder as its teeth clamped down. Then its head burst to the bark of another explosive round.

Before Max could take out the others surrounding her, Kira swooped in, removing the injured *Coin's* sickness and setting off an area of effect heal that brought her back to full as well as killing the surrounding zombies at the same time. The fact that light magic was a weakness for undead creatures had turned the fairy into a force to be reckoned with. With that knowledge, she continued to carpet bomb the place with healing spells, only stopping briefly to land and drop a few more spells into her queue before taking off again. Her killing spree was cut short when Max called up to her.

"They just keep coming, and the boss's health isn't dropping. Do you see anything from up there that might stop them?" He glanced at the lengthy bar, representing the Nightmare that ran down the edge of his forearm.

"No, but I'll keep an eye out," Kira called back before flying up to the top of the ceiling for a better view. A moment later, she shouted back down. "There's nothing out of place, well, other than the dozens of zombies pouring out of the water."

"That's not helpful." Max took out three of the creatures.

Suddenly, Kira yelled back down. "Crap! Stop fighting! Stop fighting! Stop fighting!" Her voice climbed higher with each word.

Max released the tension in his trigger fingers and looked up at her while making a point of raising one eyebrow to make his expression as incredulous as possible. "Why?"

She stopped in mid-air looking annoyed. "'Cause you just killed three and six more crawled out of there." She pointed toward the edge of the room.

Max followed her finger to the moat as six extra hungry looking forms flopped onto the floor like dead fish before pushing themselves up. He glanced around, taking a count and realizing the number of enemies had almost tripled. He let out an awkward, "Yikes," and holstered his pistols, pretending that he hadn't been exploding the creatures' heads a few seconds before.

Corvin switched up fast and cast several area of effect poison spells to function as healing for the wounded enemies to prevent his team from killing any more by accident.

"Any sign of which one is the actual Horseman here?" Max called up to Kira.

"No, they all look the same, and none of them seem to be behaving any different. I think they all are," she responded from her place, safe in the air, where she hovered with her arms folded, looking a little too casual.

"Okay, everybody, keep an eye out. I think we're missing something," Max ordered as he dodged a few more grabby hands and considered the possibility of a collective, hive-like, Nightmare. It was possible, and in a way, it kind of made sense. If it was meant to be the Horseman of Plague or Pestilence or whatever they wanted to call it, then it stood to reason that the endless supply of small enemies was supposed to represent a virus. If that was the case, then killing a few didn't matter. No. To win, they would have to find a cure.

CHAPTER THIRTY

Kira checked her mana as it drained little by little from the continued use of her wings. She had to land at some point and get a mana vial from someone before she ran out. Although, with the room below being overcrowded with the hungry undead, she didn't love the idea of going down there. She cursed Ginger for losing her bag along with her items and clothes. Then she felt bad for doing so since it wasn't really the *Coin's* fault. Actually, if she was going to be mad at anybody, she should've been mad at Carver for setting all of this up. She cursed his name. Then did it again a few more times for good measure.

Beneath her, the others changed their strategy from offense to just staying on the move while searching the arena for anything they might have overlooked, which was more difficult than it sounded, again, due to the arena's overcrowding. She watched for an opening to land.

Corvin ran to put some distance between himself and a group of determined zombies, only stopping near the center of the floor to catch his breath.

It looked like he wouldn't be grabbed for at least a few

moments, so Kira took the chance to drop to the ground in front of him.

He stumbled backward in surprise.

"You mind if I steal a vial? I'm running a bit low?" she asked, making a point of holding her hands out beside her to illustrate the point that she was obviously not carrying any on her person. She had given up on being modest. It was too late for that at this point. At least she had dried off, for the most part, making her tiny garments opaque once again.

"Oh, ah... umm," he stuttered in response before fumbling with his item bag. A second later, he presented her with two silver vials.

Kira downed one and tucked the second into the side of her underwear, drawing his eye in the process. She threw the empty over her shoulder, hitting a zombie that was stumbling toward her in the head. It let out a confused groan. She ignored it and thanked the blushing *Venom* as she turned to take off, inadvertently thanking him again with a spectacular view of her rear.

That was when a drop of water fell from the orb that sat in the center of the ceiling and landed on the head of the zombie that approached her. It winced, as if burned, its skin sizzling loud enough for her to hear it. She turned to look at Corvin who had noticed the same thing. She looked back up at the orb, feeling stupid for not checking it out sooner. She shot toward it without hesitation, leaving Corvin to tell the others of the discovery.

Once there, she stopped in mid-air, hovering just below the shape embedded in the ceiling. Her figure probably appeared as the perfect image of a traditional fairy with her lack of clothing. All she needed was a giant flower to sip dew drops from, and she would be good to go. Although, now, looking at the orb close up, she couldn't have been further from good to go.

It was damp with streaks of condensation running from its edge and collecting at its center before falling in intermittent droplets. She held out her hand to catch one, but it felt no different from a drop of rain. She licked her finger. It was just water, though it tasted clean, unlike the contents of the moat below. She reached up and touched the orb. It felt cool. In fact, it was the first thing in the whole dungeon that didn't have the same sticky warmth to it. Around its edges she noticed text, the letters worn with virtual age. She circled it, adjusting her angle to get a better look.

It read, 'For the bearer of the code, I open.' Then on the other side, 'The cold-blooded has the key.'

She pulled back a bit. "Well, Carver's not being very subtle," she said to herself as she dropped back down to the others, landing in an opening near Max. "We need some kind of code to open that thing. It says the cold-blooded has the key. Which I assume means that Alastair has what we need."

"How the hell are we supposed to get it from him? Even if we could contact him, he couldn't send it to us anyway." Max sounded annoyed.

Corvin jumped in, quite literally as he leapt over the clawing arms of one of Farn's legless zombies. "We could have one of us log out and contact him from outside."

"I guess that works. Hopefully, he'll know what to do here," Max agreed and gave Corvin the okay to head out.

The mage paused a moment, rummaging through his bag before handing all his remaining mana vials to Max.

The logout process would take thirty seconds, but during that time, Corvin would have to stay in one place until it completed. It was an opportunity that the horde wasn't about to waste.

They converged on the reynard boy like ants at a picnic, forcing Max and the others to return to killing the creatures as they swarmed.

Kira made a point of hovering above him, so her dust sprinkled his head. She watched as he held as still as possible, his long ears twitching at the sound of gunfire mixed with hungry moans.

Then he was gone.

CHAPTER THIRTY-ONE

Corvin fell away from the dream, losing and gaining consciousness at the same time until the electronic hum of his rig and the sound of people moving around him filled his no-longer-furry ears.

Bastian pushed up his headpiece and pulled himself from the rig while a man in green scrubs tried to stop him from getting up too fast. His head spun, still groggy from the dream. He called to anyone who would listen to get Alastair, then corrected himself by asking for Milo. It was hard to get names straight sometimes.

He knew that, to him, he had only been inside the dream a moment ago, but since he had been unconscious for most of the logout process and taken time to wake up, it had been longer than it felt. He glanced at a clock at the corner of one of the monitors. Ten minutes had passed since he'd left. Ten minutes where his friends were still in there fighting to stay alive. Even with the mana vials he left behind, he wasn't sure if it was enough to keep everyone going. He looked around the room at their bodies restrained in their rigs. He hoped they were alright.

Bastian sat and waited as a tech sent an urgent message into the system to contact Milo, who was probably wondering why one of the party had logged out suddenly. After about ten more minutes, the man was awake and struggling to form a coherent sentence. As soon as Milo's words started to make sense, Bastian explained the situation and asked about the code that they needed.

Milo pressed his finger and thumb into his eyes as if forcing them to adjust to the light. "Wait, what code? What exactly did it say?"

Bastian repeated the text as close as he could, not having seen it himself. He hoped he had it right, remembering how things could change when passed along between people, especially when one was a sarcastic fairy. "It said, that it would open for whoever had a code and that the cold-blooded would have the key."

Milo's stared off at nothing in particular for a moment. Then something seemed to click into place. "No, it's not a code. Well, it is. Just not that kind."

Bastian tried to follow his words but failed to make anything of them. "You're not making sense," he argued, almost sounding curt. He was too worried to remain as polite as he usually was, not with the others still in danger.

Milo tried again, "He probably means code, as in programming. But what would he ..." he stopped mid-sentence, his eyes widening. Then without another word, he ran out of the room.

Bastian followed, not sure if the man had intended for him to do so or not as they both ran down the hall in their pajamas and socks. Bastian looked down at one of his toes that stuck out through a hole as Milo slapped the call button on an elevator, the doors opening as if it had been right there waiting for them.

Milo continued to explain as they went up, "Okay, a while back, Neal gave me a drive with an item for the game on it. All he told me was that it was the key to something special. He wouldn't tell me what it was, but he said I would know when to use it. That has to be it." He paused, letting his mouth fall open. "Oh god. He has been preparing this since then."

"What kind of item is it?" Bastian asked, pulling Milo out of the horrific realization that his partner had been actively planning to betray him for quite some time.

"It's a gem or something. It doesn't really do anything. It's a marker to trigger something in the game. I looked through the code when he gave it to me, but it didn't seem like anything out of the ordinary. He was always doing stuff like that. Making random things he knew we would never use. I have a drawer full of them."

The doors opened on the top floor, and they ran down another hall into what Bastian assumed was Milo's office. It was a large, dark room with stone walls like the inside of a castle. It looked out of place after having been in the rest of the building. A dome of fiber-optic stars drew his eyes to the ceiling. It must have been expensive.

Milo dashed to his desk, a big mahogany affair covered in decorative carvings, and fished through a messy drawer of papers and other random items, including several USB drives. He tossed things on the floor as he searched, not wasting any time on being neat. "Got it!" He held up a small drive in triumph, the word "key" written on it in black marker.

It wasn't as impressive as Bastian thought it would be, but that didn't stop Milo from holding it in both hands to keep it safe as they ran back to the elevator.

"So how do we get it to the others if we can't accept a transfer?" Bastian asked.

"Neal put a block on your characters to stop us from installing anything directly through your rigs. But if this thing is part of his quest, it will probably get a pass. After that, it should just equip automatically."

They rushed out of the elevator and back to the Nemo Unit, where Milo turned back to Bastian. "You said this orb with the text around it is on the ceiling?"

Bastian nodded. "Yeah."

"Okay, we'll install it on Kira since she can get to it."

As the words left Milo's mouth, Bastian flashed back to the

conversation he'd had earlier while still in the dungeon. The one about how Carver couldn't have known that they would have a fairy in their group to fit throughout the gap beneath the door. Again, the questions surfaced, since, with all *Flight* blocked, the only way to reach the orb was with Kira's wings. *How could Carver have prepared for that?* Something felt off, but before he could say anything, Milo had already popped the drive into Seth's rig, his fingers dancing across a keyboard.

Bastian looked at Seth laying there helpless, a memory of Kira standing before him in her underwear drifted through his mind. He shuddered at the thought. It wasn't because of the obvious attraction that he had toward the fictional woman, but because of the way that he had embarrassed himself in front of her. The memory of fumbling with his items and stuttering gnawed at him. Even after meeting Seth, he still kind of knew him as Kira, no matter what she was in the real world. His thoughts were interrupted by Milo who told him to get back in so he could explain what was happening to the others.

He climbed back into his rig and lay down as a gruff nurse with a short beard helped him get reconnected. The man held up a syringe for him to see. "You've been under for a long time, so it will take a while for the system to pull back in. Do you want a sedative to get you there faster?" the nurse asked.

Bastian nodded without thinking about his own safety and held out his arm.

Milo came back over. "I have the item loading. It will take a few minutes to render so you might be able to beat it in."

Bastian tried to nod, but the sedative took hold. His head dropped to the padded headrest with a thud as the rig hummed back to life. The world spun as if it was trying to throw him off. Then there was nothing.

CHAPTER THIRTY-TWO

Kirabell cast another heal on Ginger as the *Coin* made a break for the other side of the arena where there was a bit more breathing room. She tried her best not to hit any of the zombies in the process. The last thing they needed was to spawn any more of the things. The room was already packed as it was.

In total, the team had stayed alive for a full twenty-seven minutes since Corvin had logged out, all while dodging over sixty drooling mouths. Somehow, they managed.

Kira checked her mana, noting that she was running low again. She'd already used up the vials that Corvin had left with Max and was now begging the others for whatever items they might have. Although, considering the fact that none of them were mages, it wasn't a surprise that they didn't have much to speak of.

"Please tell me you have at least a lemon drop or something," Kira landed next to Ginger, who had finally found a spot away from the dead.

The *Coin* panted while bent over with her hands on her legs for support. "Sorry," she said between gasps of air, before adding, "I'm not big on citrus."

Kira deflated. "Damn."

"I've got some hots, though," Ginger offered.

Kira grimaced and stuck out her tongue. "I'll take one." She sighed, not loving her options as the *Coin* pulled a small red wrapper from her bag. Kira took it and popped the item in her mouth, the overpowering flavor of cinnamon and cayenne pepper coating her taste buds. It actually had a greater effect than the candy items she preferred, regenerating a little health as well as mana every few seconds, but it tasted awful. Kira winced and scrunched her face. She couldn't understand why Ginger would eat the damn things by choice.

Suddenly, Kira felt the cold hands of the dead wrap around her slender neck, the surprise of it causing her to spit the fiery little ball of nasty out of her mouth with an audible, "Ptwoo." It hit Ginger in the forehead.

"What the hell?" The *Coin* wiped a bit of spit from her brow without doing anything to help.

Kira panicked. How one of the creatures had snuck up on her, she didn't know. She'd thought she was clear. Lacking her items and equipment, it wouldn't take much for the zombie to take her apart.

She spun, hoping to at least kick herself free, but there was nothing there. She grabbed at her neck and spun again, trying to pinpoint her attacker, but all she found was a confused looking Ginger, still doing nothing to help. It was at that point that she realized there was nothing grabbing her. Just a silver pendant with a thick chain looping around her neck. A large sapphire that matched her eyes sat at its center. She let out a confused, "What the what?" not forming a complete question.

"Looks like Alastair came through." Max shot another zombie in the knee. "I bet that's the key we need."

That was when Corvin got back online, his avatar appearing right where it was when he had logged off, which was now in the middle of the horde. In a heartbeat, they closed in on him. Fortunately, Farn was nearby.

She rushed the cluster of enemies, her shield plowing

through them like a bulldozer. She finished by taking the legs off three with her sword. "Nice of you to join us," she said as she helped him up and over to the rest of the group.

"What's the code?" Kira asked, expecting something more. "Is written it on this?" She struggled to look at the pendant, its short chain not letting her get it anywhere near close enough to see and probably making her look like an idiot as she tried.

Corvin stepped to the side to avoid a rotting hand that reached for his ankle. "No, that is the code. Like programming. It's made of code."

"Oh, I feel dumb." Kira cringed and placed a hand on her head. "So I what, just fly up to that orb and the thing will open?"

"Maybe?" Corvin gave her a shrug.

Kira narrowed her eyes. She was really hoping for more to go on. "Alright, I guess I might as well try it and get this over with."

Without another word, she shot straight up, leaving her friends behind and stopping just below the orb. She waited, but there was no response. She waited a few seconds more just in case. Still nothing. She glanced down at the others who were all looking back up at her in expectation, making her feel self-conscious. Kira thought for a moment, then got an idea. She clutched the silver pendant and held it out as she moved closer to the orb.

A single drop of water ran down the surface of the crimson shape from its edge, hanging for the briefest of moments before falling. It landed directly on the shining blue gemstone of the pendant, splashing against her fingertips.

Kira craned her head up at the orb, her eyebrows raised hopefully as the thing began to glow along with her pendant. "Yes!" she whooped in victory, flying out of the way. At least, that was what she meant to do. Instead, she let out a quiet, "Yeahhhh," sounding like a stoner as she drew out the word and stared straight into the orb, unable to move.

She heard Max's voice say something from below, but for some reason, she couldn't understand him as her eyes locked to the dead center of the strange light above.

It was as if the thing was staring back.

Then her mind went blank.

CHAPTER THIRTY-THREE

Max took a few steps back, unsure of what was going to happen as a circle at the dead center of the floor rose, followed by several rings around it to form a platform and stairs.

The others backed away as well.

He glanced up at his partner, her small form silhouetted by a blood red glow. "Kira, maybe you should get away from that thing."

She didn't respond, sending a wave of dread through him.

He cupped his hands around his mouth and yelled, "Kira! MOVE!"

Without warning, the orb jerked upwards, releasing a torrent of water from its edge that formed a column around the enthralled fairy.

Max leapt back to the platform, fearing the worst. Any moment, he expected to see her body slam into the ground. It didn't. He checked her health. Still full. She was fine. Then the numbers below her name shifted on his skin to form a rotating circle as if the game had begun loading a patch to her character data. It was accompanied by a number. It read one percent. Then two percent. Then three.

A violet glow shined as the light of the crimson orb above passed through the crystal blue water that had engulfed his partner. The torrent hit the floor and rushed out in all directions, flowing over Max's feet to spread out across the room toward the horde.

The zombies screeched and screamed as it cascaded over their toes and into the surrounding moat. A chorus of cries came from all around as their spawn point was cut off, purified by the falling liquid.

Max ignored them altogether and attempted to reach into the column of water in hope of finding his friend. His heart sank as his hand was met with resistance, like there was some kind of barrier surrounding it. "Damn it!" he shouted in frustration. Whatever was happening to her inside, he couldn't stop it. He tore his attention away from the center of the room and focused on a task that he could do something about. That task being brutal acts of mass zombicide. He drew his pistols and went to work.

The rest of the party did what they could to remove the enemies from the arena, but for the most part, they were just in his way. Fueled by anger, Max moved like a demon as he emptied his magazines into the helpless forms around him. He reloaded and checked the percent next to Kira's name. It was up to thirty-five. He thumbed the slide lock to chamber a round, glancing back at the column of water before continuing.

Corvin and Ginger stayed near the center, searching for a way to get Kira out of the torrent, while Farn and Kegan made sure that none of the enemies got anywhere near them.

The number below Kira's name climbed, now at eighty percent. Whatever was happening, was almost done. Max growled at the zombies with a fury worthy of his class's title, and for a moment, they even seemed scared. With nowhere to spawn, the horde thinned out, and before long, it was gone, leaving only Max in the arena, wisps of smoke trailing around him.

The others said nothing as his eyes darted back to them.

Then the rage inside him vanished as if someone had flipped a switch. In its place was dread. He holstered his weapons and ran, approaching the pillar of water just as a new exit opened at the far side of the room and the familiar voice of the darkness called out his name for a contract. He didn't respond, but it continued anyway.

"Make your offer—"

"I don't give a fuck!" Max yelled back, interrupting the first of mankind's fears. He didn't care. There were more important things to think about.

"Accepted!" the voice responded, somehow reading his input as an offer. Max ignored it, even as he felt the chill of a contract item form in his pocket.

The value on his stat-sleeve below Kira's name reached one hundred percent, then vanished, returning her status readout to normal. The orb dropped back down with a loud bang, cutting off the flow of water in sync with the completion of whatever had happened. The column of water fell like a curtain around the platform, revealing the fairy standing perfectly still at its center, her eyes closed.

Max froze for a second, then continued to run.

Her silver hair was fluffed as if it had been blow-dried after a long and comforting shower. It fell to the side with a few locks sweeping past her nose and drawing his eye downward. The silver chain hung close around her throat, its pendant resting in the delicate curve of her collarbone. Its gemstone somehow changed from sapphire to a glittering amethyst.

Max let out a heavy sigh of relief as he stepped up the first few stairs toward his best friend who at least seemed to be alright. Farn and the others gathered in behind him.

As if sensing their presence, Kira let out a slow breath, her lips parting only a little as she exhaled and opened her eyes. She looked calm, almost rested, as if waking up on a Saturday morning in a soft bed, the whole weekend ahead of her. She glanced around at the party, making eye contact with each of them until coming to rest on Max.

He responded with a stunned gasp.

Gone was the bright and tranquil blue of her eyes that had always looked out at him. In its place, a dreamlike shade of deep purple sparkled in the torchlight, matching the stone in the pendant around her neck.

Her expression grew confused as gaping mouths surrounded her. She glanced behind her, as if to see if it was really her they were looking at or if there was something interesting or possibly monstrous sneaking up on her. Finding nothing, she turned back and spoke, her voice sounding unsure.

"Umm." She tilted her head to the side. "There's something in my hair again, isn't there?"

CHAPTER THIRTY-FOUR

Questioning looks greeted the party as Max entered the bridge of the Nostromo. This was due to the almost nude fairy storming through the room in a huff.

Alastair started to speak but was promptly interrupted with a loud, "I don't want to talk about it!"

Max would have laughed, but he wasn't in the mood after everything that had happened.

On her way, Kira caught one of Alastair's *Shields* checking out the view.

She skidded to a stop and singled him out. "I'm sorry, did you not get to see my ass yet?" she shouted at the crew member, whose eyes widened and shot back up to Kira's face. "I wouldn't want to deprive you. Here, why don't you take another look." She twisted to give him a better view. The rest of the crew laughed at the exchange, then promptly shut the hell up when she glared back at them. "And you!" She stabbed a finger in Alastair's direction. "You better delete the recording of that last fight."

He nodded several times in quick succession without offering anything more. Although, from what Max assumed,

Alastair had already skimmed through the footage while they returned to the ship. So it was probably too late, and the guy had already seen everything.

Kira disappeared down a corridor, her yelling still audible. "The merchant better have clothes!"

Ginger followed to act as bodyguard for the pissed off fairy. Max figured the *Coin* felt responsible, having lost her gear back in the dungeon.

The crew relaxed as soon as they were gone but tensed up again when Max started shouting. "What the hell happened back there? What did that thing do to her?"

"I'm sorry." Alastair held his hands up, palms facing out. "I assure you, we had no idea that there was more to that pendant than a standard key item."

Max watched Alastair for a moment through narrowed eyes. With his character designed to look like a JRPG villain, Max had a hard time telling if Alastair was being sincere. He decided to give him the benefit of the doubt and released the tension in his jaw. "Just tell me what it did to her."

Alastair let out a breath and his body deflated. "The short answer is, we don't know."

A wave of anger burned through Max's chest, but he let Alastair continue.

"Ultimately, the item's code was normal, but there was a line hidden in the comments section that became active when Kira used it on that weird orb thing. It downloaded a ton of files from storage outside the system and installed it all to her rig and character data."

Farn stepped up to join Max, facing her boss. "How can that even happen? Doesn't the system need consent or something?"

"That was my fault," Alastair admitted. "When I installed the item, I bypassed it. I just didn't think—"

"That's right; you didn't think," Max said, sounding like his father. He backed off a moment later. He didn't like how he sounded. "Sorry, I'm just worried."

"I understand that. I am too. It's thanks to your team that we even have a chance here; the last thing I want is to put any of you in any danger."

Farn took a step forward. "What did the download do?" she asked, bringing the conversation back to what was important.

"That's the part we don't know. On top of running a large update, it locked us out of her rig. We can't access the system files to investigate. All we can do is monitor her vitals."

"Can we log her out and use a different rig?" Farn asked.

"No, her avatar data has been linked to it for now."

Max swallowed a lump of dread. "Is she going to be okay?"

"As far as we can tell, she should be fine. The system can't do anything to her other than affect how she connects. So it doesn't have a way to actually hurt her."

"Maybe you should wait until she's in the room before talking about her." Ginger appeared in the doorway, a wide grin on her face as she stepped into the room.

Kira followed behind, her demeanor in extreme contrast from before. She looked at the floor, saying nothing as she moved toward the group. She almost seemed more embarrassed after finding something to wear.

The merchant below deck didn't have much in the way of equipment for her race, just the starter gear that Max had only seen her wear in their first few days online. She had replaced it as soon as she could back then. It provided almost no actual protection as armor, but that was true of most fairy gear. Besides, Max didn't think that was why she had ditched it anyway. She had never actually explained her reason, but he had always assumed she'd gotten rid of the equipment because it was completely and utterly beautiful.

Thin spaghetti straps clung to her shoulders, connecting to a well-fitted bust of an empire style dress. Its pure white fabric ruffled around her knees, almost floating as she moved. Her shoulder blades were exposed by a low cut back, just enough to free her wings if the need should arise.

With the new outfit combined with the shining amethyst

pendant and matching eyes, she had become a sight to behold. Hell, to call her breathtaking was no exaggeration, considering the hush that fell over the bridge as the crew took in her transformation.

She stood at the edge of the party, arms in front of her, holding a new journal, having lost her old one, her head lowered.

"Well isn't anyone going to tell her she looks nice?" Ginger leaned forward, gesturing toward her like a mother showing off her daughter before being picked up on prom night.

Max approached, forcing the fairy to look up, her eyes shining with a depth that one would have to have seen to believe.

She looked back to the floor. "I know I look stupid."

He laughed a little and placed a hand on her head, feeling her tense on contact. His mind raced to find a comment that would adequately make fun of the situation without making her feel bad. To his surprise, all he could come up with was a simple, "You look nice." He'd even kept his tone gentle and honest.

The fairy took in a sudden breath and made eye contact with him before looking away. The corner of her mouth twitched up toward a smile for an instant before she shoved it back down and covered with an annoyed snort.

It was actually a better reaction than any Max might have gotten from a joke.

"You do look pretty amazing," Farn added stepping up to admire her.

"See, I told you it wasn't weird," added Ginger as Kira let a goofy smile have its way with her. The *Coin* took the opportunity to run her fingers through the fairy's hair, separating out three of her silver locks.

Kira pushed her away. "Cut it out."

"Oh, come on. Wren doesn't let me do this anymore. At least give me this." Ginger continued to braid her hair.

Kira rolled her eyes and submitted, then grew serious again.

"So, what's the verdict here? Should I be worried about this?" She held up the pendant that hung close around her throat. The fact that it had no clasp on its thick chain made it impossible to remove without decapitating her, which probably wouldn't work even if they tried, since the item's description only listed one thing, that its ownership was bound to her.

Alastair reiterated what he had told Max before continuing. "We don't know exactly what the update did, but judging from your connection, the techs are pretty sure you're being monitored by someone outside the system - obviously Carver."

Max scoffed. "It's not enough just for him to put us through this? Now he has to watch, too?"

"I don't think he can actually see any of you. The connection doesn't seem to be sending that much data. In fact, I'm now rethinking the entire purpose of the mission. I don't think he wants to take down the system at all. I think all that stuff on the video about not wanting to see the Somno system used for games was all bull. I think he's putting you all through these impossible tasks because he wants to make you stronger. I think he wants you to win this."

"Well, that makes sense. He didn't seem like he was motivated by revenge in the second video we saw," Max said, missing the larger point.

Alastair started to speak, but Kira beat him to it, "So what's the point of all this then? Just one big experiment?"

"That's what I'm thinking. He probably doesn't care about getting fired at all. He just wants to force us to run one of his trials for him. It makes a lot more sense than trying to get back at me anyway." Alastair shoved his hands into his coat pockets.

"I suppose that means I'm the guinea pig then." Kira pointed to her eyes with two fingers.

"Yes and no," he answered, leaning his head from side to side. "He seems to be using you as a back door."

Kira shoved her new journal behind her to cover her rear. "What's this about my back door?"

Kegan and Farn let out a laugh.

"Not that type of back door." Alastair groaned, taking a hand out of his pocket to rub his forehead. "No, he seems to be using you as an entry point to view information on the whole party, so by that, I assume you're all guinea pigs."

"That's not creepy at all," she added through a heavy layer of sarcasm.

Farn jumped back in. "What do you mean by, 'He wants to make us stronger?' I mean, we're not getting much experience from any of this. And you've seen Max fight, right? How much stronger could we possibly get?"

"Yeah, I am pretty badass." Max rested his hands on his guns.

Alastair nodded. "That's true; you are living proof of how much a person can grow when training for combat on a nightly basis. By now, your reflexes might be pushing the limit of what the human mind can do."

"I wouldn't go that far." Max stepped back from his previous boasting.

"I'm not exaggerating. The game doesn't give you any help when it comes to movement and combat other than increasing your weapon damage and your physical defense in accordance with your stats. Everything else is all you. And you must have noticed by now that it carries over into reality. In theory, you should be able to handle a gun the same no matter which world you're in. Same goes for the melee classes. I can only imagine what would happen if Ginger got in a knife fight," Alastair said with a straight face.

Ginger glowered in his direction. "What kind of places do you think I hang out in?"

Max tilted his head to the side, considering the possibility of what they might be capable of, then shook off the thought, getting back to the point. "Okay, but unless Carver is trying to turn the world's nerds into an army of combat specialists, how does that help him?"

Alastair laughed. "It doesn't. He's not a supervillain. Neal doesn't care how good a fighter you are. In fact, I don't think he cares about the conflicts that go on in the outside world at all. That's not a priority for him. All he ever cared about was this." He pointed to his head before continuing. "He wants to make your mind stronger, and I think that's why he's making you do these impossible fights."

Max nodded as if he understood the explanation. Then he shook his head. "Nope, I'm not following any of this."

The others agreed.

"Okay, let me give you a visual." Alastair took his inspector from the back of his journal and held it so that he could see Max through it. He tapped the pane of glass once, then did the same to Kira, followed by the rest of the team. He tapped it a few more times and swiped his finger toward the ships main window, where each of their status screens appeared in a grid.

Max focused on his, reading it off in his head. Most of his stats were pretty well balanced, the only one of real importance being dexterity, since it was what his gun's damage scaled off. He had been dumping every other level's upgrade points into it, and for the most part, spreading the rest across his constitution, defense, and skills while adding a few to luck every now and then.

He glanced at the rest of his team's stats. Farn had built her character around constitution, strength, and defense. Kegan was a strength and dexterity build, which made sense, since bows worked off both. Ginger had gone with dexterity and luck, and Corvin had gone with intelligence and focus.

Overall, everyone had balanced their characters well without neglecting anything. The exception being Kira since her race had been designed to be a glass-canon type build with some of her stats being soft-capped from the start.

Alastair stepped up to stand in front of the screen and gestured back to it with one hand. "Okay, so this is how you see your character."

"Yeah, and?" Max leaned against one of the railings and folded his arms.

"And this is how the game sees your character." He tapped

another few commands out on his inspector, and the screen changed.

At first, Max wasn't sure what was different. Then it was obvious. Decimal points appeared at the end of each stat, some of which actually contradicted what had been chosen. Max noticed that his luck was a little higher than what he'd set it at, making him more likely to get an item drop and less likely to get an ailment like poison. On top of that, the decimals fluctuated up and down as if they were always changing. He looked back to Alastair, who continued.

"Obviously things are a little different, but what I want you to focus on are the two new stats that appear at the bottom of each of your sheets."

Max dropped his eyes to the lines that now read *willpower* and *resistance*. The first stat, willpower, varied significantly between each party member. It also fluctuated more than the rest of their stats, jumping up and down several digits at a time one second while hovering somewhere in the middle the next. The second value, resistance, seemed to mirror the first.

"Alright, what the hell does that mean?" Max spoke the words that he assumed everyone was thinking.

Alastair stepped back to the team and lowered his voice. "Okay, this isn't really a secret or anything, but it's not common knowledge, either." He paused as if thinking of how to explain things. "So if you want a beer online, you simply go to a tavern and order one off the menu, and the NPC at the bar gives it to you. Right?"

Max nodded, unsure of where he was going with it.

"But that's just how you see it. From the game's perspective, all it knows it that you ordered option number whatever off their menu and how much it costs. It can load some less complicated items or ones that have a full profile of characteristics in its database, but other than that, the system has no clue what to do. It can't tell you how a drink tastes or smells or how it feels going down your throat. The game can't just create sensory information. It doesn't understand that stuff. But, it does understand that you do. So to find out more, the system asks your mind to fill in the blanks." He gestured to the party. "You expect a beer to come in a frosty mug, so it does. You expect it to be cool and refreshing, so it is. You expect to get a pretty good buzz after a few, and there you go. It understands beer. It will then merge the data it gets from everyone around you to form a consensus so that everyone sees it the same way and it will use that data to fill in any gaps. So if you've never had a beer, it will just ask others and then pass on that information to you.

Corvin held up one finger. "Unless you're underage."

"Of course. If you're not old enough, it filters out the effect of the alcohol, but that's beside the point because for all that to be possible, the system has to allow each of you to influence it. And your willpower stat is the measurement of how strong your mind pushes to control the dream. If left unchecked, you could potentially do anything, like turn water into wine or move objects with your mind."

"Or turn yourself into Mothra and destroy Valain," Kira suggested.

Alastair nodded. "Pretty much. So to keep that from happening, the dream pushes back, balancing its resistance against your will so that you can give it what it needs without giving you too much control. And for the most part, that works."

"What do you mean, for the most part?" Max asked, assuming he wasn't going to like the answer.

"Well, sometimes when you put a player in a situation of high emotional stress, their influence can fluctuate a little too much and the system can have trouble keeping up with that. It doesn't usually create a big enough gap to fully overpower the system or anything. But it can alter the dream in more subtle ways like increasing your stats temporarily. So there are moments where players have stayed alive or dealt more damage when mathematically they shouldn't be able to. Not only that, but the more a user does it, the harder your mind pushes. Like working a muscle, it gets stronger the more you use it. This gives the system a harder time keeping you in check."

"And that's why Carver created the Nightmares." Corvin rubbed at his eye patch.

"Yes, and since some of you have been punishing yourselves by fighting them, it's like you've been training for this quest for years. That's why your willpower stat is so high, Max."

Max compared the values. "Nice, I'm kicking all of your asses," he bragged, his value as it holding steady at around fifty-five.

"Great, like his ego wasn't big enough," Kira groaned.

In second place with forty, Corvin seemed to stand a little taller than usual, while Kira and Farn high-fived to celebrate a tie as theirs both wavered close to thirty-seven. Kegan and Ginger brought up the rear, looking disappointed but explaining that it must have been because they hadn't fought as many of the Nightmares.

Max folded his arms across his chest and let a smug grin spread across his face. "So how high would my will have to get to overpower the system and be all godlike and what not?"

"Pretty damn high."

Max's grin fell. "That's unhelpful."

Corvin raised his hand before speaking. "Has anyone ever done it before?"

"Not that I know of." Alastair looked at the ground and shoved his hands into his pockets before falling silent and creating an awkward lull in the conversation.

Eventually, Max shook his head. "Well, this is all well and good, but some of us need to log out and rest before doing anything else. We can talk more outside."

"Agreed," Alastair said.

Kira stretched and let out an unnecessary yawn. "Yeah, I better get out before I pee my pants." She froze as soon as the words left her mouth, then looked at Alastair with a worried look. "I haven't peed my pants? Right?"

He didn't answer. Instead, he grew quiet and looked back down at the ground.

"Oh god! I feel so gross now." She flailed both hands while Max burst out laughing. "Oh really, you're gonna laugh at me, mister eat-seven-tacos-before-logging-on-for-ten-hours? How did that work out?"

Max shut up without another word, not wanting everyone to hear the rest of the story.

"That's what I thought." She pointed at his chest.

Alastair started laughing as well, before adding, "Don't worry. No one has peed their pants."

Kira shook her head at him. "Not cool. Not cool at all." She ignored his continued chuckling as she navigated through the menu on her forearm to find the option that read 'sign off.' Then her face dropped.

Her amethyst eyes flicked back up to Max, then shifted to Alastair, who was still enjoying his joke longer than he should have. Her words came out with a quiver of fear. "How concerned should I be that my logout option is missing?"

CHAPTER THIRTY-FIVE

Corvin struggled to think of something to say.

Beside him, Kira sat in the captain's chair. She looked like a patient at the doctor's office waiting for a life-changing diagnosis.

Max and Farn had tried to stay with her, but she had insisted that they at least log out to use the bathroom before they regretted it.

Corvin wasn't sure why she had sent them away. The fairy looked like she needed a friend now more than ever. Although, no one knew what kind of risks they would be taking by skipping breaks when they were available, so it was for the best that they didn't stick around. Kira probably wouldn't be able to live with herself if something were to happen to them because of her. That was just the type of person she seemed to be. At least, that was what Corvin assumed when he saw the look on her face as the others vanished back to the real world. She had put on her bravest face and smiled, letting it fall as soon as they were gone.

Of course, Corvin was there with her. The recent dose of sedatives that he'd been given had left him stuck in there as well for the time being, but thanks to his short break during the last fight, he was good to go for several more hours. Although he didn't feel like his presence was doing much for the fairy other than making the silence that they sat in more awkward than if she had been alone.

He glanced down at her every now and then as she sat with her hands in her lap, waiting for Alastair to log back in to tell her if there was any hope of getting her out from the other side.

She kept checking the mission clock as if noting the passing of each minute as they stacked onto her total play time. That must have got old quick because she stood up.

"I can't sit around anymore. I'm going for a walk. Wanna come? Get some fresh air?"

"Yeah, sure," Corvin said, his pulse speeding up, not really sure what else to say before following her out of the room.

The air outside was cool as soon as they stepped onto the ship's upper deck. Kira took in a deep breath, letting it out slowly as her shoulders relaxed. A light breeze swelled around her, ruffling her dress, the moonlight passing through the impossibly light fabric creating a subtle silhouette of her body underneath.

Corvin looked away and tried to stop his tail from wagging as she stepped to the railing and leaned against it. The thing had a way of betraying his thoughts at the worst of times. He assumed that the fluffy appendage worked off impulses in his brain meant for other parts of his body, so he couldn't always control it at will.

Kira sighed, bringing his attention back to her. " I guess there are worse places to be stuck." She gazed out over the land below as they drifted through the cloudless sky.

A simple, "Yeah," was all he could think of to say, causing the conversation to die before it even started.

They stayed like that for what seemed like forever as he struggled to think of something to fill the silence, something that might distract her from her situation.

Normally, Kira was pretty chatty, always cheerful and

stuffing her face with food. He had once seen her eat seventeen peanut butter cups at once to win a bet. She was fun to be around. It was why he had always liked her. Of course, he knew that they weren't the best of friends or anything, but they had always gotten along. And yes, for a time, he may have had a slight crush. Although, he never would have acted on it. Not just because he had always assumed that she and Max were a couple, but mostly because she was pretty, and he was awkward. It was a good thing, too. That would have been an uncomfortable conversation.

Now, knowing the truth about who she really was, he felt like he understood her more. He still liked her, just in a different way. It made him want to know more about her and how she saw the world. Though that didn't change the fact that he was still painfully shy. It was a trait of his that he wished he could change, but he never figured out how. He took a deep breath and tried to be bold.

"So, I have to ask …" He placed a hand on the ship's railing in an attempt to appear casual.

The stars danced in her eyes as she gave him a simple, "Hmm?"

"What's it like? You know, being this? I mean, what you are?" He fumbled the question, but she seemed to get the point.

"You mean what's it like playing as the opposite sex?"

"Yeah." He resisted the instinct to look away.

She leaned onto the railing, resting her chin on her hands. "You know, if someone else had asked me that question, I would probably lie or avoid it. But you're probably one of the only people that won't make fun of me." She shot him a smile that warmed him inside, and he did his best to reassure her with a nod. "I guess, from a purely physical standpoint, I'd say it's …" she leaned her head to the side, "comfortable? I guess?"

Corvin opened his mouth to ask what she meant, but she interrupted him, her eyes widening while she shook her head.

"Don't take that the wrong way," she insisted.

"Okay." He held up his hands trying to convey that he had no intention of judging her no matter what her answer was.

She settled back down. "What I meant was, it's kind of nice to be small and light and to have no body hair whatsoever. Sure, there are occasional sensations that catch me off guard and weird me out. But I have a better range of motion, which helps me to fly and dodge. And I never have to worry about getting hit in the junk. So it's really not bad. Honestly..." she hesitated, "I kind of like it just as much as my real body."

Corvin watched as she stepped away from the railing and tiptoed across the deck like a dancer, lifting up on one foot and raising the other high over her head as she leaned down. It was an impressive and somewhat alluring display of flexibility. He laughed at the demonstration, and she returned to her place at the rail.

"I guess that makes sense, from a physical standpoint. But what about ..." Corvin cleared his throat, "the rest?"

"That's where things get dicey." She twirled one of the braids that Ginger had added to her hair. "I never realized how different things are. I mean, I did. I'm not an idiot. But I never thought about it. That's the part that I have trouble with."

"Okay?" Corvin said, having trouble following her.

Her eyes slid up and to the side as if searching for the right words. "Guys are hard to figure out, which I know is odd, coming from me. It's just strange to be treated so differently. It can be nice, like holding doors and such. Sometimes players even offer to help me on quests and stuff when they don't stand to get anything out of it. Part of me likes the attention. But I know damn well they wouldn't act that way if I was something else, so it ends up feeling ..." she frowned, "wrong."

Corvin stayed quiet, realizing that he'd been guilty of giving her special treatment in the past. After all, the main reason he always crafted lemon drops was because he knew she liked them. It was a sobering thought.

She continued without calling him out on it. "Other times, it's horrible. You all can be real dicks sometimes. I kinda understand why it's hard for female gamers to play without being bothered by anyone. I mean, if I had a nickel for every time a guy has sent me a message asking me to send nudes, I'd be rich. It's like there's something about the fact that I don't know their real name that turns off a filter in their heads. For example, I got this one a couple nights ago." Kira opened her journal to read aloud what was easily the most vile and depraved message that Corvin had ever heard.

"Well, that's … horrifying." He felt ashamed of his gender as a whole.

"I know, right? What kind of person sends that? And how does he think so little of me?" Her fingers tightened around the railing as she spoke then relaxed as soon as she finished. She lowered her head in defeat. "What's worse is when someone gets it in their head that they should go around touching all the women they meet online, as if they're all just begging for the attention. I mean, I like being touched sometimes. For example, the last dungeon was a bit hard on me, but Farn made me feel better with just a pat on the back. When it's from a friend and for the right reason, physical contact can be really nice." Then her eyes narrowed. "Though, I'd prefer it that Max refrains from slapping my ass. Granted, he obviously doesn't see me like that, so it doesn't really bother me. Plus, I trust him," she leaned to the side and nudged Corvin's arm with her elbow, "and I supposed I trust the rest of you guys, too." She scrunched up her nose. "Well, maybe not Kegan."

Corvin laughed and scratched one of his ears. "Yeah, probably keep an eye out for that guy."

She snickered too but sank back down a moment later. "But there are times when someone touches me, that it's like, I know there's more to it. It doesn't usually go too far. Just a hand on my arm or waist, but it feels like I don't have a choice. It just happens, and then I feel like I have to be okay with it because if I say something, I might make things more uncomfortable." She stood quietly for a moment, then slid closer to Corvin, placing her arm around his back so that her hand rested on his hip.

A tingle rushed through his back, and he stood up straight, his tail puffing up a little. "Woah, what—"

"See. It's weird, right?" She slipped away from him.

Corvin gave an awkward nod before relaxing again after the sudden invasion of personal space. "Ahh, yeah."

She smiled, her point made. Then she sank back down against the rail, turning away so he couldn't see her face. "A while back, Max and I played with a group of guys that we met through party search. They all knew each other, so it was a little weird when we first started. But we fought well as a team, and it seemed like a good party. So, after a few hours, everyone was feeling pretty comfortable, joking and talking about whatever. It was fun. Then one of them started flirting with me. Obviously, I wasn't into it, so I tried to ignore him. Then he started putting his hand on my back. At the time, my gear was cut really low, which left a lot of skin exposed for my wings. Anyway, I tried my best to move away and stay out of reach to avoid the issue, but he kept seeking me out, always switching places to stay beside me. So I started making it more obvious that I wasn't into it, like stepping away when he reached for me and what not. But he didn't take the hint, so I finally said something."

"How'd he take it?" Corvin held his breath, afraid of the answer.

"Fine, actually. I just told him it was making me uncomfortable as nicely as I could, and he apologized like a gentleman. I had been building it up in my head like it was going to be a problem, so I felt like an idiot when it wasn't."

Corvin exhaled. "That's good."

"Yeah it was, but I'm not done. About an hour later, he started doing it again. Like he somehow forgot or thought I would give in if he was persistent enough. I pushed his hand away to remind him, but he just got more aggressive. Then he put his hand on me, like really low." Kira slid her arms around her stomach as a noticeable shudder pulsed through her body. "His fingertips slipped into my dress a bit." She fell silent for a moment.

"What'd you do?" Corvin asked, his heart racing a little.

She swatted at the air beside her. "I slapped his damn hand away as hard as I could, which I'll admit isn't that hard. Then I told him to cut it the hell out, a lot less politely than I did the first time."

"Did he stop?"

She threw her hands up before dropping them to her sides again. "At that point, it became a thing, which was exactly what I was hoping to avoid. He acted like it was no big deal, and I was just being uptight. Then his friends all ganged up on me like it was my problem, like I shouldn't have been bothered since my body isn't real. Max jumped in and got between them and me, and as much as I hate to admit it, I totally hid behind him. But there were four of them and two of us, so they didn't back down. They asked Max what it was to him, and if he was my boyfriend or something. He said that I was his friend and that he didn't like how they were treating me. And you know Max, he wasn't about to back down either, so it escalated. Finally, I just said we should go, which sucked because we were almost done with the quest we had been working on all night. Then they got pissed that I wanted to ditch and got all bent out of shape about it. They said that I was an example of why girls shouldn't play games.

"In the end, Max disbanded the party right there in the dungeon, and I teleported us out, which is why the both of us have one percent negative feedback on our profiles saying that we quit early. How much does that suck? Granted, Max has plenty more negative feedback for trash-talk, so I shouldn't feel too bad about it. But there's something about being called a bitch because you don't want a guy's hand down your dress that doesn't feel great." She clenched her jaw as soon as she finished talking.

"Wow, what a bunch of—" Corvin started.

"Douche bags?" Kira finished.

"Yeah," Corvin agreed, wondering what he would have done if he had been there with her. Then he realized he had missed an important detail. "Why didn't you just tell them you were a guy?"

"Ha!" She gave a loud but mirthless laugh. "Yeah, that's another crazy thing. Back when we first started playing, I used to just tell people as soon as anything felt weird, and it would put a stop to things before they started. But after the first year, being honest stopped working. Apparently, claiming to be a man became the go-to response used by most of the real female gamers to get people to leave them alone. After a while, people just stopped believing it or not caring."

"Seriously?"

"Yeah, after that, there was a period where saying I was gay worked. Then, all of a sudden, it started making guys more interested, like they were gonna get me into some kind of fantasy group thing."

"Yikes."

"One time I told a guy that my cat had just died, and that I wasn't in the mood, which was actually true. I'd loved that cat, and I really was upset about it. But do you know what he said?"

"What?"

Kira did her best impression of what she thought a smooth-talking player sounded like. "We should go somewhere quiet, and I'll help you forget about it."

"Really?" Corvin grimaced. "What'd you do?"

"I did what any sensible person would do. I noped the hell out of there and ran away."

Corvin laughed. "Oh god, I'm sorry."

"Yeah," she said, her voice sounding tired. "You know what does work pretty well though?"

"What?"

She hesitated as if not really wanting to say despite having already started. "Okay, you can't tell anyone, like, not even Max." She glanced around over her shoulder as if checking to see if anyone else was around. "Especially not Max."

Corvin held up his hand as if taking an oath. "I promise."

She bit her bottom lip before speaking. "You know how Farn assumed Max and I were a couple."

"Yeah, to be honest, I thought so, too. Or at least, I suspected it. I thought it would be rude to ask, though."

She laughed with a snort that was somehow endearing. "Yeah, we get that question a lot actually. It's super awkward."

"Well you do make a cute couple," Corvin joked. "You fight well together, and you're always having fun. Plus, he's kind of protective of you."

"That's just because we've played together for a long time. We're at a point where we know each other well enough to strategize without talking. Plus, we have a lifetime of joking around behind us, so we can seem pretty close." She leaned away from the railing and winced, like she was preparing to rip off a band-aid. "But when people just assume we're together, I don't really do much to stop them from thinking that."

Corvin looked at her sideways. "Really?"

"Yeah, I mean, I didn't use to go along with it, but then I noticed it stopped most of the advances. Like belonging to someone else is the only thing these d-holes seem to respect, or at least, they don't want to cross Max. It may not make me feel great about myself, but I get to forget about things and play the game for the most part. Which is all I really want."

"Too bad that's what it takes."

"I know. I mean, can't I just play a game? Not every woman you meet online is looking to date. People need to take no for an answer. I shouldn't need to give a reason why not. And I definitely shouldn't need to activate my cage, like, ever."

"You've had to?" Corvin's mouth dropped open.

"A couple times." She sunk back down to the railing and sulked.

"Damn. I guess men suck," Corvin said matter-of-factly.

"Yes, we certainly do," Kira added before changing the subject. "Anyway, enough about my sob stories, what about you? How's being a fluffy-tailed reynard treating you?"

"Ahh," he dragged out the syllable, taken aback by the question. He wasn't one to talk about himself. But she had answered his questions, so it was only fair that he did the same. "I guess I can't complain. I like the ears." He flipped them back and forth. "The tail is hard to control and gets in the way, though."

She smiled. "I bet you're glad it was your robe that got caught in the door last dungeon and not your tail."

Corvin's eyes widened as he considered it. "Oh, man, that would've sucked!" He swept his tail around himself so he could hold it in his hands and stroke it.

She looked at him, biting her lip again, looking a little shy but also more like herself. "Hey," she said in a sheepish tone. "Feel free to say no to this, but can I touch it?"

His face flushed, looking down at his tail. "I guess so."

"See I asked first, like a gentleman," she explained puffing out her chest with pride.

Corvin laughed as she reached out and took the end of his tail in her hands.

"Oh my god! It's so soft. How is it this soft?" she asked, bouncing on her toes.

He shrugged, not really knowing how to respond.

She didn't let go. Instead, she sat down and leaned against the side of the steel plating below the railing. She patted the floor next to her, indicating for him to sit.

He cooperated. To his surprise, she draped his tail across her lap and stroked it like a cat. No one had ever really touched him before in-game, and it gave him a little more understanding of what it meant. It felt strange but not bad. In a way, he felt closer to her.

A chill had found its way into the air as the ship traveled to the north, and she used his thick fur as a blanket, letting out a contented noise that was somewhere between a sigh and a moan as she snuggled with it across her lap.

"How do you like being a *Venom* mage?" she asked, running her fingers through his fur.

"I guess ..." he thought about it for a moment, "I sort of hate it."

She ceased her petting and sat up straight. "Why?"

He sighed. "I guess because I don't get to do much. I know I'm useful, but I just hang around the background casting spells. I never really get the chance to stand out."

"There's nothing wrong with that," she insisted, leaning closer toward him.

"I know. It was the reason why I chose my class in the first place. Back then, I just wanted to play the game without drawing too much attention. If you hadn't noticed, I'm kind of shy."

She laid on a thick layer of sarcasm. "No way, really?"

He continued, "At least, that's how I felt before playing with you guys. Since then, I've seen what you do out there, and I find myself wishing I could be different. I want to be more fun like you and cooler like Max."

Kira snorted. "You think Max is cool?"

"I do. He's a great leader, an amazing fighter, and he carries himself like he has nothing to prove. He has a confidence that I just don't," Corvin answered, opening up to someone for the first time in years. There was something freeing about it.

"I didn't know anyone looked up to Max like that." She tilted her head from side to side. "I suppose he can be kind of cool. I've known him a long time, so I never really notice. I just remember him getting picked on in school and falling apart whenever he talked to women."

Corvin snapped his eyes back to hers, surprised by what he'd heard. "He got picked on?"

"Yeah, it's probably why we became friends. He had a bit of a rough childhood. Although, I didn't know him then since I didn't move to town until later. It's not something he hides or anything though. His father was hard on him as a kid, and he left Max and his mother without much explanation."

Corvin let his shoulders sink. "I'm sorry, I didn't know that."

"It's okay. Max is fine now, but back then, he was just a child, so it hit him hard. And you know how cruel kids can be. Once they sensed that weakness in him, they grabbed on and wouldn't let it go. By the time I started at his school mid-way through third grade, he was alone. On my first day, I saw him sitting by himself outside. I could have gone over to the other kids, but they were all grouped together, and I was afraid to introduce myself. So I just went over and sat with him."

Corvin looked at the fairy, wishing that he had met someone like her back when he had been alone. Actually, in a way, he was still alone. "And you've been friends ever since?"

"Yup. He puts up with me."

Corvin stayed quiet for a while before speaking again, debating on how much he should tell her about himself. He decided to go with vague honesty. "I got picked on pretty bad in school, too. It didn't end well."

"I'm sorry. That's crappy," she said with a sincerity in her voice that didn't quite match her words.

"Yeah, it was. But if Max could bounce back and become the badass that he is now, maybe there's hope for me."

"That's true." She stroked his tail again.

He thought for a while. "When this mission is done, I'm thinking of starting over with a different class, something like a *Blade* or maybe a *Shield*."

She went quiet for a few seconds as if weighing his choices. "I think you'd make a good *Blade*."

"Why?"

"The gear would go better with your tail."

He laughed. "You really like the tail, huh?"

"I do. I just want to lay down and roll around on it." She lifted the furry blanket and nuzzled it with her cheek.

That was when a voice called to them from the doorway. "You two are looking mighty cozy over there."

Corvin looked up in unison with Kira to find Max staring down at them, one eyebrow raised in question of their position-ing. His forehead burned as the fairy continued to nuzzle his tail as if completely unembarrassed.

She buried her cheek into Corvin's fur. "Don't judge. This is actually quite calming, which is something I need right now."

Max nodded, accepting that as an explanation. "Well, I'm glad you're calm. But unfortunately, we're all back online, and Alastair has news." He motioned with his hand for them to come back inside.

They obeyed without question, Kira giving Corvin a grateful smile.

He smiled back, this time without his heart racing.

CHAPTER THIRTY-SIX

Together once again, the group gathered around Kira at the center of the bridge as Alastair approached. She tried her best to read his expression.

He clapped his hands together. "Good news, everyone."

Kira leveled her eyes at him, not buying whatever he was selling. "And that is?"

"No one is in any danger at the moment."

"I'm assuming there is bad news as well," Kira prodded as she folded her arms across her body.

"Umm, yes." Alastair deflated a bit. "We have no way to log you out properly at this time."

"Figured that was coming." Kira dropped herself into the captain's chair and slouched, as if sighing with her entire body. Then she remembered that she was only wearing a dress. She sat up straight and crossed her legs the way she thought a proper lady should. She didn't want to give the crew another show.

Farn placed a supportive hand on her shoulder, which was appreciated.

Alastair ignored the fact that she had stolen his seat again.

"We can still get you out by cutting the power to your system, but there is a message on your rig's screen that warns against doing that. It mentions consequences, which I assume means that the virus will be released if we forcibly disconnect you. So, the question here is, what do you want us to do?"

Kira was taken aback by the question. It hadn't occurred to her that she might have a choice. "What do you mean?"

Alastair leaned against a railing to the side, looking less authoritative. "I mean, do you want to quit now? Obviously, I'd like to keep going, but I'm not going to force you to. If you want out, it's okay." His expression was sincere, though a bit hopeful.

Kira looked to Max to ask what he thought she should do, but he gave his answer before she could ask the question.

"It's up to you. We'll stick by you no matter what you choose."

Farn gave her shoulder a gentle squeeze in agreement.

Kira turned back to Alastair. "How long can I be in here before I should start worrying?"

His eyes glanced up at the ceiling then back to her. "Well, in the test that got Neal fired, he had subjects in for twenty-six hours. So you've got a little under eleven before passing that record."

She considered the time she had left, which still seemed like a lot. "Can we revisit this when I get closer? Maybe we can finish before then."

"That's reasonable." Alastair gave her a warm smile before adding, "Now, get out of my seat."

"Oh, sorry." She hopped up awkwardly and returned to her place at Max's side.

Alastair reclaimed his chair and proceeded to get himself back into captain mode. He leaned forward to address the crew. "Okay, people, we have just under eleven hours to get this thing done. After that, we'll all be out of a job. It's all or nothing, so let's get down there, and do what we do best."

The crew's determination grew despite the fact that some of them didn't have much to do other than stand around. Most seemed to be there just in case they were needed. Though the threat was real, and they probably liked their jobs, so it was only natural that they felt invested in the mission.

Standing out from the rest, Alastair's assistant, Jeff-with-a-three, seemed even more serious than usual, his attention locked on a leather-bound book, its digital ink displaying a list of the party's vitals.

Kira caught the book's contents out of the corner of her eye. It didn't make her feel better. Neither did the pitying looks she caught from the crew when they thought she wasn't looking.

In the end, it didn't matter; she had made her decision. So she just stepped closer to Max and Farn as Checkpoint employees pulled levers and turned wheels, bringing the ship down as they approached the third location. Frost formed on the windows as they grew closer.

CHAPTER THIRTY-SEVEN

Max stepped off the retractable stairs of the Nostromo and onto a snow-covered dock at the end of a long bridge. On the other side stood Castle Alderth. It was a strange place to feel relieved, but for the first time, the quest had brought him to a place he had been before, somewhere he knew like the back of his hand. Granted, it had been a long time since he had last set foot in the place.

The dungeon, if you could call something so large a dungeon, sat on the edge of a waterfall that stretched wide on either side, its waters frozen in time long ago by ice. The *City of Rend*, or at least what was left of it, lined the sides of the massive river that once flowed around the castle. In the middle of the river sat the airship dock, held up by a few pillars.

The platform was never meant to be used since it was just there to make the place look like it had once been a working city in the past. It was a happy accident that the designers had thought to connect it to the castle's main gates, giving the team a straight shot into the castle without having to travel through the surrounding buildings and streets. As it turned out, having their own ship was pretty convenient.

Spires reached into the sky like dozens of upside-down icicles as the castle loomed over the bridge. The sheer size of the place was an impressive feat. Players could spend weeks exploring it and the surrounding city. To many, the enormous dungeon was considered an entire game in and of itself, especially since it had its own storyline, but that was back when Noctem released its first expansion. The castle still saw a handful of hardcore fans, but other than that, it saw few visitors today.

Now, most of the players that chose to venture into the difficult area had done everything there was to do. Max and Kira had even run through the place multiple times, trashing all of the key items they received each time so that they could start over from scratch. Max breathed a sigh of relief that he hadn't thrown away the dungeon's keys after their last time there. *It would suck to have to unlock everything again now.*

As he stood on the far side of the bridge, the castle had the imposing yet somber presence of a tomb. Although, that was probably due to the fact that it was a tomb.

The castle hadn't always been shrouded with such a heavy gloom. Well, technically, it had, as it had only come into existence two and a half years ago, but according to the lore, it had once been one of Noctem's strongest kingdoms. Ruled by House Alderth, it had been a grand and majestic palace surrounded by a city of loyal subjects. It wasn't easy living in the cold of the northern territory, but its mages had created a spell that made the place livable. Overall, it had been a nice place to call home. That was until the Nightmares were discovered.

Back in the city's fictional past, Eustace Alderth, who ruled over the city at the time, had led a group of his bravest adventurers to challenge the Nightmare, Rasputin the Destroyer. The intent had been on securing a contract to gain prosperity for his people. They fought hard, and in the end, were victorious. That's when things went south. Eustace betrayed his subjects by offering the lives of his entire kingdom in exchange for immortality. Rasputin had accepted the trade eagerly, and in an instant, ice claimed the city, people and all.

Thousands of imaginary lives were lost in the trade, including Eustace himself, whose frozen body still stood outside Rasputin's lair in the mountains, not too far from where they were now. He did gain the immortality he sought by going down in Noctem's history as a monster who sacrificed his people for personal gain. It was a precautionary tale about the nature of the Nightmares and an example of the corruption of power. At least, that was what Max and Kira could piece together from notes and the description text of various items found in the area.

The thing that had kept players interested in the place two years ago was the huge number of secrets and hidden passages. Its mystery had even become a topic for debate, with players arguing back and forth on message boards. One side insisted that the city had been explored in its entirety and were waiting for it to be given an update to add more content to it, while the other side believed that it still hid more that had yet to be discovered. The debate continued to this day, scrutinizing things like markings on walls and courtyards that could be seen from above but no one could seem to find on the ground.

According to Alastair, Checkpoint did have something planned to bring players back to the area, but the fact that Max and company were there now as part of their quest also meant that there must be something hidden within. As it seemed, both sides were right.

Snow drifted through the deathly still air as Max walked, all warmth leaving the place as if it didn't want to stick around for what was about to go down, leaving him and his group chilled in the crisp light of a full moon as they traversed the bridge. Shadows clawed toward them from the icy spires. Max couldn't help notice that Farn swallowed hard.

Kira, however, let out a quiet, "Ahhhh," as she held out her tongue to catch an unsuspecting flake of ice that fell into her mouth. The fairy's spirits were higher than one would expect, considering her situation. She seemed to have moved on rather than dwelling on things, which was how she handled the majority of her problems. For the most part, nothing kept her down for long. It was one of the things that Max had always appreciated about his partner.

She switched up her strategy from catching snowflakes to straight up biting them out of the air, making ridiculous 'chomp' noises as she did.

Farn gave a short laugh as Kira's improved demeanor did wonders for the mood of the group, even in their bleak surroundings.

Max enjoyed her antics but shook his head at her immaturity regardless.

Kira stopped for a moment. "Hey, when I was stuck getting updated and whatnot in the last dungeon, who got the contract?"

Max slapped a hand against his forehead, realizing that he had forgotten about it with everything that was going on with her. "Oh god, I can't believe I didn't check." He shoved his hand into his pocket. The item was tiny, which added to the reasons that he had forgotten about it. A second later, he pulled out his hand to see the familiar shape resting in his palm. The moonlight glinted off its silver surface. "Holy shit," Max muttered as he checked its description in his journal. Then he promptly burst out laughing.

Kira's gaze fell on him. "What's so funny?"

He responded by holding the book out for her to read, which she struggled to do with him still laughing.

"Dude, hold still," she nagged.

He settled down, still snickering as she paraphrased the text.

Contract name: *Silver Bullet*
Type: consumable
Ownership: unbound
Usage: one-time only
Basic enchantment: none

Advanced enchantment: ability, One-Shot
Ability description: this bullet can kill any enemy in one hit, as
long as that hit deals critical damage. Range, limited.

"That's freaking awesome!" Kegan jumped to the front of
the group to walk backward in front of Max.

"Yeah, from the sound of that, you might be able to take
out a Nightmare," Farn added, sounding hopeful.

Kira continued to eye him with suspicion. "But why is it
funny?"

Max pointed to the one line at the end that she had skipped
since it didn't seem important. Then she tilted her head to the
side. "I don't get it."

Max waved his hand. "You wouldn't; you were stuck in that
column of water, so you missed my response when the darkness
asked for an offer."

Everyone fell silent, clearly thinking back to what he had
said in the heat of the moment. He read the line out loud.
"Item given to form contract: fucks – quantity: zero."

The others burst out laughing at the absurdity of the
system's wording.

Kira looked annoyed at being left out of the joke but
shrugged and laughed anyway.

The fun was interrupted by Ginger, who was holding her
sides tight and shivering. "Yeah that's all hilarious and all, but
can I get a comfort spell here?"

"Crap. Sorry," Kira said as Max was starting to feel the bite
in the air.

Players couldn't actually freeze to death, but their brains
didn't know that, so the cold could get uncomfortable unless
they had an item capable of keeping them warm. Fortunately,
due to the requirement of keeping her feet bare, Kira had
purchased an anklet long ago that did just that. So for her, the
system ignored her mind's input for perceived temperatures and
loaded a comfortable sixty degrees for the colder environments.

Kira set up a quick spell exclusive to her class that extended the item's protective effect to the rest of the party. It didn't cost much mana and stayed in effect until she canceled it or died.

"Thanks." Ginger released her grip on her sides and stopped shivering as they approached the entrance.

The cold, dead hands of the castle's frozen subjects reached out in greeting as Max stepped through the huge doors of the entryway, their blank eyes on him as if pleading for a salvation that would never come. It was a twisted sight. Horror fans must have loved it.

As soon as he crossed the middle of the courtyard, the still bodies came alive, their icy joints cracking as they dashed toward the party. The area was designed to be difficult but only for low-level play, making the attacking corpses a minor threat, to say the least. They were still unnerving, but Max drew his pistols and took them out without skipping a beat. Kegan didn't even need to help.

From there, he wasted little time, taking a shortcut and proceeding to the main hall in hope of finding something that would point them in the right direction. All he found was an empty throne since he and Kira had already beaten the bosses that appeared in the room years ago. Max stepped up the stairs toward the ornate chair and plopped down into its cushioned seat to think, slouching with an unintentional swagger, like some kind of dark king.

Lacking a second throne for a queen, Kira sat down on the step in front of him with Farn sticking close by her side.

Kegan stood in the middle of the room, his hands in front of him as if framing a picture of Max and the two women sitting at his feet. His eyes lit up with a mischievous sparkle. "Hey, Kira, turn toward Max."

"Why?" She leaned her chin on one hand and stared at him, her expression incredulous.

"Just do it; it will be funny," the *Leaf* insisted.

Kira rolled her eyes up to Max where they lit up as if realizing what Kegan had been getting at. She smiled in understanding, then placed one hand on his unsuspecting leg while gazing up at him. Her violet eyes sparkling up at him with longing.

"Dude, cut it out." Max attempted to shake her off, covering his embarrassment with annoyance.

Kegan interrupted. "Okay, Farn, you too."

She shot him a look that asked 'Are you kidding me?'

He returned it with one of his own that told her that, 'No, he was not.'

Max didn't expect her to play along, but when she looked to Kira, who was now getting into it, she must have decided to go with it.

Suddenly, Ginger ran up the stairs. "Oh, me too, me too!" She dropped down in between Max's legs and leaned against him, her back arched to accentuate her breasts. She let her head rest on his lap and reached back with one arm.

Max shrunk back on instinct, letting out a confused, "Hey, what …" His voice cracked a little.

"Just shut up and look badass," Kegan interrupted.

Max groaned and gave in, taking a breath as he pushed back his nerves, a face of cold determination in their place.

Kegan took his inspector out of his journal and centered the small glass rectangle on the scene. A small click was audible as the frame flashed, leaving a still image on its surface as if he had snatched it out of the air. He held it up to see it closer. "Awesome. You better thank me, man. I just took your new profile picture."

Max's harem dissolved and descended the stairs to see the image, leaving the king alone on his throne. Each of them touched the photo, copying it to their own files on contact, laughing as they did. The pleasant notes of Kira's voice echoed through the hall, drawing out even more laughter from the rest. Kegan sent the picture to Max, who glanced at it on his own inspector without taking it out from the back of his journal and being careful not to look too long. He hid a grin and snapped the book shut, dropping the image into his personal gallery. There would be plenty of time to look at it later.

"Umm," Corvin spoke up, clearly waiting for a moment to break into the levity. "I could be wrong, but if Carver is working off the same list that most television and games use for the Horsemen, that means that we are either here to fight War or Death. And I'm guessing from the frozen bodies and overall depressing tone here, that this is where we'll find Death."

"Yeah, probably." Max leaned on one hand with little enthusiasm.

Corvin paused. "So if that's the case, we might want to go to the castle's crypt. There is one, right?"

Kira made a face at Max that seemed to question him for not thinking of it.

He ignored her. "Good idea." He scratched his head, trying to remember how to get there. "We just go down, I think."

"Oh, that helps," Ginger criticized.

"Yeah, not vague at all," Kegan added.

Kira and Farn snickered.

Max groaned and pushed himself up from the throne. It was going to be a long walk.

CHAPTER THIRTY-EIGHT

Kira trailed behind with Farn as Max led them down several wrong turns. She made a point of asking him questions like, "Are we there yet?" and, "Are you sure you know where you're going?"

His eyebrow twitched, though he never brought up the fact that she had been there as much as he had and that she was just as lost, which would have been accurate. That was when the spherical form of an ice poplo rolled in behind them as they triggered an ambush attack. Max slapped a hand to his face.

Kira opened her mouth to speak, but he cut her off.

"I know, I forgot about it," he said between his fingers as they rested against his shaking head.

Kira let out a chuckle. "It's cool. I did too."

As far as monsters went, poplos were kind of silly since they were nothing more than a big elemental ball and their faces were always different. Some were cute; some were scary. They were pretty much the jack-o'-lantern of Noctem's monsters.

This one made an attempt to look frightening, but the positioning of one of its eyes, sitting a bit lower than the other, made it appear sort of dumb. They were probably added to the area to help counteract the overall dreary feeling of the place and keep it from becoming too depressing. Although, with an arsenal of ice spells and the ability to give *frost* status on contact, they were no pushovers. At least, they weren't the last time Kira had been there, but after two years, the creature was around a hundred levels below her party's. Therefore, it was soon reduced to a melting pile of snow. Afterward, they pushed on, encountering a few more of the things as they searched. Each time, their rotund aggressors met the same end. One was even cleaved clean in two by Farn with a single strike. Its face looked a bit confused as it parted in the middle.

This continued until Corvin spotted a spiral stairway leading down. It was there that the poplos got the last laugh by spawning at the top and chasing the team down comically. The group toppled on top of each other in a lump as a couple of the monsters rolled over them at the bottom.

Kira let out a muffled protest from underneath Max and Farn, who had thrown themselves on top of her to keep the bouncing balls of snow from touching her. Their skin turned a light shade of blue for a minute, and they gained a significant weakness to ice attacks from the resulting status effect - though Kira removed it before they had time to worry about it.

After having dealt with the oversized snowballs, Kira found herself in a dim crypt, their destination apparently reached. They recovered and continued their search without skipping a beat, clearing out a few weak enemies under the incandescent crystals of ice that lit their way.

Despite being a place filled with death and loss, the gentle blue glow reflecting off patches of frost was almost beautiful. There was a peace to the place that Kira found calming as they proceeded down the main corridor to stand before the largest of the area's tombs. It belonged to Eustace Alderth's father, who had ruled over the castle before him. If they hadn't already beaten the dungeon, they would've had to fight the old man's ghost, but since they had, all they found was his grave.

Kegan gave a short bow, placing one hand across his chest.

"You gotta feel bad for the guy. His own son destroyed everything he cared about."

Kira bowed as well. It was a respectful gesture for a man that never existed.

Finding nothing other than pity at the large tomb, the others spread out to search the rest of the crypt. It didn't take long for them to find a clue.

"Hey, what does this look like to you?" Kegan stood under an archway leading to a side path, his finger pointing up at a small bell hanging in the center.

Max stepped closer to examine it. "That looks like the bell we fought in the Famine dungeon."

"Probably means we go that way," Farn tapped it with her sword so that it rang as she passed under it.

The others split up to search the tombs that lined the narrow passage, reading the text on each for a hint. Kira noticed Farn sticking close her as if she wanted to be near, just in case something happened. A moment later, the *Shield* stopped in front of a small alcove.

"That's odd." Farn rested a hand on her chin.

"What?" Kira scanned the space up and down.

It didn't contain anything out of the ordinary, just a wide tombstone with a statue of a young woman on top. Although, it was strange that the figure sat with its back to the viewer, its face turned away toward the wall as if looking at something of interest.

Farn pointed down with an armored finger at the simple line of text inscribed on the stone. "There's no name or date on this one."

Kira raised an eyebrow as she read it. "The two most important days in your life are the day you are born and the day you find out why." It sounded like some kind of quote, though she didn't know where from. She pondered its meaning but was distracted as she noticed a circular marking on the wall behind it in the direction of where the statue was facing.

Farn noticed it too, stepping past the stone to investigate.

Kira took a step back as the *Shield* pushed on it with one hand. When nothing happened, Farn went ahead and rapped on it with the back of her gauntlet, like she was knocking on a door. Again, nothing. She shrugged and turned around to leave. Then she froze.

"What is it?" Kira asked as a shiver crawled across her skin.

Farn didn't answer her. Instead, she just called out to the others, "Guys! I think I found something!"

Max and the rest fell in behind Kira, forcing her to step closer to the stone. Each of them glanced at the inscription.

"It's Mark Twain, I think," Corvin said, inadvertently demonstrating that despite being younger than Kira, he might also have been smarter.

Farn shook her head. "Not that." She pointed to the statue sitting on top, its back to the others. "This."

Kira's eyes fell to the woman on the stone. Like many statues in the crypt, it was nude with sculpted stone made to look like cloth draped around it, probably to keep it from being too risqué for the game's overall rating. The figure leaned on one arm and clutched the cloth to its chest with the other, its gracefully curved back fully exposed. It almost seemed alive, as if it might take a breath at any second.

She had passed by the figure before, more than once even. It was just a statue. She had never given it a second thought or even a first thought. It was background, nothing more, but background or not, Farn was staring at it like it was something otherworldly.

The others squeezed in closer, and Kira stepped around the stone to make room. She fell backward as soon as she did, gasping as Farn caught her. She continued to step away from the stone until she ran out of room, her back pressed against Farn's armor, the *Shield* holding her shoulders for support. A muffled sound escaped through her fingers as she clasped her hands over her mouth, her own face looking back, carved in stone.

Its head was cocked to the side in an almost friendly manner while amethyst crystals sparkled in its eyes, filling its expression with life. A replica of her unwanted pendant hung around its neck.

"No way," Max said in a hushed tone as he joined her.

Kira removed her hands from her mouth. "How?" was all she could get out, but the implications of the word were clear.

Corvin brushed a hand against his chin. "This castle was part of the first expansion. That was two and a half years ago."

"Oh god." Farn tightened her grip on Kira's shoulders. "Carver knew it would be her from the start."

"He must have picked her back then," Corvin added.

"Why me?" Kira dropped her eyes to the stone the statue sat upon. "My willpower stat isn't even that high." She lifted her face toward Max. "Yours is almost double."

His expression turned with a sudden twist, bearing his teeth as a growl rose in his throat. "Damn it!" He slammed the side of his fist against the wall. "There has to be something Alastair's not telling us. There's no way he didn't know about this."

Ginger looked over Kira's stone doppelgänger. "How did he get it to look so real?"

"It's probably a copy of her avatar rendered in a different material," Corvin explained while reaching toward the statue's slender back. He stopped just before touching it, pulling his hand back as if it might burn him.

Kira shuddered as she imagined Carver positioning her naked body on the stone like a doll and draping only a sheet around her for clothing. A part of her felt violated, although she knew she shouldn't. It wasn't real, but real or not, she had been sitting there on that stone for over two years, alone in the crypt. She had even passed by herself and hadn't noticed. Even if she had, she just would have ignored it as a coincidence. Her eyes started to well up, but she shoved the emotion back down before she fell apart.

Max's face softened, and he stepped to her, holding up a finger in her face that snapped her back to him. "This doesn't change anything. You got that? We're still just here to kick Death's ass and save the world, nothing more."

Kira understood what he was trying to do. It was just like when he had called out to her while she crawled through that claustrophobic passage in the last dungeon, like he knew she was teetering on the edge. She closed her eyes and took a breath, letting his words sink in. Then she snorted. "Well, aren't you sounding heroic." She forced a laugh, unable to remove the quiver in her voice. She shook her head, feeling stupid at her lack of control. "Sorry, this quest is really screwing me up." She lowered her head.

Ginger stepped forward, putting her arms around both Kira and Max before pulling the two figurative brothers close and tussling their hair playfully. "It's okay; I like you when you're all fragile. It makes your cuteness tolerable, and Max is kind of hot when he gets protective."

Kira groaned in unison with Max, and they pushed her away in a unified effort.

Ginger laughed, bringing back some of the light-hearted mood from before so that Kira could move on.

She did her best to ignore the face staring back at her as she forced her own to harden with determination, only wavering a little. "Okay, we're here because Carver thinks we're badass enough to fight Death. I gotta start acting like it."

Max slapped her on the back and gave her an encouraging, "Damn right!"

She stumbled from the sudden impact and responded by punching him in the arm before turning back to the statue. "No more being a baby. Let's get this done." Her words did their best to chase away the fear in her voice, and the party got behind her, both figuratively and literally, as they packed into the small alcove. An awkward moment passed before Kira spoke again, "Now, does anyone know what I'm supposed to do?"

The group released a collective breath.

"That was anticlimactic," Kegan commented.

"I don't see *you* doing anything." Kira glared at him over her shoulder before shrugging. "Any ideas?"

"Try touching it," Corvin suggested.

"Yeah! Touch it everywhere," Kegan added.

"Touch all the things!" Farn raised a fist in the air.

Kira placed her hands on her double's shoulders, its gray skin feeling warm under her palms as if it was immune to the cold just as she was. Nothing happened. She ran her fingers along its collarbone and onto the pendant. Still nothing. She poked it in the eyes, Three Stooges style, being sure to accompany it with the appropriate comedic sounds. Clearly, that wasn't the answer.

The others watched her as she groped herself all over, bursting into laughter behind her several times.

She pushed it, pulled it, slapped it, and even gave it a kiss on the mouth, which had been Kegan's suggestion, but after everything, still, nothing happened. Finally, she plopped herself down on the tombstone next to it.

"That's it; I got nothing." She leaned to one side to rest on her arm, mimicking the statue's pose without realizing it. Suddenly, there was a click, followed by a clack, and her eyes widened. The whole stone slid into the hall, taking her with it and revealing a rectangular hole with a ladder heading down.

Kira looked around at herself and the statue trying to figure out what she had done to activate the mechanism. She felt like an idiot when she figured out what it was. "Seriously, I had to copy its pose. How the hell was I supposed to figure that out?" She hopped off the stone as the others gathered around the hole.

Max peered in. "Well, at least we know what's waiting for us down there."

"You mean Death?" Kira asked matter-of-factly.

Max set one foot onto the ladder. "Yup."

CHAPTER THIRTY-NINE

Max led his team with his guns drawn as they followed him in single file through the narrow underground passage. For a group of people about to face Death, he was surprised that the mood was rather light.

Farn opened her journal and browsed through a playlist from a music app she had purchased. She switched the output from her ears to include her whole party. A version of Queen's 'We Will Rock You' faded in combined with an orchestral score that gave the familiar song more impact and revved up the group as they broke into a run.

Kira belted out the words of the song, every now and then revealing a decent singing voice that Max didn't know she had. Ginger jumped to touch the ceiling like the grown-up that she was. The others copied her, looking like a high school football team running down the hall toward the field before a big game. Well, all except Kira who couldn't reach.

The passage came to an end, and the group spilled out into a large room with a wide stairway leading up in the middle.

Max froze, looking up at the chamber's contents. "Well, crap."

"Ha! It's not just me." Kira pointed in his direction with a wide smile on her face.

The others stood with their mouths hanging open at the forty-foot statue before them of Max locked in combat with a massive skeleton.

His form was placed low against one wall, resting on the floor as if he was in the middle of leaping backward. One leg was tucked up against his stone body while the other extended, arching over the stairs. Both arms were extended, pistols ready to fire at a skeleton dressed in rags coming at him at an angle from above. It reached out for him, its face contorted in a silent scream.

With that, Kira's mood seemed to recover from the shock of seeing her own statue back in the crypt above. She materialized her wings and flew up to land on the statue's head. "I'm not sure how to feel about the fact that yours is so much bigger than mine." She placed her hands on her hips, looking dissatisfied.

Max shrugged, resisting the urge to make the obvious joke. "At least it looks pretty badass."

"Yeah, what the hell?" Kira let out an indignant growl as she stepped onto Max's giant stone nose and sat down on it, leaning forward with a huff. "Why do you get to be fully clothed while all I get is a little sheet? Is that sexist? I'm not sure."

"Kinda," Ginger said while Farn nodded in agreement.

Corvin stepped up the first few stairs, so he was standing under the statue's knee. "Obvious sexism aside, this thing gives me a thought."

"About?" Kira asked.

"Well, Max has the highest willpower, right? So if the point of this quest really is to make one of us strong enough to over-power the system, then putting Kira in danger would certainly be a good way to create an emotional response to push you further. So maybe the whole point of choosing her is to use her as a hostage."

"Okay, so my life could be in your hands," Kira said, sounding more casual than one would expect.

It struck Max as odd that she didn't seem as worried as she had been up in the room above, looking at her own statue. *Great, like that makes me feel better,* Max thought, not wanting to worry about what might happen if he failed. "I guess it makes sense. If Carver watched our recordings, then he would know that I spend most of my time protecting you."

Ginger laughed. "If that's the case, he probably thinks you two are lovers."

"Eww." Max recoiled with an exaggerated gesture.

Kira grimaced. "Don't say lovers."

Ginger said it again, dragging out the word, "Loooovvverrrs."

Farn climbed onto the statue, standing on its lap and leaning on its raised leg. "Wouldn't it be crazy if this whole quest was just because of a misunderstanding, and Carver just thinks you two are a couple." She looked from Kira down to Max.

"Ugh." Max dragged a hand over his face. "Why the hell do people even think that?"

Farn snorted and hooked a thumb up at the fairy. "Well, she is sitting on your face right now."

"Ha! Nice." Kegan called out as Farn let on that her sense of humor was a little dirtier than Max and the others had thought.

Kira looked down at the placement of the statue's nose. "Yikes." She shifted her view back to Farn. "At least I'm not standing on his junk."

The *Shield* looked down as well, her boots planted on top of his massive stone crotch. She snorted. "So I am." They both laughed, though neither of them made any motion to move.

"Okay, you two, off my statue." Max waved his hands in a shooing motion, like they were a couple of unwanted pigeons. They obeyed begrudgingly, and Max snapped a quick picture of the scene with his inspector, getting a sideways look from Ginger. He shrugged back at her. "What? When am I gonna be back here again?"

Not wanting to waste any more time, he began his ascent. A wave of tension coursed through his spine as soon as he set foot on the stairs. It seemed to travel down through the others, replacing the levity with a more serious vibe. If it wasn't obvious enough that he was almost to the boss, the massive stone skeleton on the ceiling made it clear as he passed it. Its bony arms stretched out past him, the fingers of one hand gripping the side of the stairs, so he had to step over its joints.

"This isn't unnerving at all." Kira tiptoed close to its jaws as if she was trying to sneak by.

Surprisingly, after the spectacle below, the top of the stairs ended in a small room with an even smaller door. The others piled into the space like clowns going on a road trip, making Max feel cramped with them pressed up against his back.

"What's going on up there?" Kegan shouted from behind.

Max took position next to the narrow door. Farn took the other side without needing to be told. He nodded to her. She nodded back. Then he pushed the door open, and the two dashed in to secure the area.

Fresh air filled his lungs as he found himself outside again. Max scanned his surroundings, finding decorative gravestones and statuary scattered about. High walls towered on all sides with no doors or windows to be seen, the faces of gargoyles staring down at them from above. The only way in or out was the small door of a mausoleum that they came from.

Max motioned to the doorway, telling the mages that it was safe, or at least, it was for the time being.

Kira and Corvin emerged followed by Ginger, her dagger at the ready. Kegan brought up the rear, arrows in hand, his arm twitching. They weren't about to be taken by surprise again.

Snow fell softly across the graveyard. Silence fell equally so. Max broke it, looking up at the moon. "The sky is open. Do we have *Flight?*"

Kira swiped open her spell-craft menu and shook her head. "Nope, just me again."

Suddenly, the door they came from slammed shut on its own, the implication being clear. They had to survive to escape.

At the center of the cemetery stood one grave larger than the rest. On top, a robed statue perched, casting a long shadow in the light of the full moon. The air was still, without a trace of wind. If Max wasn't so adept at sensing movement, he might have missed it. The figure at the center turned.

He sprang to action without bothering to tell his team of the target, not because he didn't think of it but because he didn't need to. They were already falling into formation before he got a shot off. He fired at where he thought the hooded figure's head would be and his guns barked, tearing through the silence and echoing off the high walls. A metallic clang followed as the bullets impacted against a blade, now held in a skeletal hand in front of the figure.

It had moved almost too fast to see, effortlessly blocking his shots. The figure paused a moment, then stepped down from the ornate grave marker that it had spent the last two and a half years waiting for them on.

Max grinned. It would be rude to disappoint it.

CHAPTER FORTY

Max's heart skipped a beat as the skeletal figure's robe fanned out, its tattered edges floating in the still air with each movement like it was underwater. The white bone of its skull peeked out from under its hood. Then, from underneath the gray cloak, it drew a long, unmistakable weapon. The sight of it somehow filled Max with satisfaction as if he wouldn't have felt right about the fight if Death didn't have his traditional scythe.

In its other hand, it held a short sword with which it had blocked Max's last attack. Well, short wasn't really the right word for it. It was actually larger than most swords, but due to the fact that the intimidating figure stood almost twice as tall as a normal person, the blade looked small in comparison.

The group, clearly still feeling confident, prepared to rush the boss. Then it revealed two more arms, each with a different sword. Then two more, bringing the total to six.

Kegan let out a short, "The hell?"

"It's certainly well-armed," Kira remarked, getting a grin from Farn.

Max rolled his eyes.

In the next few seconds, shots rang out, arrows flew, and

spells were cast, but after it all, Death stood unaffected, its six arms blocking everything with an impenetrable defense.

Max called to Corvin, "Any chance of your basilisk eye slowing this thing down?"

"Sorry, it only works on things that actually have eyes. Empty sockets won't cut it."

Max frowned before returning his gaze to the hooded skull of their foe. It looked calm, almost tranquil. Then it was on him.

It closed the gap in an instant, blades swinging with precision. He dodged twice but took a hit from one of the swords. It hit hard, cutting away around twenty percent of his health. He took another. It was fast. The familiar tingle of Kira's magic touched his skin as a healing spell swirled around him. A fraction of a second later, two arrows flew at the boss from where Kegan stood behind him. They didn't land, but they forced it to block, saving Max from being hit by the scythe and buying him a couple seconds to put in some distance. Try as he might, he just couldn't get away. Again, it wound up its scythe. He was out of options.

Without warning, the world around him vanished, and Max fell into the same gloom as before when fighting the spiders in the last dungeon. Everything came back just as fast, and he stumbled backward landing on his rear again, the frozen ground crunching underneath him.

Farn stood in his place, bracing against her shield to take a hit that was meant for him. He glanced at the shift beads that encircled his wrist as another bead faded from black to red. He grinned and pushed himself up from the snow. He had to pay her back for saving him.

A look at his forearm showed her health drop by at least a third from the attack even with her shield's damage reduction. Max did the math in his head. Her shield absorbed around ninety percent of the damage, meaning that the hit would have done well over three times her total hit points if she hadn't blocked it. The scythe must have been different than the boss's other weapons. If any of them were to be hit by it, they would be killed outright. Judging by the look on Farn's face, she'd realized it too. She kept its focus on her anyway. There wasn't an option not to. She didn't bother attacking; there wasn't enough time. It was going to have to be up to him.

Max fired, his bullets causing little more than a few sparks as they ricocheted off the thing's blades. Kegan's arrows had the same effect. Its defense still seemed impenetrable. They had to find a way to slow it down. If not, all the time Farn was buying for them would just go to waste.

A steady glow of light circled the *Shield* in repetition as Kira cast heal after heal to keep her health high enough to continue the struggle. She couldn't keep it up forever; Max was sure of that. Eventually, Kira's constant healing would draw too much attention.

As soon as he thought it, the hollow eyes of the skull turned toward the fairy, her mouth silently forming the words 'Oh crap' as she saw it, too. Then it was in front of her. Farn yelled from behind it in an attempt to draw it off, but it shrugged off the taunt and drew back a sword. The blade hit the ground just as Kira escaped into the air, her wings shining through the dark sky.

Max let out a breath that he hadn't realized he'd been holding. He just hoped it couldn't follow her. It didn't. Instead, it opened its mouth and screamed, a red glow gathering in its jaws. Energy swam toward it, like lightning in its teeth, brighter and faster than Max thought possible. It fired.

A beam of deep crimson cut through the air with pinpoint accuracy. All the maneuverability in the world couldn't save the fairy; there wasn't time to react. It hit her square in the chest, throwing her back against the wall before sweeping up across one of the castle's towers.

Kira's most recent bone charm was obliterated, her singular protection gone. She fell almost forty feet, far enough to kill her, or it would have been, if Farn hadn't caught her out of the air, the two of them rolling as the *Shield* used her body to take the impact. She was getting good at catching the fairy.

Max fired again, trying to buy them time, but it wasn't enough. Then a rumble from above drew his attention as a tower crumbled to pieces, having been hit by the blast as well. It fell as if cleaved clean through by the beam. Rubble crashed to the floor of the graveyard, sending him running for cover. Max hoped he was lucky enough for Death to be caught in its own destruction. He wasn't.

He dove a few feet from Farn as she released the fairy, who was somehow unharmed after everything. Clouds of dust filled the graveyard, making it hard to see.

"I guess he doesn't like it when people get out of range." Kira coughed. Her jaw dropped as she tried to speak again, a silver blade glinting through the dust as it began to settle.

Death seemed to appear from nothing, scythe held aloft. Farn reacted, throwing Kira to the side so that she rolled in Max's direction. He caught her as the massive blade came down, burying itself deep into the ground, mere inches from Farn's head.

Despite the depth with which the weapon had penetrated the frozen earth, the skeleton didn't even struggle to pull it back out.

They got back to their feet, Farn again putting herself between the Nightmare and the squishy fairy behind her. It was the right move, even if it brought them right back where they started. If they lost their healer now, it was over.

Max glanced to Kira who was dropping heals into her queue with one hand while absentmindedly twisting the ring on her finger that tied her life to Farn's in a one-way bond. It was clear what she was thinking. Max didn't want to have to use the rings either. Fortunately, Farn seemed to have the thing back under control for the moment as she deflected with her sword and blocked with her shield, holding Death's attention on her.

Max took the brief opportunity to retrieve an item from his pocket. They were out of options, and if there was ever a time to use a bullet that could kill anything, this was it. He ejected a magazine and snapped the tiny item in on top before jamming it back in and racking the slide.

Power surged through him as soon as the round slid into position, his arm feeling like he'd shoved a fork into an electrical socket in the best way possible. Something inside of him clicked into place, and he took a deep relaxing breath. He could do anything with that bullet, like he had become the hero of all the movies that he had ever quoted. His doubts fell away. Even if Kira was a hostage, it didn't matter. He could save her and the world at the same time. All he had to do was land a critical. He wondered what his willpower stat was in that moment. It must have been high. After all, he was Max-freaking-Damage, and he was about to shoot Death in the face.

The others continued their assault from all sides, but the large health bar at the edge of Max's sleeve had only dropped a hair, each of them doing little more than chip damage to its limbs. He watched for his opening. He only needed one.

Looking desperate, Ginger tried something outside the box, firing her grappling hook at the boss. It caught one arm, and her eyes lit up. The skeleton must not have registered it as something to block since it wasn't an actual attack. She yanked the line, and for a second, the Nightmare faltered. Its arms swung wildly, still blocking attacks from Kegan, but for Farn, who was right in front of it, the millisecond of unbalance gave the *Shield* an opening. She slipped through its almost unbreakable defense and thrust her sword between its ribs. Bones cracked as she twisted the blade.

It cried out and dropped to one knee, stabbing one of its swords into the ground for support. Then it pulled back on the arm that Ginger held with her line. The tension yanked the *Coin* off the ground, tossing her across the cemetery where she impacted hard with one of the statues, shattering it to pieces.

Farn attempted to pull her sword out and escape, but Death grabbed her hand, leaving one of his swords stuck in the ground. It whipped her around like a rag doll and pulled her off the ground, holding her tight against its chest like a child clutching a favorite stuffed animal. She struggled to get free, but it had her in a literal death grip. The humor was lost on her as her face flooded with panic. Then Death reached his scythe arm around her, keeping her close in the rough embrace, its bony arm across her chest.

Death paused, like it was savoring the moment, its four free limbs still keeping up its defense as it lowered the blade of its scythe to Farn's throat. She screamed as it became obvious what was about to happen. The cold edge of the weapon snatched her breath away as it touched her skin, freezing her scream in an awful sounding croak.

Then she was falling, the attack interrupted as Max rammed the skeleton with everything he had, taking a few hits in the process. He couldn't stand off to the side anymore. Hell, he wouldn't have been much of a hero if he'd let things go on like that much longer. He smiled as Farn dropped to the ground safely, even as his health fell below ten percent.

He got back to his feet, ignoring his dwindling hit points. It was okay; he didn't need them. He had his bullet. He dodged a blade, distracting the boss with a few rounds from his other gun. He had to wait until he had the shot. He ducked another strike then sidestepped to avoid another. Finally, he let out a wild laugh and thrust his pistol up, a few feet from the thing's skull. He added one word as he squeezed the trigger, "Smile."

Everyone froze as the shot rang out and reverberated off the walls.

Max stood, stunned, his wrist clutched by a skeletal hand. Wisps of black smoke drifting from the muzzle of his gun as it pointed just to the side of Death's head. He couldn't believe it. He was Max-freaking-Damage, and he just fucking missed.

CHAPTER FORTY-ONE

Max froze in terror as his mind processed what had just happened.

It was gone.

The most powerful contract he'd ever had, wasted.

That feeling that he could do anything. That confidence. It was all a lie. He had seen that damn statue below, showing him in all his epic glory, and it had messed with his head, stroking his ego just right.

His eyes darted to Kira who was saying something that he couldn't hear. *I'm so sorry*, he thought. She trusted him with her life, and he had screwed it all up. He was an idiot, and now he was trapped. He glanced back to Death, its blade piercing his chest as he felt the warmth of Kira's magic race to beat it.

It wasn't enough to save him. He knew that. Magic could only do so much. So it came as a surprise when he fell backward in the snow, the form of Death towering over him before turning away.

Max was right. Magic couldn't have saved him. At least, not anything normal. Which was probably why Kira hadn't used anything normal. Instead, she'd used a contract. Max recognized it as the one that she had been given for sacrificing herself to save an NPC during the Sengetsu fight years ago. The one that she had used earlier that night to open a door in the Famine dungeon. The one that she had promised not to use again. He glanced to his forearm. His health readout was full and accompanied by every buff icon in the game. He'd also gained a hefty regeneration effect that would last for the next five minutes. His mouth fell open. She had actually torn him from Death's embrace, but like Farn's *Blood Shell* ability that had cost her life earlier that night, it too came with a price. That price being that it affected the whole party except the caster, and now, after using all her remaining mana, the overpowered spell gave her the full, undivided attention of Death. It would be impossible to draw the boss off her. In short, it was suicide.

Max looked up to Kira from his place in the cold dirt, the residual glow of the contract's power still fading from her form.

She gave him a slight shrug as if to say, "Oops."

Death reacted, streaking toward the fairy, its scythe swinging back in anticipation. The glow around her simply blinked out as the curved blade struck her at near blinding speed.

Her body hit the wall two dozen feet away with an impact so great that Max felt it through the ground. She slid down almost in slow motion, landing on her feet for a moment.

He looked to Farn as she glanced down at her ring. He wasn't sure how to feel. He didn't want to lose either of them, but it was too late for that. Any second, the *Shield's* life would be cut down to just a few minutes in exchange for Kira's, her sacrifice giving her the power to make a difference in the time remaining.

Max's throat tightened as the *Shield* placed her hand to her chest and closed her eyes, waiting for whatever might come. Then she snapped them open again. Something was wrong.

In the distance, Kira dropped to her knees, her limp hand opening. The recently removed ring slipped from her grip, bouncing off a stone as it fell to the frozen ground. The cold bite of the air rushed back to him as the comfort spell she had cast earlier faded away.

Farn let out a sob as she tried to form words.

Max looked to his party readout. The digital ink confirmed it, just a red zero out of fifty showing as Kira's name faded away. It was over. They couldn't win.

Then things got weird.

Kira fell to all fours, but to his surprise, she didn't disappear. He glanced again at the digits below the space where her name had been. It read zero, but it didn't disappear either.

Eerie laughter echoed through the graveyard, its source difficult to determine as it bounced around the high walls. It was unnerving, and it was coming from Kira. Another glance at her health showed something else. The readout shifted and merged to form what looked like the number eight. It rotated and stretched into a symbol he recognized, infinity.

Max's jaw hit the ground as he realized what was happening. He squinted at the fairy, looking for the pearl hanging from her earing. It was gone. It was the first contract that either of them had gotten, the one that had dangled from her ear for years. Kira had always said that she was saving it for a rainy day, and today, it was pouring. As the items description had instructed, she must have swallowed it a moment before to save herself from Death's retaliation. Once a part of her character, it could bring her back from death.

She didn't come back alone.

Max looked to the space where her name had been, woven into the design of flames on his wrist. His skin burned as letters reappeared, each carving themselves out in heavy black ink. He knew the name - Rasputin.

Kira stood as the pure white fabric of her dress faded into an equally pure black, so dark that it seemed more like the complete absence of light as if it was drawing it in and snuffing it out. Her hair changed to match as her violet eyes gained a quality that was somehow menacing on her gentle face. In her hands, she held two wickedly curved black daggers. They gleamed with excitement, somehow light enough for her to wield.

She spoke, "I can't heal like this, so try not to get killed." Her voice was hard and layered, carrying a tone of something darker, like it wasn't just her in there.

Death stood, looking confused, its focus still on her. It didn't stay that way long. The Nightmare shot toward her at full force like before, but this time, it was met with resistance. She deflected its hits with her blades while taking others. Crimson streaks of light appeared across her body each time she was struck. She ignored them and struck back with a ferocity that Max had to see to believe. It was beautiful.

He thought back, trying to remember what Kira had said when she had read him the contract's description years ago. She had lost all the abilities she had as a *Breath* mage, but in their place, her strength and dexterity values got a boost. Granted, even with the buff, she still seemed to be on the weaker side, making it hard for her to deal damage. That didn't stop her from trying.

She spun, slashing at her foe with relentless aggression. Each movement maintained the same graceful quality that she had for everything else but with an added, eager brutality that made her attacks look more like a savage dance.

Max pushed himself up. He couldn't let her do all the work.

The others piled on, getting a few hits through while Kira kept the boss busy. Although, even with her acting as a pint-sized damage sponge, it was still slow going, and judging from the five-minute countdown appearing next to her infinite health value, Rasputin's effect wasn't permanent. Even worse, they still couldn't land a critical hit to the damn thing's skull. It was to a point where the only one of them actually doing decent damage was Corvin. Although, the only thing he could get to stick was a low-level poison spell that he had to keep recasting every few seconds to keep active against the boss's resistance. Nevertheless, Kira kept up her assault on the towering skeleton, becoming more of an annoyance than anything else since all she could do was chip away at its limbs.

Eventually, the thing seemed to realize that it couldn't hurt her either and stopped trying, only attacking when she got close to landing a hit. It swatted her away like a mosquito again and again, but she kept coming back for more regardless. It didn't take long for the boss to get fed up with her. It dropped one of its swords and reached low under her defenses to scoop her up by one of her ankles.

If Max hadn't still been upset about missing his shot earlier, he might have laughed as Death lifted his partner off the ground and held her upside down.

The fairy shrieked with surprise before letting out a ridiculous sounding growl and shoving one hand up against her body to keep her dress from falling over her head. Max assumed it was just to keep the garment out of her face rather than to protect her modesty, considering everything that had happened in the last dungeon. She swiped at its bony hand, doing practically no damage as it carried her around to keep her out of the way while it went after the rest of the team. Although, that also meant that it wasn't paying much attention to her, so when it lunged at Corvin with a blade, she took her opportunity.

"Ha! Take that, dickass!" yelled the ridiculous creature as she cracked the boss in the back of the head with a dagger, emitting a sound that made Max cringe as her dagger scraped against bone. To his surprise, the Nightmare reeled from the hit, losing a large chunk of health as she landed a solid critical. She laughed, beaming with pride at her accomplishment.

It turned its hollow eye sockets in Kira's direction and paused for an instant, just long enough for her to get out the word, "Sorry?" Then it slammed her into the ground hard enough to crack the frozen earth around her. The fairy released an appropriate, "Ouch," as it lifted her back up and dropped her into an open grave like an empty can into the trash. That was when Corvin's poison damage ticked the boss's health just below fifty percent. From there, things changed.

Death stopped attacking and dashed backward, letting out an ear-splitting scream. Max shrank in place at the sound. The only one who didn't flinch was Kira who just yelled back as she crawled out of the grave she'd been deposited in.

The hooded Nightmare's call was answered on all sides as the various statuary came to life. Max spun in panic, gray forms surrounding him. At the same time, Death began firing off his beam attack in quick succession. It didn't seem to be aimed at anyone, but it struck the area enough to be a major obstacle and create an uneven terrain as it carved up the earth.

In the midst of the sudden chaos, Max found himself forced together, back to back, with Kira, who laughed like a psychopath. Somehow, it made him feel better, having her there to support him after he'd failed so completely just a minute before.

The statues were like miniature bosses in and of themselves, each presenting a significant problem. If it wasn't for the left-over regeneration effect and stat boosts from Kira's first contract, Max would already be picking out one of the open graves for himself. Even with that, it was still a losing battle, the others cornered by blasts from the boss's death ray. That was when an echo stone fell from the sky. On impact, it played its message.

"Find cover, fast!" Alastair's voice yelled from the stone on a loop as two transport ships buzzed through the open sky. Their boss must have decided to get off his ass and help, which was only right considering how things had developed.

Max tightened his grip on his guns, not really wanting to hear the man's voice since he was pretty sure they'd been misled by him at some point. It was going to take all his self-control not to punch the guy the next time they were face to face.

The two ships looped back and slid open their doors. Max did a double take as each ship revealed a Checkpoint employee harnessed in and gripping the handles of what looked like a large Gatling gun.

The sky erupted with a hail of bullets, cutting down the

surrounding enemies while Max and the others scrambled to find cover. The ground around him splintered apart as the gunners above did their best to avoid any friendly fire. Although, with the movement of their aircraft, their aim was less than perfect.

Max ducked behind a thick gravestone and yanked Corvin into its protection by his tail. Farn followed their lead, using her shield to cover their backs. In his peripheral, he caught Ginger leaping into an open grave while Kegan drew his other silver arrow and fired it in behind her. Max could actually hear Ginger's annoyed shouting over the din around him as the *Leaf* teleported into her hiding place. From the sound of it, he'd landed on top of her. Behind them, Kira ignored it all, still trying to murder a statue with Rasputin's temporary daggers.

Debris flew through the air as Max huddled close to Corvin and Farn, trying to keep their bodies as compact as possible. He didn't even know guns like that existed in the game. Evidently, Alastair had been saving something special for himself. The barrage paused while the two ships looped back around for another pass. The echo stone's message had stopped, having been destroyed in the attack.

"Everyone okay?" Max peeked over the stone at his back.

"I'm good," Kira answered as if she'd been caught in a light rain, her voice still carrying a darker tinge.

Max looked back to the open grave off to the side. "Kegan! Ginger! You alive?

Two heads poked out. "For the most part," Ginger replied, shoving Kegan back to his side of the hole.

That was when Max noticed that Death had stopped firing its beam attack. As to why, he had no idea. He called to the others, and they regrouped near the mausoleum for better cover while they waited for the gunner's next pass. Most of the statues were in pieces, and the few that remained were brought down by a couple well-placed arrows from Kegan.

The ships returned a moment later, this time taking aim at the giant skeletal form that now stood facing the sky. The high-pitched whine of their guns spinning up blurred together with another loud scream from the massive boss as it gathered energy in its jaws. The gunners didn't even get a shot off before another crimson blast streaked through the sky, detonating both ships in its wake.

"At least it was helpful while it lasted," Max commented, looking around at the remains of the statues that were no longer a problem.

With the attack ships dealt with, Death returned to the fight, its health still at fifty percent.

One look at his wrist told Max that they didn't have much time left as Kira's contract timers ticked down. It wasn't looking good. Then he had a thought.

Max shoved in a fresh pair of mags and converted their contents to explosive rounds. Remembering how much damage Kira had done with her single critical hit, he wondered if they even needed to use something special to finish the skeleton off. In fact, after doing some quick math, he was pretty sure they didn't. All he really had to do was land a few more criticals without screwing up. That was easier said than done.

He called to Ginger, "When I say now, can you snag its arm again with a line again?"

"Ah, yeah, but that didn't work out great last time."

"I know, just be ready." He hoped he was right.

"Kira, can you continue to annoy the thing and grab its other arm?"

"That's what I do best," she chirped in a voice laced with madness.

"Kegan, can you ..." Max paused upon noticing the *Leaf* standing off to the side looking dumb.

Kegan shrugged and pointed to his empty quiver.

Max groaned and continued, "Can you just jump on an arm or something?"

"Sure. Why not?"

"Farn, can you do the same?"

"Got it!" she grunted back as she took a hit to her shield.

"Leave its scythe arm free," Max added to everyone, who all looked at him incredulously, "and, Corvin, keep up the poison."

The mage nodded without saying a word, downing another mana vial.

With a loose plan in place, Max fired off a couple shots. They detonated, blocked by the boss's six arms. He expected it, which had been the reason he'd converted his mags to explosive rounds. He knew he couldn't land a clean hit, but he figured he could at least get some splash damage through, just enough to draw the Nightmare's attention.

Farn motioned to get between them, but he called her off with a glance as Death rushed him, its scythe raised high above its head.

Max struggled not to panic, holding as still as he could. Then he yelled, "NOW!"

Ginger fired a line, hooking a skeletal limb and yanking the thing off balance again. Kira followed suit, leaping into the whirlwind of blades and wrapping her small body around its opposite arm so that it fell to its knee. Before it could do anything else, Kegan and Farn grabbed two more limbs from behind. It had to be strong enough to shake them off, leaving Max seconds to act, at best. He unloaded one pistol into its sternum, not risking a shot at its head until he was sure. He had to be.

Suddenly, Death dropped its remaining sword the same way it had when Farn had struck it in the chest. Then a bony hand clamped around Max's wrist. He panicked. It wasn't that he hadn't expected it. In fact, it had been what he was waiting for. No, what worried him was that he had assumed that Death would go after the hand that had just fired. It didn't. Instead, it grabbed the one still carrying a fully loaded pistol, leaving him with an empty gun as it squeezed his hand in a way that forced him to let go of the one he still needed. The weapon fell to the ground, leaving him unarmed as the massive skeleton flipped him around like a dance partner and gripped him tight against its chest. All the breath rushed out of him. He couldn't believe it. He had screwed it up again!

Ignoring everyone else, Death lowered its scythe to Max's throat, and he tried to grab at the blade with his free hand on instinct, as useless as the act might've been. The voices of his party reached his ears, sounding slow and drawn out as he realized he was about to die. For him, it was over. He just hoped that they could figure something out without him.

Then, just as the scythe touched his skin, a beautiful face stepped into view, Corvin. Max could have kissed him when he saw what he held. His dropped pistol almost floated back to him as the mage tossed it.

Max caught the gun and smiled, his free hand pointing it up, the muzzle rammed against Death's unsuspecting jaw. He couldn't miss. Normally, he would've had a snappy one-liner to say, but instead, he just pulled the trigger. His virtual eardrums almost burst from the shot fired as gunpowder filled his senses. He could even taste it. He didn't see the bullet hit, but the limbs of bone holding him tight let go. He turned on his enemy, gripping Death's ribs for stability and pulling himself closer as he emptied the gun into its mouth. The Nightmare let out an ear-splitting screech as it fell forward onto him, bones coming loose in his hands as they all came down in a heap.

The robes of Death fell over his body, plunging him into darkness along with everyone else holding onto the thing, and for a moment, Max wasn't sure what was happening. Limbs jabbed and poked in search of a way out, occasionally finding a sharp piece of bone. Then Max found himself looking up at Ginger, who was crouching down, holding up an end of the tattered fabric so that she could look under. Corvin was behind her bending on one knee.

"Did we win?" Max asked the *Coin* from his place lying flat on his back.

Ginger snorted. "No points for style, but I guess so."

From under the writhing layer of ragged darkness, Kira howled, "I swear I will kill the next person that touches my ass. I am so not even kidding." From the dark tinge in her voice, she sounded like she might actually do it. Her daggers poked up, tearing a fairy-sized hole in the robe that she poked her upper body out of.

"Sorry, that was me this time," Farn said as she tried to wriggle her way through the same opening beside her.

Kira glared at her sideways, her daggers held at the ready. "Oh, really? That's a pretty dangerous confession right now." Her weapons dematerialized in her hands and her hair faded back to silver, making it obvious that her contract with Rasputin had just ended. She let out a disappointed sigh.

Farn laughed. "What was that now about you being dangerous?"

Kira folded her arms. "Well, I guess I can forgive you."

"That's good 'cause it was me last night, too," the *Shield* added, her mouth curling up in a mischievous smile.

Kira sputtered, having trouble forming words.

Farn shrugged. "What? We'd just met; I wasn't gonna own up to it."

"Well, now that the mystery is solved, we should get back to the ship. I need to get some answers from our boss," Max said just before the familiar voice of the darkness called out a name.

"MaxDamage—"

"Yeah, yeah," Max interrupted the darkness as if it was his mom telling him to take out the trash.

"Make your offer!"

Max held his arms out wide and lifted his head to the sky as if about to speak to the heavens themselves. "I give fucks, quantity, zero."

CHAPTER FORTY-TWO

Max strode onto the bridge with his usual swagger, wearing Death's cloak around his shoulders like a trophy. The tattered ends of the dark fabric dragged on the floor as he walked. The cloak had no stats or enchantments attached to it, which was disappointing. Actually, it wasn't even equipment. It had just become a piece of crafting material, the same as the scrap of cloth that Farn had offered up as worthless earlier that night, but it looked cool, so Max wore it regardless. Not to mention that his item bag felt a little heavier with the weight of a new contract item.

The win may not have been pretty, but it was still a win. Despite that, Max struggled to keep a smile on his face as Alastair stood, grinning like an idiot, clearly proud of the help his men gave during the last fight.

The man waggled his eyebrows at him as if asking for approval as the party filed onto the bridge behind him.

Max's smile wavered as he approached, the corner of his mouth beginning to fall as he clenched his fist. Only when he was almost within reach did he allow the mask to drop, his face twisting in anger as he closed the gap.

Confusion hit the unsuspecting mage as Max drove his fist into his face at full force, launching the man much further than one would expect.

Alastair fell back into his chair, one hand against his face in shock. He was lucky Max wasn't a class that recognized his fists as a weapon.

"How the hell did Carver know that you would pick us?" Max yelled at his temporary employer with a rage in his voice that told the entire bridge to mind their own business.

Alastair squirmed backward deeper into his chair. "I don't know what you're talking about."

Max didn't buy it. "That castle has been there for years, so how the hell did statues of Kira and I end up in it?"

Alastair's eyes darted back and forth. "I wasn't aware there was."

That answer didn't satisfy Max either, but he did lower his voice, continuing in a quiet tone that was somehow even more threatening. It was time for the truth. "How did he know back then that you would pick us for his quest? What is it you're not telling us?"

Alastair hesitated, then sighed, letting his body sink into his chair. "You're right."

A look of panic washed over Jeff-with-a-three's face. Max caught it in his peripheral. Whatever was coming next was big.

Alastair continued, "I honestly didn't consider the possibility that Carver needed you two specifically. When this whole thing started, I didn't even know what to expect. That much I swear to you. But now that I know more, you might be right. He may have known I'd contact you." He sat up in his chair, still rubbing his face.

"How?" Kira stepped to Max's side.

"I wasn't lying when I said you were some of the best players available. But we have millions of users online, so obviously there are others out there with track records just as good as yours or better. However, you two are ..." Alastair paused to choose his words, "different."

Max tensed up at the word. "What do you mean, 'different?'"

"Let me ask you, do you know how the Nightmare's contract reward system works?" Alastair asked matter-of-factly.

Max breathed a simple, "No," through his teeth.

"Neither do we." Alastair threw up his hands. "At least, not entirely."

"What do you mean, you don't know?"

"Oh sure, we know how it was supposed to work. A player offers an item, and the darkness gives them something in return from a preselected list based on their class and what type of item was offered."

"Yeah." Max gave a nod, following the explanation.

"Notice, I said, that the player is supposed to offer an *item*," Alastair emphasized the word, "but not everyone offers an item, do they?" He turned his eyes toward Kira.

"Umm, no." She fidgeted with the fabric of her dress, looking guilty.

"And what did you offer the darkness every time it called your name in the past?" Alastair asked the question, making it sound like she had done something wrong.

Kira responded in a quiet, sheepish tone, "I offered forgiveness." She paused before defending, "I thought it would be cute. I didn't think it would accept it."

"And it shouldn't have. The game doesn't understand things like concepts. It should have just repeated the question until you gave it something normal." He raked a hand through his hair. "But it didn't. And that was how you broke the contract system. From that point on, if anyone offered something other than an item, such as a month of their life or their left eye," he looked at Farn and Corvin before continuing, "the system errors out and asks the player's subconscious for an answer instead. It then tries to adapt it in some way that will work within the game, which is how you end up with crazy abilities or weird items. It can't even store those contracts on our system since it doesn't know what to make of them.

Instead, it drops it into your brain along with all the imaging data for the game."

Kira clutched her pendant absentmindedly. "Why did it accept my offer if it wasn't supposed to?"

Alastair let out a sigh and took a step away from Max, probably making sure he was out of punching range. "That's where I may not have been completely honest." He hesitated, glancing at Max for a response before continuing, "When I told you that I didn't know of anyone that had ever overpowered the system with their will, I may not have been totally honest."

Kira covered her mouth in disbelief as she took a step backward. "Oh my god."

"It was one of us," Max finished her thought before adding, "Who?" in a tone that demanded a straight answer.

Alastair's eyes fell away from Max, hitting the floor before rising back up to Kira. He didn't have to say more.

Max felt like an idiot as everything fell into place. It had never been about him or his willpower. It didn't matter that his stat was higher. No, it had been about Kira from the start.

"How?" The fairy shook her head back and forth. "My will isn't even that strong."

Alastair shifted in his chair. "Most of the time, that's true. But there are times when it fluctuates. And in your case, it can do so wildly. In your fight against Rasputin, your will dropped to zero then shot up past Max by double, so while you may not have meant to, you did push your thoughts out enough to alter the system."

"And that's why you picked us? Because you thought she could influence the quest to help us win?" Max stepped forward, feeling his anger rise once again. "Didn't you consider that you might be playing right into Carver's hands?"

Alastair flinched at the sudden movement. "Yes! I thought that if I was going to pick people to do this, I should pick someone that could do the impossible. And you're probably right; it was exactly what Carver wanted. But I swear, I didn't know this would happen, and I never——"

"I don't care!" Max shouted over him. "We're running out of time, and you put Kira's life at risk!"

She shrunk back and tightened her grip on her pendant as he said the words that everyone had been avoiding.

He ignored her and continued to yell, the night's frustrations pouring out of him all at once. His failures and fears overpowered him until he lost track of his point altogether. His shouting grew less productive from there, leaving the others standing uncomfortably, unable to interject.

Alastair did nothing but apologize, which only pissed Max off more. Finally, one word put an end to his tantrum.

"Stop," Kira's voice came out soft, sounding sad and a little frightened as she continued, "Alastair didn't know, okay. He didn't do this to me on purpose." She avoided making eye contact.

"It doesn't matter!" Max tried to explain, refusing to let it go and yelling at her by accident.

She flinched before shouting back. "You're right; it doesn't matter! None of it does. I don't care, okay. I don't have much time left and shouting at Alastair isn't going to help!" She spun on her heel without giving him a chance to respond. Then she was gone, her bare feet padding their way out of the bridge.

Max stood, stunned. He had been so mad at Alastair for lying, and if he was honest, it had hurt to find out that he wasn't important, that the quest wasn't about him. It had all just overwhelmed him, and he'd let it take over. He hadn't stopped to ask or even think about how Kira felt. It wasn't like she was dying, but there was a chance of it, however small it might be. From her words, it was clear she was thinking about it no matter how well she hid it, and like an ass, he had just blurted it out in a tantrum because of his wounded pride.

They had always been together, ever since the day back in school when they'd met, and no matter what she looked like, she was his best friend. Even when he was in a bad mood, she was always there with a joke to cheer him up. But now, she was actually afraid for her life, and he hadn't even noticed. Not really.

He'd just been so caught up with the idea of being a hero that the danger hadn't even registered. He thought he could brush it all away with a few confident words and save her from whatever lay ahead. There just wasn't a reason to truly worry.

Max lowered his head.

He was an idiot.

Alastair started to speak, but Max held out a hand to stop him.

"We're done. I'm sorry I hit you," Max finished, losing hold of his anger.

Alastair nodded, accepting the apology without questioning it.

Max turned toward the door but stopped, noticing the expression on Farn's face as she, too, looked to the exit. Her eyes said it all - she was worried about the fairy. She even leaned in the direction of the door with one foot half up as if she was about to take off running, but for some reason, she stayed put.

His shoulders fell. "Would you mind checking on Kira? Tell her sorry for me." It was like he'd pulled up a nail that had pinned her foot to the floor, her body shrugging off a weight as she rushed after the fairy.

Max would have gone himself, but Kira and Farn seemed to have grown close during their short time together, and it was clear that the *Shield* valued the budding friendship. Still, if he was honest with himself, he was just afraid.

Whenever he and Kira had a disagreement in the past, they would just joke about it and move on. There was never a need for anything else. Then again, they had never been put in a situation like this before, and Max didn't know what to say. It was more emotional than their partnership got.

He sighed and pulled off the gray cloak that he had been so proud of before. He didn't deserve it.

CHAPTER FORTY-THREE

Farn stepped out onto the deck, her pace slowing as she realized it was empty. Kira must have flown away as soon as she had gotten outside. She pulled out her journal and checked her map to make sure the fairy was at least still aboard the ship. She breathed a sigh of relief. The map wasn't quite large enough to give a precise location, but it showed enough to know that Kira was near the back of the craft. She turned and continued walking.

She couldn't imagine what Kira was going through. All she knew was that she liked her and hoped that they might stay friends when the quest was done. Of course, that would first require her to live through the night. She shoved the thought out of her head. If it came to it, she would pull her from her rig in the Nemo Unit herself. The idea set off a chain of realizations that ended with the fact that Kira wasn't real to begin with, just a character played by Seth. Farn wasn't sure how that made her feel. She shook off the question and stepped onto the rear deck.

Farn scanned the area. It was empty, too. She glanced back at her map to confirm that Kira hadn't moved. She hadn't.

That's when she heard the slow notes of a song she recognized. It was the theme from a video game Farn had played as a child, one that she had loved. It wafted down with the breeze from on top of one of the cabins, giving her a nostalgic feeling that brought her back to a time when things were simpler and she wasn't quite so lonely.

She climbed a maintenance ladder on the side of the cabin that was more for decoration since there wasn't any real need for maintenance on the ship. At the top, she found Kira.

The fairy sat with her legs folded, plucking the strings of a small harp while resting her chin on the instrument.

"Since when do you play the harp?" Farn climbed onto the roof and worked her way across on her hands and knees for stability.

Startled, Kira stopped playing and wiped her eyes to make a futile attempt to hide the fact that she'd been crying. "I felt I should learn to play it since this dumb game pulled it from my subconscious."

Farn sat down beside her, noticing her tears but not mentioning it. "That's a contract item?"

"Yup."

"What does it do?"

"Plays music," she answered matter-of-factly.

Farn laughed at the obvious answer. "That's it?"

"Yup," Kira repeated. "No other purpose. I do find it calming, though, so I guess there's that."

"Max said he's sorry." Farn changed the subject.

"That's nice," Kira responded without offering more.

Farn hesitated before asking the question in the front of her mind, "Are you okay?"

Kira sunk down and hugged the harp. "I'm scared."

"There's nothing wrong with that." Farn leaned back on her hands. "Being stuck here would scare anyone."

"I know, but that's not why. I just don't want the responsibility. I liked it better when I thought I was being used to encourage Max. I could deal with that. He might be an idiot, but I trust him. He can save the world and look cool doing it. I'm sure of that. But me, I've never excelled at anything in my life."

"I'm sure that's not true," Farn argued.

"It is, and what's worse, it's not even because I can't. It's that I don't try hard enough. I never have. Not back in school or dating or even work. Sure, I could have tried to break my way into an illustration career, but that just seemed too hard. So instead, I go to a dumb job that I hate every day because it's easy. I know that about myself. It's what I do. Life is simpler when all you have to do is stand in the background and crack jokes." She sniffed and plucked a few strings. "Even now, I'm not afraid of failing or even death. I just don't want to be important. I liked it better when I thought I was a hostage. What the hell does that say about me?"

Farn didn't know how to answer, so she sat quietly while Kira played a sad song from an old JRPG. They both must have played it because Farn recognized the tune.

We really are alike, she thought before blurting out, "I almost didn't accept this mission."

The song stopped. "Why?"

"I was scared, too." Farn looked up at the stars. "The idea of working on something so important with people I didn't know terrified me."

Kira picked up the song again, looking a little less depressed. "Do you regret it?"

Farn shook her head and answered a quick, "Nope," before looking away to avoid eye contact for what came next. "I got to meet you."

Kira snorted, a smile finding its way back to her lips for a moment before retreating back inside her. "Thanks, but I'm nothing special. Not really. I only stand out because I'm a goon and Max convinced me to make a weird character."

"That's not true. You're amazing and fun." Farn leaned forward and pulled her legs up to rest against her chest armor.

"And you're nice to me." She bit her bottom lip to form a period at the end of the statement.

Kira stopped playing again and cocked her head to the side. "Why wouldn't I be?"

Farn shifted uncomfortably, almost regretting bringing up something personal and feeling torn as she realized that she wanted to tell her more. "I know that sounds weird. But I kind of don't have any friends. I haven't for a long time. I'm not good at making them."

"Oh." Kira resumed playing as Farn cringed at having put herself out there. The fairy plucked a few strings before adding, "That's stupid."

"Sorry." Farn lowered her head.

"Oh no. I didn't mean it like that." Kira sat up straight and shoved her harp down into her lap before turning to face Farn. "You're fine at making friends. I mean, we're friends, right?"

Farn's cheeks burned, and she looked away into the distance. "I think so?" She let a tell-tale inflection of doubt enter her voice.

"Oh god. I hope so at this point! I practically let you see me naked. If that doesn't say we're friends, I'm not sure what does."

Farn laughed. "I think everybody saw that, so by that logic, you're BFFs with the whole crew of this ship."

"Ugh, don't remind me." Kira sighed as Farn relaxed. Then the fairy gave her a quasi-fist bump that tapped their rings together.

Farn was glad to see it back on her finger.

"I'm happy just being BFFs with you," the fairy added.

"If you're not careful, you're gonna make Max jealous." Farn laughed some more.

"Nah. He's more of a bro. That's different. Besides, I think I can speak for him as well when I say he'd be happy to be your friend too. And hey, he's single, so you know, there's that." Kira waggled her silver eyebrows.

Farn smiled, not really considering the option but happy

that she had someone that she could talk about such things with. "Does that mean you're not mad at him anymore?"

Kira waved her hand away. "I was never really mad. He gets tunnel vision when he's angry, so he didn't notice I was upset. He just freaked me out is all. I'll get over it, provided I don't die or something." She fell silent again.

"Do you regret it?" Farn leaned a little closer. "The mission, I mean."

Kira tapped her fingers on her harp for a long while. "Maybe. Or, at least, a part of me does. I'd be stupid not to. At this point, no matter what happens, I'm not going to come out of this the same as when I went in." She put her instrument down beside her and leaned back. "But I don't want to lose this world. And as scary as things have been, it's also been fun. So part of me really wants to keep going. I like this party. I want to do less frightening quests and go to taverns with everyone, and we can't do that if we stop here."

The Nostromo suddenly leaned to the side to adjust its course, reinforcing her words and reminding them both that they were still on their way to another fight.

Kira grabbed her harp as it started to slip away down the incline of the ship's cabin and clutched the instrument with both hands rather than holding onto something more stable. The result was that she began sliding toward the edge as well.

Farn reached out, catching her by the back of her dress, causing the fairy to let out an awkward laugh as Farn's fingers touched the skin of her back.

"Maybe we should go back with the others," Farn suggested, trying to be the responsible one.

Kira nodded. "Yeah, maybe."

CHAPTER FORTY-FOUR

Max turned toward the door of the bridge as Farn and Kira entered, the *Shield* giving him a nod to let him know that he was off the hook. He let out a sigh of relief, noticing that the fairy had found her smile again. He smiled back in apology, grateful that she didn't need anything more. It wouldn't be fun for her to stay mad anyway.

"Just in time. We have some good news for once," he said before giving the floor back to Alastair, who stood from the captain's chair. He wasn't quite over the fact that their boss had lied to them, but for Kira's sake, he put the conflict on the shelf for the time being.

Alastair cleared his throat. "How familiar are you with the lore involving the lost city of Sierra?" His question was met by a room of shrugs. He sighed. "Really? Nobody? Not even Corvin?"

The reynard's ears twitched in a way that somehow expressed confusion.

Alastair pushed a hand through his hair. "Alright, that's disappointing. There's a bunch of quests that mention it." He opened his journal and sent a file into the large window at the front of the bridge as if it was a theatre. "This is a rough trailer for our next major expansion. We planned to release it this holiday season." He tapped play, and a voiceover started.

"Over four hundred years ago," it began.

"Skip it!" Kegan yelled out, provoking a sharp look from Alastair as the trailer continued.

An enormous dragon appeared on screen, scales glowing with a fire that raged from within. It was joined by a second, bearing shards of ice protruding from its back. Both were far larger than any dragon that Max had ever encountered. Hell, they were larger than the airship they rode on.

The voiceover stated that the two dragons were, in fact, kings of their kind, and there wasn't room for both of them. As long as they lived, Noctem would never know peace. Their conflict split the dragons of the world into two opposing sides that laid waste to all that got in their way. They fought for ninety-nine years in what became known as *The Dragon War*.

Cities fell as the people tried everything to put an end to the relentless violence, but it seemed nothing could quell the beasts. Then, on the hundredth day of the hundredth year of the war, the city of Sierra and its citizens, the deru, found a way. With their vast knowledge of the elements, they crafted four crystals that could seal away the two dragons, but in the process, they sealed away their own city along with themselves.

The trailer showed the dragons clashing in the center of a broken and devastated city as the earth around it began to shake. The ground puckered and cracked until shards of rock ripped through the surface, surging up and to the center as they crashed into each other. One piece after another layered together until a shell formed over the dragons, trapping them below the surface, only letting one final burst of flame escape. All that remained was a barren scar on the landscape, a mountain of lifeless stone. The video held its view and the scene aged before Max's eyes as it was reclaimed by nature, becoming an innocuous piece of land covered with flowers and trees.

Thus, the entire deru race and the War Dragons blinked out

of existence. The screen went dark. Then the words, '*until now*' appeared in sync with the voiceover. A short shot of the two dragons rushing toward each other flashed, then it cut to a party of adventurers, not unlike themselves. They stepped up at the end to signify the players of the world facing the return of the creatures. The camera rotated around them to show a sky growing dark with swarms of smaller dragons clashing, their winged corpses falling like meteors across the land. Fade to black.

"Okay, the point is?" Kira inquired.

"That's where your next waypoint is. Sierra, the lost city," Alastair explained.

"If it's lost how do we go there?" Ginger asked with her arms folded.

Alastair rolled his eyes. "Well, it's not actually lost. We know where it is. It's been in development since the beginning. The story was going to be that it had been hidden, sealed inside a mountain."

"Not one full of lava this time, right?" Max butted in.

"Umm no, there's no lava?"

"What about magma?" Kira joked.

"What?" Alastair asked before adding a frustrated, "No," and continuing, "but it is almost a functioning city at this point. We've been building it little by little with each update to avoid downtime when we launch it. Otherwise, we would have to shut down the servers for over a day to load a whole city at once. We were going to unveil it this November as a new kingdom to be claimed, along with the deru as a new playable race."

"Oh cool," Corvin said, leaning forward on a railing.

"There is one small problem." Alastair held up a finger.

"Of course there is." Max threw up his hands.

Alastair's face grew serious. "The War Dragons are still in there."

Max raised one eyebrow. "Like, tearing shit up and what not?"

"No, no, nothing like that. They're petrified in the city's

center, like statues, but ..." he exhaled and took a step forward, "my guess is that they won't stay that way once you get in there. I mean, they are called the 'War Dragons,' so they have to be the Horseman of War."

Max nodded, expecting nothing less. "Okay, that isn't so bad. At least, we know what we're going up against, which is more than we can say about everything else we've faced so far. And we've fought dragons before." He turned to Alastair. "What kind of weaknesses do these things have?"

"Umm, none." He dropped his hands to his sides.

"Of course." Max rubbed at the bridge of his nose. "Any other helpful tips then?"

Alastair leaned his head to the side and folded his arms. "They aren't really fightable creatures. They don't even have health bars. They're meant to fight each other indefinitely. We were going to have them get free and wreak havoc around the world for a few months. When that got old, we planned a small expansion of quests to craft more crystals and seal them away again. It was supposed to be an event to bring players from all over together for the good of the world with multiple parties wielding their own crystal. It was going to be awesome." There was a sparkle in Alastair's eyes as he spoke. Then his expression changed as he sunk back into the peril that the world was currently facing. "But if you do have to fight those things, I don't really see a way that you can win by normal means. I mean, one hit from them does at least a hundred times all of your hit points combined."

Max sighed. "So what you're saying is that it will come down to Kira's willpower. That is what Carver wants, right?"

Alastair nodded. "I agree. This is the last of the Horsemen; I think he's betting everything on pushing her far enough to take control of the system." He turned to Kira. "If you can do that, you shouldn't have trouble killing them."

"Well, crap. No pressure." She plopped down into Alastair's chair. "I don't even know what I'm doing."

The group fell silent. She was right. Talking about bending

the game world with her mind was one thing, but actually doing it was something else entirely.

Farn spoke up. "I think you can."

Kira bobbed her head in a mixture of nodding and shaking back and forth as if trying to nod but not having the confidence to commit to the gesture.

"I do, too," added Corvin. "You're forgetting that you still have that pendant, and it's still running all kinds of stuff that we don't know on your rig. My guess is that all of that might help you."

Max considered it. "True. I can't imagine Carver making us come all this way, only to have us fail and send it all crashing down."

The others agreed.

"Alright, we'll cross that bridge when we come to it. So how do we get to this place?"

"That's going to be a bit tricky." Alastair shoved his hands into his coat pockets. "Normally, we just teleport there, but since you can't right now, you'll have to use the back entrance."

"And that is where?" Max asked.

"Well, it's invisible, so that's helpful. I'll have to go down with you and show you exactly where it is." Alastair waved his hand. "It will make sense when we get there." Excitement returned to his eyes at the prospect of getting to help.

Max let his hands fall to the butts of his pistols. "Something tells me we're not going to like this."

CHAPTER FORTY-FIVE

The Nostromo groaned with reluctance as it flew low into an area between two nameless mountains, letting the team out as close as possible to their destination.

Alastair climbed down the rickety rope ladder, feeling uncomfortable asking Kira for a *Flight* spell after being caught in a lie that affected her. She didn't seem mad about it, but then again, she didn't seem like the type to get mad in the first place. Either way, he didn't want to press his luck.

As soon as his feet touched the ground, he sent out a couple party invites to his two *Shields*, SpoilerAlert and FireDrill, who were both employees like Farn, each having characters unrelated to the company.

Jeff-with-a-three brought up the rear, looking just as boring as usual. The severe elf had a habit of bringing the mood down, and if Alastair was honest, he'd always felt like the guy didn't like him. His eyes always seemed to be judging him, though he'd never said anything to confirm the theory. Despite that, Alastair couldn't argue that he was easily the best assistant that had ever lived. His memory was perfect, and he simply owned the position, like he had been born for it. So when he thought about it, the elf's performance was worth a few judgmental looks and a sour disposition. That didn't stop him from adopting Kira's new name for him with enthusiasm, though.

Max took one look at him and his small party and laughed. "What's with the red shirts?"

Both of his *Shields'* eyes widened at the implication, but Alastair waved his hand to reassure them. "You're just here to help out. You'll be fine."

Each of them stood completely rigid, like they'd been lashed to a pole. If anything, his interaction with them only made it worse, which made sense. He was their boss, and there was always a little fear in that relationship that he had a tendency to forget about. There wasn't much he could do about it, so he started up the mountain.

Alastair led the two parties up a path that, at some points, grew so narrow that they could only pass in single file. He apologized for the difficulty on reflex. It had actually been a deliberate choice to keep people from finding the place while it was still in development. The odds were low that anyone would be exploring the area to begin with, but they weren't taking any chances. They'd even taken the effort to place a high-level monster further ahead to act as a guard.

Kira glanced at the mission clock, then stared off into nothing for a moment, eventually letting out a sigh along with the word. "Seventeen." She must have been adding up her total time.

Farn stepped close to her and nudged her in a playful manner. "How you holding up?"

"Okay, I guess." Kira folded her arms. "I'm assuming I peed my pants back in the real world by this point, though."

Farn laughed, then looked to Alastair as if asking him to confirm.

"I assure you, you haven't," he promised.

"What makes you so sure?" Kira questioned.

He paused. "Well, when I was logged out earlier, Max told me to have nurses put in a catheter before that happened."

Kira stopped in place, all the color draining from her face. "What the hell, Max? Don't tell people to do things to my bathing suit area without asking."

"Take it from someone who knows, it's better than waking up with a surprise," Max said, his arms folded in front of him as he walked. "Plus, I thought it would be funny when you found out." He leaned his head to the side as if pondering the humor, then he nodded to himself.

Kira placed a hand on Farn's shoulder. "I need you to do something for me."

"Sure, anything," the *Shield* said without hesitation.

"When this is done, I need you to log out before me and tell them to take it out before I wake up. I'm going to pretend it didn't happen."

Farn nodded.

"Okay, great. No need to speak of this again." Kira picked up her pace.

Alastair smiled a little at the exchange. That fact that they could joke around with each other in such a tense situation made him a little envious of the camaraderie that the party had with one another.

He hung back so he could walk side by side with Max as if leading the others together as a team. The *Fury* seemed to have committed to getting things done rather than fighting, a fact that Alastair appreciated. "Thank you," he said in an attempt to mend things between them.

"For?" Max said without taking his eyes off the path.

Alastair kept his view on the ground as well. "For doing all this. I know things haven't gone entirely to plan, but you and your team have been amazing."

"Well, you are paying us." Max kept up a business-like front.

"True. I guess as far as mercenaries go, you're worth every penny."

Max let out a single laugh. "I hadn't thought of us as mercenaries, but I guess it fits."

Alastair chuckled as well. "Sounds kind of cool, too."

"I'll add it to my resume."

Alastair smiled, feeling a little better that he at least got a laugh out of the *Fury*. He really did appreciate everything they'd done for his company, and he hadn't meant to lie to them. He had a legal team telling him to keep his mouth shut after all, so it hadn't been up to him in the first place. At least, that was what he'd told himself. Only part of him believed it.

In truth, he wasn't sure how far he would go to save Noctem. He loved the players, and Max and Kira were perfect examples of who he cared about, but it was his world. He couldn't just let it be destroyed, and now, with Kira's neck on the chopping block, he wasn't sure what he would do if he had to choose between his life's work and her. That sobering thought left him wondering if he was as good a person as he had thought or if he was just as bad as Carver. He shook off the question, leaving it unanswered as the path came to an end with a small cave in front of them.

The entrance was nondescript. In fact, it didn't look like anything at all. It wasn't supposed to, so in that regard, it was perfect. If Max or the others had come across it at any other time, they probably would have kept walking. Upon entering, the cavern inside was far larger than one would expect, the path leading to a wide rock bridge cutting through the center. Dangerous looking stalagmites covered the floor far below.

Kegan let out a slow whistle as he looked over the edge. "My money's on one of the red shirts falling. Any takers?"

"Seriously?" Alastair glared at him as the two *Shields* exchanged looks that one could only describe as regret.

"I'll take you up on that," Ginger joined.

Alastair crossed his arms and tapped one foot, making sure she noticed.

Ginger shrugged at him defensively. "What? I'm betting they'll live. That's good, right?"

He rolled his eyes and continued along the path.

At the end of the bridge, the cavern wall split into a large opening, a soft glow coming from within. In front of it sat a small furry creature. Alastair hadn't seen it in a while, not since they had first started building the city in secret.

It was hard to tell what it looked like until they moved closer. It sat with its legs crossed and its head down, its face covered by two bat-like wings that topped off the creature's head in place of ears. As he approached, it stood. Its movements were sloppy, almost like it was drunk. The wings parted and flopped back revealing two enormous bulging eyeballs and an equally large mouth. A wide toothy grin took up most of the thing's head. Its bluish fur was speckled with gray and covered a small potbelly that stuck out as the creature stood upright on its hind legs. It cocked its head from side to side like some kind of fidgety mental patient. It was hard to tell if the designer who'd created it meant for it to be scary or cute. It seemed to be both.

"We've been calling it a misfit," Alastair said behind one hand, leaning toward Max as if trying to keep the creature from hearing him.

"Is that the guard you were talking about?" he replied.

"Yeah, it's supposed to be a standard cave dwelling enemy that comes with the expansion. But this one is a little different."

"How so?"

Alastair smiled. "For starters, it has about twenty times its normal health and attack values, which makes it appropriate for a party of players at around level one hundred and ninety. It will attack anyone that tries try to get past it, which is what we're doing."

"What the hell, man?" Max shouted, before hushing his voice back down when it echoed through the cavern.

Alastair dismissed his concerns with another wave of his hand. "Don't worry; this is why I came along. You guys just need to sit back and relax for once. I have this." He patted his GM armband and winked.

Max paused for a second, then shrugged. "Okie, dokie.

Have fun." He stepped back to stand out of the way with Kira, who was tilting her head from side to side, mimicking the misfit's movements.

Alastair stepped forward, grinning wildly as he called to the *Shields* in his party. "Here's the plan. I just need time to set up one GM ability, so I need you two to keep it off me." He motioned to the two guards who were both equipped with pretty standard armor around level seventy.

The expression on both their faces made it clear that they were able to do simple math, and any way they added it, seventy was never going to equal one hundred and ninety.

"Oh, relax. I've done this before," Alastair said in an attempt to reassure the two men.

Jeff-with-a-three said nothing but gave him a look that felt just as judgmental as usual.

FireDrill didn't know SpoilerAlert well. Sure, they had met at an office holiday party two years ago, but that was pretty much it. Although, when they ran into each other in a conference room the previous day, along with several other employees from all over Checkpoint, they had sat next to each other regardless. He had feared the worst since talk of the controversy with Carver, and the possibility of layoffs was heard around the room. He hadn't thought the conflict between creators had affected the company that much, but there he was. What else could it have been?

A moment later he was shocked when Milo Parker himself, a man that he had never met in person, had entered the room. He was even more shocked when he had asked the room's employees to work on a special operation within the game as the characters they played in their off hours.

He'd signed the nondisclosure buzzing with eager excitement, especially since they came with a generous bonus for participation. Then Milo played a video on the conference room's projection system. Well, it didn't work at first, which required IT to come in and mess with the connections. Milo had brought in muffins and coffee while they waited. Eventually, the projector was up and running, and Carver's face appeared on the screen. That's when he learned what they had all signed on for. He was horrified. Layoffs were the least of everyone's concerns. Instead, the collapse of the entire company was on the line. Failure wasn't an option for him or the world, for that matter. He had to do his best.

Out of the chaos that followed, he had found a friend in the *Shield* that stood by his side as SpoilerAlert, the two of them bonding over the course of the night. They even found out that their wives knew each other, both working in the human resources department. Plans of double dates were made, provided they made it through the mission and still had their jobs.

They cheered together when Alastair made his first speech on the bridge. They laughed together after that ridiculous fairy had caught Spoiler checking out her ass, and they felt the virtual loss of friends when the Horseman of Death shot down their attack ships only an hour before.

Now, standing side by side with his new friend in front of his company's CEO, FireDrill activated his shield gauntlet and drew his sword, a cold sweat on his brow and conviction in his heart. He glanced to Spoiler, getting a nod in return. They were ready.

Alastair set his target, the misfit responding in kind with a focused glare. FireDrill braced himself as the strange monster rushed forward, determined to stop it at all costs.

His boss wasted no time in opening the special menu linked to his GM armband, which essentially made him a GM on top of his class as a *Cauldron* mage. FireDrill assumed the man would never use it during actual gameplay, giving him the benefit of the doubt since that would be cheating, but now, it was the only way to move forward.

Little more than a rudimentary development console, the GM menu allowed Alastair to make small changes to the world on the fly. It bore no decorative elements or fantasy styling of any kind since, not being available to the public, there was never a need to make it look nice. So, unlike everything else in Noctem, which had been designed to keep players immersed in the illusion that the world was real, it just appeared as a simple blank rectangle in the palm of its user's hand. Although, despite its simplicity, it was still powerful, or at least it could be, provided there was time to do a little coding.

The misfit's mouth opened wide in a sort of silent laughter as its eyes focused on the *Cauldron* mage attempting to set up a command to destroy it.

Spoiler moved first, putting himself between them, his gauntlet's barrier glowing. He planted one foot as the strange creature rushed forward, its large, yellowed teeth coming straight for him. Then, at the last second, the damned thing jumped feet first, impacting with his shield. For a moment, time slowed as the horror of what was happening sunk in. The attack didn't carry much damage, and Spoiler had blocked it well, but the force of it was more than anyone could have anticipated, not to mention the angle was bad. Spoiler's back leg buckled as he slipped back.

FireDrill reached out, his fingers falling just short as his friend and co-worker was launched over the side, their eyes meeting as he fell. FireDrill clenched his fist and turned to face his comrade's killer.

It swayed before refocusing on Alastair who was still tapping away at the small window in his hand.

FireDrill's eyes widened, his heart skipping a beat. He wasn't sure if he could stop it. He made a choice, deactivating his shield and dashing forward, dropping into a slide on one knee just in time, his sword held in front to force the misfit back.

Again, it leapt, but this time, face first. Its impossibly wide smile came at him, its silent laughter filling his mind. Teeth clamped down on his blade, ripping it from his hand.

Panic coursed through him. He just hoped he'd bought enough time as the creature flipped in the air, its hind legs impacting against his chest.

Alastair ignored the second *Shield* as he disappeared over the edge, his scream cut off by the jagged stalagmites below. Despite losing his two guards, he remained calm.

Jeff-with-a-three made no motion to help.

Max took a step back as the misfit retargeted again.

Kira and the rest of the party followed suit, backing away in unison.

Alastair finished his sequencing and closed the window just as the thing closed the gap. Then he grinned, almost as wide as the creature before him. He snapped his fingers. The attack carried no effects or animation, but the thing fell dead at his feet, its wing-like ears falling limp over the madness of its face. It was a little anticlimactic, but regardless, Alastair blew on his fingers like they were the muzzle of a recently fired gun. "Told you there was nothing to worry about."

Max leaned over the side where the two *Shields* had fallen. "Dude, that was cold."

"I did choose the name Coldblood. I do what has to be done." Alastair continued walking toward their destination, letting Max watch as he walked away. *That will hopefully make him think twice about throwing another punch.*

A treasure chest waited in the chamber beyond, and Ginger wasted no time, popping it open with a set of lock-pick tools. Inside sat six full-size bars of hard mercury, each being worth around nine hundred dollars. Her face lit up.

"Sweet!" she squealed.

The material had no real use in the game. It was just mercury, enchanted to remain in solid form, but since it could be traded to Checkpoint for real money, it encouraged exploration and kept the players engaged, even if it was a rare find. After all, who could resist a good treasure hunt? Besides, money was something that Checkpoint had no shortage of.

Alastair tapped the chest with his foot. "We had to put something valuable here in case someone made it past the misfit somehow. Couldn't have anyone suspecting the real reason for this place."

Max ignored him, glaring down at Ginger as she took a bar of hard from the chest. "We didn't earn that."

It surprised Alastair. He didn't expect Max to be so honorable.

Ginger sucked her teeth at the *Fury*. "Yeah, I don't really care."

Max continued to judge her with his eyes.

"But ..." she started to say as Kira joined in.

The fairy's eyes settled upon the *Coin* like two wide pools of glistening water.

"FINE!" Ginger fell victim to the sad puppy act and tossed the bar back into the chest before slamming the lid shut. "You both suck."

With that done, Max changed the subject, "So where's this invisible entrance?"

Alastair pointed at the back of the cave behind the chest. "Right there."

Max approached the rock wall and placed his hand on its surface. "Feels pretty solid to me."

"Of course it does. You literally have to run into it for it to let you through. We figured no one in their right mind would do that." Alastair kept his voice even to ensure that it was hard to read.

Max squinted and raised one eyebrow at him. "Okaaaay." He took a few steps back and got into a runner's stance. He glanced back at Alastair.

He waved his hand as if to say, get on with it.

Max faced forward again and pushed off, holding his arms in front of himself just in case.

Kira burst out laughing as the *Fury* impacted with the wall, tumbling backward to the floor.

The others held still as death, their eyes shifting back to Alastair.

He didn't really intend to go through with the prank, but at the last second, he thought of Kira and what she had laying ahead of her. He couldn't predict what would happen in the next fight. At that moment, he just wanted to hear her laugh.

Max sighed. "Okay, I guess I deserved that a little."

The others joined the fairy's laughter when they saw it was safe to do so, which only made her laugh harder.

Kira wiped a tear from her eye and leaned against the cavern wall to recover. She let out a short yelp as she fell through the solid rock behind her as if it wasn't there.

Max lost it immediately, clapping and rolling on the ground like an idiot. "Now that is the best thing I've seen."

Alastair snickered too, feeling a little like part of the team again.

Kira stamped back through the wall. "Okay, I get it. Karma's a thing."

"Yeah, and it's awesome," Max agreed, still on the floor holding his sides.

Kira shook her head and stormed off through the wall again. Farn let out a few last chuckles before following.

Alastair approached as well, hoping that he might be allowed to stay with the team a little further. His heart sank as his hand felt solid stone against his virtual skin.

"I guess this is where we part." He offered a hand to Max, who took it, forming an unspoken truce as he helped him up. Then, still holding his hand, Alastair spoke. "Seriously, thank you. For everything."

Max smiled. "Anytime." He paused. "Jackass."

Back in the city of Valain, two *Shields* respawned with no way of returning to the Nostromo without a specific teleport spell. They sighed and turned to each other.

"Want to stop by a tavern, get a drink?"

The other nodded. "Hell, yes."

CHAPTER FORTY-SIX

Max passed through the stone wall, leaving Alastair behind on the other side of the intangible rock. It was cold as he slipped through the rock like a ghost. With no light source within the construct of the wall, he was blind until he reached the other side, where a dim glow hit his eyes and his foot caught something soft but firm. He fell forward, arms flailing as, again, the sound of laughter filled his ears. He growled a sigh and looked back to his feet, where he saw a giggling Kira stretched across the floor of the entrance. As annoying as her continued pranks were, she was still hard to be mad at. She was probably just coping with her situation.

"Fool me twice, shame on me." He chuckled to himself as he got back to his feet and offered a hand to his partner. She accepted, and he lifted her to her feet.

From there, Max led the group down the newly discovered tunnel for a short distance before coming to an opening where, all at once, they fell silent as Sierra came into view. Max's knees actually trembled as he uttered a quiet, "Holy shit."

Spanning for what seemed like miles, the subterranean expanse filled a cavern so large that it seemed impossible. Even its edges branched out into a network of caves, reaching like tendrils into the surrounding rock. Max always knew that the developers of Noctem had a policy of go big or go home, but this was something on a whole new level of imagination.

The cavern was covered with dozens of towers of all sizes, rising from the floor as they tapered into points at their tops. Strangely, they had no walls. Instead, they consisted of layered rings, supported by heavy girders and wood beams. Each was filled with smaller buildings as if every level was a small village in and of itself. Alone, the towers would have been impressive, but the fact that more hung from the ceiling like stalactites, mirroring their counterparts on the floor, rendered the view breathtaking. The structures above and below reached toward each other, sometimes overlapping like the teeth of the dragons imprisoned within. Some even connected in the middle as if they had grown together over time. The rest were joined by a series of lifts dangling from heavy chains while tracks wove through the city for what Max assumed was some kind of train.

Somehow, though housed within a cavern of stone, the place felt warm and inviting like a hearth. Massive crystals hung throughout the space, their glow chasing away the shadows. In a way, the city seemed almost industrial, like its people had learned to use magic in an entirely different way from the rest of the world.

Kira stood, bending to the side to view the hidden city upside down while letting out a slow whistle as she wobbled on the balls of her feet.

The path from the secret entrance ran halfway up the wall of the cavern before reaching a bridge that took them down to one of the towers. From there, Max could just barely make out the shape of the two dragon kings between the structures. Their forms were still locked in some kind of eternal struggle, jaws open as if letting out a never-ending roar of frustration at their fate as the city surrounded them on all sides.

"Damn. Can't see much, but they're definitely big."

Finally, after coming to terms with how small he felt before the city, he continued, becoming the first player to set foot in Sierra to declare the lost city no longer lost. To his surprise, the layers of each tower were populated by NPCs, each a member of the never before seen race, the deru. Their skin ranged from blue to gray, but overall, they looked human enough. The only major difference was the strange crystalline formations poking out from their hair behind their ears. With each crystal colored to match one of the world's elements, it was easy to guess that their race had some kind of affinity system built into it.

Corvin raised a few thoughts on the subject, wondering about some of the possibilities out loud, especially for mages.

Judging from the towers and the number of workshops they passed, it also seemed likely there was an emphasis on crafting for the deru. It was as if they were Noctem's version of dwarves despite the fact that they weren't short. Hell, if anything, they were taller than most races.

The city's inhabitants paid no mind as Max led the party through the walkways that circled their towers. When he approached to engage any of them, they gave him a gentle smile and lowered their head politely. Apparently, none of them had any dialogue set up yet.

"Any thoughts on how we trigger this thing?" Max questioned the group.

Shrugs from all around told him that they had none.

He shrugged as well. "I guess we just head toward the center for now."

Kira walked slower the closer they got, her breathing speeding up noticeably with each step as he looked back to check on her.

"How you doing? Feeling godlike yet?" Max asked over his shoulder, half-joking as to avoid putting pressure on the fairy.

She placed a hand on her chest. "Maybe?" she said with an upwards inflection that made it sound more like she was asking him.

"Actually, we might do okay here," Corvin jumped in.

"How so?" Max asked.

"This is a city, not a dungeon, meaning we aren't limited to the items in our bags; we can access our entire inventory. I don't know about you, but I have a ton of stuff stored."

Kira looked over her item list. "I have fifteen bone charms that I made earlier with the loot we farmed last night. That's a lot of free hits." With that, her breathing settled out.

Ginger hopped back to the fairy. "Hey, if they have any item stores set up here, I'll buy you anything you like since I lost your other stuff. I know you probably can't wait to replace that dress."

Kira let out a simple, "Meh," before adding, "I'm getting used to it, and it's easy to move in."

"Fine with me. Saves me credits." Ginger folded her hands behind her head as she walked. "I like the new look better anyway."

Kira smiled and twirled one of the braids in her hair.

Max hadn't really paid much attention to her new gear, or more accurately, he had tried his best not to since he didn't want to be caught staring again. Although, as desirable as her appearance might have been, if he was honest, she looked a little ridiculous in a fight, like she had worn the wrong outfit to the battle, forgetting her armor at home. Max chuckled at the thought; it actually seemed like something she might do. Her dress was common for fairy gear, though, all fluff and no toughness. He'd always found it annoying, like his poor partner was forever doomed to get the short end of the stick, never looking as cool as someone like Farn. His attention drifted to find the *Shield* with the corner of his eye to take a closer look at her gear. The ends of her tunic swayed as she walked, and Max couldn't help but notice how detailed the embroidery of her sash was.

Of course, that was the moment Kira chose to look in his direction, following his line of sight with hers.

Max flicked his gaze away, pretending that he was looking past the *Shield* at something in the distance.

Kira narrowed her eyes so that slivers of purple focused on him accusingly.

His head itched as heat prickled across his scalp. Fortunately, they came across a bridge, allowing him to blurt out, "A bridge!" He swept his arm out toward it as if they might have missed it without him there to point it out. "Ah, looks like it will take us to the towers closer to the dragons."

Kira rolled her eyes and stepped past him across the walkway, letting him breathe a sigh of relief, a feeling that was short-lived.

The bridge did indeed take them closer to the dragons, their hulking forms just as intimidating as Max had expected up close. The pair of beasts stood frozen in stone in a wide circle lined with glowing lanterns around its outer perimeter. Four shrines sat spaced around its edge. They had to be where the crystals that kept the War Dragons sealed away were housed.

Max found what he thought was a lift station and pulled a lever to call it up. What arrived was no elevator. Instead, a line of mining cars rolled up alongside the tower, wrapping its train around the level like the boarding zone of a roller coaster, which in retrospect, should have been his first clue that he should hold onto the handrails.

He turned back to the others as if to ask their opinion. Farn responded by hopping in and holding out her hand toward the narrow benches that faced in both directions as if she had saved him a seat. He shrugged and joined her with Kira nestling in alongside him. Ginger jumped into the next car, leaving room for someone to join her. She looked surprised when Kegan and Corvin took the car behind her.

Max found a lever at the front that read 'up' and 'down' on either side, along with several tick marks in between the words that he paid no attention to as he pulled it all the way toward down. The train started with a hiss, like air lines releasing steam, and it slowly began traveling along the rail that circled the level they were on.

Ginger stood, leaning over the back of her car to talk to the pair behind her while Max turned and rested his arm on the edge of his. The ride was relaxing, as he looked forward, watching the track. Then he grinned.

"Hey, Ginger." He kept his voice in monotone, so it would be hard to read.

"Yeah?" she answered, without even looking over her shoulder at him.

"You may want to sit down."

"Eh, I've ridden a train before." She brushed him off.

He didn't argue, but he did grin wider.

Kira arched an eyebrow at him and followed his eyes to the track ahead of them before letting out a solid, "Nope," and motioning to take flight. Max responded by grabbing the back of her dress and pulling her back down beside him as the train dropped.

"I hate you!" she cried as Max laughed, getting his payback for her tripping him earlier as they shot toward the ground below at an eighty-degree angle.

Farn raised both arms in the air and let out a long, "Whoooooo!"

It didn't take long for them to reach the bottom since apparently the tick marks on the lever that Max had ignored indicated speed.

The brakes kicked in as Farn's shouting shifted into a, "Woooah no," as she tumbled on top of Max and Kira in front of her.

"That was awesome." Max laughed as he peeled off his fairy companion, who had given in and huddled tightly to his side. "You want to go again?"

She didn't answer, opting to glower at him with every fiber of her being instead.

He turned to check on Ginger, only to find her car empty. Behind it struggled the rest of the party, who now had an upside-down *Coin* to wrestle with, her feet sticking up as she squirmed. Judging from the uncomfortable look on Corvin's face, it wasn't hard to figure out where her head had landed. He let out a yelp as she hit him somewhere sensitive, to which

Kegan responded with a few inappropriate comments that were followed promptly by Ginger kicking him in the head. There was some question of whether it was an accident. Soon after, they were all back on their feet, ready for whatever was next.

On the floor of the cavern, tents populated the wide streets between the towers, some selling a variety of crafting supplies and items while others offered games like ring toss and darts. Of course, there was also enough street food to make Kira drool. It reminded Max of a carnival midway. As if the deru, being trapped underground for so long, had set aside a part of their city for fun. It was a clever way for Checkpoint to fit another type of entertainment into the world's lore.

The place was empty now, save for the few NPCs wandering around and manning the tents, but Max could imagine what it would be like after its release. Looking up at the city, he couldn't help but be amazed as it seemed to fold over on itself. He hoped that they'd be able to come back and see it full of players later. His thoughts were interrupted by a low whine behind him, like an animal whose paw had been stepped on. He turned to find Kira struggling to get the attention of one of the deru operating a tent that sold fried dough covered in powdered sugar. It gave her the same gentle smile and nod that Max had gotten earlier.

The fairy looked back to him, her face somehow sadder than it had ever been. "The transaction system hasn't been set up yet."

Max groaned. "You'll live."

"But there's so much, and I can't eat it."

Max faced her and put one hand on his hip, the dragon kings looming behind him. "Would you really want to eat a bunch of fair food right before fighting these jerks?" He hooked a thumb back at the War Dragons.

His words hung in the air for a moment. Then all hell broke loose.

CHAPTER FORTY-SEVEN

Screams drifted through the air from beyond the city's center like a bump in the night that begged for investigation. Kira flinched and spun toward the two War Dragons, expecting to see them breathing fire and ice in her direction, but there they were, still as petrified as ever. She turned, taking note that the deru around her were closing up shop as if something was coming.

They moved with a frantic energy, their gentle smiles nowhere to be seen. Nearby, a small girl with light blue skin cried out, only to be picked up by a woman, a plush toy left behind. It was a well-worn stuffed lagopin with one ear hanging by a thread as if it had been loved by the girl a little too much. Kira couldn't help herself. The fact that the child wasn't real didn't occur to her as she snatched the toy off the stone. She couldn't bear to see the kid lose something so precious.

She ran to catch the pair before they made it more than a few feet, getting a few confused looks from the rest of her party in the process. The mother spun as Kira approached. She took they frayed animal from Kira's outstretched hand and passed it to her daughter, who clutched it tightly in her arms. The woman motioned to leave but stopped to give Kira a grateful nod. She smiled back as the deru's eyes fell to her pendant, a momentary look of pity crossing the woman's face before she turned away. Fear rolled through Kira's stomach before her thoughts were interrupted by Corvin who stood a few feet behind her.

"Is this an event of the expansion, happening early?"

Max drew his pistols. "I don't think so. Look at how detailed the deru's reactions are now. It's like they're being controlled by a different algorithm. No, I think this is the quest taking over. I'm betting that whatever is coming is all Carver's doing."

An explosion went off in the distance, and with a glance, he told Kira to get in the air to investigate. She took flight without question as deru soldiers rushed out of the towers and made their way into the center of the city. They gathered around the four shrines that held the crystals that sealed the dragons. Obviously, they didn't want the beasts getting loose. She tried to count the troops, coming up with a number around three hundred.

From the air, Kira could make out figures in the distance between the towers on the other side of the center. Puffs of magic and fire erupted around them every now and then. "Monsters are coming!" she yelled back down to the others. "I can't tell what kind from here!"

"Scout ahead but use the towers for cover!" Max shouted back up.

Kira flew toward the disturbance, circling around the structures and making sure to stay out of range. Her feet touched down on a platform above, and the sound of battle erupted as an army of creatures poured into the street. They weren't ghouls or goblins but something else. They wore gear similar to an adventurer, almost looking like players themselves.

She fell to her knees as her mind refused to process the scene. Finally, the horrific reality sunk in. They were players. She didn't know how or why, but actual people were attacking the city. The whole place had become a giant invasion event. Sierra was under siege.

Kira took flight back toward the center, passing over the street on her way. The deru, unarmed save for the soldiers, stood against the players as if hoping to hold them off, protecting their city with their lives. Kira watched in shock as her fellow adventurers cut them down without hesitation. Men, women, children. It didn't matter. They weren't real, but it tore at her heart regardless. Her vision blurred with tears as she turned back to the others who were already surrounded by the madness.

From there, she did the only thing she could. She activated whatever spell she had in her queue and supported the city's force on the ground.

CHAPTER FORTY-EIGHT

Max stood with his mouth hanging open as the deru soldiers guarding the crystals fanned out to form a wall around the shrines to meet the incoming army. They were tough, but there were too many players, and the situation was clear that they weren't going to keep the invaders back for long as their city was torn apart.

The two factions ignored Max and his team. The players were disorganized, like they had been dropped into the place without a plan and told to fight. At the same time, the deru regarded his party as allies, probably marked as friendly for the sake of the quest. Max's fingers tightened around his pistols. He had to do something, but he didn't know what. Then near the far side of the center, Kira caught his eye. She swooped down on her way back, touching the ground for a moment to set up a heal on a group of deru guards. She dropped a few more spells into her queue and took flight again. He let out a breath, grateful for his partner since seeing her told him what should have been obvious.

His eyes shifted to the rest of the party. "We have to help. What else is there?"

Without another word, he took aim and raced to aid the overwhelmed defenders, getting numerous confused looks from the invading players as he pumped rounds into their unsuspecting numbers. Using the confusion to his advantage, he and his team got the drop on most of the adventurers they encountered.

Luckily, it seemed that their levels were much lower than their own. Hell, luck probably had nothing to do with it. No doubt Carver had only lured in weaker players to make sure that Max's team wouldn't be killed outright before Kira had a chance to figure herself out. Although, despite the level difference, a critical hit was still a critical, and in PVP, anything could happen. Eventually, someone would get too close. Max had to be careful.

Ginger threw out the spider egg that she had taken from the Plague dungeon and a smaller version of the spider that they had fought earlier burst from within. It proceeded to attack any player that she targeted. Corvin pulled the fabric from his face and used his left eye to hold the stronger players in place while Kegan dispatched them. And Farn, well, she just charged shield first into entire parties, throwing them off balance while the deru finished them off. Max looked up just in time to see Kira streak by, casting spell after spell, supporting the defending ground forces. Then she fell.

The fairy dropped out of the sky, hitting the ground hard and losing her bone charm in the process. Max saw her go down, but he didn't see why. She hadn't been hit; he was sure of it. No, it was like she had just been switched off. She was fine one moment, and then she wasn't.

He sprinted toward her, dropping as many of the unguarded players as he could in his path. If she hadn't been shot down, then that meant something was wrong. A sick feeling coursed through him as his imagination ran wild. *What if she'd reached her limit within the system? What if she was hurt for real, or worse?* He should have forced her to quit earlier. They shouldn't have risked it. His mind raced with possibilities, possibilities that he wasn't ready to face. He missed the feeling from before, when he rode high on his ego, back when he thought he had the power to save her. Now he just felt helpless. His eyes welled up as he tore through the players between them like paper, shooting people in the back before they realized he wasn't on their side. Finally, he found her.

Farnsworth had beat him there and knelt over his friend, her shield covering them both. She moved aside to give him room and looked up at him through tear-filled eyes that begged him to do something.

Kira lay on the cobblestone, eyes shut tight, clutching her chest with both hands. She looked like she was in pain.

Max called her name several times, but all she did was lie there, her small body taking rapid breaths like a dying animal clinging to life. He touched her throat for a pulse before realizing that it was a stupid thing to do since his mind would only interpret what he expected to feel. Instead, he slapped her on the cheek, his hand coming away wet with tears as they flowed in an endless stream down her face. His heart charged into his throat.

That was when some of the invading players caught on that there were traitors in their midst. Heads turned toward Max and his broken partner one by one. He could almost see the recognition of an easy target on each of their faces.

The rest of his party converged to block their path and Max passed the responsibility of protecting Kira to Corvin, who rested her head on his lap and wrapped his tail around her to provide some form of comfort while his basilisk eye held potential threats at bay. He winced but never looked away.

Max exchanged a look with Farn, carrying everything that he needed to say as the players rushed them. They couldn't let a single one through.

CHAPTER FORTY-NINE

Farn screamed through the chaos for the players to stop, her voice raw and cracking. When they failed to listen, she cut them down in a display of ferocity that she didn't know she was capable of.

Her shield deflected a blow from a large man with a thick beard. She followed with a strike to his leg, knocking him flat on his back. He tried to roll away, but she plunged downward through his chest before he could escape. Their eyes met as he disconnected, the life in them fading in the space of a breath. She paused in shock as the glowing particles of his body dispersed from around her blade.

Taking advantage of the momentary opening, a young woman, a *Leaf*, attempted to catch her off guard by firing two arrows at her while she was exposed. They pierced the back of Farn's shoulder, but she moved just in time to avoid a critical that could have killed her. Ignoring the arrows, Farn launched her sword with both hands in the direction of the attack. Clearly not expecting a counter at distance, the *Leaf* failed to dodge the flying blade, and the impact launched the small player backward into another group, pinning her to an unlucky mage and killing them both in a lucky hit.

Unarmed, Farn sprinted to reclaim her sword. She plowed into a group on her way with her uninjured shoulder, knocking a few over. The arrows in her back dug in, causing additional damage as her momentum forced her into a roll. Before she could recover, a *Coin* lunged in her direction, a short dagger in his hand. With her sword still several feet away, she grabbed her attacker by the collar as he fell upon her, his dagger piercing her abdomen. The pain, though dulled by the system, sent a wave of nausea through her body that took hold in her stomach. She slammed her back against the ground, positioning the *Coin* so that the arrows in her shoulder pushed through her and into his heart. It hurt more than expected.

Weapons clashed and players shouted as Farn rolled off the body, glowing particles drifting from the lifeless form as she pushed herself back up with a grunt. Despite the pain and sick feeling in her gut, she charged ahead, shoving down players to get to her weapon. She fell hard as she reclaimed it but recovered to one knee as four players closed in. She glared up at them from a crouch, her sword ready, two arrows still in her shoulder. Wisps of her loose black curls fell across her field of vision as she glared daggers at them, her heart full of passion, determination, and rage.

With a short motion of her blade, she snapped the ends of the arrows from her back and ripped the tips from her chest with her free hand. She popped a health vial, pulling the stopper with her teeth.

The surrounding players took a step back.

CHAPTER FIFTY

Max ducked behind Kegan and Ginger for protection to retrieve a pair of crimson magazines from his item bag. He had only received them an hour ago as a result of his most recent contract, but there wasn't time to waste debating whether to use them or not. He just hoped they did what he thought they would. He tapped the mag release on both guns, not bothering to catch or pick up the spent magazines as he slammed in both of the red ones. He placed both pistols against his forehead and breathed the words, "Explosive rounds."

As a class, *Furies* weren't well suited for PVP since their damage weighed on criticals and players wore better armor than most enemies in the game to protect them, making it harder to land one without getting close. Normally, range was his primary advantage, but now, it became more of a double-edged sword. Not to mention the fact that a *Shield* could rush him without much risk. He was left with little choice. It would take everything he had to keep his partner safe.

He stood baring his teeth, causing a couple of the invading players to change their minds as they turned and focused on the deru guards instead. He stepped in front of his friends and raised his pistols. He released the slides and they snapped forward into place, the first round of each mag moving into position to be fired. A timer reading five minutes appeared within the tattooed flames on his wrist below his status to signify that the one-time-use contract ability of the magazines had been activated. He had read over their vague description earlier. It only consisted of two words, *Unleash Hell.*

His guns, Mary and Anne, both contract items as well, weighed on his mind now that he knew they had been pulled from his subconscious instead of from a list of pre-programmed items. He had always liked pirates, even read books about them, so when he'd taken down a Nightmare named Rackham, based on a famous real-world captain, his mind must have made the connection without him realizing it.

Mary Reid and Anne Bonny, historically, were also pirates. Two of the few female ones. They had sailed with Jack Rackham, or Calico Jack, as he was called due to his preference for colorful clothing. While history remembered the man - who was, in truth, a terrible pirate, surrendering early in his career only to be hung - it often overlooked these two women, the ones who deserved better. The women who fought alone and refused to surrender while the rest of the crew cowered below deck. Their story had always stuck with Max.

Now, with the knowledge of how the contract system worked combined with how the quest had been going so far, he couldn't help but wonder if the weapons he carried reflected his own insecurities as a leader. If, in his mind, he only saw himself as a man hiding below deck while others carried the burden. Either way, none of that was important now. Mary and Anne, the pirates, were long gone, leaving only their memory in his hands.

Max never used the select fire switches on the pistols since there hadn't been a need to turn their safeties on before. Noctem was a game, after all. Why bother being responsible? But as stated, the pistols were contract items, and so they had a third, unlabeled option. He thumbed their switches all the way down and fired.

Hell erupted from his hands as the pair of pistols unleashed an unending stream of explosive rounds in a continuous spray of destruction. With both guns set to fully-automatic, stacking with the five minutes of infinite ammunition that the magazines provided, on top of his custom rounds skill, he might as well have been Death himself.

The machine pistols roared, breathing fire and smoke from their barrels as if they were an extension of his own body. A few other players fired back as he raged against the limits of the system. He might not have had the wild spikes in willpower that his Kira did, but his was still high enough to squeeze every last bit of power he could from the game. He moved faster, terrified of what might happen if he didn't as he acquired targets with both hands independent of one another. The fear of losing his best friend pushed him further than any Nightmare had before. His hands burned as the ends of his pistols glowed red from the heat of constant firing. He didn't stop.

In the crowd, Max glimpsed the face of a young *Blade* that he recognized. Among the invading army was DarkA55a55in, leader of the party that he and Kira had rescued a day prior. He looked at Max confused, clearly questioning why he was opposing the player's advance. The boy's expression changed to terror as Max closed the gap, executing everyone between them.

He holstered his left pistol, Anne, and grabbed the boy by his collar. He didn't stop there. Instead, he pushed him backward at least ten feet into some kind of fruit stand. Wood cracked as produce spilled to the ground.

With his right gun, Mary, he fired at two nearby players, dispatching them both in a torrent of death without taking his eyes away from his captive. Satisfied that they would have a moment to talk without interruption, he pushed the glowing barrel of his gun into the kid's face. "Why are you doing this?!" His voice came out rough, strained from overexertion.

"It's an event!" the kid squealed back, grabbing at Max's wrist.

Max pulled back, lifting his captive up before slamming him back down and crushing a few apples with the boy's weight. "What event? Who sent you?"

Tears welled up in the kid's eyes. "I don't know; I just got a system message. Everyone did."

Max looked at him with an intensity that not even he knew he possessed. It was a look that demanded more without him needing to ask, prompting the kid to spill information like blood from a wound.

"It just said that there was a one-time event here. An evil race of creatures had trapped two dragons, and we had to set them free to restore balance or something like that. It said there were rewards."

"How'd you get here?" Max growled as he fired blindly at three players behind him, hitting them all with the sheer quantity of bullets that poured from his gun.

"It came with a teleport crystal," the kid responded, trying to get his footing as Max held him down.

He pulled the player away from the now broken fruit stand and threw him to the ground. "You idiots!" He leaned over him. "If those dragons get free, this world will end, and my friend will die!"

The kid's eyes widened, clearly unsure if he had fallen into something real or if Max was just good at role-playing. "What can I do?" He shoved himself up from the stone, changing sides.

Max leaned in close and breathed his words at the boy, his low tone still even more frightening than his yelling, "You pick up your sword and protect this city."

At a loss, the kid said nothing back. Without another word, Max disappeared into the fray, leaving the boy alone to choose a side.

Suddenly, an explosion detonated at the far end of the field, taking out one of the shrines. The chain of lanterns that surrounded the center went dark. There was no stopping Carver's quest now.

Max scrambled back to his partner, her helpless body still clutching her chest in pain as she gasped for air. He commanded the others to form a wall around her. They obeyed without question. There was no way in hell he was going to let the army of fools that charged toward them lay a finger on his friend.

To his surprise, the remaining deru guards abandoned their pointless defense of the other three shrines and fell back toward him, forming a second defensive wall around the party. No, not around the party. Around Kira. It was as if they recognized she was important.

Hundreds of players surrounded them at once after they finished with the remaining crystals, and with time still remaining on his limitless ammunition, Max fought alongside the deru forces. Farn and Kegan followed while Ginger fell back to Corvin as a last line of defense.

A broken shard of crystal, snapped from the head of one of the city's guards, clattered to the ground near at Max's feet as he and his team fought with everything they had. In the end, hits were taken, and ground was lost. Without a healer, it was only a matter of time. Then things got worse.

CHAPTER FIFTY-ONE

Kira's heart raced faster than ever before, her fingertips feeling like ice against her skin. No matter how heavy she breathed, she couldn't get enough air. Her lungs ached, and her throat burned as the voices of Farn and Max reached her weakly through the sounds of battle that surrounded her.

She felt Max slap her. His hand was wet against her cheek. She realized she was crying. It made her want to shrink into nothing as tears pooled around her face. Despite that, she also wanted desperately to see him. She just couldn't open her eyes. In fact, she couldn't move at all. It was like she had lost all control of her body. She needed to respond. To say something. To do anything. But she couldn't. She just laid there, frozen in place, gasping for air as war raged around her.

Something warm and soft fell across her body as she heard Corvin's voice telling her everything would be okay. His words wavered in the middle, and he let out a choking sound as if he was in pain.

Farn yelled in the distance, sounding angrier than Kira had thought possible since the *Shield* had always been so kind to her. Then the sound of endless gunfire drowned out everything else.

Her friends were all fighting. No, not just that, they were fighting for her, and she could do nothing to help. She was like a lead weight tied around their necks as they sank together. The very idea that Carver thought she could do anything was absurd. She couldn't believe how wrong he was.

The ground rumbled as the sound of gunfire faded, only to be replaced by the roars of centuries-old rage. Sounds reverberated through the ground to her shaking body, and heat blasted her skin. The fire was then snuffed out by a freezing cold that chilled her to the core. Hundreds of screams filled her ears; many cut off midway, silenced in an instant. Then the world faded, towers falling somewhere far away.

She curled into a fetal position as her mind ran wild, still lost in pain and darkness. *This is it*, she thought as despair set in. The fabric of her dress coiled around her legs as she curled tighter. She was disappearing. Half of her just wanted to let go, while the other half screamed at her not to. She searched herself for something. Something to grab onto. Something to bring her back. A thought, a sound, a memory. Anything.

It was okay, none of it was real anyway. Or was it? She needed to go back to the fight, but she felt like, maybe, she was free, like she might wake up in her body back in her rig. A body that was strong and real. That was what she wanted, wasn't it? It would be so easy.

She wasn't sure which body she wore. Maybe both. She couldn't tell. They both felt the same anyway.

Then, through it all, she felt something. Her hands pressed against her chest, one overlapping the other. On her finger sat something cold. Something she couldn't let go of. It bound her to her friends, to the world, to everything. She couldn't leave. Not yet. She focused on the thought, on the others fighting to save her, and on herself at their center.

With all of her will, she pulled away from the peace of the dark toward the fire, ice, and violence. She inhaled, the pain in her chest fading as hot air filled her lungs. She opened her eyes and felt the system's resistance fall away from her mind. Something flooded around her, waves caressing everything that she was, accepting her will as a part of something larger. Her mind flowed into it.

CHAPTER FIFTY-TWO

The fighting slowed to a stop as the contract timer on Max's sleeve reached zero, the slides of his pistols locking back empty. A deep rumble drifted across the battlefield, followed by the sharp crack of fracturing stone. The shell of rock that encased the two dragon kings crumbled, falling in large shards as the two Nightmares, each a Horseman of War, began to move.

Players fled in all directions to escape the debris that flaked off the beasts as they took in their first breaths. The ones that didn't make it were simply crushed. Max watched as confusion settled on the faces all around him. Some of them looked stunned, clearly not understanding what they had done. Others, the slower minds in the mix, actually cheered when they saw that their mission to free the dragons had been successful. They stood in awe as the two enormous beasts shook off their bodies.

The towering kings of ice and fire looked to each other as if unsure how to start after waiting for so long. It didn't take them long to figure it out. The sound of their roars shook the ground they stood on as if the entire city was quaking in fear. The players stepped back at a loss of what it meant. Then it was clear.

Fire engulfed entire towers as one of the dragons attacked, its jaws snapping at the other with the built-up frustration of their long but fictional slumber. With one stumble of its leg, dozens of players were crushed. A second later, a hundred more were killed as a tail whipped across half the city's center. Players ran for their lives as their mistake became clear, only to find that there were no exits. Max noticed a few mages attempt to teleport, looks of frustration and fear on each of their faces, finding their spells blocked. There was no escape.

The towers above burned and fell, crashing into the ones below in a cacophony of destruction and death. Screams from the players blended with the deru's as the city was ripped apart at the seams.

The fighting stopped completely as players scattered, the flood of panicked adventurers making it difficult for Max to move in the chaos as the dragons leveled half of the city in under a minute. He struggled to find the others, his sense of direction getting thrown off as he struggled to find a safe path through. Then, just when he thought he caught a glimpse of Farn and the others, the sound of steel buckling met his ears. He turned, the shadow of a tower consuming his surroundings. It fell in what seemed like slow motion, hitting another on its way down. The only thing he could do was run. He didn't look back as debris flew over his head like a wave in the ocean.

Blasts of ice and fire erupted all around him as he lost sight of the others. He checked his stat-sleeve. They were alive, barely. It was only a matter of time before the War Dragons fight reached them. They couldn't win. His thoughts fell back to Kira. He had to get her out of there.

He frantically shoved people out of the way as the last of the deru guards came into view. He was almost there. Then one of the warring kings crashed into the ground behind him. He turned just in time to see its massive head slam against the cobblestones a dozen feet away, smashing them to rubble. The other dragon's jaws clamped down on its throat as it screamed out in pain. The force of its breath blew him off his feet, throwing him to the ground like he was no more than an ant. No, worse, he was nothing. All the bullets in the world wouldn't be enough to stop them. He closed his eyes, expecting the worst.

Then a sound rang out, crisp and clear, like a string from Kira's harp, somehow still audible over the din of the chaos. It hung in the air as if singing a single note of a song. Along with it, a wave of invisible energy swept past him like nothing that Max had felt before. It was clean and soothing. He opened his eyes to see the dumbfounded faces of the players surrounding him. Even stranger, they had stopped running. The War Dragons would be on him in seconds, but they weren't. In fact, they seemed to hang there, frozen in time. The air grew still, almost silent.

He wasn't going to question it. He ignored everything and scampered back to his feet, sprinting to Kira's side. The deru parted to let him through. He stopped short as soon as he met her violet eyes.

She looked calm, her face tranquil as a nonexistent breeze ruffled the semi-sheer fabric of her dress around her. Corvin sat on the ground supporting himself with his hands, looking up at her as if stunned. She glanced down at him, making contact with his left eye. It had no effect. An electric quality filled the air, growing stronger as Max approached. She looked normal with no in-game animation or sound to accompany her other than the fading chime, but it was clear to him that she'd stopped the dragons. Hell, even the flames that burned around her had paused mid-flicker as if locked away in time.

Her eyes returned to him, and in them, he saw power. She didn't speak, which would have worried him, but something inside him told him it was okay. Instead, she gave him a knowing smile. Then she shut her eyes tight, her nose scrunched up adorably.

A seconded note sounded along with another pulse of strange energy. Then everything just felt right.

Max couldn't believe his eyes. The fire and ice were nowhere to be seen. He glanced back at the dragons. They were gone too - as were the hundreds of players that had surrounded him a second before. It was as if they'd never been there to begin with. He blinked twice taking in the scene.

The towers were all back where they belonged, the deru continuing with their day safe and sound. The destruction of the battle was just a memory.

Max turned back to Kira. He tried to speak, but the words got lodged in his throat.

She smiled back at him again as if she already knew what he wanted to say. Then she collapsed.

CHAPTER FIFTY-THREE

Wyatt pushed himself up from his rig, struggling to balance himself as he shoved through the fog that hung over his waking mind. His eyes burned, and his mouth tasted foul. Beside him, a wall of nurses blocked his best friend from view. He tried to stand but almost fell, still out of it from his time as Max back in Noctem. Across the aisle, he saw Marisa pushing her Somno unit off her head as well.

The others remained motionless, having stayed inside with Kira in case she woke up there.

He got to his feet with a few frantic motions and tried to push his way into the group beside him. He demanded to know what was going on and caught a glimpse of Seth laying as still as death. His heart froze. Then he saw the readout on the screen next to him, the one that showed Seth's vitals. He didn't know what he was looking at, but he knew that the squiggly line meant that he was at least alive.

Doctor Narang caught his eyes, but instead of giving him answers, he yelled to one of the nurses to get him out of there.

Marisa got to his side as a man in scrubs apologized and explained that they needed room to work.

At first, Wyatt resisted being escorted out, but he gave in when he realized that he wasn't helping. A few seconds later, he was out in the hall, being told that they would be allowed back in when the doctor knew more about what was happening. The doors closed, too thick to hear anything more from inside.

For a while, Wyatt couldn't bring himself to move. Instead, he just stood there taking short breaths, unable to form a coherent thought.

Marisa threw her arms around him, hugging him until he calmed down.

It was awkward, being held, especially considering that they were both in their real bodies. As Ginger, she was always teasing him, but now, it was different. There was compassion in the act. It helped him relax, and he breathed a heavy sigh.

"Thanks for coming with me." He cringed as his voice came out with a croak.

She let go, looking into his eyes for an instant before glancing away. "I saw the screens." She leaned against the wall beside him. "He's alive, and his vitals looked normal."

Wyatt raised his head. "You sure?"

She nodded. "His heart rate was a little fast but not overly so, and his blood pressure was fine. I'm no doctor, but I know that much."

Wyatt fell back against the wall, releasing a slow breath. "Thank god. I don't know what I'd do if …" He didn't finish the thought.

"Do you think we should tell them to pull the plug when they come out to get us?" she asked. Then she waved her hands, crossing them in front of her face. "I mean pull the plug on her rig, umm, not Kira." She shook her head. "I mean Seth. Whatever his name is."

Wyatt would have laughed at her flustered stumbling, but he couldn't with his friend laying in the other room. Instead, he gave her a weak smile to let her know he understood what she meant. He didn't answer her question, though. "Sometimes I call him by the wrong name, too."

"Really?"

"Yeah, he always responds by accident," Wyatt added.

"That's kinda funny. Like when people say 'you too' when a waiter says 'enjoy your meal.'"

He smiled, remembering something. "Seth does that all the time at the movies when the guy scans his ticket. I always make fun of him for it."

She looked at him sideways. "You two go on a lot of movie dates?"

"Yeah, I like dumb action stuff, and he'll watch pretty much anything if he can make a joke about it. He's easy going like that, always happy to go with the flow as long as he gets to have fun. It's probably why we do everything together. He encourages me to do things, and I drag him along for the ride."

Marisa smiled. "You do complement each other, in a weird codependent sort of way."

Wyatt grimaced. "It sounds bad if you say it like that."

She dismissed him with a wave of her hand. "Meh, there's nothing wrong with it. You just fill in each other's weaknesses. Honestly, I'm a little envious. Most married couples can't figure that out."

Wyatt scoffed. "Well, I guess we have been friends since we were kids. It's not surprising that we rely on each other." He paused before continuing, "I think that's what makes this so hard. He's always been there for me, even when things got hard. But now that we're in the middle of something that actually matters, I feel like I don't have what it takes to get him through it. I'm afraid I'm going to fail him."

Marisa fell silent for before speaking, "You're an idiot." She threw Wyatt off guard, resembling her online persona.

"What, why?" he asked, confused.

She rolled her eyes. "So Carver threw a wrench into your little bromance. You two will be fine. But maybe tonight isn't about saving her, I mean him or whatever." She chewed her upper lip. "Sorry, but that is really hard to get straight. Anyway, maybe tonight, you just have to be there for your friend."

Wyatt let himself rest against the wall, not quite sure what to say to that. Then he sighed. *Could it really be that simple? Am I really that dumb?*

Marisa grinned like the *Coin* she was. "I'll take your silence to mean that I'm right." She sounded satisfied as she reached into the pocket of her pajamas and pulled out her phone. She sent a quick text before adding, "Sorry, I figured I should tell my kids I'm out. They must be awake by now."

"Oh, no problem," Wyatt said, grateful for the change in subject. "I'm sure they're worried about you."

She shrugged. "Yeah."

"They seem like good kids," he added.

Marisa folded her arms and leaned her head back against the wall, looking up at the ceiling. "Wren can be a smart-ass sometimes, and Toby could really try harder in school, but there are moments when they make me proud to have spawned them. And they appreciate what I do for them. So that's nice."

"They know what you do for a living then?" Wyatt asked, only half paying attention, still worried about Seth. He wouldn't have asked it otherwise.

She raised an eyebrow at the question. "They do."

"How does that go over?"

Marisa shrugged. "I don't tell them much about my nights, and they obviously don't want to know the details. Although I had 'the talk' with them a few years back, so they know what happens when two consenting adults get together. Plus, they're at that age when supervision becomes less about keeping them from using the scissors, if you know what I mean."

"Is that why you didn't let them stay home alone during all of this?"

"Pretty much. Wren is still a little awkward with guys, but Toby has a girlfriend. I had to turn the hose on them a week ago." Wyatt managed a weak chuckle at her wording as she continued, "And I don't mean that as an expression either. They were making out on the front porch. I guess because I was in the house, they seemed to think that I wouldn't notice if they didn't come inside." She let out an indignant snort. "Seriously, like I was never a teenager. Anyway, I went to the backyard and hooked up the garden hose to the faucet on the back of the house. Then I dragged it through the kitchen and living room to the front door where I opened it and let them have it."

Wyatt knew she was trying to make him laugh to take his mind off things, but still, it worked. He couldn't help but grin as she beamed with pride. "That's umm, some solid parenting."

"I thought so," she grinned before whispering, "but I don't think his girlfriend likes me now."

Finally, he let himself laugh outright. It wasn't really that funny, but her unapologetic tone displayed how similar she was to her character. "What made you pick a *Coin* for a class?"

Marisa stopped at the sudden question. "Umm, I don't know. I guess because the starting gear looked kind of nice."

Wyatt gave her a judgmental look. It wasn't the answer he expected. "Really?"

"Well, I didn't make the character to play with." She dug a toe onto the floor. "I've never been a gamer or anything before now. I was struggling to make ends meet, and things were feeling a little hopeless for me back then. So when a friend told me about what kind of money I could make at a brothel online, I got myself a system. It wasn't even a hard decision. I gave myself a hot body and a pretty face and picked whichever starting outfit looked best, which was apparently the *Coin's* default gear.

"I don't know what I expected, but the Everleigh club welcomed me in, and from there, I moved up fast since ..." She froze for a second, clamming up. A moment later she continued regardless, "I don't hate what I do. The club is run well, and I always feel safe. So, in a way, it's probably the best job I've had. Plus, I'm kind of good at it." She gave an awkward laugh with a smile that touched her eyes. "It wasn't long before I was making money like crazy. I did the math and realized that I didn't have to work every night, and that left me with a lot of free time. So I dug my unused dagger out of my inventory and made my way out of the city."

"And you just went with things from there?"

Marisa nodded. "I never understood how satisfying games could be. Noctem has been liberating, and not just because it gave me a job or because it gave me back the time in my life that I lost working nonstop and going gray from stress. There's just something about swinging through a forest by a grappling line and fighting monsters that makes me feel alive."

Wyatt nodded. "Plus, you get to steal stuff."

She gave him a wide grin that suited her. Then she let it fall. "But nothing lasts forever. And right now, making sure Kira is safe comes first. Even if it means losing that freedom." She didn't bother to correct which name she used anymore.

Wyatt started to speak but stopped as the door to the Nemo Unit opened. From it approached the nurse that had escorted them out. "Is he okay?" Wyatt stepped forward, forgetting everything else and not giving the man a chance to speak first.

The nurse looked away as if he wasn't used to talking to a patient's loved ones, like he was only out there because the doctor was too busy. He took a quick breath before answering, "We're not sure."

CHAPTER FIFTY-FOUR

Kira didn't sleep. Instead, it was more like she had ceased to exist. She was dormant. Then, suddenly, she wasn't. Consciousness flooded back. The feel of a comfortable bed around her told her which world she was in without needing to open her eyes. After all, beds had no purpose in a virtual world where no one slept. She wasn't groggy, but she wasn't fully aware either. She rolled onto her side and nuzzled her face into a pillow, her silver hair falling across her cheek. Her mind snapped awake as sensory information rushed in, telling her which body she inhabited. She opened her eyes.

Farn leaned over the bed from a chair at its side, a hopeful look on her face. Corvin and Kegan stood in a doorway behind her. Farn hesitated as Kira hoisted herself up, running one hand through her hair, brushing it from her face.

She looked around the medium-sized room, its simple luxury surrounding her. "Where am I?" She raised herself further.

The dam holding Farn back broke, and she lunged forward to embrace her, being careful not to squeeze Kira too hard against her metal breastplate. "You're okay!"

Kira returned the hug, more to comfort her worried friend than to seek it herself since she wasn't sure what had happened. She leaned her head into the *Shield's* neck, letting her cheek touch her skin.

Kegan stepped out of the room and yelled down the hall. "She's awake!"

Farn released her and looked down at her hands as she let them fall to her lap. "You're in Alastair's room on the Nostromo."

"Why the hell does he have a bedroom on an airship?" Kira focused on the least important detail of the moment.

"Alastair felt a ship should have a captain's quarters," Corvin answered from the door.

"I think it's for entertaining." Kegan formed air quotes around the word entertaining.

Feeling somewhat disturbed to be wrapped in Alastair's sheets, Kira tensed. "Oh god, I hope not." She forced an exaggerated shudder to make Farn laugh.

The *Shield* cracked a smile but let it fall just as fast.

Kira sighed, allowing a worried expression to creep back. "Anyway, what happened?"

Farn's face went blank, and she looked toward the door.

Kira's concern grew. "I mean, we won, right? I did the thing. Overpowered the system and what not. Carver got what he wanted; the quest should be done. So why am I still here?" As soon as the words left her mouth, she knew the answer. It wasn't over.

The sound of someone running down the hall grew as the metal grating of the floor rattled with each step. Alastair swung into the room, one hand gripping the side of the door to stop his momentum. Farn moved from the chair to the foot of the bed, making room for him to sit down.

"Oh, thank god!" Alastair said, catching his breath.

Kira looked up at him, for once completely serious. "Spill it. I stopped the dragons. Why am I still logged in?"

His breathing returned to normal, and he sat down, putting

up a calm front. Although, something about the way he avoided making eye contact with her told her that he might be faking it. She grimaced and folded her arms in front of her. She wasn't buying it.

"True, you did stop them." He focused on the bedsheets. "I don't understand how you did it, but you transported the War Dragons to opposite ends of the world and set them on flight paths that will never meet. As for the players that attacked Sierra, you sent the ones that survived back to their individual spawn points.

"We've pinned the whole thing on Carver by reporting that the event was a misguided attempt at revenge for his firing, which was kind of true in a way. It's not the best PR, but opinion has turned a little in my favor, seeing as Neal just sent a couple hundred players to their deaths. We also kept all your names out of it by saying that we used an emergency protocol to stop the event and cancel it out. Not many people saw you down there in all the chaos, and we removed all recordings of what you did. So you don't have to worry about anyone finding out it was you."

"Quit stalling." Kira leaned forward, using her arms to support herself. "What's the problem?"

Alastair placed his hands on his knees and took a breath. "Well, there are two problems." He shifted his gaze to look her in the eyes as he spoke. "When you took control of the system and stopped the dragons, the quest didn't end. Instead, it gave another waypoint. We're circling it a few miles out as we speak. It's some kind of large storm in the middle of the ocean. You beat all the fights that Neal listed for completion in the quest log, so we assume that whatever's in there is the last step. We just don't know what that is."

Kira glanced at Farn, who still looked worried, before turning back to Alastair. "So, what happened to me? Why'd I pass out?"

Alastair took another breath as if giving her time to prepare herself. "You had a seizure."

Kira's chest tightened at the word.

"That's what made you fall initially and why you couldn't move. We don't know what the cause was. It could have been triggered by whatever that pendant did to your rig or just because you've been logged in for too long."

Reminded of the issue of her login time, Kira glanced at the mission clock on her wrist. She gasped. "Twenty-eight! I've been unconscious for almost …" she paused to do the math in her head, "ten hours! What the hell? Why didn't you cut the power and get me out?"

Alastair cringed. "That's the second problem. I did."

She wasn't even angry at the statement. How could she be? It made no sense. She just cocked her head to the side with a confused expression.

He continued. "Your brain activity went wild during the seizure. So as soon as you stabilized, I made the call to force the shutdown. There was too much risk to continue, even if it meant failing the quest. So we cut the power and pulled you out. We think that was what caused you to pass out."

"And whose brilliant idea was it to put me back in?" she asked in disbelief.

He shook his head. "We didn't put you back. Your rig is still powered down."

"Then how the hell am I here?" She let the pitch of her voice rise to a shrill note.

"We don't know." He looked down at his lap. "When we cut the power, your avatar should have lagged out and disappeared. But it didn't. Instead, shutting down your rig seemed to cause some kind of error that disrupted your brain activity and knocked you out for a while, but even with that, your connection status to the system stayed green the whole time."

Kira glanced to the faces around the room in desperation, but apologetic looks were all she got. "How is that possible?"

"I wish we knew. The system can't actually do anything to you physically. Doctor Narang rushed in a whole team of colleagues and tons of equipment. They're still trying to figure things out. All we know right now is that there's a ton of activity going on in parts of your brain that people don't normally use. The techs think that whatever Neal did to your rig accelerated the effects of being logged in for too long, and somehow, your brain is has learned to emulate a connection system on its own as a result of that."

His words echoed in her head. "So what does that make me? Wi-fi?" She didn't expect an answer.

"I'm sorry." Alastair looked back up to her face with pity in his eyes. "I never thought anything like this was even remotely possible, and it looks like everything we knew about the effects of being logged in for too long may have been wrong. Neal must have been withholding information from the beginning. So, at this point, we're in uncharted territory."

Kira ignored him and pulled a pillow close, hugging it to her chest tight. "I can't. I just can't right now."

Farn slid up to her and placed a hand on her back. "It'll be okay. We'll figure it out."

Kira gave up on keeping appearances and sunk into the *Shield's* side as she wrapped an arm around her.

Alastair went on about the situation, but his words faded into the background hum of the airship's engines. It didn't matter what he was saying. In just a couple hours, the system would collapse with her inside it. She let her mind run with the thought, teetering on the edge. Then she buried her face in the pillow and screamed.

She let the muffled sound go on until she ran out of air, her cry drifting away to silence. She stayed like that for a while, and the others let her be until she lifted her head. She held frighteningly still. Then she hit Alastair in the face with the pillow as hard as she could.

"What the– Hey!" he blurted out as he struggled to raise his arms in defense before she had time to hit him again. Which she did several more times. "I'm sorry!" he cried.

"I know! I'm not mad at you!" she shouted back, contradicting her actions. "I'm mad at the situation!"

"Then why are you hitting me?" He shielded his head against the fluffy assault.

"Because I can't murder the situation!" She couldn't hit him hard, but still, it made her feel better.

Suddenly she heard a voice from beside her.

"Hey, Kira?"

She stopped for a moment, turning toward Kegan as he swatted her in the head with a second pillow.

She stumbled to the side glaring at him before hitting him back.

The *Leaf* returned the attack, then threw his weapon to Corvin, who seemed to understand his intent. Sometimes, when faced with more than you can handle, you just have to let go and give in to whatever distraction you can find.

Corvin struck the fairy in the back of the head, sending her into the mattress with a soft 'wump.'

Alastair stood, his hair a mess from having been wailed on with his own bedding. "What the hell is wrong with you people?"

Corvin answered by hopping onto the bed and whipping him in the face twice. Kira took advantage while his back was turned, grabbing his tail and letting out a laugh as she yanked him back. She unleashed a furious pile-driver down upon him. He toppled off the bed at Alastair's feet, throwing his pillow up to the vampiric looking mage in an unlikely alliance that took the fairy by surprise. Alastair got on board quickly after that. It was hit or be hit. He swung, then threw his weapon to Kegan, ducking a projectile as Kira threw it. The pillow sailed over his head, hitting an overly serious elf in the face as he walked in the door.

Kira snorted as Jeff-with-a-three took the hit, his eye twitching as stared into the room, clearly unamused.

Finding herself unarmed after throwing her weapon, Kira faced Kegan head on as he pointed past her at some imagined place in the distance like a baseball player stepping up to the plate, predicting where he intended to hit the ball. Kira turned to where he pointed, then back to him, realizing that she was the ball. He swung, and she fell to the center of the bed with an involuntary squeal that made her laugh.

Farn shook her head, looking down at her laying in the mess of blankets, and for a moment, Kira thought the *Shield* might say something responsible to put a stop to the ridiculousness.

Instead, Farn reached down and grabbed the edge of the bed's comforter, which was now untucked. She then pulled it up and over Kira's head, using her weight to hold her down as she flailed. Then she gathered the other side of the blanket to form a crude sack.

Kira squirmed, like a cat playing under the sheets in an attempt to find a way out.

Farn held her up so only her back was still on the mattress until she tired out. "You calm now?" the *Shield* asked.

Kira let silence answer back as she hung almost upside down with her dress tangled around her. She folded her arms across her chest in defiance even though no one could see her. Farn shook the sack a bit, dislodging an uncooperative, "Maybe." She shook it again, and Kira gave in, letting out a laugh, followed by a cheerful, "Yeah."

"Good," Farn said without releasing her.

"You're enjoying this, aren't you?" Kira asked from her place in the sack.

Farn let out a laugh that sounded a bit too excited. "I kind of like having a little prisoner."

"Well, that's vaguely inappropriate," Kira said before adding, "Thank you for making me feel better. Although, I am going to bite the first person I see when you let me out of here."

The *Shield* tightened her grip. "Okay, I'll just make sure to point you at someone else."

"That's fair." Kira accepted her captivity, settling in as if resting in a hammock. She then asked abruptly, "Where's Max?"

Alastair stepped in. "He's on his way back in. We thought you'd wake up out there in the real world, so he logged out with

Ginger to be there when you did. They've both been by your side this whole time."

Kira smiled at the sentiment and wiped away a tear that no one could see. Then she took a breath and found her resolve. "Okay then. In less than two hours, Noctem will crash, thousands will lose their jobs, and I will probably die. We should probably get going. Agreed?"

Farn shook her again. "Hey, don't go making it sound so bleak."

"Sorry." Kira pointed from within the sack toward where she thought the door was. "Anyway … onward!"

Farn snickered, then hoisted her onto her back and carried her toward the deck. Apparently, she wasn't ready to let Kira go.

CHAPTER FIFTY-FIVE

Max rushed onto the bridge only to find it empty save for Checkpoint's employees. He glanced to Ginger, who shrugged. Then he looked to Jeff-with-a-three, who was standing in a corner, his expression as serious as ever.

The tall elf barely acknowledged him but held up one hand pointing in the direction of the deck.

Max gave a nod in thanks and made his way outside.

The others were grouped by the railing, Kira standing at their center, staring off into the distance with a blanket wrapped around her. The sight of her sent a pang of guilt through his chest. He couldn't believe he'd been waiting in the wrong world when she woke up. She must have been scared, especially after hearing everything that was happening to her. He ran toward her at full speed, not caring how it looked.

His heavy footsteps announced his presence, and she turned to face him without hesitation. Behind her small form, a storm filled the horizon. Hell, calling it a storm was an understatement. It was closer to a hurricane. Dark clouds blanketed the night sky while lightning flashed and rumbled in the distance.

Max started to speak, but Kira held up a hand, cutting him

off. "I know. There's a lot to talk about, but we gotta save it for later. The clock's tickin'." She didn't need to say more.

Hours of tension drained from his body. "Sorry I'm late."

"You should be," she chirped with a warm smile. With that, all was right again.

Max stepped to her side and looked out toward the storm. "Damn! They said it was big. But man!" He turned to head back to the bridge. "Well, we can't hang out here all day." He waved his hand for the others to follow, taking charge of the team once again.

Kira fell in beside him with the end of her blanket dragging behind her.

"Okay, listen up, people!" Max called out in a commanding voice as he stepped through the doorway, gaining the attention of everyone on the bridge. He started to say more but was cut off by Alastair.

"Excuse me. It's still my ship."

"Oh sorry." Max stepped aside and motioned with one hand to the captain.

Alastair took over. "Okay, listen up, people! It's all hands on deck. We're gonna finish this." He plopped down in his chair and pointed toward the storm. "Take us in."

The bridge sprang to life, and the ship leaned to one side as it turned into the wind, turbulence growing as it approached the edge of the swirling hurricane. The crew looked nervous. They probably hadn't tested what would happen to an airship in such extreme weather conditions. The craft did have a damage gauge after all, which meant that it could technically be destroyed. A loud pop came from the side of the room, and all heads turned in its direction, where Max found Ginger tying herself down with a line that she'd fired at the floor.

Alastair gave her a judgmental look. "Would you not put holes in my ship?"

"What?" She held out her hand to the room. "There are no seat belts."

He tilted his head to the side, letting the gesture turn into a nod. Then he shifted in his seat to grip the armrests better. It was probably a good idea. Corvin and Kegan both grabbed onto the handrails near the door, while Kira took her place at the center rail in front of Alastair. Max stepped next to her, Farn joining him as well to bracket the fairy on either side. Alastair ignored the fact that they blocked his view.

Their caution proved necessary as a bolt of lightning hit the ship, and it lurched in one direction, dropping enough to throw everyone off balance. The main navigation team clung to their consoles and the uniformed helms-woman at the wheel struggled to stay standing. She let out a nervous laugh as she regained her stance. Max could see a bead of sweat run down one of her curled horns.

The Nostromo pushed forward, groaning in protest as its engines fought for momentum. Its design probably hadn't been created with the current situation in mind, which made the ship nearly impossible to handle. The wind hit hard, and the helms-woman looked terrified as she fought to keep the ship going in a straight line. The moonlight disappeared as the clouds surrounded them in a blanket of black-gray gloom. Violent thunder cracked while lightning lit up the sky in bright bursts all around them. The storm scorched the ship on all sides as it tossed the vessel about like a toy.

Kira clung to the rail with both hands; her head ducked as if it would somehow help the craft's progress. Max found a better grip as well, his arm crossing Farn's behind the fairy's back in unison to grip the bar at her sides. He wasn't going to let anything happen to her, not when they were so close.

"Down forty percent damage," one of the flight crew announced.

"We've lost an engine!" called another.

Windows blew in and shattered glass covered the floor, sparkling like stars with each flash of lightning. The Nostromo pitched from left to right, its engines proving no match for the changing air currents. The water below roared as it swirled along with the storm, joining the deafening cacophony of broken glass, rain, and wind. Then it faded. The gusts died, and the ship stabilized, still leaning to one side.

Max blew out a long-held sigh of relief. They had made it, the ship limping into the eye of the hurricane on its last legs. Glass crunched underfoot as the crew began to move about the cabin once again.

"Everybody alive?" Alastair stood from his chair and scanned the room. "Nobody fell out, right?"

Max glanced around the bridge to make sure no one was missing. He couldn't really tell. It wasn't like they had taken a head count before going in. At least, his team was all accounted for. He pried his hands off the railing and stepped toward the door. Farn held a moment longer before releasing Kira from her protection.

Max led the party out into the destruction that was once the ship's upper deck. Boards were torn from its surface and dark scorch marks littered what remained. A section of rail had been completely lost, as were several equipment crates. Behind them, an entire hatch was missing, somehow ripped away by the wind. He glanced at his mission clock, only an hour thirty left. He gritted his teeth, then walked to the side to look down over the edge where he blurted out a sudden, "Holy crap," impressed by the magnitude of what lay below. The others came to see as well, each gasping as they did.

The ocean fell away into an immense vortex of swirling water, a deep hole at its center. The sea spray made it impossible to see far, but a crimson glow illuminated it from underneath, pulsing like it was alive.

Max trembled. "What is it?"

To his surprise, Alastair had an answer, exhaling the words, "It's the Sphere." Then he whispered, "My god, Neal has it running somewhere."

"What's the Sphere?" Max demonstrated that he hadn't been paying attention earlier.

"It's a testing platform," Corvin answered, demonstrating that he, of course, had been.

Alastair placed a hand on the rail. "I recognize that red light. It's the default color of the sky there. It was the first thing Neal showed me when he created it. I always found it unsettling. I tried to get him to change the color, but he never got around to it. Or he just didn't care to. Either way, it's not something I could forget."

"What's it like in there?" Max questioned, trying to find out more about what might be waiting for them inside.

"No way to know," Alastair held his free hand, palm up, offering nothing helpful. "It's a temporary environment used for testing. It's not part of the system. There are no set rules there."

Max furrowed his brow. "So if we go through, we won't be in the game anymore?"

"Exactly." Alastair snapped his fingers and pointed at him without taking his eyes off the portal below. "When I said there are no rules there, I meant it. We always used it under careful monitoring."

Max swallowed. "Meaning that Carver could do anything to us in there."

Alastair nodded. "And there would be nothing you could do to stop him. He could use your own minds against you if he wanted. It could be a nightmare."

"Literally," Kira added the obligatory descriptive, getting a groan from everyone else.

Alastair looked to each of the party's members. "Still want to go?"

Max appreciated being given the option to back out, but he knew none of them would take it. Hell, if anything, they looked more determined than ever as they all nodded in unison.

"Alright then." Alastair clapped his hands. "Don't worry too much. Neal is a jerk, but he's not evil. So I can't imagine him doing anything too horrible in there."

Kira dangled her arms over the rail. "At least we have that going for us."

Max leaned further over beside her for a better view of the pulsating portal, its glow feeling like the heartbeat of Noctem itself. "So how do we get down there? I'm guessing this thing isn't gonna make it through." He gestured to the airship.

Alastair looked back at the bridge as the ship listed to one side. "I'm kind of wishing that we didn't get our transport shuttles shot down earlier."

Kira swiped open her spell-craft menu, then closed it again. "We have *Flight* available."

Max grimaced. "I guess that means we fly."

"Well, that settles it." Alastair slapped one hand against Max's back. "We'll try to get you as close as possible." He turned and headed back to the bridge to give the order.

Max didn't envy the helms-woman for having to lower the airship into the maw of the swirling vortex. With an engine down, it couldn't be easy to keep the craft away from the sides. It had to be like playing a game of Operation while drunk.

The horizon disappeared as they sunk below the ocean's surface where red streaks of light revolved around them as if pulling them closer. It was terrifying but also beautiful. The deafening white noise of the surrounding water drowned out the sound of the ship's engines, forcing everyone to shout over its volume.

Despite the pressure and fear, Max found himself smiling as an energy filled the air, transferring to the rest of his team standing on deck.

Kira leaned over the rail, her mouth open in an excited smile, her eyes sparkling. She laughed as the wind blew through her silver hair.

The ship slowed its descent to a stop, signaling that the moment had come. Max made his way to the damaged section of rail where it had been torn away by the storm, leaving them an ideal diving platform.

Alastair returned to the deck from his place on the bridge, most of the crew following behind to send them off. He didn't give another speech or further words of encouragement. He would have had to shout it over the sound of the water anyway. Instead, he just placed one hand across his chest and bowed.

Max returned the motion and signaled to the others to do the same. Kira curtsied, getting a few smiles from the other side. Somehow, it all felt right, giving thanks to the crew that had supported them throughout the night, like a proper good-bye.

Max turned to the edge with Kira joining him, placing one hand on the end of a broken section of rail as she stepped toward the abyss.

"So this is it," she said matter-of-factly.

"Yeah," Max agreed.

"Final dungeon," she continued.

"And?" he asked.

"Point of no return."

"Your point?"

"Anybody need to buy some last-minute items?"

"No," Max answered.

"Anyone want to play a mini-game one last time before we go?"

"NO!" the others answered in unison.

She brushed away the thought with one hand. "Okay, just felt like I should ask. You know, for tradition."

Corvin laughed.

Max rolled his eyes. "Okay then, magic us up and let's get going." He looked over his shoulder at the crew who were still watching them. It was clear that they had not expected to be standing there that long. "Oh god, they're all still watching us. Now it's awkward."

Kira smirked as she snapped open a caster, the glowing glyphs of her menu sliding into place as she brushed her hand against them, adding the glyph that selected the whole party. The spell activated, giving her friends a full two minutes of *Flight*. She stepped back to the edge. "As much as I hate to admit it, this has been one hell of a quest."

Max got ready to jump. "If it wasn't for the whole apocalypse thing, I would've loved it."

She smiled over her shoulder at him. "Let's end this right."

"Yeah, this is a game after all, so let's play it." Max held up one wrist.

She tapped the back of her hand against his without saying anything more.

Max glanced back at the others. "Okay, we have less than two minutes before the spell wears off, so stay close and move fast."

They nodded as one. Then, without hesitation, they dove into the unknown.

Max straightened his body to pick up speed and clenched his right hand to push the *Flight* spell to its limit. The others followed his lead with Kira darting between. Flashes of red illuminated their faces as they streaked downward. Together, voices shouted into the void, some of them calling out Carver himself. They were coming, and there was no stopping them.

The roar of water drowned out the others' words as the sea spray swirled around Max's body, soaking him through. He pushed through it into the flares of energy at the bottom of the ocean. Light and dark somehow consumed him all at once, and silence filled his ears, louder than anything that he had ever heard as the world turned inside out.

His head pounded with pressure as the details around him blurred. He scanned his surroundings for the team, finding brief glimpses of his friends before losing track of them. The crimson light hit his eyes so bright it blinded him. Then, just as quickly, the void consumed him as darkness swirled around him. His wet skin felt cold, so cold it burned. Unable to make out anything more than shapes and colors, he searched for the light of Kira's wings. He thought he saw something, but it blinked out before he could get close. He glanced at his party's stats on his sleeve. Everyone's health was full, and there was still a minute left on the *Flight* spell. Then the numbers scrambled, his party's names fading from his skin as the digital ink crashed altogether. The magic that kept him airborne failed along with it.

Waves of energy pulsed past him, throwing him into a

spiral. Up was down, left was right. It didn't matter; he had no idea anymore. Something brushed up against him in the confusion, and he almost drew one of his guns on reflex. He probed the blurring darkness with his hand, catching hold of something solid. It clasped his wrist. A brief flash of light showed Farn, her mouth forming words that he couldn't make out. He matched her grip, closing his fingers around her wrist to anchor them together. He fought to communicate but couldn't push his words through the roaring silence of the abyss. Another wave of energy hit hard, loosening his grip. Then another. Her hand slipped away, his arm reaching out, her fingertips touching his just before another wave crashed into them. Then she was gone, swallowed by the void. Everything faded.

Back in the real world, thousands of miles away from where their bodies lay in their rigs, a server in a nondescript building, in an almost random city, hummed to life. It ran its one and only file. Seven users logged in.

CHAPTER FIFTY-SIX

"What the crap?" Max said as he came to.

A light but overcast sky filled his view as he lay flat on his back on an uncomfortably hard surface. He squinted for a moment to let his eyes adjust before pushing himself up with his hands, the feeling of coarse pavement against his palms. He cocked his head to one side, looking at the ground as his vision came back into focus. A white painted stripe ran parallel to his leg. He followed it with his eyes to its end near a steel pole embedded in the pavement. The familiar shape of a basketball hoop at its top.

"What the crap?" he said again, more confused than ever.

He glanced to his wrist, but the overlay of stylized flames was nowhere to be seen. He reached into his pouch for his journal, flipping it open to a random page. It was blank. He flipped further, and so was the rest. "I guess that means no logout," he said out loud, not so much to himself but more to fill the silence of the empty basketball court that he now sat in. The realization of what it meant to lose the option to escape sent a chill down his spine, and he sympathized with Kira, who had already been in the same situation for hours.

He got to his feet and closed his eyes for a second, listening and standing statue still. He drew his guns with the same practiced speed that he always did, aiming in opposite directions while he scanned the area to get the lay of the land. The court was surrounded by a forest of towering trees that he didn't recognize, each almost as wide as a car. To the side sat a small, rusted jungle gym, complete with monkey bars and a swing set. The view of the trees, towering overhead, gave him vertigo as the overlapping trunks made it impossible for him to see anything beyond them. He pulled his vision back to the basketball hoop in front of him. A well-worn ball rested a few feet away. He shrugged, holstered his pistols, and picked it up.

Max missed the basket for the fifth time. "How am I this bad at this?" He opted to bounce the ball and wander over toward the playground. He tucked it under his arm as he stepped onto the mulched area that surrounded the swings. Aside from the play equipment, there was nothing else to give him any clue of where he was. He assumed he was somewhere in the Sphere, but as to why it looked like a playground or where the rest of his team was, he had no idea.

"Well, I assume that we've been split up for a reason." He hoped his friends were okay.

"How long have I been here?" It had felt like fifteen minutes, but without his stat-sleeve, he had no way to be sure. It would've been nice if he could have figured a way out of the purgatory that he seemed to have been dropped in, but that kind of problem-solving was more Kira's or Corvin's wheelhouse. Mostly, he just shot things.

He placed the basketball on the ground to explore the area. He rode a merry-go-round, swung on the swings, and climbed on the monkey bars. He also attempted to use a teeter-totter, but that didn't go so well as he was alone, and it took two people. He must have looked foolish sitting on the low end as it rested on the ground. "Well, this is depressing." For a moment, he wondered how far he could launch Spalding - if he placed him on one end and jumped on the other from the monkey bars. Spalding was now what he was calling his basketball-shaped friend.

Max then raised his voice an octave to mimic Kira as if she had been by his side. "Spalding is an entirely uncreative name for a basketball."

He frowned to himself. "How about Jasper?"

Imaginary Kira was satisfied with that.

He wished she was there.

"Any ideas?" Max looked to Jasper.

The basketball sat on the ground, useless, as usual.

He turned away from the ball. "Why am I here?"

The place was unrecognizable to him, but there was something about it, something that he just couldn't put his finger on. He wasn't sure why, but it did feel connected to him in some way.

"There has to be a reason. Right?"

Jasper ignored him.

"Fine, be like that."

It hadn't been long enough for him to start talking to inanimate objects for real yet. That would take another few hours, at least, hours that he didn't have with a deadline looming over him as imposing as the surrounding trees. He couldn't check, but he knew time was slipping away with each moment that passed.

Then he noticed it.

It was small and unadorned, just a plain wooden structure in the shape of a house. It stood near the edge of the playground, a good distance from everything else. He staggered as memories flooded back, hitting him all at once. How could he have forgotten? His voice slipped out quiet as he realized where he was.

"Oh no."

Ginger sat up with a start in a hospital bed, skittering back against the wall as fluorescent lights buzzed above. She knew exactly where she was. She still had nightmares of the room, or at least she would if she didn't login to Noctem every night. The sterile walls and scratchy sheets reminded her of the worst moment of her life. She had avoided hospitals at all cost ever since. She told herself it wasn't real, that it was just something Carver had told the Sphere to pull from her memory, but it didn't matter. The guilt and grief she'd felt in that moment were real. Nausea swam through her, causing her to keel over onto the bed. She clutched her stomach as she was dragged back to that night so many years ago, the night that she'd killed her daughter.

Of course, she hadn't really killed Wren; she knew that now, but back then, after waking up in the hospital without the child that she had carried inside her for six months, she was sure she'd lost her. What was worse, it had been her fault. She'd been working sixteen-hour days between two jobs to pay for health care and to keep her first child fed. Her insurance hadn't covered much, so it had taken everything she had to make ends meet. Exhaustion had caught up with her, and she'd fallen asleep at the wheel while driving home. She'd almost died in the accident, which had forced the doctors to prioritize her life over that of her child since the baby was unlikely to survive being so underdeveloped.

Because of her negligence, Wren entered the world almost three months premature after having been in a serious car accident. No one expected the child to live. When she'd realized what she had done, she screamed and cried for hours before the nurses could get her to calm down.

Now sitting in the recreated room, Ginger cursed Carver for forcing her to relive that night. It didn't matter that Wren surprised everyone by living, Ginger still carried the guilt of her mistake with her every moment of every day and every time she saw Wren's hearing aids or picked up her asthma prescription. Both conditions were a direct result of her lack of proper development in the womb. She wanted to hold her daughter, to say she was sorry. Instead, she got up and dried her eyes. She swore back then never to fail her children again, and she wasn't about to start failing them now. She tried the door; it was locked. She tightened her jaw. She was going to get out of there.

Corvin sighed as he stood in the hallway of the high school that he attended for two years before being expelled. He shrugged. It wasn't a surprise.

He made his way toward locker two-eleven, letting his hand brush against each of the combination locks that hung from the metal doors that lined the wall. In a way, it was liberating, not having anyone there with him. No insults or shoving from his peers. Just an empty hall.

He hadn't exactly been Mr. Popular in high school - his love of old video games and anime hadn't given him much common ground with the majority of his fellow students. His situation was exacerbated by the fact that he hadn't grown until much later. He was short and scrawny back then, and paired with bad skin and allergies, he had a target on his back from day one.

Looking back, though, things hadn't been that bad for him then. Sure, there was Mark Bogdan, one of the popular kids, that had relished in any opportunity to bully him, but mostly, it was just jokes about him being adopted, gay, or never having a girlfriend. Only one of which was actually true. He wasn't gay, although his fathers were, so that solidified that rumor even though it shouldn't have. It wasn't like their relationship had any bearing on him, and he had participated in some awkward teen dating. Not much or anything meaningful, but he had at least kissed a girl by age sixteen.

Ultimately, it was just his pride that suffered back then. Although, on rare occasions, it had become something physical. Mark had once pushed him and his desk over in the middle of class, while the teacher had his back turned, of course. And Mark did slap his books out of his hands like any self-respecting bully should do from time to time. Still, that was pretty much as far as it ever went. It wasn't fun, but he had lived with it. It was high school, after all. What else could he do? Then one day, he screwed up.

Corvin still remembered exactly what he had been thinking about while he was staring out the window in class that day. He had been thinking about what kind of giant robot he would want if he could choose. With Metal Gears, Gundams, EVAs, and even that pink one from Nadesico, the options were near limitless. He was not thinking about Jill Roskham, Mark's girlfriend at the time, who sat in front of the window, and he certainly was not staring at her. Well, technically he was, but he wasn't trying to. She just happened to be in his line of sight while he imagined the possibilities of space-mech combat. This explanation didn't carry much weight though when Mark had confronted him at his locker, the same locker that he stood in front of now.

Spinning the dial of the small silver lock to six-six-five, he pulled it open. He was impressed at how well the Sphere simulated his memory. Even the stickers inside were the same, but now that he stood in the recreated spot that had destroyed his life, it bothered him. He turned away from the locker, a sick feeling in his stomach. Even though the hall was empty, he could swear he could hear Mark yelling.

Students had swarmed around him back then, preventing his escape, like sharks smelling blood in the water. Not believing that it had been just an awkward misunderstanding, Mark had shoved him back into the open locker hard. Corvin remembered the pain in the back of his neck where he had hit the shelf inside before slipping to the floor.

The crowd of boys had towered over him as he sat on the cheap linoleum. He remembered their shouting, their fevered energy feeding into each other, adding fuel to the fire. Then they stopped. Their eyes wide, like several deer in headlights. A look of sheer terror filled their faces. Corvin hadn't known why in that moment, but a second later, it had been obvious to him, too.

The gun had fallen from his locker and landed next to him with a loud clank against the floor. He had looked at it, then back to the boys above. The implications of why he might have brought such an item to school were as clear to him as they had been to the others around him. He had opened his mouth to speak, but a boot cut off his words.

Now, sitting in the same spot simulated by the Sphere, Corvin ran his tongue across the place in his mouth where three fake teeth had replaced the ones he lost that day. Upon seeing the gun, Mark and the other boys had let loose. They were no longer bullies. In their eyes at the time, they had to protect their classmates from him, a deranged psychopath, bent on gunning down innocent students. There was no need to be gentle, and they had held nothing back.

Corvin had woke days later handcuffed to a hospital bed after having suffered fourteen broken bones and a head injury that had almost killed him. He had later read posts online from while he was unconscious, calling for the doctors to let him die. He ran his hand through his hair feeling the area on his head where a scar would have been in the real world.

He was promptly expelled from school and villainized by the media. He was an unstable boy who didn't get along with others, according to the interviews with Mark and his friends, who had been hailed as heroes for acting fast and risking their lives to prevent yet another tragedy in a long line. It didn't matter that the gun wasn't loaded, or that its barrel had been filled with lead, making it little more than a paperweight.

The charges against him were dropped when it was discovered that the officer that had logged the gun into evidence, never examined the weapon long enough to see that it was a stage prop. They'd just popped the magazine out and thrown it in a bag.

Corvin had borrowed the blank pistol from a neighbor that

had used it for a student film. He had done so on the request of a teacher that was directing a school performance of Romeo and Juliet based on that horrible version set in modern times. It was supposed to be edgy. Corvin had been helping to build sets for the play and had agreed to help acquire the prop despite feeling uncomfortable with the request. Unfortunately, the teacher that had asked him to do it decided to cover their ass and deny any involvement. So the school considered him as acting on his own and with poor judgment. His fathers both fought for him, spending a fortune in legal fees, but in the end, the expulsion held. Few ever found out that the gun was fake. Him being innocent wasn't an interesting story.

The teachers and police that should have protected him weren't there. Society had failed him. Most people would have become bitter or cynical, but even after all that, Corvin didn't change. He just accepted the things that he couldn't help and moved on. It took him two years of hard work to rebuild his life, and during that time, his only real escape was Noctem. It was somewhere he could go that didn't know him. He made friends like Max and Kira that didn't judge him, friends that now stood with him in defense of a world that had tossed him aside two years before. Noctem was worth something to him. It was something that he was determined to hold on to. He sat on the floor with one leg stretched out comfortably, an artificial red stain beside him where he had spat out his teeth.

Kegan came to, his head pressed against the cool tile floor of a hotel bathroom. The last thing he remembered was plummeting through a hole in the world. What he did not remember was drinking an enormous amount of alcohol and eating something covered in jalapeño peppers. Nevertheless, the room spun as he lunged headfirst toward the porcelain to expel said jalapeños. Confused and dizzy, he let himself fall to the side into the space between the bathtub and the toilet. His head throbbed, and his mouth tasted worse than he thought possible. It was one of the worst hangovers that he had ever had, and for a moment, he forgot all about the mission.

The shaken *Leaf* focused on breathing to keep his surroundings from spinning. In his condition, his mind locked up, making all thought difficult. He pulled himself up, gripping the side of the bathtub for support and made his way to the sink to rinse his mouth before splashing some water on his face. It made him feel more human. Although, the well-tanned elven male looking back at him from the mirror reminded him that he was not human. At least, he wasn't while he was logged in.

His thoughts came back to him, kicking his mind back into gear. Where he was, how he had gotten there, and what they had come to do began to repopulate his brain. His headache faded as he tried to figure out what was going on. *Why the hell am I hungover?* He questioned himself. He hadn't touched a drink in years. Not since. "Oh," he said out loud as he started to work it out.

Leaning on the door frame, Kegan hesitated, afraid to enter the bedroom beyond. He knew what had been waiting for him the first time he'd been there, back when it was real. He just hoped the Sphere wasn't able to recreate everything that he remembered. He didn't want to have that conversation again. He worked up the courage to step inside.

The bed was empty. He breathed a deep sigh of relief. Granted, the rumpled sheets still had plenty to say all on their own as did the empty vodka bottle on the floor. He picked up the glass vessel, feeling its weight in his hand. It was heavier than he remembered.

Of course, he thought. Leave it to Carver to program the Sphere to load up a memory of his biggest regret. He paused for almost a full minute, then threw the bottle against the wall, its pieces shattering across the room like pixie dust.

Farnsworth lifted her head off the dining room table of her childhood home. The scent of extinguished birthday candles wafted through the air, filling her head with memories. A cake sat in front of her, eighteen half melted candles on top. Her eyes widened at the sight of it, and her heart broke all over again. She recoiled, knocking over the cheap Ikea chair she sat in. It hit the wall with a hollow *thunk*. She stepped away from the table until her back pressed against the white painted wall. She flicked her eyes around the room, the same way she would search a dungeon for threats. She was alone. Without hesitation, she made a break for the front door. She tripped over an ottoman on her way through the attached living room. The momentum sent her falling into the door with more force than intended. She fumbled the deadbolt and turned the knob. The door swung open.

Farn's heart sank as she burst through the exit, only to find herself back in the same house. Well, not entirely the same. The adjoining dwelling was the same but mirrored, with everything positioned in the reverse of what she remembered. She felt dizzy from the jarring nature of the scene. Even the text of a discarded magazine on the coffee table was backward. She stood still, realizing that there was no running from the place. Her heart raced as a light sweat broke out on her forehead.

She had expected a fight or a dungeon to be waiting for her in the Sphere. She was ready for that, but this she was not prepared for. What made it worse was that she was alone, just like she had always been. If she at least had Kira or Max with her, she would have been able to laugh off the memory, but alone, she was left with it playing over in her mind. The things she said back then. What she had asked for. And how bad it had hurt when she didn't get it. All of it.

Smoke wafted from the candles, filling the air with a wish

that still hung in her mind, a wish that it had crushed her when it hadn't come true. She hadn't celebrated a birthday since.

Kira opened her eyes, taking in the expanse of the Sphere. Its crimson sky stretched out over a lifeless landscape of dark stone as far as she could see. It was empty but, somehow, not depressing. The ground felt cool and comfortable under her bare feet. It was quiet but not too quiet. Just peaceful. Like death. Not the type of death that people feared, but the sort that gave release and rest to those who needed it.

A gentle breeze slipped past her, weaving through the fabric of her dress to caress her body underneath. She let out a squeak and her face flushed from the intimate feel of the air on her skin.

"I always liked this place," a voice said from behind her.

She would have spun around with panic at the sudden realization that she wasn't alone, but the calming effect of the place relaxed her and gave her a kind of strength that she didn't fully understand. It was as if something in the place was calling to her. Besides, she didn't have to look to know who stood behind her.

She turned slowly, moving one foot at a time, allowing her dress to float in the air around her legs. She looked the man in the eyes, a defiant smirk on her face as she spoke his name, "Carver."

CHAPTER FIFTY-SEVEN

I wonder if I could get close enough to kick him in the dick? Kira thought, facing her enemy for the first time. She held back. The avatar in front of her looked nothing like the man that she had seen in the short videos at the beginning of the quest as if it had been randomly generated to save time. Still, there was something similar about him. She couldn't quite put her finger on it. He was elven, with pale skin and short messy hair the color of chocolate. He wore the robes of a mid-level *Venom* mage loose around his body like a bathrobe. He looked comfortable as if style was secondary, almost needless for him. In his hands, he held a simple rectangle of black glass the size of a standard tablet computer. Its surface was polished to a flawless shine, without so much as a fingerprint marring its face.

"Obviously, I apologize for the inconvenience that you have been through over the last two days," he said as though he was putting in effort to choose his words.

Kira wanted to throw his apology back in his face, her fists along with it, but there was so little time, and she didn't have much strength anyway. Furthermore, she didn't want to show her frustration in front of him. That might've made her appear weak. She wished more than ever that her friends were with her, but standing there in front of a man that threatened two worlds and her life in the name of science, she didn't seem to have a choice but to go at it alone. This thought led her to another. She wasn't weak. True, she may not have the physical capabilities of Max or Farn, but she did have other advantages. She was still an enchanting creature with a quick wit that, at times, had left people speechless.

She didn't respond right away. Instead, she looked to the side at the horizon. "It's not much to look at, but it's peaceful." She ignored his apology. She tilted her head, considering the view longer than necessary, hoping to make Carver question whether or not he should speak again or wait for her.

He seemed to be waiting.

She glanced back to him, turning on the charm and giving him a good look into her eyes. Eyes which he had only made more striking by changing their color.

Carver let out a brief, "Ah," before continuing.

A direct hit!

He recovered. "Have you ever had a dream that seemed to last for days?"

"Sure." She didn't hesitate to keep him on his toes.

He paused and glanced around before explaining. "Well, that's essentially how this version of the system works."

Kira thought about his words. "Meaning that you and I are talking here, but the mission clock is no longer ticking?"

"Yes. Time is currently passing at a much slower rate than you're used to. So you may use this opportunity to ask me anything you want." His voice sounded calm and polite.

Kira noticed the difference. It was the complete opposite from what she'd heard before in his videos. He hadn't seemed like a man that gave much thought to others, so his regard for her was out of place. It couldn't have been that he liked her or even respected her, but there was definitely something. Then she got it. He needed her. She asked her question. "Why are you here?"

He looked flustered at the vagueness of the inquiry. "To help you."

Kira let out a laugh. "I see that. But why? I mean, you put us through so much, and now, you show up to explain everything like a villain in a movie."

Frustration bubbled under his skin, cracking his mask, like he just wanted to get on with things. The welcoming attitude fell, revealing one that was more suited to him. "Things have not gone according to plan. I didn't think Alastair would choose you over his world and cut the power to your rig. He was supposed to leave you there, and he might have ruined everything. So I need to understand your mental state to know if you can be salvaged, and the best way to do that is to talk to you."

Kira laughed again, putting less effort into appearances as well. "What did you think would happen? You can't predict how people will behave. You're not some mastermind, controlling people from the shadows."

He sighed. "I realize that."

She nodded as she channeled Max's attitude. "Okay, you wanna talk? Let's talk."

"Right to the point, I appreciate that." Carver raised the obsidian tablet that he held and punched in a few short commands. Then he motioned behind her to where two crushed velvet sofas bracketed a low coffee table.

Kira raised an eyebrow at the out of place furniture, sitting there in the open space as if it had always been there. "That wasn't there before, right?" she asked, knowing the answer already.

Carver shook his head and sat down.

Kira motioned to join him but stopped, almost forgetting to smooth her dress behind her so that it didn't bunch up as she sat. She was getting used to the garment. She wasn't sure how she felt about it. Suddenly, the world around her began to move. She froze on the sofa while her surroundings swiped to the side at an impossible speed. There was no wind or inertia. In fact, she got the sense that she wasn't even moving. Her fingers clung to her seat for balance anyway.

The red sky blurred into a white ceiling and the rocky ground became a surface of smooth cement. Walls materialized from the ground up as the world slowed to a stop.

"A little warning next time," she said with a hint of irritation as she sat in the windowless room that now surrounded her.

"Sorry," Carver said out of expectation more than anything else. He dropped his tablet on the table unceremoniously and leaned back.

Kira eyed the device.

"You wouldn't know what to do with it." He didn't bother to move it out of her reach.

She returned her attention to him. "So how long have you planned this for?"

"From the beginning," he answered as if it was obvious. "As I said, I created this system to do more than play games. Before I had even met Milo, I was running tests for this on small groups. But things were too slow, and I didn't have the funds to do much more. I needed to expand and increase my testing pool. Noctem did that for me."

"So, the whole game is just one big experiment. To do what?"

Carver's eyes focused in on hers. "To find you."

She snorted at his seriousness. "Yeah, I know all about the little obsession you have with me. So my willpower value is all over the place. Why does that make me special?"

"First of all, you're not special. Not really. Since getting access to the millions of players that Noctem had to offer, I was able to find plenty of others like you. You were just the easiest one to get Milo to choose, so here we are."

"Well, you don't have to be a dick about it." Kira frowned and turned away.

He ignored her. "And second, calling it willpower is misleading. That's an arbitrary name that Milo thought of. It doesn't really mean what you or he thinks it does." He leaned forward.

"No, it's more than that. It's a representation of you as a whole. Your thoughts, emotions, fears, creativity. It's everything that makes you, you. In short, it's your identity."

"Ha!" Kira gave a mirthless laugh. "Have you seen me?" She ruffled her dress. "I mean, I'm not exactly a guy with a strong sense of identity?"

Carver looked annoyed as if she had just said something stupid. "Technically speaking, gender is strictly not binary. That's just how the majority of people think based how they are taught. So when you declare that you're a guy, I have to ask, are you?"

Kira looked at him incredulously. It was a simple question. One that she would have answered on reflex, but when she opened her mouth to speak, she stopped, finding the words missing. Her mouth remained open as she followed his line of thought. She remembered back to when she had first logged in as Kira. It hadn't really felt any different. Sure, she had been more comfortable expressing herself differently which was what created her as a character, but she hadn't felt any more or less tied to her new body than she had to her old. Eventually, she just thought of both bodies as hers. Her mind ran around the thought in circles of belated self-discovery. Then it was obvious.

It wasn't really new information. She had known she was different. She just hadn't ever defined it. She hadn't needed to, and it had been easier not to. If there was one thing she had a habit of, it was doing what's easy. She dropped her head back against the couch with a sigh. "Like I didn't have enough to think about," she responded, not really answering his question but making it clear that he was on the right path before adding, "You suck, you know that?"

He rolled his eyes. "Don't be overdramatic; there's nothing wrong with lacking a gender. In fact, that's actually a small part what makes you useful."

Kira snorted. "What the hell does that mean?"

"It means that you have all the right aspects to make up a strong and complex personality, but none of it's tied to anything. You are simply you, so it doesn't matter if you're male or female or even human, for that matter. And that makes you adaptable, which is why your willpower stat fluctuates more than others. Not only can you influence the system, but you also let it have more control over you as well. And for what we're trying to do here, you'll need both. You have to be strong enough not to lose yourself but also flexible enough not to break."

"And I'm no good to you broken."

He nodded. "And that's why this quest had to be hard on you. It was designed to push your limits and force you to explore your concept of who you are. Like stretching before a race."

"Yeah, thanks a lot for making me cry. I hope that makes you feel real good about yourself." Kira made sure her tone was extra snarky.

"That was unavoidable." Carver didn't seem like he cared. "I need this project to succeed, and at this point, so do you."

"And what is this project? What did you do to me?" She let a bit of anger taint her voice.

He paused to choose his words as if being intentionally vague, "I've helped you open a door."

"A door to what?"

"To your mind."

"And what if I just close it back up? Lock it tight and throw away the key?" She gestured tossing something over her shoulder as she leaned forward.

Carver folded his hands together. "That isn't really an option."

"Is that because I can't or because you won't let me?" She narrowed her eyes.

"Both actually. There is more at stake than you're aware. And if this works, you may be able to help a lot of people. People that would never have had a chance without some sacrifice on your end. So, I'm sorry, but giving you a choice is not possible."

Kira grimaced at his choice of words. "Sacrifice? How about you do it your damn self."

"I lack the necessary flexibility needed of a proper subject. Besides, I've already given up too much of myself to this system." He sank in his seat.

"And how did that happen?" She arched an eyebrow, curiosity getting the better of her.

His expression changed, making him almost look sincere. "I started developing this system only a couple years before I met Milo."

"So?"

"So, doesn't it strike you as odd that in such a short amount of time, we could have built a system that is literally decades ahead of anything else we currently have?"

She thought about it, tapping her foot against the coffee table. "I suppose."

"Good, because it should." He raised up, puffing out his chest. "Why no one has asked that question yet, I have no idea. The truth is that it took over seventy-five years to develop."

Kira cocked her head to the side to do the math. "So what? You're gonna tell me you came from the future?"

He laughed for the first time in their conversation. "No, that would be ridiculous." He leaned back. "Remember I told you that time flowed differently here?"

"Yeah."

"I haven't told anyone that detail before. In fact, I kept it pretty well hidden. Not even Milo knows. I always left the flow of time alone when others were in here testing." He rubbed a hand on his pale chin. "You can get a lot done in a short amount of time when you can stretch a week into years. The downside is that, over that time, being alone, you can lose yourself, or at least, I did. I don't remember who I was back when I started or what I cared about. All I have now is a goal. To be honest, I don't know what I'll do if this succeeds. I won't have a purpose. I might just break. But I can't stop. And I can't let you stop either."

"At least that explains your lack of social skills," Kira commented with her most irritating smile.

Carver laughed again. "True enough."

A small part of her wanted to comfort the man who now seemed more broken than threatening. "Is that what could happen to me if I don't continue?"

He sighed. "It's one of the possibilities. There are others. None are good."

They both grew quiet.

Kira should have tried to run or fight, but deep down, she knew it was already too late. Going back wasn't an option. Plus, she could already feel it, something out there in the system. The something that had found her when she pushed her will into it earlier. She hadn't realized it, but it had been there, reaching out from the dream ever since. Now, in the calm of the Sphere, it was clearer. She couldn't ignore it.

She let out a long sigh, sounding defeated. "If I can't go back, I might as well go forward."

"Good," he said, returning to his normal tone, though it was warmer than before.

"So, what do I have to do?"

He picked up his tablet and glanced over some readouts before looking back to her. "To be honest, I'm not sure."

"What?" Kira sat up straight, her mouth hanging open.

"I've never come this far before, so from here, it will be up to you and the system to work something out." He stood from his place on the sofa.

Kira tensed as his actions told her that her time was coming to an end. "Did you find out what you needed from me?" She got to her feet, following his lead.

He paused before answering, "No. But I think things will be okay. I'm not really one to trust my gut, but I feel that you were the right choice."

"Any advice?" She attempted to stall.

Carver tapped his chin with his tablet, then spoke, "It's not about overpowering the system like it was down in the lost city with the dragons. That was just to get you ready, to help you open the door. For what comes next, you'll have to let go."

Kira wrinkled her nose. "I don't like the sound of that."

"You'll do fine." He gave her an affectionate smile like he was teaching her to ride a bike.

She reached out to grab his arm. "What about my friends?"

He looked down at her hand. "You'll have to find them on your own. Once you do, you'll be ready. Think of it as a final warm-up," he said matter-of-factly.

She let go and rolled her eyes.

"Oh, and don't take too long. They're all currently trapped in their worst memories," he finished as he turned away from her.

"Wait, what?" she blurted out as the room around her vanished. She wasn't sure if the world had moved or if she had. All she knew was that she was back under the red sky of the blank Sphere, alone. "Great, just great."

A few minutes of nervous pacing later, Kira sat on the ground, wishing Carver could have at least left her a sofa.

"Okay, might as well try." She took a deep breath, filling her lungs with the crisp air around her. She stayed like that for what seemed like hours. Her eyes closed, almost motionless, pushing out with her mind. She remembered what it had been like earlier in the lost city when she had sent her thoughts into the system. Somehow, it had accepted her, letting her in and embracing her until she could feel it all around her. Now, she could only feel it in the distance of the Sphere, drifting without purpose as if it had no more idea of why it was there than she did. It was stronger now, but it seemed less accepting, pushing back against her thoughts in reflex. Her brow furrowed as it matched her like a mirror. It wasn't working. Her mind just wasn't that strong.

Whatever was out there, it seemed to want as much from her as she did from it. She thought back to what Carver had said, that it wasn't about overpowering. It was about letting go. She had ignored his advice, not liking how it sounded, but now, it echoed in her head. She still didn't like it, but what choice did she have. She had to trust that it wouldn't tear her apart.

Kira exhaled and opened her eyes to look up at the sky above her. It seemed to look back at her. She leaned back, placing her hands on the ground behind for support as she laid down flat. She let her body and mind relax and stared into the crimson light, almost letting it consume her. The ground against her back faded away as she drifted from her body, the whole of herself resting against the membrane of system's resistance. She didn't push, and neither did it. Instead, it waited.

She swallowed hard to keep back her fear as the thing pressed against all that she was through the open door in her mind. Then she invited it inside.

Back in the Nemo Unit, Milo stood helpless. He had logged out when he'd received the message from the techs monitoring the team, telling him that they had transferred to an unknown system.

The medical staff rushed equipment around the room to where Seth lay in his powered down rig, forcing Milo to stand off to the side. His eyes locked on the readout of the main console that showed the party's vitals as guilt rolled over him.

Kira had flat-lined.

CHAPTER FIFTY-EIGHT

Max sat in the small enclosed space of the wooden playhouse, staring out at the empty playground. An ache of loneliness crept into his chest, bringing him back to the time in his life before he had met Kira. He bounced Jasper, the basketball, against the crisscrossing beams that made up the wall and wondered how many days he had spent hiding like that back then. He wasn't weak, not anymore, but that didn't change the fact that he used to sit alone every day at school, trying to go unnoticed. It didn't change the fact that it still bothered him.

He caught the orange rubber ball with both hands as it bounced back to him. Then he pulled it in close to rest his chin on its worn, dimpled surface. He was close to giving up. He had tried to leave but found that all directions led back to his starting point. Either the Sphere had a way of creating an infinite number of playgrounds, or it just kept loading the same one in his path. He wasn't sure which. Either way, it didn't matter. He wasn't getting out, and that terrified him. Not because he was trapped, but because it was only a matter of time before it broke him. It was a realization that shook him to the core. It had been too easy to beat him.

He let out a defeated sigh. From what he could tell, he had been there for at least a few hours. "I guess it's game over for Noctem." He acknowledged the fact that the mission clock must have run out long ago. He paused for a long while unsure of what it all meant.

"I wouldn't be so sure," a voice said from outside.

Max looked through openings in the wooden structure for its source. There was no one there. He sighed again, figuring that the time had come for him to start losing it. A rustling came from behind him, like Kira smoothing out her dress to sit down. It struck him as odd that his mind would choose to hallucinate a sound that he had only heard a couple times.

"Can you hear me?" the gentle voice said again, this time from close behind him as if she was sitting against his back, just outside the house.

He laughed. "Yeah, but to be honest, I prefer my hallucinations to keep quiet." Her imagined voice said nothing for a while, and Max placed his chin back on the basketball in his arms. "That's better."

"What's up with the cake?" asked imaginary Kira.

Max sat up, confused. "What cake?" he asked back in annoyance at the idea that his mind couldn't even be bothered to give him a hallucination that made sense.

"Umm, sorry. I wasn't talking to you. Hang on, Max," the voice said.

His eyes widened. "Holy crap! Is that you, Kira? Where are you?"

"Oh, crap," Kira's voice said, sounding flustered. "Everybody, stop talking for a minute."

Max closed his mouth.

"Kegan, shut up. Everybody means you, too." Her voice still sounded close.

Max looked for her but saw nothing. He reached out toward where he thought she would be, and for a moment, he touched something warm and soft.

She squealed with abrupt laughter. "What are you doing,

man; you're lucky that was my back." She paused. "Okay, Farn, that is not my back, quit making it weird. I'm starting to think you're doing it on purpose."

Max laughed.

Kira blew out a huff. "Okay, people. I get it. I can see you, but you can't see me. You can stop poking at me. I'm kind of in five places at once. It's confusing enough without having to deal with that." A second of silence went by. "Kegan, if your hand moves one more inch you're gonna pull back a stump."

Max climbed out of the fake wooden house, still holding the basketball absentmindedly. Then the playground was gone and so were the trees and pavement and everything else. In their place was Kira standing under a crimson sky. His eyes welled up the moment he saw her, and he couldn't stop himself from smiling.

An overjoyed Farnsworth rushed past him to embrace the fairy, picking her up in a tight hug.

Max glanced around. The others were all there too.

"Okay, okay, you can put me down," Kira complained.

Farn placed her feet back on the ground and wiped a tear from her eye.

"What's with the ball?" Kira arched an eyebrow at Max.

He looked down, realizing that he had somehow brought his basketball shaped friend with him. "Ahh," he said, unsure of how to explain. "This is Jasper."

She shook her head at him. "Okay, that's a little weird."

"Never mind that, how did you find us?" Max asked.

She looked puzzled, like she didn't know what to say. "Umm, I don't really know how to explain it." She looked up to the sky. "I'm not alone anymore."

Max eyed her with suspicion but didn't push the subject. They could talk about it later. "So, what happens now? I mean we ran out of time, right?"

"No. Time doesn't work the same here. This all could be happening in just a few minutes, so we should still have plenty left." She stopped as if hearing something that he couldn't. She seemed a little out of it.

Max bounced Jasper once. "That's good."

"And trippy," Ginger added while Kegan nodded in agreement.

Kira's attention wandered. It seemed to take effort for her to pull herself back to them. Like she was trying to think about too much at once, and her brain couldn't handle it. She looked serious. "I'm sorry I couldn't get to you sooner. I know it hasn't been fun for you here."

"Better late than never." Max shrugged, pretending like he wasn't just about to lose his mind moments before.

"That's true." She laughed, her smile returning.

It warmed Max to see her after his time alone. "So I assume we've got a boss to take out here before we head back." He bounced the ball from one hand to the other.

A low rumbling from the ground answered him.

"You had to say something like that, didn't you?" Ginger said as the rock around them broke apart in a glowing burst of light that forced Max to close his eyes.

Upon opening them, he found that the earth below his feet had been replaced by a clear pane of glass a few hundred feet wide, a slight glare from the sky being the only indication that it was even there. Max dropped to his knees clutching the ball tightly as everything below fell away into the same swirling vortex that they had traveled through to get there. The dark blue of Noctem's night sky showed through the bottom as the rock of the Sphere's surface twisted and flowed deep into the impossible opening beneath him. It was at least a thousand feet down.

"I really wish the floor wasn't transparent right now," Max yelled over the volume of the portal as he stood up. The glass under his feet squeaked with each movement as if it might crack at any second.

"I'm still blaming you for this!" Ginger yelled in his direction as she and the others steadied themselves, each dealing with the vertigo of the view.

"Can we get out through there?" Kegan pointed down.

"You should be able to," Kira said, as if something else was telling her the answer. "All you have to do is jump." She pointed to the edge of the platform off in the distance that was a little hard to see.

Max snapped his eyes back to her, anger flaring as he caught her wording. It sounded like she didn't intend to go with them. "What do you mean by that?"

"Carver told me that I had to work things out here. I have to stay. But the rest of you can get out if you leave now."

"When the hell did you talk to Carver?"

"It's kind of a long story."

He moved toward her. "Well, there's no way we're leaving you here. So you can cut that crap right now."

"Yeah," Farn stepped to his side.

Kira frowned and chewed her lip but didn't argue.

"Umm, guys! Something's here," Corvin pointed toward the center of the glass platform.

Max followed the line of his finger with his eyes.

The stone sat a few dozen feet away. He recognized it instantly, having seen it earlier, just before the fight with Death. It was the tombstone from the crypt below Alderth Castle, complete with a clone of Kira sitting on top. Max squinted at the figure then gasped. It wasn't stone. His vision snapped back to Kira who stood calmer than he expected. He looked back to the stone. The figure was gone. Then suddenly, it was standing in front of them. He didn't see it move. It just sort of appeared a few feet from Kira. For a moment it stood there, its pristine skin almost glowing, covered only by a semi-sheer strip of white fabric that seemed to drift around its body, making no effort to hide much.

"What is it?" Farn shifted her stance, ready to fight. "Another nightmare?"

"No," Kira said without turning away from her copy. Its

face remained emotionless as she looked at it, tilting her head to one side. It mirrored her.

Max noticed Kira's bottom lip tremble for an instant. She shook it off and nodded as if accepting something unavoidable. Then, to his horror and disbelief, she took a step toward it.

"What are you doing?" He flung out a hand in her direction.

Kira said nothing as if she couldn't hear him, her face falling into the same blank stare as her copy as it matched her stride to close the gap between them.

Max was moving before he realized it. He didn't know what the thing was, but one thing was clear, it wanted his friend. Just before it touched her, the basketball left his hands. Whatever made him decide to throw the ball at the thing, he had no idea. He had guns. He could have shot it. Something about raising a weapon at something that looked like his best friend removed the option from his mind.

Jasper, the basketball, hit the naked fairy clone in the face, then bounced off at an odd angle. The copy stumbled backward, the attack causing no real damage other than making Max look rather stupid. Farn stepped closer to the real Kira, her gauntlet held in front even if her barrier wasn't active.

The thing recovered, looking confused as if it didn't understand the situation or why it had been struck. Then it scrunched its face in anger as a loud metallic ping emanated from it. A wave of invisible energy swept past him, feeling similar to when Kira had done the same thing to stop the War Dragons earlier. Then it felt different.

Pain, sudden and endless, ripped through Max. Not the dulled pain of the game, but real, excruciating, unbearable pain. It was as if every nerve in his virtual body screamed at once. He went limp, and his mind collapsed. Everything hurt: his teeth, his organs, his head. Hell, even his hair. He hit the glass in a lump, unable to control himself as he spasmed against the squeaking glass. Inhuman screams erupted from all around him at a volume that he wouldn't have believed if he hadn't heard them. They were the screams of creatures or beasts, primal and raw. His mind drained as he realized that one of the screams was his own.

It was as if someone had set his brain to receive the maximum amount of pain possible. In fact, that was probably exactly what was happening. It was worse than any torture ever created by man. Even if he could somehow survive it, he would never recover from the trauma. None of them would. It had already destroyed him the moment it started.

Max writhed in a puddle of his own saliva as his mind tried to escape his body. Sounds bled through, from where he didn't know. There was panicked shouting and the clanging of equipment carts. The pain in his body tore him to shreds, and he slipped through a veil in his head toward the noises that pierced through from someplace else. He couldn't make out what the voices were saying, but he focused on one anyway in an attempt to cling to something before it was ripped away from inside him.

He didn't choose which voice to focus on, but in retrospect, he must have. It was Milo's. More importantly, it was Milo's real voice, not Alastair's. He hadn't noticed that they sounded different before, but they must have because he knew they were. Suddenly, he wasn't sure which world he was in. The pain surged through his every fiber, but he also felt his rig against his back. Then he heard it.

The sound had been seared into his memory by dozens of movies. It whined, piercing his ears as his thoughts tried to comprehend it. A voice yelled, "Clear!" The noise thumped, then began to whine again. His mind clicked into place as the medical team struggled to defibrillate his friend. He didn't have to see to know it was Kira they were trying to save. He focused on a single thought, grabbing onto it through the screaming and the pain. He had to find her. He had to let her know he was there, that she wasn't alone.

Max screamed from somewhere in his mind. Somewhere that had remained sane. It sounded human, if only a little. He pushed against the blinding agony, fighting to see at least a glimpse of what was happening. The glass was cold against his face, and he struggled to open his eyes. A few seconds later, he realized they were already open. They were dry and aching as if they wanted to burst from his skull to escape his fate. He shifted his head until he found Kira only a few feet away. It may as well have been miles. Farnsworth seemed to be thinking the same thing as she clawed her way toward the fairy at a snail's pace. Then he saw the copy still standing there, wearing his friends face.

It might have been the agony coursing through every cell of his body, but something was off about the creature. His mind raced through a maze of synapses, trying to work out what it was. Then it was clear. So clear that he couldn't believe that he'd trouble seeing it. It looked scared. It wasn't the terror in his friends' faces around him, but a fear that came with a lack of understanding, like a child that had crushed a butterfly by accident. It hadn't meant to hurt them. How could it even know what pain was? It wasn't human. It was something else, something born from the system. Something that couldn't seem to exist alone.

Max glanced back to Kira, who was somehow forcing herself off the glass. Her silver hair hung in her face as she raised her head. She looked to be regaining some of herself through the pain. He wondered if she was aware of the danger she was in. Farn still crawled closer. He followed her lead, scraping his way forward. A glimpse back showed him Ginger, struggling to aim her grappling line at the creature from the ground. She bared her teeth like an animal as she fired.

The copy vanished just as the line passed through the space where it had been. It reappeared on its knees, its eyes only inches from Kira's.

Max's heart sank as the two fairies knelt face to face, like a mirror. He pushed toward them despite the knowledge that he would never make it in time. Out of the corner of his eye, he saw Farn. She wouldn't make it either. She must have known it was pointless, too, but she didn't stop either. Max focused his attention back on the two Kiras kneeling on the glass. A voice in his head told him to draw his guns, to save her. It screamed at him, telling him that he could stop it. It was right. All he had to do was pull a trigger, but before he could act, both fairies closed their eyes and leaned forward, their foreheads touching for an instant.

Suddenly, the voice yelling inside his head was drowned out by another chime that hung in his mind, this time softer, almost kind. Almost beautiful. Like the string of a harp. The clone of his partner vanished in a swirl of shimmering dust that encircled the remaining fairy, joining together with her own as her wings materialized for a moment before fading back into her body. Then Kira fell motionless to the glass.

A wave of energy swept past Max as the steady note hummed in his head. He could feel it reach into his mind, silencing the signals causing the pain and erasing not only the torment but also his memory of it. He knew he had been in agony seconds before, but he couldn't remember it. The trauma faded from his thoughts like a dream as his senses returned to their razor-sharp state of normalcy.

Max flicked his eyes toward Kira's unmoving body. He wasn't sure how, but he knew the gentle sound was her trying to save him and the others. He just hoped she hadn't paid too high a price to cause it. On instinct, he glanced at the digital ink on his wrist to check her health. It was full, fifty out of fifty. He did a double take as he realized his stat-sleeve was active again. The mission clock blinked red at its edge with just under ten minutes remaining. It stopped ticking, then disappeared altogether. They had done it. The quest was finished.

Max glanced down at the portal back to Noctem's servers, its blue glow filling him with hope. Then his heart sank as a second portal formed above in the sky, the clouds swirling in the opposite direction of the ground below. A deep crimson shining down, creating a space of violet energy surrounding them in between. Max stared up at it, realizing who the new gateway was meant for. He scrambled to Kira, meeting up with Farn at her side. The others were still trying to get their bearings when the menu options inked onto their forearms navigated automatically to their logout tabs. Anger pulsed through Max's mind as the text on his arm that read, sign off, was highlighted.

"Oh no, you don't!" Max yelled, looking down at his unconscious friend. "You're not going up there. I'm not leaving without you!"

He had to get her out of there. He had to bring her home before he was forced to log out. Max glanced to the edge of the glass platform, its edge too far away to carry her. He'd never get her through the portal in time. He dropped down to lay on his side next to Kira and pulled her small body close against his chest. He was out of options.

Farn followed his lead, laying down and sandwiching the fairy between them.

He drew one of his pistols and placed the muzzle against the glass surface that supported them. A desperate hope beat in his chest. *If I can break the glass, we can fall back to Noctem, together.*

He locked eyes with Farn. "Whatever you do, don't let go."

Farn nodded as the others gathered around, understanding what Max intended to do. The logout timer read twenty seconds.

Max didn't know if the glass was several feet thick or paper thin. He didn't even know if it could be broken. All he could do was hope. He tilted his head down, bringing his lips less than an inch from Kira's ear and whispered. "I know I can't save you. So I'm asking you to save yourself." He closed his eyes and tightened his finger on the trigger with one word in his mind. He repeated it over and over, "Please." Then he squeezed.

LOGS

Checkpoint Systems message boards, one day after mission completion.

Topic: what the hell you idiots

ChronicTheHedgehog69: I know the topic already says what the hell you idiots but I feel the need to say it again. WHAT THE HELL?! YOU IDIOTS! I lost a level! An entire level when I died trying to fight those freaking war dragons. What I want to know is how the hell does a company that probably makes a billion dollars a day let a disgruntled employee into their system to mess with it. I'm ready to quit here.

EMPIREriot: My god, man. Use a comma.

WeWantsTheRedHead: I'm a little surprised at this too. I mean how bad is their security? And should I be concerned? Although, that fight was pretty intense. I almost don't mind that I got stepped on by a thousand foot tall ice dragon. I wish Carver had let the expansion play out as it was supposed to. I kinda get why they fired the guy.

HelveticaNue: Did anyone see that jackass who was fighting against us in there. How the hell does a Fury get something as broken as full auto pistols with what I'm guessing was infinite ammo? If anyone knows how he got them, let me know.

WeWantsTheRedHead: I thought that was awesome. I actually got stepped on partly because I was watching him like an idiot. I don't know how to get those abilities, but I assume it was a contract. So they were probably only one-time use, which would make it a little less broken.

ChronicTheHedgehog69: Dude was probably cheating...

AerithNOOOOOOO: I don't think there is a way to cheat in Noctem... just sayin.

ChronicTheHedgehog69: THIS POST HAS BEEN FLAGGED FOR INAPPROPRIATE LANGUAGE

AerithNOOOOOOO: Plus that guy wasn't alone, there was a Shield with him tearing shit up. She had two arrows sticking out of her back, and it didn't even slow her down. She killed me. I'm pissed I died, but I gotta admit, she was pretty damn badass.

ChronicTheHedgehog69: What the hell made them turn on us anyway. They tryin to troll?

DracoKiro: I don't think so, I saw a fairy on the ground with a reynard kneeling over her. The Fury and Shield looked like they were protecting them.

ChronicTheHedgehog69: That's bull. I didn't see that.

HipstersSuck: You were probably too busy getting killed. I saw the fairy too, but she was standing right before we all got kicked back to spawn. It's weird though, there's no pictures of her anywhere online.

HelveticaNeue: Checkpoint wiped everyone's recordings of the event. That's why there are no photos.

ChronicTheHedgehog69: Sounds like they're trying to cover shit up.

Message written and sent three days after mission completion.

To: MaxDamage24, Farnsworth, GingerSnaps, Corvin, and Kegan

From: Alastair Coldblood

Subject: Thank you again

Hi, everyone. Sorry I haven't been able to reach out to you until now. I've been fighting with legal for the last couple days. They've decided to keep the events of the mission quiet and are aggressively drafting additional documents for everyone involved. You should be receiving a packet to sign and return in the next couple days. I know it's probably the last thing you want to do right now, though. On the upside, I convinced them that doubling your payout would help to ensure your cooperation, so there's that.

I still have a lot of work to do here, but it looks like everything should return to normal thanks to you. I really can't express how grateful I am. I mean, you literally saved a world. I know it wasn't easy, and I know that in many ways, you might never be able to look at Noctem the same. But I want you to understand that it still exists because of you. I know none of you have logged in since everything happened. I don't blame you for that, but I hope you will come back when you feel ready.

We are still working to find Carver, but we've had little luck. He seemed to have a well thought out plan to disappear in place before he started the whole thing. I know none of us will forgive him after what he did, but to be honest, I'm not sure we'll ever find him. I know that's not good news, but I told myself that I wouldn't keep anything from you again. Unfortunately, that means the bad news goes unfiltered. Anyway, I hope to see you again. Until then, I'll keep you informed.

-Alastair Coldblood

Message written and sent seven days after mission end.

To: MaxDamage24, Farnsworth, GingerSnaps, and Kegan
From: Corvin
Subject: Trying something new

So I just logged in and changed my character class to a Blade. I'm now level one again. I know that seems drastic, but I felt like after everything that happened, I needed to change. I really wish Kira could see me right now. She said that Blade gear would look good on a reynard. She was right. It's pretty cool. Plus, I got a new eye patch and it looks pretty badass. You guys need to get back on, I could use some help getting levels.

-Corvin

Message written and sent seven days after mission end.

To: Corvin
From: Kegan
Subject: RE - Trying something new

That's awesome! Blades do great in PVP; I could teach you a thing or two. I'll get on tonight and help.

-Kegan

Checkpoint Systems message boards ten days after mission completion

Topic: New development at Alderth Castle

MandalorianMan: I know that this is probably going to reopen a can of worms that should be left closed, but I feel I have to make note of it. I have always been on the side that thought that Alderth Castle had been explored fully. But now, I'm not so sure. I went there with a girl I know to, you know, 'do stuff,' since not a lot of players go there anymore. We went down in the crypt (she's kind of goth) and noticed something weird. One of the statues was gone.

Puddin: Way to add in that detail about gettin some. Classy.

partytillyoupuke: Congrats on gettin some! Very proud. But seriously, which statue? Is it the one without a date on the gravestone?

MandalorianMan: Yup. It just has a quote. The stone is still there, but the statue sitting on it is gone.

Puddin: Okay, now I'm curious. What's the quote say?

partytillyoupuke: Awesome! This is going to settle one of the biggest arguments I had with my boyfriend. I've been telling him that statue was important for like, a year. The quote is from mark twain, it's something like, the most important days in your life is the day you're born and the day you find out why.

TheUnseen: That statue is gone?! Thank god I took a picture of it last time it was there. It's wicked cute. I've had her as the wallpaper of my phone for the last year.

EMPIREriot: Wow, keep it in your pants bro. It's a statue.

TheUnseen: Sue me, it's of a fairy. I think they're pretty.

AerithNOOOOOOO: That is true. But more importantly, I read on the boards, that a fairy had something to do with the whole war dragon debacle a couple weeks ago. I wonder if they're related. Or maybe I'm just reading too much into it.

Puddin: Definitely reading too much into it.

MandalorianMan: I'm not so sure, the timing does line up.

partytillyoupuke: OK I just messaged my boyfriend. We're gonna check out the crypt tonight.

Puddin: Nice. Let us know what you find. And hey, if you don't find anything, at least it's a quiet place to 'do stuff.'

partytillyoupuke: Classy.

Message written and sent two weeks after mission end.

From: Farnsworth
To: Kirabell
Subject: BFFs

Hey, Kira. So I guess I'm sort of rich now thanks to you. I thought about quitting my job, but I figured that would be a crappy thing to do. Besides, Milo keeps popping into my office to hang out. Apparently, we're friends now. I think he's just hiding from his assistant, though. Also, my coworkers get all freaked out every time he comes in, which is pretty funny.

I haven't logged in since the mission. I don't know why. Corvin has been trying to get us all back online, and while I'd like to, something wouldn't feel right without you there. Max hasn't logged in yet either, although I haven't talked to him much since. I don't know if he'd admit it, but I don't think he wants to log on without you either.

I know we didn't really spend much time together when you actually think about it, but you were my first friend in almost a decade. So not seeing you for the last two weeks sucks. I know that my lack of friends was mostly my fault for not putting myself out there, but you didn't let that stop you. I'm still thankful for that. I guess what I'm trying to say is, I miss you.

-Your BFF Farnsworth

Message written and sent fifteen days after mission end.

From: Kegan
To: Ginger
Subject: OK YOU WIN
Fine, you win. I'll pay for the damn feathers.
-Kegan

A letter, written on actual paper, by hand, and driven by car over significant distance to a post office in Montana by an overly serious assistant named Jeff. Photocopied and overnighted to five people.

To: Wyatt, Sarah, Marisa, Bastian, and Kevin
From: Seth

My dearest friends, the wilderness is harsh and unforgiving. Words cannot express my longing for home. I have tried, to no avail, to rally my weary mind with thoughts of our victory and the wealth that we each have obtained through the sweat of our brow. I pray that when I return home, I will still be the person that you have come to know and love.

Okay, I can't think of any more old-timey things to write, and my commitment to this bit has faded.

Hey, guys! I will say one thing: internet quarantine sucks. They have me in a literal cabin in the woods, in freaking Montana of all places. There is no electricity. I poop in a hole. It is less than ideal. I am bored out of my mind.

The point of this, as you know, is to let my brain return to normal by keeping me away from any possible online connection. And that would be fine, but one of the idiot doctors also recommended keeping me away from ALL electronic devices of any kind. I don't even have a DVD player. For the love of god, people, I have been READING. Okay, truth be told, I'm really getting into this book I found here. It's about sexy vampires and werewolves. It has a really nice love triangle in it ... and I just threw up in my mouth a bit. Have I mentioned I'm bored? On the upside, I've invented a new game. It's called, throw things at trees. I'm thinking of pitching it to Milo for his next big expansion.

I made Jeff play chess with me yesterday, and he's surprisingly good at it. Not good enough to beat me, but at least he tried. He did bring me some printouts of my messages though, and I miss you too, Farn. What I wouldn't give to spend one minute hiding under your shield like a coward right about now.

Anyway, they're bringing me back in tomorrow for tests. If

all goes well, I should be home and back online soon, I hope. But don't wait for me. Get on there and have fun. Especially you, Max, I know you're just sitting in your room in the dark. You just saved a world. Two, if you include all that economic stuff that Milo was yammering on about. So get online and enjoy it.

-Kirabell/Seth

Wyatt sat in his room in the dark with only a small lamp illuminating the letter that he had just finished reading for a second time. He snickered to himself as he placed it down on his desk. He picked up his phone, bringing up the Noctem messaging app and logging in as MaxDamage24. He scrolled through his friend list, selecting the name that read Farnsworth. They hadn't messaged much since the mission, mostly because he wasn't sure what to say and didn't want to make it awkward. Making it awkward was kind of his specialty. He started typing anyway.

"Hey, Farn. You want to log on tonight and meet up, maybe just hang out at a tavern?" He cringed, realizing it sounded like he was asking her on a date. He deleted the message and started again.

"Hey, what's up? I was thinking of logging on. Probably not gonna do much since Kira isn't back yet, but I thought I might catch a movie or something. Wanna come?" His finger hovered above the send button as he wondered if he sounded reasonable. He deleted the text again.

"Hey, just read Kira's letter, sounds like she might be back soon. Let's all get back on when she's ready. We made one hell of a team, should be ready for anything." He sighed as if disappointed in himself. Then he hit send and went to bed.

EPILOGUE

A young reynard woman sat in a comfortable chair facing the window of a small, dim office in Valain's citadel. She hadn't turned the lights on, partly as to go unnoticed, but more because she was used to lurking. She leaned back with one foot on the windowsill, spinning herself back and forth, her chin resting on one hand. She was waiting patiently, but she was also bored.

Her long ears pricked up at a sound from beyond the closed door. Most people wouldn't have noticed it at all, but she was not most people. She studied the sound. Footsteps coming toward her. They were quick but not hurried as if mindful of the time. They could only have belonged to one person. She ceased the motion of her chair as the man outside approached the door. It swung open, revealing an elf wearing a severe expression. "I see our security is apparently lacking," Jeff-with-a-three commented, closing the door quickly but gently enough not to make a sound.

She tilted her head in acknowledgment, letting the moonlight highlight her features. "An intern let me in; you should really screen them better."

"You're in my seat." He pointed to the chair with his eyes.

"I'm aware." She gave him a predatory smile.

He sighed but didn't argue, sitting down in the chair oppo-site his desk. "You could have just sent me a message. I would have come to meet you. I do work for you after all. Not to mention, now isn't the best time to be trespassing in the citadel. What with all that just happened."

She arched an eyebrow at his tone. It was familiar but cautious, as if he regarded her like a wild animal that might leap at him without warning. It made sense. She meant him no harm, but she also knew he was aware of what she was capable of, in both worlds.

She grinned. "I'm a hands-on kind of super villain. Plus, I know this was a hard operation, so I felt it important that I came to see you myself."

"And what if it had been Alastair who had walked in and not me? I am still posing as his assistant, and he never knocks you know," Jeff-with-a-three asked.

"I would have handled him." She slid the hem of her skirt high up her leg to show him a little too much of a slender thigh, a pistol strapped tightly to it. She hadn't worn her normal gear, but she was always ready for anything.

The elf looked at her skeptically. "So, you would have just shot him in the face then?"

She slid her skirt back down. "Possibly, or maybe I'd just hide under the desk until he left. You'd be surprised how often that works. I'm pretty sure that's how Batman does it."

"I bet." He didn't even crack a smile.

She frowned. She'd thought it was a solid joke. "Anyway. I didn't sneak in here for banter." She dropped her leg from the window and turned to face him head-on. "Status report?"

He sighed and placed his hands on the arms of his chair, his fingertips pressing into its leather pads. "It's a mess, but I think it's salvageable."

She nodded in approval. "Well, it was a long shot to begin

with, so that's not bad overall." She looked up and to the side, weighing several variables in her head.

"How's Carver?" the elf asked.

"He's settling into his new lab. It's good to have him back in the fold," she answered with a wink, being intentionally vague as she leaned forward against the desk. "So how is our little test subject doing?" She got to the meat of her visit.

"Well enough, all things considered. We played chess a couple days ago."

"Did you win?"

He sighed. "No."

"Must be good." She let a hint of respect into her tone. "More importantly, is the beta still running?"

Jeff-with-a-three shifted to the side and tapped a finger on his chair. "Carver let her go into the final phase with the rest of her party rather than keeping them separate like he was supposed to. One of them was able to pull her out of the Sphere before it had a chance to finalize. Not sure what Carver was thinking."

"I think he has a soft spot for her. His reports always seemed to. Did the quarantine have any effect?" She changed the subject back to the matter at hand.

"Unfortunately, yes. After testing yesterday, we found that the process has stopped, but she is still bonded to the beta, so if she logs back in and gives it any more of herself, it should pick up where it left off."

"So, we just need to make sure that happens." She pondered her options. "How long will it take?"

"From what I understand of Carver's work, it will depend on the subject herself. It could take days or years. She could give into it at any time, really," he explained.

She fell silent for a moment. "Keep her monitored from inside for now, and report anything that might be important."

Jeff-with-a-three nodded. "Should I get a retrieval team ready, in case it happens soon?"

"No, not yet. I don't want to risk being noticed by moving

on things prematurely." She stood and made her way toward the door, indicating that her visit was coming to an end. "We'll wait and see for now."

His face somehow grew even more serious. "Do we have the time for that?"

She paused as her hand touched the door. "We're going to have to."

ABOUT D. PETRIE

D. Petrie discovered a love of stories and nerd culture at an early age. From there, life was all about comics, video games, and books. It's not surprising that all that would lead to writing. He currently lives north of Boston with the love of his life and their two adopted cats. He streams on twitch every Thursday night.

Connect with D. Petrie:
TavernToldTales.com
Patreon.com/DavidPetrie
Facebook.com/WordsByDavidPetrie
Facebook.com/groups/TavernToldTales
Twitter.com/TavernToldTales

ABOUT MOUNTAINDALE PRESS

Dakota and Danielle Krout, a husband and wife team, strive to create as well as publish excellent fantasy and science fiction novels. Self-publishing *The Divine Dungeon: Dungeon Born* in 2016 transformed their careers from Dakota's military and programming background and Danielle's Ph.D. in pharmacology to President and CEO, respectively, of a small press. Their goal is to share their success with other authors and provide captivating fiction to readers with the purpose of solidifying Mountaindale Press as the place 'Where Fantasy Transforms Reality.'

Connect with Mountaindale Press:
MountaindalePress.com
Facebook.com/MountaindalePress
Twitter.com/_Mountaindale
Instagram.com/MountaindalePress

MOUNTAINDALE PRESS TITLES
GameLit and LitRPG

The Completionist Chronicles,
Cooking with Disaster,
The Divine Dungeon,
Full Murderhobo, and
Year of the Sword by Dakota Krout

A Touch of Power by Jay Boyce

Red Mage and
Farming Livia by Xander Boyce

Ether Collapse and
Ether Flows by Ryan DeBruyn

Unbound by Nicoli Gonnella

Threads of Fate by Michael Head

Lion's Lineage by Rohan Hublikar and Dakota Krout

Wolfman Warlock by James Hunter and Dakota Krout

Axe Druid,
Mephisto's Magic Online, and
High Table Hijinks by Christopher Johns

Dragon Core Chronicles by Lars Machmüller

Pixel Dust and
Necrotic Apocalypse by D. Petrie

Viceroy's Pride and
Tower of Somnus by Cale Plamann

Henchman by Carl Stubblefield

Artorian's Archives by Dennis Vanderkerken and Dakota Krout

APPENDIX

CHARACTER STATS

MaxDamage24

TITLE: Nightmarebane
HOUSE: None (Ronin)
LEVEL: 114
RACE: Human
TRAIT: Versatile – All stats develop equally.
CLASS: Fury

STATS
CONSTITUTION: 92
STRENGTH: 54
DEXTERITY 166
DEFENSE: 72

WISDOM: 0
FOCUS: 0
ARCANE: 0
AGILITY: 18
LUCK: 33

ACTIVE SKILLS

SLOT 1: Custom Rounds, level 6 – Convert a magazine to a different type of ammunition. May be used once per magazine.

SLOT 2: Last Stand – Fire an empty pistol by creating bullets from your hit points. Duration lasts until death or reloading.

SLOT 3: Heavy Metal – Drastically decreases range and increases recoil enough to damage the wielder and make firearms difficult to handle but grants +75% damage.

PERKS

SLOT 1: Dual Wield – Allows a second pistol to be equipped. -5% damage output for each missed shot with an off-hand weapon for a maximum damage penalty of -40%. Penalty lasts until both weapons have been reloaded.

SLOT 2: Last Chance – The last round fired from a magazine deals +50% damage, increasing the likelihood of finishing an enemy before needing to reload.

SLOT 3: Quick Draw – Any shot fired within two seconds of a weapon being drawn from a holster will gain +25% damage.

Kirabell

TITLE: Nightmarebane

HOUSE: None (Ronin)

LEVEL: 114

RACE: Fairy

TRAIT: Fragile – Receive a significant bonus to arcane, wisdom and focus, however strength and constitution are soft-capped. Physical capabilities are also limited due to character size.

CLASS: Breath Mage

STATS

CONSTITUTION: 4

STRENGTH: 0

DEXTERITY 0

DEFENSE: 45

WISDOM: 142

FOCUS: 133

ARCANE: 0

AGILITY: 70

LUCK: 41

PERKS

SLOT 1: Dual Cast – Allows a second caster to be equipped. Spells cast with off-hand cost 20% more mana.

SLOT 2: True Flight – Wings are the mark of a true fairy.

SLOT 3: Wellspring – Increase the potency of spells while a fairy's bare feet are in contact with the ground.

Farnsworth

TITLE: Resolute

HOUSE: None (Ronin)

LEVEL: 111

RACE: Human
TRAIT: Versatile – All stats develop equally.
CLASS: Shield

STATS

CONSTITUTION: 164
STRENGTH: 98
DEXTERITY 42
DEFENSE: 176
WISDOM: 0
FOCUS: 0
ARCANE: 0
AGILITY: 6
LUCK: 9

ACTIVE SKILLS

SLOT 1: Blood Shell (CONTRACT) – Create a shell of blood that can defend against any attack for one minute, after which the user dies.

SLOT 2: Taunt – Gives weight to your words to draw the attention of an enemy. PVE only.

SLOT 3: Feral Edge (CONTRACT) – Unleash your inner beast.

PERKS

SLOT 1: Damage Absorption, level 5 – Your shield blocks 90% of damage taken.

SLOT 2: Annoyance – Increases the likelihood of getting an enemy's attention by attacking it.

SLOT 3: Protector – Increase defense by +15 when standing between an enemy and a party member.

Kegan

TITLE: Deadly Wind
HOUSE: None (Ronin)
LEVEL: 105
RACE: Elf
TRAIT: Control – At creation, choose one stat to receive a bonus for each upgrade point used and choose two stats to receive a soft-cap.
CLASS: Leaf

STATS

CONSTITUTION: 89
STRENGTH: 125
DEXTERITY 90
DEFENSE: 80
WISDOM: 0
FOCUS: 0
ARCANE: 0
AGILITY: 45
LUCK: 21

ACTIVE SKILLS

SLOT 1: Camouflage, level 3 – Temporarily change your skin and equipment's coloring to blend into a variety of terrains. Must be holding still.

SLOT 2: Piercing Strike – The next arrow fired will continue moving through your target to hit another behind it. The arrow will continue until it runs out of momentum or hits an obstacle. Each consecutive hit decreases damage by -10%.

SLOT 3: Light Foot – Remove all sound produced by your movement for five minutes for better stealth.

PERKS

SLOT 1: Speed Chain – Increase damage by 5% for each arrow fired within three seconds of the last.

SLOT 2: Charge Shot – Increase damage by 10% for every second you hold the bowstring back.

SLOT 3: Sticky Quiver – Arrows will not fall out of your quiver.

Corvin

TITLE: Nightmarebane
HOUSE: None (Ronin)
LEVEL: 121
RACE: Reynard
TRAIT: Nine Tails – All nine attributes gain a bonus equal to half your lowest.
CLASS: Venom Mage

STATS

CONSTITUTION: 74
STRENGTH: 33
DEXTERITY 20
DEFENSE: 66
WISDOM: 27
FOCUS: 98
ARCANE: 110
AGILITY: 22
LUCK: 20

PERKS

SLOT 1: Awareness – Hear better than most.

SLOT 2: The Empty Hand – Increase the potency of all magic while not equipping a weapon.

SLOT 3: Hidden – Decrease the likelihood of drawing the attention of an enemy while casting.

Ginger Snaps

TITLE: Purse Taker
HOUSE: None (Ronin)
LEVEL: 104
RACE: Human
TRAIT: Versatile – All stats develop equally.
CLASS: Coin

STATS

CONSTITUTION: 89
STRENGTH: 60
DEXTERITY 105
DEFENSE: 70
WISDOM: 0
FOCUS: 0
ARCANE: 0
AGILITY: 65
LUCK: 61

ACTIVE SKILLS

SLOT 1: Blur – Decrease a target's ability to target you. PVE only.

SLOT 2: Paralyze – Immobilize a target after a successful backstab. Removes critical hit bonus.

SLOT 3: Five Finger Discount – Will cause an NPC to turn around. Common items are fair game.

PERKS

SLOT 1: Grappling Hook – Fire a line from a wrist mounted launcher.

SLOT 2: Sticky Fingers – Any material taken from an enemy can be converted to an item to be used or sold.

SLOT 3: Backstab – Increase damage by 150% when doing it from behind.

APPENDIX

BESTIARY

Nonhostile Creatures

LAGOPIN – Being half rabbit and half bird, these mounts are seriously fun to ride. So, saddle up and hang on tight.

JEROBIN – A small kangaroo-like race, these sentient creatures are often seen working in the cities of Noctem.

Basic Monsters

SCALEFANG – A large lizard bearing a mane of bright feathers. They attack with their entire bodies from their tail to their teeth. Their rotating elemental weakness makes them particularly hard to deal with, especially in large groups.

BASILISK – An enormous black snake with a paralyzing stare. Avoid direct eye contact at all costs.

GHOUL – These animated corpses of the dead are known for their physical attacks, but they have been observed using magic as well.

POPLO – A spherical manifestation of elemental energy, capable of a number of spells that match their affinity.

MISFIT – A cave dwelling monster that likes to bite and kick.

Quest Specific Monsters

SILVER ANGEL – A silent observer who watches those who travel down the spiral.

PLAGUE TOAD – Wet, slimy, and vicious, these creatures exist to eat. They will try to lure you in with their tail and attack from below. They especially like easy targets.

Nightmares

RASPUTIN – This mad monk exists to tear and rend all asunder, earning him the title of Destroyer.

SENGETSU – Sometime sacrifices cannot be avoided. It is up to you to fear them or not.

KAFKA – Change is necessary for growth, but will that growth create a monster?

RACKHAM – Not all battles can be won, but that doesn't mean you should accept defeat.

Quest Specific Nightmares (The Horsemen)

FAMINE – The bell of Famine rings a steady rumble in one's stomach. Nothing can be eaten in this Nightmare's dungeon.

PESTILENCE – The horde is coming and it's hungry.

DEATH – Like a force of nature, this nightmare claims everyone in the end.

WAR – The embodiment of war, this Nightmare consists of two dragon kings locked in combat for centuries. There is no stopping them. It's best to just run.

CITIES VISITED

Valain

The unofficial capital of commerce, Valain runs like a well-oiled machine. Its citizens work hard and party hard. This city and its territories are the only parts of Noctem that are fully under the control of Checkpoint Systems. (Current Ruler: Alastair Coldblood, Lord of House Checkpoint.)

Lucem

The city of light, Lucem stands as a shining example of what can be done through clever negotiations and diplomacy. Artist and entertainers have flocked to its peaceful and vibrant streets. If you're looking for a night out, you can't do much better. (Current Ruler: Leftwitch, Lady of the House of Silver Tongues.)

Sierra

Lost for generations, the city of Sierra hides below ground where it's people, the Deru, thrive and innovate.

Tartarus

While now an official city, Tartarus defies logic by existing in the wilds on the dark continent Gmork. It has been constructed of entirely farmed and crafted materials. Enter at your own risk.

Rend

Once the sister city to Torn, the majestic kingdom of Rend fell to the greed of its ruler, who attempted to offer the city to the Nightmare Rasputin to form a contract. Its palace, Castle Alderth, has become a frozen tomb, home to nothing but death and darkness. To this day, it remains waiting for the day that someone breaks its curse.

CLASS LIST

Melee

FURY – Fast, loud, and full of style. In the right hands, this class can dish out an impressive amount of damage. That is, if they can actually hit their targets.

Weapon: pistols

LEAF – At home sniping from the trees, this class will attack from where you least expect it.

Weapon: bows

COIN – Don't take your eyes off this class for a second, lest you find yourself a few items lighter. Coins excel at stealth and mobility.

Special equipment: grappling line

Weapon: daggers

BLADE – You can't argue with a classic. This swordsman class is best suited for attacking.

Weapons: sabers, rapiers, and katanas

SHIELD – Built to last, this class specializes in protecting others.
Special equipment: shield gauntlet
Weapon: straight swords

WHIP – A trainer class capable of keeping a familiar.
Weapon: whips

RAGE – Known for its capability to equip anything as a weapon, this class is built for all-out attacks.
Primary weapons: anything and everything

FIST – This unique class has two different paths. On one hand, the MONK is capable of infusing their hits with mana. On the other, the THUG is a brawler through and through.
Weapons: gloves, brass knuckles, and their bare hands

RAIN – Death from above. This class can use their mana to augment their movement, often launching themselves into the air to attack when least expected.
Weapon: polearms

Magic Users
BREATH MAGE – This frail but kind class can keep their party alive through whatever the world may throw at them.
Special equipment: casters
Weapons: clubs, canes, and additional casters

CAULDRON MAGE – Specializing in destruction, this mage class is slow but dangerous.
Special equipment: casters
Weapons: clubs, canes, and additional casters

VENOM MAGE – This mage class excels at slowing the enemy down, weakening a target, and causing damage over time.

Special equipment: casters
Weapons: clubs, canes, and additional casters

Made in the USA
Columbia, SC
25 July 2024

be36d349-f90b-437e-8e76-5b4df34aea6fR01